Watch

Jaymes Logan

THE GIRL WITH SEVEN FIRST NAMES

JAYMES LOGAN

ARGOSY PRESS
KANSAS

First published in the United States of America
by Jaymes Logan 2011

ISBN: 978-0-9852258-0-3

Published by Argosy Press
719 Main Street, Apartment A, Hays, KS, 67601
www.argosypress.org

Cover Design by Kaycee Wilson
Edited by Jessica Robbins
Formatted for publication by Zachary Kastens

For my mentors Greg Luthi,
Adam Desnoyers, and Laura Moriarty.

For my wife Sarah,
without whom this book would not have been possible.
The window cleaner was her idea.

For my mom and dad,
without whom I would not have been possible.

And for my son Jayson,
who will love this when he's older.

PROLOGUE

Fate After Breakfast

THEY WERE SIX. Four women, one teenage girl, and one little girl, all with no memories and no experience of any kind. They had no parents, no place of residence, no friends, and no possessions. Their ideas and interests were programmed into them; they had unique identities, but they weren't responsible for developing them. This was the first place any of them could recall ever visiting, and the other five were the only people each had ever seen. They had knowledge, desires, opinions, complete and distinct personalities, each perfectly unique from the others. Not one could tell how she knew what she knew or why she was who she was. Each had only one thing in common, and that was the game.

They sat at a small wooden picnic table in the middle of nowhere—and not like lost on the highway, somewhere in an endless field of wheat or deep in the mountains nowhere. Literally, the middle of nowhere. The space around them was an abyss of white—above, below, all around. There was ground, but only in the sense that the metal chairs the women sat on weren't falling, and there was sky, in the sense that there didn't seem to be any kind of ceiling. On the table was a variety of very tasty-looking pastries, muffins, bagels, fruits, juices, milk, and coffee. The women ate and drank their breakfast together, three on each side of the picnic table. Each wore a paper nametag just below her right shoulder that said, "Hello, my name is," and her name.

On one side sat Tracey, a sixteen-year-old brunette wearing a pink sleeveless top and a matching miniskirt. She had a wide grin on her face and bright, wide eyes as she ate a plain bagel which she had broken up into fourths. At the rate she nibbled at it, it was clear she probably would eat only one of the four pieces. Laura sat next to her, a tall twenty-something with a thick, Amazonian build. She had already had two muffins and was biting into a partially-peeled banana. Her eyes shifted from one person to another, studying each, looking for any sign of weakness or uncertainty on the part of her opponents.

Then there was Krystal, another girl in her early twenties. She was petite, had short, blond hair, and she kept looking down at herself and then at the others as if afraid someone might tell her she was in the wrong blank white void and kindly ask her to leave. She had a muffin on her paper plate but hadn't taken a bite yet. She might not have even liked muffins but had probably only taken one because it was the item the majority of the group had selected.

On the other side of the table was Kay, a tall redhead, middle-aged, who sat up with excellent posture and was evenly buttering her plain muffin with a plastic knife. She was even-tempered and seemed not to have a care in the world. It was difficult for anyone watching to tell if she was even aware of the others in the room. Next to her and across from Laura sat a woman named Sandra with red fire in her eyes—a thick, muscular woman with wild, red-orange, unkempt hair. Her age was impossible to tell—certainly older than Tracey, but beyond that was anyone's guess. She ate her muffins and strawberries quickly and methodically. Slice, bite, chew. Slice, bite, chew. Her eyes shifted from one girl to the next, much like Laura's, except she looked like she might pounce at any of them at any moment.

And finally, there was Alicia, a little brown-haired girl no older than eight who slowly nursed a carton of orange juice. She looked positively terrified of everyone.

After they had been eating in silence for about half an hour, Kay stood up and addressed the group. She was holding a mysterious white envelope with gold writing on the outside. In a calligraphy script, the writing said, "To The Six: Best Of Luck. You Know What To Do."

"I don't know how I know this," Kay said, "but I'm supposed to read what's inside." She spoke slowly and professionally, as if she addressed the public for a living. She pulled open the envelope and revealed a card folded in half. She unfolded it and read, "You each hold the power to prove who is the greatest. We leave it to you to settle the dispute. No pressure."

"Is that a joke?" Laura asked.

Krystal chuckled nervously, "I thought it was kinda funny."

Sandra's animalistic gaze turned into a demonic smile. "I'll be the only one laughing when this is over. I mean, when you're all, you know, dead, and I'm not, and I win."

"This isn't about killing each other," Kay said. "We all know the rules."

"And we don't really know what exactly we're all capable of either, or even if we can die," said Krystal. She looked for approval from Kay and smiled when Kay halfheartedly glanced in her general direction.

"But if we can, I imagine accidents will happen," Sandra said. "Just saying."

"Rules or no rules," Laura told her, "if you try something, it'll be the last chance you get." Their eyes locked and they froze in what could have been a century-long staring contest.

"I don't want to be here," Alicia said. "Do we have to do this? I don't think I can do this."

"You guys are like a cosmic daytime soap," Tracey said. "I

don't know why I know what that is, but that's what you are. Seriously, lighten up. Eat more muffins. We've got one purpose; it's in all of us. So let's just get out there and play the game. No use, like, crying or whatever."

"Didn't figure I'd be with Miss Pompom on anything," said Sandra, "but I agree. Let's do this thing."

They all agreed, some more hesitantly and some more hastily than the others. With no past behind them and only the contest ahead, they had no choice but to move forward. Kay opened a small, silver box in the center of the table. Inside was a round red button.

"See you ladies inside," she said and pushed the button down with both hands, one pressed on top of the other. Six round, swirling vortexes opened, each dozens of feet in diameter, creating an array of colors all across the spectrum. They completed a large circle around the group. Each player was required to step into a different portal, and not one knew where she would end up. This was the first of many rules they all knew with no idea as to where that knowledge had come from. And there was also the cardinal rule: with the exception of their opponents, they were not to speak of the rules or the game to anyone.

The six got up from the table, proceeded toward the portals, and, though all completely different in every way, they each stepped blindly and obediently into their destinies. The game, the most important game to ever be played, had begun.

CHAPTER 1

Franklin Can't Think Like He Used To

DR. FRANKLIN BRYCE WAS NERVOUS ABOUT HIS NEW PATIENT, RAJEL CHIROK. The patient seemed friendly enough, even with the orange skin and the bat wings, and in the first few minutes they spent together in Franklin's spacious fourth story office, Franklin learned that they both had an affinity for American cartoons. That broke the ice a bit, but as Chirok continued to lay more and more of his troubles out in front of him, Franklin felt increasingly ill-equipped to help him. After all, Rajel Chirok was from another dimension called Nixothia, and Nixots were impervious to telepathy.

Several years earlier, Franklin's former patient named Stephen Zarcadmium had surprised him with a gift: the ability to read minds. It was a thank you for helping him through a suicidal depression. And in doing this, Zarcadmium also introduced Franklin to the existence of alternate dimensions, which changed his life forever. Shortly after that, Franklin was hired on at Vlakdormat Psychiatric Services, a firm in Abott City that existed specifically for helping beings from alternate dimensions to cope with life in a new place and for helping human beings to cope with the fact that there really were alternate dimensions. After years of using telepathy in his sessions, Franklin couldn't imagine going without it all the time. He often felt it was the only thing that made him able to keep up with the countless species and cultures he dealt with on a daily basis.

Rajel Chirok sat in a big black armchair across from Franklin, who sat in an identical big black armchair. A long glass table separated them. Chirok had two regular, human-looking arms and two other appendages connected to his large wings, just like a bat. He looked uncomfortable. The furniture in this dimension must have been quite different from what he was used to. He kept readjusting his wings and shifting his weight from side to side.

"Tell me more about your wife," Franklin said.

"I don't even recognize her anymore," Chirok answered.

"Why is that?"

"She got a body-switching operation."

"Oh. So you *literally* don't recognize her anymore."

"Don't get me wrong. I know she's still the same person and everything's still in the right place . . . but she doesn't have the same things. Her eyes are the wrong color, and her wings are all wrong."

"How did she come to the decision to get the operation?"

"It's this huge fad in Nixothia right now. You meet someone, you both look at each other's bodies, you each like something the other has, and you make a trade. I think my wife only did it because she wanted to be a little shorter."

"Shorter?"

"It's considered good luck for women to be really small in Nixothia. Midgets get all the attention. But I think I got the short end of the straw."

"Well, obviously."

Chirok struggled to contain his frustration. "Meridosa used to have the most beautiful wings."

"Do you still love her, Mr. Chirok?"

"Of course I do. I just don't know if I can handle her looking like another woman."

"Is she acting any differently?"

"No, not really. I mean, she slides under the cat door now, but all short women do that."

"Give it time. You'll get used to her new appearance. But let her know that it bothers you and that you need time to adjust."

Chirok nodded slowly, as though he had expected this advice but knew Franklin was right anyway. "Sure. I'll try."

Franklin smiled, impressed with himself for getting so far without knowing what Chirok was thinking. Before talking about Chirok's wife, they had already discussed his fear of pinecones (since they didn't exist in his dimension) and they had dug deeply into the psychology behind Chirok's chronic habit of sleeping straight through every single Nixothian holiday. In each case, Franklin managed to give Chirok some semblance of guidance.

"Before we go, I'd like to go ahead and pay for my first month of sessions," Chirok said, digging frantically through his pockets. The confinement of the armchair made him slap himself repeatedly in the face with his left wing as he moved around. He finally got up out of the chair, reached into his back pocket, pulled out a small white envelope, and handed it to Franklin. "I'm afraid I'll forget if I don't do it now, and then I'll get behind on my bills, and—"

"No, that's fine," Franklin said. He and Chirok got up from their armchairs, Chirok thanked him, and they said their goodbyes. Once Chirok had left, Franklin sat behind his small oak corner desk, laced his fingers behind his head, and leaned back to relax. He was finished with his patients for the day and, while he still had a pile of paperwork he wasn't especially looking forward to, he was relieved.

He closed his eyes and imagined how the session with Chirok might have gone had Chirok not been a Nixot. Franklin would instantly have wowed him with the knowledge that Chirok had a fear of pinecones and was worried that his wife wasn't quite his wife anymore. Chirok would immediately have been put at ease because he had found someone who understood exactly what he was going through, since, after all, Franklin would be able to put all of his problems in exactly the same terms and use exactly the same language Chirok would have. There would have been no probing, no embarrassing questions, no nodding and smiling, pretending he really understood his patient's pain when he was really just trying not to laugh at Chirok's seemingly absurd situation. No matter what the problem was, it never sounded ridiculous when Franklin could actually *feel* his patients as they talked to him.

Franklin felt a small, quick breeze as something brushed past his head. He opened his eyes to see a folded piece of blank white paper floating just above his desk, close enough to give him a paper cut if it really felt like it. It slowly unfolded itself and then the flat paper began to spin around in midair. As it did so, it started to fold itself again and then to rip along the front, then along the sides, then at the back. The top and the sides met and it became a perfect cube, somehow holding itself together without any tape or glue. *I had no idea they made checks that could do that,* Franklin thought, and then he instantly felt stupid for thinking it.

The cube spun faster and began vibrating violently. As it did, Franklin's head started to throb, first like he was a piece of slate being hit with a chisel, and then with searing pain like the double-kick bass in a death metal song. He grabbed both sides of his head and reeled forward until the pain was so unbearable that he fell out of his chair. His head struck the front of his desk. That happened so fast he didn't have time to come up with an analogy for this new kind of pain before he dropped to the floor and blacked out. The last thing he saw before he fell unconscious was the paper cube shooting toward the daylight behind his spacious office windows.

His secretary, Bethany, found and woke him a few minutes later. The paper cube was gone and he realized, looking up at her and not feeling anything from her, that either she had finally embraced every blond stereotype there was—and there truly was nothing behind her grapefruit-sized eyes—or the cube had somehow taken his telepathy with it. Bruised and dumbfounded, he was barely able to make a complete sentence.

"Your mind . . . there's nothing there."

"Thanks," Bethany said sarcastically.

"No . . . I mean I can't read you."

"Maybe you should buy a thinking aid."

Under other circumstances, he might have considered it, but he knew it wouldn't help. As Bethany lifted him off the floor and helped him out of the office and into the hall, his conversation with Rajel Chirok played over in his mind. Chirok had been convincing, but now Franklin recalled noticing something in his eyes—a certain calculation—as they talked. He realized that Chirok was analyzing him, looking for clues in case Franklin was on to his scheme. And by the end, when he was sure he had Franklin fooled, Chirok had whipped out his secret weapon and got out of there as fast as he could. He probably didn't have a phobia about pinecones or a wife. Rajel Chirok probably wasn't his real name. He might have not even liked cartoons.

Franklin's wife, Lera, discovered his missing telepathy only three days later when she found an ad for it on Interdimensional eBay. It turned out that Chirok was a superpower dealer. He stole people's abilities and sold them for premium prices. Franklin tried to tell the investigations division of Interdimensional eBay that Chirok was a thief, but Chirok had somehow forged a legitimate-looking receipt with Franklin's signature saying that Franklin had sold his telepathy. He must have used some kind of magic forging spell. They were hard to come by, but considering Chirok had managed to convince Franklin that he was a patient in need of counseling, Chirok was obviously a professional with major connections throughout the multiverse. And even if Franklin had been able to prove it, there was no interdimensional law, and alternate dimensions weren't officially recognized in any country in Franklin's dimension. Chirok could only be prosecuted in Nixothia, his own dimension. And from what he knew about the complex and convoluted justice system of Nixothia, Franklin doubted it would be a big priority for them.

Franklin sat at his computer and watched the auction, sweating, as the price of his telepathy rose and rose. He could feel it slipping further and further away in that final hour as he refreshed his web browser every few minutes and watched the time tick away. The auction had started at a price Franklin couldn't possibly afford and it ended at an equivalent of $50,000. In that last moment, as he read the words "This auction is now closed," Franklin wondered if this was the first time Chirok had stolen telepathy and if he had ever kept that power for himself. He wondered if Chirok was reading his mind before he left, knowing how important the ability was to Franklin's career and his lifestyle. Above all, Franklin wondered if Chirok knew he was ruining his life and if that information made him reconsider his plans, even for a second.

The next day, Franklin called in sick for work.

CHAPTER 2

Domestic Robot Problems

SIX MONTHS LATER, FRANKLIN FOUND HIMSELF VISITING KRAWKSON KLUB MORE FREQUENTLY THAN HE USED TO. Krawkson Klub was a place for people in Abott City of all interdimensional races to unwind. The club was named after its owner, who thought spelling everything with a "k" was clever. But that wasn't why people from dimensions all over the multiverse went there. They went because Krawkson had drinks you couldn't get anywhere else, like the Threpnoidian Dragonfly. Franklin didn't know a thing about it, beyond that it was made in a dimension called Threpnoidia, and he didn't have the slightest idea what was in it. It tasted good and gave him a buzz, and that was all that really mattered. And since, after having the same drink every week for the last four years, his eyes hadn't popped out of his sockets and he hadn't imploded, he wasn't too worried about it.

Most people also didn't come for the entertainment. At the moment, a pair of Quaxor twins from the Bramzit dimension was on stage doing a hideous karaoke rendition of "I Will Survive." They sounded like a herd of cows. Their deep, droning voices would have made them sound like only two cows had they only had one head apiece, but since there were six between them, they sounded like an entire herd.

"If I owned this place, I'd hold auditions before I let anyone with that many heads on stage," said a voice next to him. Franklin turned his head to see his best friend and colleague William Vanderhorst who was wearing a red Hawaiian shirt with an orange tie. It was the same thing he had worn to work.

"I didn't expect to see you here this evening," said Franklin, shaking his hand. All William seemed to talk about lately was video games, and Franklin had figured he'd be at home playing. But he was glad for the company.

"Still working on Final Fantasy, or is it Castlevania now?"

"Nah, I borrowed one from a patient of mine who occasionally vacations in Dimension 0.485."

Franklin nodded. Dimension 0.485 was one of the closer alternate Earth realities. Most of the history was exactly the same—Lincoln had still been murdered, the Allies had still won World War II, the Star Wars prequel trilogy was still awful—but some things changed a little.

"So what's this new game you're playing?" Franklin asked.

"Bounce Destruction Mayhem. It's a cross between Super Mario, Tekken 3, and pogo sticks."

Franklin raised an eyebrow. "Pogo sticks?"

William took a seat next to Franklin. "So how are things at work?"

Franklin was used to pretending he wasn't having any trouble with his patients, but the truth was, he spent all his free time reading up on the culture and behaviors of the species of each new patient, and sometimes it was barely enough. He often felt like a calculus teacher who never made it past college algebra.

"I'm getting a new patient tomorrow," Franklin said. "A human. Young guy. Regular case of realizing how screwed up the world is."

William took a sip from his glass. His drink was the color of mustard and was almost of the same consistency. Franklin didn't think it looked very appetizing, and he found himself less curious about its composition than he was about the Threpnoidian

Dragonfly.

"Do you mean he's finally coming to terms with the fact that most governments are corrupt and people get murdered a lot—or the other kind of screwed up?"

"Oh no, the other one. I'm not sure what he's seen, but whatever it is, my secretary said he sounded pretty traumatized. What about you?"

The twins had finished singing, and the audience was quietly and politely applauding. Franklin and William set down their glasses, lightly clapped three or four times each, and resumed drinking.

"I got a patient with fantastiphobia," said William, smiling proudly.

Franklin almost choked on his drink. Fantastiphobia was the fear of too many things going one's way. He had read about it, but he was always suspicious about whether it actually existed.

"Yeah, it's fascinating. I can't talk about his specific case, of course," William said.

"Of course."

"It turns out he was just fine when everything was going wrong, but now that things are perfect, he's getting emotionally unstable."

"It's a good thing he found us," said Franklin. "Otherwise he might have been put on medicine or something."

William shuddered at that and took a long drink from his mustard-like beverage. "Medicine. I think it has created half the mental conditions it was supposedly designed to relieve."

"I wish more Earth doctors would take a page from our book," Franklin said. "Of course, then they'd have to admit there were such things as other dimensions."

"And if they did that, you and I would probably have more work than we could handle."

Franklin laughed and raised his drink. "To the multiverse," he said. They clinked their glasses together.

"And to the best job in this dimension," William added. "Or, at least, the most interesting."

Franklin couldn't argue with that.

"*Normal* is a word that is in no way whatsoever worth bothering to define," Franklin told his new patient, Calvin Stanley. Their session had just begun and Calvin had already asked him to define *normal.* Franklin knew their conversation wasn't likely to end well. "Even the attempt at developing an opinion on the subject has driven more people mad than any actual mental illness. If normal could truly be defined, then normal would seem extremely abnormal, except we wouldn't call it abnormal. We'd call it normal."

Calvin looked confused.

"And since this is a concept we can hardly wrap our minds around, we must simply accept that anything can and does happen, logic is always logical except for when it isn't, and if it doesn't seem possible, it probably wasn't possible before it happened."

This was Franklin's best explanation, one he had practiced in front of the mirror when his wife wasn't home a dozen times and one which, he would readily admit, wasn't much of an explanation at all. But considering that he lived in a world where the majority of people either chose to ignore that portals opened somewhere everyday or were too stupid to notice, there wasn't much else he could say—certainly nothing very comforting.

What is normal? It was one of his least favorite questions, and he was used to getting less-than-positive reactions to his answer. He really needed to work on that speech, especially when dealing with someone like Calvin, who had just found out his mother was a robot.

Calvin was a short, single, well dressed, well groomed tax preparer who spent the majority of his time reading encyclopedias and competing in Scrabble championships. He was the worst sort of person to suddenly learn that his mother was a robot.

"Mom's a robot," he said for the fifth time, dumbfounded and blinking a lot.

"And you find that . . . difficult to accept?" asked Franklin.

"How is it even possible? I didn't know there *were robots,* much less that they were having children. Much less, even, that they were having *me.*"

"Stranger things have happened," Franklin said. He immediately wished he could gobble the words back up the moment he said them.

"Like what?" Calvin asked. He folded his arms and looked out at the city through Franklin's massive office window.

"I don't think you really want me to answer that," said Franklin.

"No, really, I do. What could possibly be weirder than being the son of a freaking robot?"

"First of all, she may be a robot, but she's still your mother. And no, you don't want to know. At least, not yet. Take it one step at a time. But while you're getting used to the idea, it's very important that you don't tell anyone."

"Not like they'd believe me anyway."

"Most people wouldn't, no. But trust me, for your own sake.

Your mother is an HR120."

"A what?"

"Human replica, model 120. That means two very important things for you. First, she can do absolutely anything and everything a human being can do."

"I know that much. What's the other thing?"

"If she finds out you know, she's programmed to kill you."

Calvin went wide-eyed and froze. "Oh. I thought you were a therapist, not a sci-fi enthusiast."

"It isn't science fiction," Franklin said. "It's the truth. It's my job to know these things—if I didn't, I couldn't help you. And half the problems my patients have would probably be just as traumatic for me. The first step in helping you cope with this situation is to make sure you don't do anything to get yourself killed."

Franklin told Calvin about the HR120s, how they posed as real people all over the world and how no one knew just how many of them there were or who built them. Vlakdormat's intelligence on them was extremely limited; since they could do anything a human being could do, it was impossible to tell how many of them there were. From a few recorded incidents, all Franklin and the staff at Vlakdormat knew was that the HR120s would go to any lengths to conceal their existence from the world.

"So I guess that means that I'm not a—"

"No," said Franklin. "You're not a robot. As I said, the HR120s can do anything a human can do. That includes having human children."

"That's weird."

"They're incredibly sophisticated. How did you find out about her?"

Calvin stood up and started pacing the bright blue, carpeted floor. Franklin picked up his clipboard and began writing as Calvin spoke. He wasn't really taking any notes, but he found that it usually made his patients feel better to think he was.

"She started . . . malfunctioning," said Calvin. "I came home to visit and she made dinner. Half way through her tuna casserole, she asked me how things were going at work. I told her, she nodded, and then she asked again. I asked her if everything was all right, but she just ignored me and asked a third time. She kept repeating the same question for ten minutes before she finally snapped out of it and went back to her tuna."

Franklin looked up from his clipboard. "And you surmised that she must be a robot, just from that?"

"No," said Calvin. "A couple hours later I peeked into her room and saw her unscrewing a panel on her arm with a screwdriver."

"That would do it." Franklin rubbed his chin thoughtfully. "Mr. Stanley, I have an exercise I would like you to try."

Calvin leaned forward. "I'll do anything."

"Leave the country."

"What?"

"Your mother is not only an HR120, she's apparently a broken HR120. I have no idea what she might do to you when she sees you next."

As if on cue, Franklin's thick glass office door opened. Standing behind it was a tall, brown-haired, middle-aged woman wearing a stunning red dress and heels with her arms folded in front of her.

Calvin stepped back from the door. "Mom. What are you doing here?"

It was Virginia Stanley, the HR120 herself.

"I've been looking for you," she said. "We need to talk."

Franklin immediately stood between them, staring Mrs. Stanley squarely in the face. "No one is going to die in my office. I specialize in domestic disputes. Let's settle this calmly."

Mrs. Stanley raised her hand and swatted Franklin to the ground like an abnormally large fly. Then she grabbed her son by the throat.

"Now what . . . what did I say, Mrs. Stanley?" Franklin said from the floor, coughing.

"You said there would be no death in your office. Unfortunately for you, Asimov's Three Laws of Robotics are complete bunk. I was not programmed by a human. I am not programmed to obey humans. And I am not programmed to permit useless therapists to solve my 'domestic disputes.' I am, however, programmed to do *this*."

The HR120 proceeded, calmly and unmercifully, to squeeze her son's throat more tightly. HR120s had three times the strength of humans. Franklin couldn't hope to save Calvin by himself and Calvin's windpipe would be crushed in seconds. Franklin looked up at his desk and remembered a security protocol he'd never thought he'd need. He struggled to get up off the floor and then he reached for a drawer behind the desk. He pulled out a small red leather book and frantically paged through it until he found what he needed: the positronic deactivation switch. Then he got up into his chair and pressed a small button on his desk. It flashed red and beeped.

He shouted the security code for the positronic deactivation switch—code alpha 392—hoping the HR120 was too distracted with Calvin to pay any attention. When security heard that code, they would activate a device that would send a signal to shut down any positronic activity—anything with an artificially intelligent brain—in the building.

After five more seconds of watching Calvin writhe in pain and struggle for oxygen, Virginia Stanley opened her hand and let him fall unceremoniously to the floor. He was dead. She turned to face Franklin, who was still bent over his desk.

"You know I'm an HR120?" she asked. Her arms transformed into two enormous, sleek, metallic guns.

"That's kind of obvious by now," said Franklin. What was taking security so long to turn on the switch? She should have already been deactivated.

"Just checking. Now I am authorized to kill you. No hard feelings." She lifted one of her strange weapon arms. A line of green lights on the sides of each gun flashed rapidly, and Franklin looked around frantically, wondering in which direction was the smartest to jump. But he never had to make that decision because the guns didn't fire. Virginia froze, and, after several seconds, she dropped to the floor. The lights on her weapon arms stopped flashing. Her eyes went blank.

"It's about time," Franklin said aloud. He left his office and stormed over to his secretary's desk.

"Sorry the positronic deactivation protocol took so long, boss," said Bethany. "The place has never been infiltrated by robots before. The security guys had no idea what code alpha 392 was. They had to look it up."

Franklin's face went red with fury. Nothing like this had ever happened in his five years at Vlakdormat.

"My patient *died,* Bethany."

"Oh. Finding out his mom was a robot must have been too

much for him."

"No, his *mom* was too much for him." Franklin put both hands on her desk and leaned forward, angrily. "How the hell did an HR120 get into this building?"

"That lady I sent in was an HR120? But she came in here yesterday, remember? You booked her appointment. . . . She was your one o'clock, . . ."

He slammed one of his fists down on her desk and instantly felt bad about it. He shouldn't have been taking this out on Bethany. Despite how insensitive she was, she wasn't to blame. He remembered Virginia now. She had looked different with gun turrets for arms—which made Calvin's death not only extremely depressing, but also Franklin's fault. He turned to leave.

"It's not like you could have known what she was. I mean, only a *telepath* could possibly know if a person were an HR120. . . ."

Franklin turned back and narrowed his eyes. Bethany looked away and pulled out some paperwork.

"Sorry, I forgot. Still a touchy subject. Okay, got it."

He sighed and turned away again.

"There's always time travel," Bethany called behind him.

"I almost got fired last time, remember?"

"So I guess I'll cancel all your appointments for this afternoon?"

"I guess so," he answered and walked into the elevator.

CHAPTER 3

The Purple Cloud

FRANKLIN WALKED INTO HIS REASONABLY LARGE BRICK HOUSE IN HIS REASONABLY QUIET NEIGHBORHOOD, WISHING IT WEREN'T HIS WIFE'S DAY OFF. Lera met him at the door in a rather provocative black dress that accentuated her slender, young-looking body. Lera looked like a twenty-five-year-old dancer with her slender legs and long red hair, but her actual profession was linguist. She knew several interdimensional languages, loved to translate them, and she always insisted on looking fantastic while she did so.

Lera was not only significantly taller than Franklin—she was also almost three centuries older. She was from a dimension called Verullia, and, while Verullians weren't immortal, their average lifespan was about a 1000 years. (The men usually only lived to be about 850.)

She was surprised to see Franklin home so early and immediately asked him what the trouble was. He hated that they lived in a house with a staircase immediately in front of the door —she could trap him right there if she wanted to and he wouldn't have anywhere to run. She stretched out her arms across the narrow hall playfully, trying to cheer him up. Considering what she was wearing, he wished he was in a better mood. He ducked under one of her arms and walked up the stairs into the living room. But he knew he couldn't avoid her forever. Sooner or later, he would have to tell her what had happened at Vlakdormat. He took off his shoes, sat on the leather couch, and picked up the remote control.

He turned on the black widescreen flat panel television he

rarely watched. He flipped through the channels, certain there wouldn't be anything on at two in the afternoon, but hoping for some sort of distraction. Lera sat beside him.

"Really," she said, "what happened? Not another death threat, I hope."

"Not exactly," said Franklin.

"Let me guess, then. A robot broke into your office, killed a patient, and you stopped it just before it killed you."

Franklin sighed. "Yeah, that's about right."

"I thought that's what that look meant."

Franklin shook his head. "It's not fair. Why do you still get to keep your superpowers?"

Being a Verullian, Lera possessed an uncanny sense of intuition. She couldn't read minds, but she had an amazing understanding of body language and tonal inflections that, combined with a gland in her brain that humans didn't have, allowed her to pick up on things no one else could possibly know. It was like having an extremely advanced hunch, and hers were nearly always right.

When Franklin had still been telepathic, it had been a strange role reversal for him. She could almost always tell what he was thinking just by looking at him, and, since Verullians weren't susceptible to telepathy, she was the only person close to him whose mind he couldn't read. He had once asked Lera why he couldn't read her mind, and she had just shrugged and said her species was too awesome to be affected by mental powers. She then claimed Verlluians were also immune to high temperatures up to 150 degrees, cat allergies, and the cuteness of babies. It was often impossible to tell when she was joking.

Franklin's eyes returned to the television. There was a still picture of a dark green leafy plant sitting in a dull, flesh-colored pot. The image never changed. He wondered if entertainment had degenerated so far that there was actually a whole channel devoted to this.

Lera said, "Don't take it out on me. Nobody gave me my ability."

Franklin turned off the TV and slumped on the edge of the couch. "I worked hard for that telepathy. And anyway, that isn't the point."

"Isn't it?" Lera sat closer and put one of his hands in hers. "You think you could have stopped that man from dying if you could still read minds?"

"I just . . . I've never lost a patient before."

Lera nodded. "Doctors have to deal with that all the time."

"I'm a *therapist*, not a surgeon. My patients' problems aren't usually so immediately life threatening."

"It wasn't your fault. What kind of robot was it, anyway? Wait, don't tell me. HR120."

Franklin glared at her.

"Sorry." She thought for a moment and then abruptly stood up. "Maybe you should take some time off."

He shook his head and continued slumping. "I can't do that."

"Why not? You obviously need it. You've got plenty of vacation built up. Just take a week and then—"

"I can't take time off because I'm going to quit."

He couldn't believe he was saying it out loud. The thought hadn't even crossed his mind until now, and he suddenly realized there were no other options. Despite his hope that he could somehow survive at Vlakdormat without telepathy, he knew he wasn't cut out for it anymore. His job was about more than mere psychology—it was an adventure.

It wasn't simply about having a superpower either. William wasn't supernatural, but he had grown up traveling around with his parents to other dimensions. (They were both painters and they had embraced the multiverse for inspiration. They weren't especially good painters, and they barely made enough income to support themselves, but at least William had the benefit of decades of knowledge and experience.) Franklin had learned a lot in five years, but it wasn't enough. He wondered if William would have known Virginia Stanley was an HR120 by just looking at her.

He vividly remembered the night he last saw Stephen Zarcadmium. Franklin was up late catching up on some paperwork when the strange, fat man knocked on his office door. Zarcadmium had been to see him every week for almost a year, until he was finally stable enough to work through things on his own. They hadn't seen each other for a couple of months; the last time they had spoken, Zarcadmium was putting together his own small landscaping business.

He never expected to see Zarcadmium again, but it turned out that if he hadn't, he never would have worked at Vlakdormat or met his wife. In five minutes, Stephen Zarcadmium had opened the portal to Franklin's future.

"What can I do for you?" Franklin asked. Zarcadmium was grinning from ear to ear and it made Franklin uncomfortable. This was a man who had once considered electrocuting himself in his own bathtub with a microwave.

"I'm here to do something for you," Zarcadmium said. "You helped me learn to live in this world after mine had

disintegrated into nothingness."

"I appreciate that, but I was only—"

"Don't say you were only doing your job." He paused. Zarcadmium had always been a very passionate man. "You have no idea what you did for me. My world literally disintegrated. Into. Nothingness."

Franklin was concerned. This man was dead serious.

"I never told you because I knew you wouldn't believe me. I usually keep my true origins to myself—it's easier for everyone that way. My world was called Corvadia, and now it's gone."

Franklin stood up and pushed his chair into his desk. "So when you said that the sun would never shine again and that the rivers of your life were drying up and that the dung beetles had drawn their last breath . . . you weren't being metaphorical?"

"That all happened," Zarcadmium said. His creepy smile had returned. "And I may never have gotten through it without you. I'm here to give you something for your trouble, Dr. Bryce."

"You've already compensated me for—"

"It wasn't enough," Zarcadmium said. "I can give you something that will change your life."

He lifted his arms into the air and a small, swirling, purple cloud appeared over their heads. It grew until it had engulfed the ceiling. And all at once, as Franklin looked into Zarcadmium's familiar eyes, one gold and the other a hot pinkish color, the idea that Zarcadmium might not be from Earth began to make some kind of sense.

"I don't know what that is, but I don't think I have room

for it in my house," Franklin said.

Zarcadmium laughed. "Don't worry. This won't hurt."

The cloud struck Franklin with a strange bolt of green lighting, and he was surprised to find that Zarcadmium was right—it didn't hurt—but it made his head feel like he had been thinking too hard. After a few moments, the cloud began to dissipate, and Franklin was disoriented; he seemed to see three of everything for a moment. When everything came back into focus, Zarcadmium told him to try and read his mind. Before he even thought about how ridiculous of a request that was, Franklin recited the first two full paragraphs of Moby Dick and he was amazed; he had never read it.

"That's your gift," Zarcadmium said. "You're about to have the chance to look at people's psyches in a way you never knew was possible. And you're going to meet people, like me, from places you never knew existed. Welcome to the multiverse."

And just as one man had opened that incredible portal of wonder and possibilities for Franklin, Rajel Chirok had closed it. Without his telepathy, Franklin was rock climbing without any gear.

He had only ever quit one other therapy job, and he'd done so to work at Vlakdormat. After tomorrow, the only extradimensional thing in his life would be Lera. She tried to talk him out of it, and after an hour of listening to her tell him how talented he was even without telepathy, about all the people he had helped—like Zarcadmium—he still couldn't get past the logic that the patients at Vlakdormat were different from the ones he had seen before he had worked there. There was a difference between helping people who *thought* that they were seeing talking trees and people who were actually *seeing* talking trees.

So Franklin resigned from Vlakdormat and he quickly found work at a smaller office. After only a couple days, he was already missing the resources that had been available to him at Vlakdormat. After all, having the means to send a chronically depressed patient to a pocket dimension had always been quite a time saver. (Once they had spent a day in a dimension made entirely out of bread, home didn't seem so bad.)

After two weeks of "normal" patients, it would have been easy for Franklin to pretend things were like they had been before Zarcadmium. But then he met a woman named Helena Kathryn.

She came to see him after screaming at a man at a bus stop that she was a six-year-old girl who had lost her mother and wanted to go home. She looked about Lera's age (if Lera were human), and the only way he could have described her was *perfect.* Not perfect in the sense that she swept him off his feet at first sight—he wasn't ready to leave his wife and run away with her. She was attractive, to be sure, but she was perfect in that she had absolutely no physical blemishes.

Her teeth were bright white and perfectly straight. Her shoulder-length hair, the color of chocolate mousse, was cut perfectly even and there wasn't a strand out of place. Her face was absolutely symmetrical and she wore no makeup. There was nothing to cover up—no acne, no moles, not even so much as a freckle. Franklin certainly wasn't accustomed to noticing these sorts of physical details in his patients—it was unprofessional—but Helena looked like she had been sculpted rather than born.

She seemed to have associative identity disorder (commonly known as multiple personality disorder), but he had dealt with similar cases in the past in three or four different species. It wasn't her actions that scared him.

It was her name.

After his experiences with beings from other dimensions, Franklin had come to realize one of the bizarre constants of the multiverse. No matter what dimension they came from, people with two first names were always trouble. And not trouble like saying embarrassing things in public or knocking over shoe stores. They were trouble like stopping the world from spinning, or causing every person who had ever said the word "voluptuous" to suddenly disappear like they'd never existed. There was no doubt about it. Helena Kathryn was going to be *trouble.*

Franklin shook her hand as she walked into his new office. It was on the ground floor of the building and was quite a bit smaller than his last office. He missed his glass coffee table, his spacious window and the gorgeous view of the city. His new office had one very small window that looked out into a parking lot and just enough room for two semi-comfortable armchairs, a desk, and a wastebasket. He couldn't even use his old coat rack; now he had to hang his coat on a hook on the door.

"I've been looking for you, Dr. Bryce," said Helena.

"Really?"

"I hear you specialize in unusual cases. You were recommended to me by one of the officers who picked me up at the bus stop. He told me he had a sister who came to you after swearing a car had tried to eat her."

Franklin remembered the patient. A thirty-something woman who had a bad run-in with a farquid, a common pet in the Navwisque dimension with the ability to mimic metallic objects. He had an impossible time convincing her that what she had seen was a real creature and that she wasn't actually going insane, despite having just completed a lengthy drug rehab.

"What's your problem, Miss Kathryn?"

"I have multiple personalities," she replied.

Franklin nodded. "The little girl who was bothering the man at the bus station. That wasn't you."

"No, that was Alicia. She's six years old and is perpetually lost and frightened."

"How long have you had this other personality?"

"As long as I can remember," she said, "which isn't long at all. Just a few months ago, I found myself in the middle of a field outside the city. I had no memory, a wallet, a driver's license, and six other personalities in my head."

Franklin took off his glasses, pulled out a handkerchief from his shirt pocket, and cleaned his lenses. "Six?"

"Yes," said Helena. "And every one of them knows exactly who she is. Everyone except for me."

Franklin leaned forward with his pad and pen in hand. Considering her bizarre situation, he found it odd how incredibly calm and patient she seemed. The other multiple personality cases he had encountered were unfocused and lacking in self-confidence. Helena just looked confused.

"I wonder if I could meet one of them."

"I was hoping you would," Helena said, nodding. "I've always known how to call them. I don't know how I know, but I know."

"Which one will I be meeting?"

"Tracy. Most people find her obnoxious, but at least she's not insane."

"You consider yourself insane?"

"No, not me. One of the other personalities: Sandra. She thinks pain and death are hilarious. I try not to let her out if I can help it. People don't share her sense of humor."

Franklin wondered what exactly she meant by that. Had she actually killed someone? "No, I suppose they wouldn't. Why don't we keep Sandra waiting for another day?"

Helena closed her eyes for several seconds and then opened them again. Her serious expression suddenly became lighter, cheerier.

"Tracy?"

She jumped up and shook his hand like he was a good friend she hadn't seen in years. Franklin was now convinced that something severely traumatic had happened in Helena's past—and it most likely involved cheerleading.

"Oh my God! I've been, like, so looking forward to meeting you. I gotta say, you look absolutely fab. It must be the hair."

"Tracy, I'd like to—"

"You know, being stuck inside someone else's head is so weird. Like the other day, Helena was in a mall, and I was like, 'Hey, Helena, let me take over so I can shop,' because I'm, like, so much better at that than she is, and—"

"Tracy, if we could just—"

"Well, anyway, I'm just glad she finally decided to come see you. We all knew a shrink was a good idea. Well, all of us except Sandy, of course. God, she is *hopeless.* She's probably, like, a cannibal or something and just, like, none of us knows it."

"Tracy, can I speak with Helena again please?" Franklin asked, deciding to make it a personal policy from then on to never accept patients with two first names.

"Yeah, no prob. But I don't know why she always gets to steer this boat."

Tracy rolled her eyes, closed them, and after a short time, Helena was calm and collected once again. They seemed like two remarkably different women.

"What do you think?" Helena asked.

"I think I'm going to have to keep you here as an inpatient for a while," said Franklin.

"That's probably a good idea."

CHAPTER 4

The Long Chase Begins

LATER THAT EVENING, FRANKLIN AND LERA WERE IN THEIR LIVING ROOM STARING AT THE FAR WALL, WHICH WAS THE ONLY ONE IN THE ROOM WITHOUT A FAMILY PHOTO OR A HANGING PLANT OR A VERULLIAN STATUE OF SOME HISTORICAL SIGNIFICANCE FRANKLIN WASN'T AWARE OF. He was staring because he was thinking about Helena. He wondered where she came from and what could have triggered the onset of six multiple personalities *and* total amnesia. Lera, on the other hand, was looking at the wall because it was a popular game in Verullia called Veritzu. He had never understood it and she had never been able to explain it to him, other than to say that concentration was key and if your eyes moved in the slightest, you lost ten points and had to start all over.

The phone rang and Franklin immediately jumped up from his chair. Lera didn't as much as flinch. Franklin shook his head at her and answered the phone. It was William.

"How's that pogo stick game working out?" Franklin asked.

"I beat it yesterday," said William. "Bought the sequel."

"What's it like?"

"Same as the first one, but take out the pogo stick and replace it with a flamingo."

"I can't begin to picture that."

"Anyway, that's not why I'm calling. You've got to come back to work."

"I quit."

"You have to un-quit. Dr. Grothman, the guy who took your place. . . ."

There was a long pause. "Yeah. . . ?"

"He has kind of killed off half your patients."

"What?"

"He's got this weird philosophy. No matter what his patient's going through, the answer is always suicide."

Franklin couldn't believe what he was hearing. How did this guy get hired in the first place? After all, Vlakdormat had a strict policy about new hires; they always had to go through Gordon, the mind probe, who could immediately tell if someone's intentions were less than honest. Surely this new guy would have been filtered out.

"How did you find out about it?" Franklin asked.

"One of his patients ratted him out to me . . . right before he went and offed himself. Apparently Grothman's very persuasive."

Franklin couldn't imagine how their boss, Dr. Caslom, could possibly be buying Grothman's story. "What's Caslom doing about it?" he asked.

"Nothing. I think Grothman must have some kind of persuasion powers." Vlakdormat was an equal opportunity employer. They couldn't refuse to hire someone for having superpowers. A new hire had to sign something saying he wouldn't use his powers against anyone, but if Grothman had powers, he might have persuaded Caslom not to make him sign it. "Luckily I haven't run into Grothman, or I wouldn't be making this phone call," William said.

"Meet me at Krawkson Klub tomorrow night at seven," said Franklin. "Don't do anything—I'll have a plan by the time I see you."

"He might kill someone else before then."

"Try to make sure he doesn't. I need time to do some research. Besides, I can't get off work for this. They would never understand."

"Franklin, you are coming back, right?"

"I'll help you get rid of this guy. That's all I can promise."

Franklin hung up the phone and looked at his wife. She was still staring at the wall.

"Did you hear all of that?" he asked.

"Suicide bad. Evil persuasive doctor. Got it. Now please. I'm trying to concentrate."

Franklin went to bed. This had been a weird day, even for him.

It was six o'clock the next afternoon. Franklin was finished with his last appointment and was locking up his office. He was due to meet William in an hour but he wasn't thinking about Dr. Grothman, despite the fact that Dr. Grothman was killing off his old patients. As he headed down the hallway toward the parking garage, all he could think about was Helena Kathryn.

He had met another of her personalities that day, Krystal. She was an absolute genius. She had extensive knowledge of math, science, and history. She spoke of ancient Rome and string theory and computers, and she even knew precise equations that could be used to open doorways to specific dimensions. She seemed to know a lot of things Helena didn't.

Why had these personalities manifested themselves? It would take a long time to get to the bottom of it, but he didn't want to rush her and risk further psychological injury. She was living proof that anything was possible. Franklin was afraid he might say something to her that would trigger further amnesia or force one of her personalities to come out, like the apparently-homicidal Sandra, or even cause her to develop an eighth personality. He knew all of that was unlikely, but he couldn't begin to explain what might have happened to Helena. He had never come across anything like it, even at Vlakdormat.

Franklin's thoughts were interrupted by a strange, mechanical buzz coming from inside the walls around him. He put his ear to one of the walls and he could hear the sound more clearly. It grew louder and louder. In a moment, it grew so loud that the wall began to vibrate. Franklin took a step backward. It could be the electric company, he thought. Though most people weren't aware of it, the electric company was run by a clan of greedy and rather nasty creatures from the Pliscott dimension. When people failed to pay their bills, the Pliscotts' penalties involved more than simply turning off the power.

The whirring sound stopped, and four janitors wearing light gray overalls phased right through the walls and surrounded Franklin, two on either side. They each raised an arm like Nazis.

"Good evening," said Franklin.

All four upraised arms transformed into large, red-glowing energy weapons.

"I must regretfully inform you," one of them said, "that we have come to destroy you. We hope your last day has been pleasant and rewarding, and we can assure you that your death is necessary and is in no way meaningless whatsoever."

They definitely weren't from the electric company.

Franklin folded his arms. These were HR120s. "If this is about Virginia Stanley, you could have come after me before now."

"This has nothing to do with that incident," said the same

HR120.

"But now that you mention it," said one of the others, "that was very rude of you."

Franklin quickly leaped under one of the robot's legs and slid across the tile floor. One of the HR120s fired, missed, and blew apart the legs of the HR120 Franklin had just slid under. It collapsed to the floor and started firing at him. Soon, all four of them were firing at him. He had managed to get to his feet and take off down the hallway.

He dodged several thin blue blasts of energy, but a couple of doors and parts of the wall vaporized. He knew he couldn't outrun four HR120s on foot. His only chance was to get to his car and hope he could start it, back it out of its spot, and either get it out of the parking lot before they could catch him or run them all down before they blew up his vehicle. It was a horrible plan. It would never work.

It took him a while to realize that they had stopped firing. When he heard the crunching of metal and the sound of sparks flying behind him, he stopped running. He turned around to find three of the HR120s lying in a jumbled mess on the floor. Helena Kathryn was holding the legless HR120's flaming head by one hand, smoldering wires dangling beneath it.

"How did I do that?" she asked, which might have been Franklin's first question, had he not been astounded to find himself still alive.

CHAPTER 5

Priorities

THE ONE THING FRANKLIN HATED ABOVE ALL ELSE WAS IRONY. Irony seemed to always find a way to turn his life upside down and to change things when he least expected it. It even managed to make his life weirder than it already was. Irony was ironic, really.

For instance, he had just quit his job at Vlakdormat, a center of therapy for the supernatural and the interdimensional—and for the human beings who were on the verge of mental breakdowns because of the realization that one of those two things existed. He had found a job as a therapist at a *regular* mental health facility, and it was the last place on Earth he expected to meet a woman with seven multiple personalities, amnesia, and the ability to rip HR120s to shreds with her bare hands. Yes, irony was his greatest enemy, next to, perhaps, the robots that were trying to vaporize him. Them, and the therapist with persuasion powers who was killing all of his old patients.

Helena rode shotgun in Franklin's navy blue Ford Taurus as he turned up his windshield wipers and squinted to see the road through a vicious rainstorm. He planned to take her to Vlakdormat after his meeting with William. Perhaps the Unexplained Phenomena Wing could help make sense of her newfound abilities. But he had to take care of one incredibly dangerous problem before the other, and right now he just hoped he wouldn't hit a light pole on his way to Krawkson Klub.

"Why is it that it always seems to rain when something dramatic and dangerous happens?" Franklin asked aloud.

"You're agitated," Helena said from the passenger's seat.

"Thanks for pointing that out."

"You struck me as such a calm man. Considering the kinds of people you deal with on a regular basis, I might have thought you would thrive under these circumstances."

"Robots aren't trying to kill you," said Franklin.

Helena looked down at her hands. Franklin briefly looked over at her and thought he detected a hint of sadness. "Somehow I don't think that would affect me in the same way," she said.

Franklin sighed. A therapist being insensitive: another irony.

"How did you know I was being attacked?" Franklin asked her.

"I left a sweater in your office. The inpatient attendant wouldn't let me go after it until your sessions were over."

"It's a good thing you came when you did. I promise, we'll find out what's happening to you."

"How are we going to do that?"

"I can take you to Vlakdormat. They're pretty good at figuring out these things."

"But this isn't just about psychology anymore. I physically destroyed those robots. I shouldn't have been able to do that."

"You'd be surprised what they can do at Vlakdormat."

A short time later, Franklin made a hard left off the road and drove toward a clump of trees. Helena glanced at him questioningly as they headed straight for the trees.

"Relax," said Franklin. "We're here."

Instead of crashing, they drove through a dimensional aperture disguised as a clump of trees, which led to Krawkson Klub. If Franklin hadn't been driving at a speed of thirty to thirty-seven miles per hour, he would have smashed right into a tree trunk. Pocket dimension apertures were accessed by obscure conditions like these, so that people couldn't just wander in accidentally. Most people wouldn't have known what to do with themselves once they were there. Franklin wasn't certain if this was achieved through a magical spell or a very complex hologram (both of which existed and could be used for such a purpose) but Krawkson was rich enough to afford both.

They were now in a large parking lot in front of a brick building with flashing neon signs. The sky was completely clear —no rain, no clouds, not even stars. Franklin explained to Helena that Krawkson kept a five acre artificial pocket dimension on his keychain, and that's where the dimensional aperture had transported them. Anyone in Abott City who knew it was there was welcome, and no one who was unaware of the multiverse would wander in and find out about it the hard way.

"So we're smaller now?" Helena asked.

"Technically. As soon as we go back through the aperture, we'll be our normal size again."

"So what if the owner accidentally smashes us?"

Franklin hadn't really thought about that before. "I doubt that would happen. It wouldn't be good for business."

"A night club? You were talking about a night club?"

"This isn't Vlakdormat. I have to take care of another problem before we can go there. Besides, Vlakdormat isn't open again until tomorrow."

Helena folded her arms. "You are the worst therapist I've ever known. Granted, you're the only one, but I'll bet I could pick up a phone book right now and find a better one."

Franklin raised an eyebrow. "Look, I'm sorry, but this is important."

"Whatever."

"You aren't Helena, are you?"

She laughed. "*Laura.* You may not realize this, *Doctor* Bryce, but the rest of us are people too. We have needs, just like she does. And we want to get to the bottom of whatever the hell is going on just as much as she does. Probably more. It might be easy for her to be calm and patient all the time—she's not watching everything from the sidelines. I want results, and I'm going to get them."

"Laura, please. Everything that I'm doing is in your best interest."

"Oh yeah? Then what are we doing at a nightclub? Do you remember what Helena did to those robots back at the crazy house? I could do three times worse to you. Maybe *four* times worse."

She was obviously nervous and afraid but was trying to look tough. She was also right—if she had the mind to try and hurt him, Franklin almost certainly couldn't stop her. But he stood his ground; he thought the best way to deal with these other personalities was to make them respect him. If he could align his priorities with theirs, he might not be in immediate danger every time one of them took over.

"The facility I'm going to take you to has been infiltrated by a man with the ability to force people to do anything he says. This man may have the ability to take over the city, and more. We're here to meet someone who can help me remedy that situation. If I don't take care of that problem *first,* we'll never solve yours or anyone else's. Do you understand?"

Laura didn't say anything for a few minutes. "Okay, that's a twist," she finally said. "We'll do it your way. But I want you to remember something, *Doctor* Bryce. There are six more of us in here. Helena, for whatever reason, gets to have control of our body most of the time. Occasionally, one of us can get out, but she's stronger than us. We seem to be wired that way. But all six of us—and pay attention now, because this is the part where your skin goes all crawly and dramatic violin music plays in the background—all six of us can hear everything Helena hears. We can see everything she sees, taste everything she tastes, et cetera, et cetera. Which means anything you do to her, you do to us. So be careful. You have no idea what we're capable of."

Her eyes shut and slowly opened again. Helena was back in control.

"I'm sorry," said Helena. "Some of the others are . . . less patient than I am."

"Well, I am patient," Franklin said. "I can handle them."

"I thought you were angry."

"With the robots. Not with you." He smiled and she nodded, then stepped out of the car. Franklin followed, and they headed for the entrance to Krawkson Klub.

When they entered, their ears were filled with the screeches of what some ungodly creature from some ungodly dimension called singing. It was more reminiscent of a high school fire alarm. Franklin inwardly cursed himself for scheduling this meeting here, and he doubly cursed himself for scheduling it during karaoke hour.

"Franklin," came a voice from behind them. He and Helena spun around to see William, who, judging by the half-empty glass of mustard-colored drink in his hand and the awkward and clumsy way he was walking, had already been there a while.

"Isn't this music fantastic?" William cried over the screeching of whoever or whatever was on stage. It was an eight-foot-tall cucumber with no visible mouth. Franklin had never seen one before and he couldn't tell where on its body the screeching could possibly be coming from. It was safe to say that it didn't need a microphone and wouldn't have been able to use one if it had one. William would have agreed that it was horrendous had he not been drinking. Franklin had never seen William like this before, but it didn't seem entirely beneath him, either.

Franklin tried to ignore the mouthless creature and he shook William's hand, which was more difficult than usual; William kept missing it and Franklin finally grabbed it and held William steady on the fourth try. "William, what are you doing? We had an important meeting planned."

William snickered and took a swig from his glass. "We're about to try and stop an extremely dangerous madman who has the ability to kill us both just by telling us to go throw ourselves down an elevator shaft, right?"

"Yes. . . ."

"Then what have I got to lose? If I'm leaping to my doom, I might as well have a good time the night before."

Franklin grabbed William's glass away from him as he tried to take another swig and William gave him a resentful glare. "William, we aren't going to die," Franklin said, "as long as we get to work. Now, be polite and introduce yourself. This is my friend, Helena Kathryn."

William looked at her and he suddenly forgot about his drink. He brushed his long blond hair back with one hand and popped his fingers. He did his best Barry White impression. "Well hello there," William said, and Franklin wished he had the luxury to pretend they didn't know each other. "You know, Franklin here's married. I'm not."

Franklin shook his head but it didn't faze Helena at all. She held out her hand as if William were a consummate professional.

"I'm a patient of Dr. Bryce," said Helena.

William's interest in Helena vanished as quickly as it had appeared. "A patient? Franklin, you brought a *mental patient* here?"

"William, please," said Franklin.

"It's all right," said Helena. "It's a valid concern. You see, I have amnesia. I don't remember anything from before the last six months."

"Oh," said William. "I guess that's different."

"I also have six other personalities in my head."

William tore his glass out of Franklin's hands and took another drink. "We're dead."

"And I can tear the robots apart with my bare hands," said Helena.

William suddenly appeared more sober. "Robots?"

"HR120s," Franklin said.

"Oh, wait. You guys got attacked by *HR120s*?"

"That's right," said Franklin.

"And she can—"

"Yes. And they'll probably be sending more, so—"

"Wow," said William. "Okay. Never mind. The mental patient can stay."

The three of them got a table as the screeching cucumber finally finished its song. Franklin started to breathe a sigh of relief, which he quickly took back as soon as he spotted the Quaxor twins taking the stage.

Franklin pulled out a thick paperback book from the inside pocket of his trench coat and flipped to a chapter toward the middle. It was an interdimensional reference guide called the

Nitzu Trivisknot; he had borrowed it from Lera's personal collection. He used her books to look up interdimensional species' abilities, habits, and cultures when he couldn't get enough information from reading patients' minds. The *Nitzu Trivisknot* had the most information on telepathy and mind control.

"William, I need to ask you some questions so we can narrow down Grothman's powers. Does he require any tactile contact when using his powers?"

"No, I don't think so. It seems like he just has to make eye contact."

"He must be telepathic," Franklin said.

"How do you figure?" asked William.

"How else could he have bypassed Gordon?"

Franklin had never been a powerful enough telepath to hide anything from the mind probe—not that he would have tried—but more powerful telepaths could do things like trick a Landorn. If Grothman was telepathic, he could keep Gordon from knowing he had persuasion powers. Franklin flipped forward a few pages.

"I've got it. He's Threpnoidian."

"Threpnoidian? They make fantastic drinks *and* they have mind powers? Lucky ducks!" said William.

"How can you be sure?" asked Helena. "Is that the only race that uses persuasion through telepathy?"

"It is now. There used to be several of them," Franklin said.

"What happened to them?" asked Helena.

Franklin read on for a moment. "They controlled each other to death. Apparently, races with this ability historically kill themselves off because it's impossible to enforce any laws. I don't like you, I tell you to go kill yourself. Someone doesn't like me, they tell me to go kill myself. If you're mentally stronger than me, you don't die, and I do. Either way, we all end up killing each other."

"Surely at least some of those races invented *morality,*" said Helena.

"You'd be surprised how many haven't," William said. "Some interdimensional races aren't that creative."

"Even the deeply moral and religious species haven't been able to fight off the temptation to kill people they don't like," Franklin said. "According to this, it's just the nature of people with that ability."

"But then why haven't the Threpnoidians killed each other off?" Helena asked.

"Their power only works on other races. They can't use it against each other."

"Makes sense," said William. "So how do we stop Grothman from using it on us?"

"Window cleaner," said Franklin.

"That doesn't make sense," William said.

"I know, but that's what it says. All we have to do is spray ourselves with window cleaner and he won't be able to use his powers against us."

"So what's the plan?" asked William.

"We spray ourselves with window cleaner, we go to Vlakdormat, we find out why Grothman's doing what he's doing, and then we send him to Dimension 13.2."

"You do know," said William, "that its entire population was killed off by a nuclear holocaust, right?"

"Exactly. I think isolation is the best way to go. Of course, I'm not at Vlakdormat any longer, so if you have a better idea, then by all means. . . ."

"I don't understand," said Helena. "Shouldn't Grothman be sent to the authorities in his own dimension to stand trial? This isn't the kind of crime the American government is fit to handle."

"No, absolutely not," William said.

"We can't send him back to his dimension because we don't have any way to open a portal that goes there," Franklin said. "The Threpnoidians have ways of blocking that sort of thing. Most people think it's because they're afraid of people stealing their secret drink recipes."

CHAPTER 6

What Window Cleaner Is For

FRANKLIN, HELENA, AND WILLIAM WALKED THROUGH THE MAIN LOBBY OF VLAKDORMAT TOWARD THE ELEVATOR. Franklin would have preferred the element of surprise, but Vlakdormat—being a center of mental health for beings from all over the multiverse and holding secrets that would compromise the mental health of most humans—had an extremely complex and effective security system. Breaking into the building would have been impossible.

Franklin had missed Vlakdormat more than he realized. He felt comforted by the familiar smell of coffee and doughnuts, the various interdimensional beings—doctors and patients—who walked through the lobby to their appointments, and the poster on the wall that read, "Insanity Is Relative."

He had already worked in the regular world for too long. That world ignored the strange things that happened every day and quibbled and bickered about its politics and its television and its carbohydrates and its other such things that didn't make a pebble of difference in the grand beach that was the multiverse. Working in that world again had made him feel like a fish in a bowl. He knew there was a world outside of the bowl, but the fake plants and sunken pirate ship tried to make him forget about it.

Before they reached the elevator, a spiny-tailed Vaklock beast stepped in front of them. It was seven feet tall and slightly resembled an armadillo. It had a gray outer shell and rough fur. The three of them stopped in their tracks and Helena instantly stood in a fighting stance, ready to defend them.

"How have you been, Tramsey?" asked Franklin, holding out

his hand. Helena looked at him and eased her stance.

"Pretty good," the Vaklock responded in a deep growl. His English was barely understandable, though he was perfectly fluent, and Franklin figured the others probably couldn't make it out. He only knew what Tramsey was saying because he had gotten used to the accent when Tramsey had been his patient.

Which meant that Tramsey was potentially under Grothman's influence.

"Still going to your PEA meetings?" Franklin asked the Vaklock.

"PEA?" asked Helena.

"People Eaters Anonymous," William whispered.

"Every week," said Tramsey. "And I'm still clean, too. The cravings are getting worse, though. Doctor Grothman gave me a great suggestion about alleviating them."

Franklin took a deep breath. He knew what was coming. "What's that?"

"I'm going to go and kill myself. In fact, I'm on my way to do that right now. You guys can join me if you want."

"No thanks. I think we have something that might help you even more."

Tramsey shook his massive head. "No way. Doctor Grothman said there's nothing more effective."

Franklin turned to Helena and William, who were standing on either side of him. This was the time to test their plan. "Fire."

The three of them raised their bottles of bright blue window cleaner and squirted the Vaklock, each emptying half a bottle. Tramsey stared at them, confused. He was entirely unaffected.

"Was I dirty?" he asked. He wiped off some of the cleaner

that was dripping down the front of his shell. "Well, thanks, I guess. Wouldn't want to go take the big plunge without going through the wash first. Ciao." He waved at them, turned around, and walked away.

"I don't understand," William said. "That should have worked."

"There are only two possibilities," said Franklin. "Either window cleaner doesn't work on Vaklocks. . . ."

"Or we bought the wrong brand?" asked William.

Franklin pulled out the *Nitzu Trivisknot* and thumbed through it again. "Or this cheap English translation has a typo."

"Wait a minute," said William. "You used an *English copy* of an interdimensional reference guide written in *Brallnak*?"

Franklin had only grabbed the book because of its contents—he had completely forgotten which language it was written in. Brallnak was one of the most difficult interdimensional languages in existence. There were a hundred ways to say the same word depending on the context. Sometimes vowels and consonants even switched places depending on context. If his copy had been translated wrong, there was no way to tell where the mistake was.

Helena did not look happy. "Are you saying we may have brought the window cleaner for no reason?"

"He's saying that we might have needed a box of Cracker Jacks, for all we know," said William.

"Okay, look, don't panic," said Franklin. "I just read the book. It was the best reference we had. I doubt Lera has anything in the original Brallnak."

"That's because it's so frustrating that most of the copies got burned or eaten," said William. "Wish I hadn't been drunk last night, now. Maybe I would have noticed what you were reading and we could have avoided this whole getting-us-all-killed thing."

Franklin ignored him and looked at the section in the *Nitzu Trivisknot* about Threpnoidians. He read it over again carefully and found nothing new.

"I didn't read it wrong. It says to use window cleaner."

"We did that. Maybe there's another step," Helena said.

"Shake well," Franklin read.

"Not helping," said William. "We've got to do something. The Vaklock is on his way to off himself as we speak. Not that I'm a big fan of the Vaklocks or anything, but he has been going to rehab and all."

The floor began to quiver slightly beneath them, and Franklin was positive that it was because of the man wearing the giant shiny red robot suit walking toward them.

"Greetings," said the man in the robot suit. It was at least seven feet tall and covered Grothman's body from head to toe, probably to protect him from precisely what Franklin was planning. Behind the vaguely tinted glass of the robot's domed head, Franklin could make out three small black horns protruding out of Grothman's Threpnoidian forehead. His skin was cranberry red and his hair was long and black. He stopped a few feet from the three of them, and one of his robot feet made a slight indention into the floor as he slammed it down. His head made a high-pitched whine as it looked down at each of them.

"I would have been here earlier, but I just found out you were here," Grothman said through a loud speaker built into the robotic suit's head. "And you've brought window cleaner." Its giant arms folded in front of it. "Impressive."

So it wasn't the window cleaner the *Nitzu Trivisknot* was wrong about. It was how they were using it.

"How did you know we were here?" Franklin asked him.

"Your patients aren't the only people under my persuasion. Dr. Caslom told me you wouldn't be especially happy if you discovered that someone using my therapeutic techniques had obtained your old position. So I've had people watching in case you returned." Grothman and his massive armored suit lumbered closer and loomed over them menacingly. "Some people have no respect for new and innovative ways of doing things."

"Why are you doing this?" Franklin asked as he looked around for some way to gain the upper hand. Everyone in the lobby continued to go about their business as though nothing unusual was happening. It seemed that Grothman's influence stretched to everyone in Vlakdormat by now. It was a good thing William had figured him out when he had, but now that Grothman's suit had them pinned against a wall with nowhere to run, and now that the one plan they had was useless, there wasn't much left they could do about it.

"Your patients are hopeless, Dr. Bryce, as most are." Grothman smiled deviously. "Many of them allow themselves to fall into a vulnerable and unstable mindset, incapable of social functions and are therefore worthless to society. That kind of self-defeating way of thinking is intolerable, and there is only one way to remedy it."

"You're right, Dr. Grothman," William said, sarcastically. "Survival of the fittest. That *is* a brand new idea. Wish I'd thought of it."

"I don't see any point in debating with you," said Dr. Grothman. "After all, there's really only one way to sway you."

Grothman closed his eyes for a moment. "You agree with me now, don't you?"

It all suddenly made perfect sense to Franklin. His patients were weak-minded and irrelevant. The only way to help them overcome this was to let them take their own lives, to make way for others who could handle the bizarre and ironic nature of the world.

"Let's help them all," said Franklin. "Let's *kill* them all."

"Dr. Bryce?" said Helena.

"He's right," William said. He and Franklin stood together, opposite from Helena. She shook her bottle and sprayed them both.

"That's not going to help," Franklin said. "There's no point in arguing anymore. Dr. Grothman is right. We need to find all of the patients and help them. Let's go."

"Actually," Grothman's voice bellowed, "that's not exactly what I had in mind. You can't handle the truth, either, can you?"

Franklin shook his head. It was true. Everything Dr. Grothman said was true.

"You're weak. You lost your telepathy, the only thing that kept you stable. But you never really were stable, were you?"

"No," Franklin said.

"You can change all of that. You can cure yourself."

Franklin nodded. It made so much sense. Just a little death would perk him right up. He'd never have to feel sorry again. He would be a new man.

"Okay," Franklin said. "I'll kill myself. Thanks for your help."

"Don't mention it," said Grothman. "I'm only doing my job. Now you let me know how that works out for you, all right?"

"Can I help?" William asked.

Grothman smiled. "In fact, why don't you join him?"

William shrugged. "Sure. Sounds like fun."

Franklin began to walk away with William. His mind had never been clearer.

"Now, you . . ." Franklin heard Grothman's voice from behind him. "I'm not sure what to do with you. . . ." Franklin didn't think anything of it. All that mattered was suicide. His cure. He wondered if Tramsey was waiting for him. It would have been awfully nice for the three of them to all jump to their deaths together.

"You can't read my mind, can you?" said Helena. Franklin and William reached the elevator and waited for the door to open.

"What are you?" Dr. Grothman asked, "An android? A Nixot in disguise?"

Franklin heard a loud crash and then a scream came through Grothman's speakers. Franklin glanced over his shoulder and went wide-eyed with horror. The nice man who had so kindly suggested his demise was lying on the floor in a jumbled heap of robot suit. Helena was sitting on her knees on top of the twisted metal, hanging on to what was left of the helmet with one hand and raising the other hand above her, balled into a fist.

"Hello. My name is Helena."

"W-why? Why aren't you—"

"No. My turn to ask a question. Why would a Threpnoidian trying to control a mental health facility wear a huge protective metal suit?" Helena ripped Grothman's helmet off with her bare hands and threw it to the ground.

"Everyone," Grothman yelled. He didn't sound nearly as threatening without his sound system. "Everyone listen to me! Stop trying to kill yourselves, stop whatever it is you're doing, and *destroy* this woman! She doesn't believe in our cause. She is *evil!*"

Franklin and William instantly left the elevator as the door finally opened for them and went to Grothman's aid. They were no match for someone who could rip apart thousand-pound metallic suits, but Dr. Grothman knew what was best for them. He was the best therapist Franklin had known. He wondered how much the bill for his suicide would be.

But before he and William could reach her, Helena lifted her spray bottle and squirted Grothman in the face. The Threpnoidian screamed and rubbed his eyes like a toddler who had used too much shampoo. The room was instantly in an uproar of noise and confusion. Helena climbed down from the robot suit and joined Franklin and William.

Dr. Grothman's powers had worn off, and suddenly Franklin thought suicide was as stupid an idea as he would have only minutes earlier.

William pushed a small, red emergency button on the wall and yelled for security to put a force field around Grothman. Instantly, a wall of energy was erected around the Threpnoidian, who slowly dragged himself the rest of his way out of his robot suit with great effort. Franklin could make out several large cuts and bruises on his dark red face and his arms.

Franklin couldn't help but think of Laura right then. She had been right—Franklin had no idea what she and her other personalities were capable of. He was grateful to Helena for stopping Grothman, but after today, he wasn't in a hurry to meet any of her other personalities.

William reluctantly walked up to Helena and nervously held out his hand. Helena shook it. He looked both impressed and dismayed, much like Franklin felt. "I don't know how you did that . . . but nice work," William said.

"Dr. Bryce," said Helena. "I think you need a new copy of the *Nitzu Trivisknot.*"

William threw his hands in the air. "Seriously, man. I know Brallnak is tough, but how could that translator confuse 'spray the Threpnoidian' with 'spray yourself?' Good thing we weren't supposed to use hydrochloric acid or something."

Franklin walked up to the force field and stared at Grothman, now bruised and battered, sitting on the ground and nursing a sprained ankle.

"You're fired," Franklin said.

"I don't believe you work here anymore," Dr. Grothman said tauntingly. "You want to know why I do the things I do? I'll tell you. We're not so entirely different."

"I've never used my position to murder people."

"Yes, okay, besides that. I am a real therapist, you know. Or at least, I used to be. I used my powers to help people, just like you. I always knew what they thought, how they felt, and when I was done with them, they were always better for it. But like you, I couldn't use my powers when it really counted. You read the *Nitzu Trivisknot.* Remember what it says about Threpnoidian powers?"

Franklin didn't want to answer. He was beginning to guess where this was going. "They don't work on other Threpnoidians."

"Exactly. Now, I never used the persuasion part on my interdimensional patients, at least not at first. Just read their minds. But then I fell in love. Got married. And a couple years later, my wife got depressed for no reason. She started seeing a therapist. There wasn't anything he could do to make her better.

There was nothing I could do, either. She stopped going to work, stopped eating. She even stopped going to bars, and in Threpnoidia, you know someone's lost it when that happens. If I could have, I would have used all my power to make her happy again. She jumped off a bridge. She did it for no reason at all. And that's when I realized that anyone who needs a therapist is just delaying the inevitable. I'm the only one in our profession who really cures anyone, Dr. Bryce. And after what you've been through, you should understand."

Franklin let Grothman's words ring in his ears for a moment. Then he smiled and shook his head. "It's a good thing I don't buy your philosophy," he said, "because you're one of those people who needs therapy. And I'm going to make sure you get it."

Good old irony was striking once again. Here was a therapist who needed more help than all of Vlakdormat's patients combined.

"William, why don't you have a talk with Dr. Caslom to decide how to proceed with Grothman's treatment," Franklin said. "But don't forget my vote."

"Nuclear holocaust dimension. I got it," said William.

"I'm going to take Helena down to the Unexplained Phenomena wing and see what we can find out about her."

Helena nodded, and they headed for the elevator. William took the stairs and was already gone before the elevator doors opened.

"Dr. Bryce," said Grothman from behind them. "Before you go, I want you to know one more thing. I might not have my powers now, but I was in your mind long enough to know everything I need to know about you."

"I'm happy for you, really," said Franklin.

"No you're not. You're jealous. We are very much alike, whether you choose to realize it or not. But the real difference is that I still have my ability, and the real irony is that you've never realized the single reason all of these terrible things are happening to you. Losing your telepathy. Being attacked by HR120s. Even me, showing up and killing your patients. It's because of your *name*, Franklin Bryce. You know, the age-old constant of the multiverse? You have *two first names.*"

Franklin froze. He had been so worried about working with Helena, but he had exactly the same curse she did. It had never occurred to him in his entire life that Bryce could be a first name. He had never really met any Bryces.

Grothman pushed a button on his watch and a swirling red portal appeared above him. It sucked him and his broken robot suit into it, and then disappeared. His watch had a built-in portable aperture that went to some pocket dimension, and even if Vlakdormat security could trace it, he'd be in his own dimension by the time they did. And since Threpnoidia had a powerful portal blocker, they had no way to go after him.

CHAPTER 7

Something You're Not

FRANKLIN AND LERA SAT IN THEIR LIVING ROOM, TALKING ABOUT THE EVENTS THAT HAD TRANSPIRED OVER THE LAST TWO DAYS. Franklin's life was being turned upside down, and, as usual, his wife didn't seem to be bothered by it at all. It wasn't that she was unsympathetic, she had once explained. It was just that she was 312 years old and had been married eighteen times. She was rarely surprised by anything.

"I can't believe you never told me I had two first names," Franklin told her.

"It never came up. I just figured you knew. It is *your* name, after all. I wasn't going to hold it against you. I didn't figure being married to someone with two first names would be any more dangerous than being married to a lava man."

"Not the lava man again."

"I'm just saying. You or a lava man? What's more dangerous?"

"I'm not sure anymore. Calvin Stanley. All those patients at Vlakdormat. I can't help wondering how many other people I'm going to get killed."

"You're just a victim of circumstance. None of this is your fault, and you know that."

It was weird coming from her, but Lera was right. Besides having two first names, which he couldn't control, he wasn't responsible for anything that had happened in the last few weeks. But he certainly felt responsible.

"I think it's Helena you really need to worry about," Lera said.

"What?"

"She's powerful, and she's unpredictable. Don't tell me you aren't worried she might be dangerous."

He couldn't. He wondered if her intuition told her he had been thinking the exact same thing.

"What is she?" Lera asked.

"I don't know. I took her to the Unexplained Phenomena Division, and Dr. Drake ran some tests, but he couldn't explain her."

"That's why they call it the *Unexplained* Phenomena Division. Maybe if they changed their name they could actually explain something every now and then."

"She checks out as human, but there's obviously more to her." The only thing Dr. Drake had been able to tell him for sure was that Helena didn't have classic multiple personality disorder. The scans of her brain showed seven distinct personalities all crammed into one cranium. It looked like it might have somehow been done intentionally, and Dr. Drake thought that whatever had been done to her might have caused her amnesia.

Lera was about to say something else—and it was probably something sarcastic judging from her expression—but the doorbell rang. Franklin went to the door and opened it.

"Here is your pizza," said a young man wearing a red uniform with a matching hat. He pushed the box toward Franklin.

"You've got the wrong address. We didn't order a pizza."

"Oh. Well, I lied," said the man, opening the box. "This isn't a pizza."

The box transformed into a hideous, whirling machine of terror. Six blades sprung out, three on each side. The box lid became a handle for the pizza man to grip it with, and the blades spun around on top of it like a buzz saw. Two nozzles shot out of the top and started spraying fire into the air. Luckily, the pizza man hadn't stepped inside the house yet.

Lera came to the door behind Franklin.

"We didn't order one of those, either," said Lera. Her eyes grew wider as she looked at the pizza man. "Hey, that's an HR120."

"What was your first clue?" said Franklin. He expected the robot to lunge at him, but instead, it stared at Franklin's wife for a long time. Then the whirling, fire-spitting death machine transformed back into a pizza box.

"Sorry to bother you nice folks," said the HR120. "Have a wonderful day."

The HR120 walked to its car and drove away.

"What exactly just happened?" Franklin asked her as he closed the door.

Lera looked as though she had just come into some money. "Guess I just have that effect on people." She opened a drawer in the coffee table and pulled out a phone book. "You want to order a pizza?"

Franklin sat with Helena on a wooden bench in a park, just a few blocks from Vlakdormat. It was getting late, and they had been talking for a long time, trying to make sense of everything that had happened. Franklin knew that a conversation was inevitable and he thought the cool autumn air might do them both some good. It hadn't occurred to him until just then how much time he spent indoors.

Franklin was bringing Helena up to speed on some of the

things that had happened just before he met her. After he told her about Virginia Stanley, she froze.

"And she could do anything a human could do?"

"Anything except be read by a telepath. . . ."

Franklin immediately realized where this was going.

"You're describing *me* perfectly."

Franklin quickly shook his head. "I've never known an HR120 to have amnesia or multiple personalities."

"But you don't really know much about them at all. No one does. What if I am?"

"If you were an HR120, you would have already vaporized me for knowing about you."

"Still. . . ." said Helena.

"We don't know," Franklin reluctantly agreed. "There's no real way to know, short of opening you up and looking for wires."

"HR120s don't bleed. I do. Not easily, but I do."

Franklin sighed. He knew Lera was right to be suspicious of her, considering what she was capable of. A part of him was, too. But whatever Helena was, he was certain she had no ulterior motives against him. She had shown him nothing but appreciation, and she had helped him protect a place and some people that he deeply cared about. "You saved my life. I think I owe you the benefit of the doubt."

They sat in silence for several minutes. An older couple walked by and kindly waved at them. Franklin halfheartedly waved back.

"They have no idea what happens every day in this city, do they?" Helena said when the couple was far enough away.

"No," said Franklin. "The evidence is all around us, but most people choose not to know."

Helena nodded. "And your job is—was—to help those who did choose to accept it to live in the world the way it really is."

"Among other things, yes."

Helena looked at him for a long time. "I think you made a mistake."

"Excuse me?"

"Leaving Vlakdormat."

Franklin sighed. "You wouldn't understand. Without my—"

"You don't need it. Even now, when you discover some new or frightening thing, you adapt. And you help others to adapt. You weren't at Vlakdormat when you met me. This is still your job. No matter where you are, it follows you."

Franklin shook his head. "If I went back, you wouldn't be my patient anymore."

"Get us both transferred. Vlakdormat needs you, and we both need Vlakdormat. It can disable HR120s."

"Yeah, when security remembers the code."

"Stop trying to be something you're not."

"Something I'm not?"

"Normal, Franklin. Stop trying to be normal."

She was so convincing that he wondered if she had somehow obtained Grothman's persuasion powers. After a long time, Franklin nodded. He couldn't fool himself for a regular guy any longer. After all, he did have two first names.

"I don't even know if they'd take me back."

Helena smiled. "They do happen to have an opening."

CHAPTER 8

The Grand Victory of Lasteria

THERE WERE VERY FEW THINGS IN FRANKLIN'S LIFE THAT HADN'T CHANGED SINCE HIS INITIAL INTRODUCTION TO ALTERNATE DIMENSIONS. At first, he hadn't expected *everything* to be different. Certainly meeting other species and having a beer in a pocket dimension had been new. But the little things—like watching television, paying the electric bill, or going to the grocery store—shouldn't have changed.

But five years later, a therapist again at Vlakdormat and married to a woman from another dimension, Franklin realized the truth: nothing in his life could ever go back to the way it used to be. He was even more aware of it now that he had to keep his wife close to him when he wasn't at Vlakdormat. She and the positronic deactivation switch were the only things he knew of that could protect him from the HR120s.

"All right," said Lera, holding her hands impatiently on her hips. "I've been kind. I've asked nicely. Now, I'm telling you. Give me the milk. Now."

"I have as much right to this milk as you do," said a putout-looking woman. "I'm a wife with a household to take care of. I'm a human being, just like you."

Lera had been fighting with this woman over the last gallon of two percent milk in the grocery store for almost five minutes. Franklin thought about stepping in, but he didn't want to make the situation worse. Sometimes Lera's skin gave off an intense, almost neon red glow when she was angry, and people tended to stare at them when that happened.

"I'm not human, sweetheart. Don't let the exterior fool you."

Franklin's eyes widened. "What are you doing?"

Lera ignored him. "I'm not leaving without it."

"You can't have it," the other lady said. She was a heavy-set woman about twice Lera's size but was obviously still intimidated. Lera had that effect on a lot of people. When she and Franklin first met, he had a sneaking suspicion she knew something very intimate and personal about him. He later discovered that was entirely true. Lera immediately knew something about *everyone* she met. In Franklin's case, it was the fact that, as a teenager, he liked to fall asleep to the flashing of a strobe light.

"I'm a Verullian. You have absolutely no idea what I'm capable of."

"Lera, please," said Franklin, "not in the grocery store."

Lera finally looked at him and laughed. She flashed her red glow for dramatic effect. For a split second, her skin was bright red as if she had thousands of watts of electricity in her bones, and it showed straight through her khaki capris and her brown top. "Of course not, Franklin." She said, "I wasn't talking about *that*. It would be insane to do something like *that* in public."

The woman holding the milk looked concerned. "Oh, God, you're one of *them*, aren't you?"

"Yep," said Lera. "So you know exactly what I could do but won't do in public."

The woman nodded slowly, looked around, and then handed Lera the milk. "It was nice talking to you folks. Really."

She stared at Lera for a moment and then sprinted off down the aisle. Franklin forcefully grabbed their cart. and he and Lera started walking in the opposite direction.

"I can't believe you did that."

Lera nonchalantly scratched *milk* off the grocery list. "Now it's time for cereal."

Franklin abruptly stopped walking and stared her down.

"What?" Lera said.

"You know what. You flashed her."

"I did not."

"You know what I mean. And you told her you were Verullian."

"She can handle it."

"How do you figure? She took off in a panic!"

Lera shook her head. "That's what I mean. The woman thinks she was abducted by aliens."

"Aliens? How did. . . ? Your intuition."

"Exactly. I did the glowing thing to make her think I was one of the aliens. And presto! We get the last gallon of milk."

Franklin frowned. "So I have to know. Was she really abducted by aliens?"

"I doubt it. I was getting the vibe that these were the crop circle kind. Most people, no matter the dimension, aren't really into crop circles. The best way to tell if it's a real abduction is if they're the kind of aliens who spray paint graffiti on mailboxes. The Wixeens include vandalism and abduction as part of their religion."

"Weird. But about drawing so much attention to yourself—"

"I know how to handle people, Franklin. You worry too much."

"You're right. Killer robots are after me. Why should I be worried?"

"You shouldn't be."

They slowly started moving again and Franklin looked for the cereal aisle.

"They've already tried to kill me twice," he said. "They'll find a way to get through you and Vlakdormat."

Lera smiled and affectionately rubbed her fingers across Franklin's shoulder. "But until that happens, you and I will just have to spend a little more quality time together."

Franklin was still annoyed, but he couldn't help but smile back. He could never stay angry with Lera for very long.

"Just do me a favor," said Franklin.

"What's that?"

"Don't flash anyone in public again."

"You sound jealous."

Franklin glared.

"All right. I'm sorry. I'll only flash you from now on."

Eva Crill's office was strange, but then so was Eva Crill. She had been at Vlakdormat several years longer than Franklin had. Not only did she counsel beings from other dimensions—she was obsessed with them. Her office was filled with treasures and trinkets from all over the multiverse, including a yellow fluffy floating hat she had bought in the Repzoth dimension (which she occasionally "wore" just a few inches above her head), a horridly graphic painting of *The Grand Victory of Lasteria* from the Kalket dimension (which was actually a massacre that had killed most of the Kalkets' ancestors—but since they had all been ruthless and unpleasant people, it was widely considered to be the best thing that ever happened to them), and a sarcophagus. Franklin had no idea where the sarcophagus had come from, but he never cared to ask. Knowing Dr. Crill, there was probably still a corpse inside.

"A pleasure to see you, Dr. Bryce!" she burst out upon his arrival. Helena was already there. "Miss Kathryn was just telling me about your epic battle with Dr. Grothman."

Dr. Crill overstated everything, and not just in conversation. She was wearing a black and red coat with a long pointed collar that came up past her cheeks and made her look like a vampire, and she wore her thick violet hair up in the shape of a cone. Eva Crill was human, but it was hard to tell upon first glance.

"It was hardly epic," said Franklin, "and Helena did most of the work."

"She is extraordinary, isn't she?" said Crill. "You're lucky to have her as a patient, Dr. Bryce. I would almost kill to work with such a baffling case."

Franklin looked at Helena, but she didn't seem offended. He had warned her about Crill's eccentricities before the meeting and had explained that Crill was a specialist in memory retrieval. The Unexplained Phenomena Wing had technology that might have helped to locate Helena's missing memories, or, at the very least, determine why they were missing, but nothing they tried had worked. So Franklin had reluctantly called on Crill to use her magic.

"How exactly are you going to find my memories?" Helena asked her.

"Perhaps 'memory retrieval' is a bit misleading," Crill said in her high, shrill voice. "If your amnesia were severe enough, the memories might very well be wiped out completely. Erased, trashed, eradicated. We couldn't very well find something that was *eradicated,* now could we?" Crill shook her head. "No, no, no. In these cases, we use magic to surf backward through the fabric of reality and find the actual *events* that took place before your tragic amnesia."

"Time travel?"

"Not time *travel*, exactly. More like time *watching*. I have a Matrulian skull—quite amazing, really. Looking through the skull's eyes, I can find any moment of your life and then play that event back so that you can see exactly what happened. I've even devised a way to hook the thing up to a big screen TV so we can all watch. And the sound quality is fantastic!"

"So it won't bring the memories back," said Helena.

"No, not really. But it will do the next best thing. You'll be able to go back and catch all the episodes of your life you missed —from the comfort of my own home, while eating a bag of popcorn."

"And this is the only option?" asked Helena. She seemed disappointed.

"What do you mean?"

"It would take a long time to watch my entire life on a screen. Is there any way to upload the information into my brain, like they were memories?"

Crill frowned. "Must you take the fun out of everything? Must every patient make that suggestion? I was looking forward to a good show on my brand new big screen TV."

"My memories might be private," said Helena.

"You don't know that. Who knows what you were like before? You might have been an open book."

"I doubt it."

Crill sighed. "Yes, we can upload whatever we find directly into your brain. But it will take several sessions. We don't want to overload you."

"Are you sure her mind can handle it?" Franklin asked Dr.

Crill. "She has six other personalities taking up space in there."

"The limits of the human brain are endless," said Dr. Crill, "We simply don't want to give her too much information too quickly. But there is no limit to how much knowledge can be processed incrementally. I put a different encyclopedia in my head every week. Granted, most of my thoughts are now in alphabetical order! But it's worth it."

Franklin gently took Helena by the arm. "Dr. Crill, if you would excuse us for a moment?"

"Certainly, certainly. I need to feed Rufus before we get started, anyway."

"Rufus?"

"My pet velociraptor."

Franklin stared at her in disbelief. "Your *what*? You're keeping a velociraptor at Vlakdormat?"

Eva Crill rolled her eyes and leaned against an unlocked case of sharp and deadly ceremonial knives from various dimensions. "Yes, Dr. Bryce, I'm a complete lunatic. No, of course not. I keep Rufus in a pocket dimension. I'll return in precisely four minutes and thirty-eight seconds." She pulled up her long sleeve and set a timer on her watch. Then she walked straight through the large canvas painting of *The Grand Victory of Lasteria,* revealing the aperture into her pocket dimension.

"Can *you* use this magic skull, Dr. Bryce?" Helena asked.

Franklin held back a laugh. "I'm sorry, I can't. Don't worry. Dr. Crill is a professional. She's not going to come back wearing a giant red robot suit or anything."

"I don't trust her. She's going to have access to my history. We have no idea what she's going to find."

"I know. But from what I've heard, it takes a certain kind of mind to access the Matrulian skull, and she's the only person here who can do it. She's your best option."

"You're saying that you have to be practically insane to use it?"

"Basically, yes."

"I almost hope my past turns out to be completely dull."

"I can see how you might."

When Dr. Crill returned four minutes and thirty-eight seconds later, she was wearing an entirely different outfit, this time a bright yellow dress with a matching conical hat and with a giant python slithering around her neck.

"The right outfit for the right occasion," she said, stroking the snake with two fingers.

Franklin looked at his watch. He was already late for his next appointment. If it had been anyone else, he might have been worried about whether Helena would survive her session with Eva Crill, but the one thing he knew for certain was that Helena could take care of herself.

CHAPTER 9

Delusions of Villainy

"I'M SORRY I'M LATE," FRANKLIN SAID AS HE SAT DOWN ACROSS FROM HIS NEW PATIENT. Miles Flastcaster, a skinny freckle-faced college age young man, was standing in front of the office window, which was cracked open slightly, enjoying a breeze. He had his hands on his hips and he was nodding to himself. For a moment, Franklin wondered if the patient was conducting his own therapy session and how well it was going. Flastcaster was wearing a bright orange, one-piece jumpsuit with a large utility belt around his waist and a mask to match, and it was all made entirely out of duct tape. Franklin immediately picked up his clipboard and pen. It was going to be one of those days.

"That's all right." Flastcaster said, "I was admiring the view. You have a beautiful office, sir."

"Thank you," said Franklin. Flastcaster scowled and cursed under his breath. "I did it again."

"You did what again?"

"That's why I'm here. I really need your help."

"What's the problem?"

"I *complimented* you. Why can't I just keep my big mouth shut?"

"You don't think you should be giving people compliments?" This was a new one to Franklin, even at Vlakdormat.

"It isn't . . . it's not *evil*!"

Franklin nodded. The only people he knew of who might have considered it evil to give a compliment were from the Drawkcab dimension, but they were backward about everything.

Flastcaster ran a hand through his curly blond hair and then leaned his head on his hand. "I need you to help me stop being so nice."

"Why?"

"I don't want to be nice at all. I want to be *bad.* Aren't you wondering about the suit?"

"I wasn't going to mention it."

"But you were wondering. I think it's dumb, too, but I want to get it right. I want to be a real super villain. I want to rule the world."

"You're unsatisfied with your life so far. That's fair. But are you sure being evil is the answer? What else are you good at?"

"Not much. Mostly, I just read comic books and watch war movies."

Franklin might have guessed that. "Then perhaps you should try developing a talent involving your interests."

"I'm already doing that. I want to rule the world. It's not like it's illegal or anything."

"No. . . ." Franklin hesitated. "No, wanting to rule the world isn't illegal. But have you considered how realistic it is?"

"My father always said it's the attempt that matters."

"Yet until now, you've spent all your time reading comics and watching war movies?"

"I never really paid much attention to my father," Flastcaster admitted. "But I'm tired of being useless, so I set the highest goal I could think of. If it's not realistic, maybe I could try taking over a little town somewhere and then work my way up."

Franklin took off his glasses and massaged the bridge of his nose. "I'm not sure being too nice is really the problem. Are you sure being a super villain is what you really want?"

"You're missing the point," said Flastcaster. "I've already

made up my mind. My only problem is that I don't know *how* to be evil. I really think becoming evil would fix that."

"I don't think it's in anyone's best interest for me to help you overcome your good nature so you can try to take over the planet."

"Oh. Really?"

"I don't think so."

"Sorry to bother you then."

Flastcaster stood up and walked toward the door, and his duct tape suit made a loud crunching sound with every step.

"We still have some time left," said Franklin.

"I came to the wrong place. I'm sorry, really. I know you want to help, but look at me. I'm apologizing and speaking in a soft, comforting tone. I really need some help. I just want to be evil!"

Flastcaster left and closed the door behind him. Poor kid. He was smart and able. He just needed some direction, and Franklin was afraid that the direction he'd chosen would either lead to the barrel of a gun or the bars of a jail cell. He pushed a button on his desk and called security. He asked them to keep an eye on Flastcaster, hoping he could prevent him from doing anything stupid, at least for a few days. He hoped Flastcaster was going through a temporary obsession, glorifying a larger-than-life idea because it was easier than living his real life. Considering what his life had been up to this point, Franklin thought there was a good chance he would decide being a super villain was too hard and quit before he really tried. But just to be on the safe side, he had security secretly put a CVT (a cloaked visual tracer) on him. The CVT was an invisible tracker that would tell security where he was and provide a video feed so they could see what Flastcaster saw, without him spotting the tracker.

Franklin still had five more patients left. He hoped his session with Flastcaster wouldn't set a precedent for his entire day. But on a positive note, at least he would have something interesting to tell William when they met at Krawkson Klub later that evening.

Since Flastcaster had left so abruptly, Franklin decided to take the remaining time before his next appointment to rest for a while. His life had been nonstop insanity over the last month, and he was beyond stressed. He hadn't been sleeping well. His thoughts were almost always focused on the HR120s and on Helena. There were so many questions he didn't have answers to, and he wasn't used to so much mystery in his own life. His job was to help others solve their own inner mysteries.

Questions other people had were easy. ("Why do I feel this way?" "How do I cope with the fact that there's a fairly active interdimensional portal in the middle of my basement?") These were pretty easy for Franklin. He was trained for questions like that. But his own questions were quite a bit harder. ("Why are androids out to kill me?" "How is it that I didn't notice I had two first names until I was thirty-six years old?")

Franklin leaned back in his chair, closed his eyes, slowly breathed in and out, and tried to clear his mind. Three minutes later, Bethany's nasally voice was ringing in his ears.

"Boss? Are you there?"

He opened his eyes, frowned, and pressed another button on his desk.

"It's Dr. Crill. She called for security a couple minutes ago. They're in the pocket dimension in her office, trying to contain her pet velociraptor. It attacked her."

"What?"

"Helena Kathryn tried to kill Eva Crill. And you might not have to worry about your three o'clock. Helena's missing."

When Franklin entered Crill's office for the second time that day, he found her in entirely different spirits. Her conical hat was lying in the middle of the floor, her hair was a mess, her makeup was running, and her tacky yellow dress was torn in the back. The snake was gone—probably hiding behind the sarcophagus. Crill was the kind of woman who, regardless of her bizarre nature, was known for being able to handle a lot of stress. But now she looked positively traumatized, exactly as one might expect to look after being attacked by a velociraptor.

"Everything is under control," a security guard told Franklin upon his arrival.

"Not until we find Helena."

"Understood, sir. Dr. Crill says Helena came back here from the pocket dimension. We have search teams covering the grounds."

"Good. Let me know as soon as you find her. Try not to hurt her." He said it before it even occurred to him that they probably couldn't get within ten feet of Helena if she didn't want them to.

"Yes, sir."

"And please be careful. She's unlike anyone you've known."

As the security team began to move out, Franklin knelt down in front of Crill, who was sitting on a leopard print couch, sipping something that looked like tar that was violently bubbling at the top.

"She tried to kill me," Crill said.

"I know. Can you tell me what happened?"

Crill set down her drink, which bubbled over onto the table.

"It isn't just her memories. Helena's *timeline* doesn't go back before her amnesia."

"You're saying there are no events before six months ago?"

Dr. Crill nodded slowly, and Franklin knew there couldn't be a mistake. Matrulian skulls never failed. The Matrulians were an ancient, extinct race who had been tightly connected to the fabric of time. They could physically move backward or forward through any single person's timeline at will, but they couldn't change anything. They could go as far back as when the person became a sentient being, or as far forward as the person's death. This property was inherent in their genetic makeup, which was why their skulls, with the help of magic, could now be used to view time, as long as someone with an especially Matrulian personality used them. Franklin couldn't imagine what Eva Crill had in common with the Matrulians, but he had often wondered if that similarity had anything to do with their extinction.

Franklin asked, "And Helena attacked you when you told her this?"

"I never had the chance to tell her anything," Crill said. "She grabbed me, without any provocation, and dragged me through *The Grand Victory of Lasteria* and into my pocket dimension. She ripped open Rufus' cage with her bare hands. I managed to contact security before he did too much damage." She started crying. "I just don't understand. I've tried and tried, but apparently there's just no taming a velociraptor."

Franklin handed Crill a tissue and waited until she had composed herself a little. He felt bad for her. This was a side of her he had never seen before. He was somewhat surprised to learn that she had feelings at all.

"Eva, listen very carefully," said Franklin. "I need to know what changes you noticed in her personality. I know you only spent a short time with her, but are you sure it was Helena? Or was it another personality?"

Eva Crill slowly stood up and narrowed her eyes at Franklin. "I don't know. All I know is that she's dangerous. As far as the Matrulian skull is concerned, she's only six months old. She has seven personalities and superhuman abilities. Do you know what that sounds like to me? It sounds like she was *created,* not born, maybe for some terrible purpose we can't begin to understand. I don't think you have any idea what you've let in here."

She had a point. Franklin was responsible for Helena, and he had left her alone with someone she had expressly told him she didn't trust. He had to be more careful. If they could get Helena back to Vlakdormat, he would make sure new precautions were put into place. But Franklin didn't want to think about that now. The most important thing was finding Helena before she hurt anyone else.

"This is my fault," Franklin told Crill. "It won't happen again."

She relaxed a little and put a hand on his shoulder. "I trust you to do the right thing."

He left Dr. Crill's office and headed for his own. He was glad to be out of there—he felt more uncomfortable with Crill now than he had earlier that morning. He cancelled the rest of his appointments for the day and immediately went to work looking for Helena. This was his mess and he was determined to clean it up. He just hoped it wouldn't get him killed.

"Dr. Bryce," came a voice from his desk only a few moments later. "This is security. We've spotted Helena on the CVT you requested this morning."

"What?"

"She's in a car headed downtown. And she's with the gentleman wrapped in duct tape."

CHAPTER 10

On the Job Training

FRANKLIN FOUND HIMSELF RIDING SHOTGUN FOR HIS FIRST TIME IN A VLAKDORMAT SECURITY CAR. William sat behind him, having asked to come along as soon as he had heard about Helena. It was a black four door American car, and it had absolutely everything: an mp3 player, a GPS, plenty of cup holders, gun turrets, ejector seats, a cloaking device, and even a Gatorade dispenser. It was like riding in a giant Swiss army knife.

"This thing can even make you breakfast if you don't have time to stop," said Agent Strexit from the driver's seat. He was a tall, muscular man with a square jaw, a blond crew cut, and he wore a black suit and tie. "But it doesn't make doughnuts. We're not cops."

Vlakdormat security didn't have a lot of respect for local law enforcement, who tried to cover up anything and everything that might prove the existence of alternate dimensions. But it was painfully obvious that almost everyone on the force had seen something they couldn't explain. Most of them were in denial about it, and Franklin had never seen a single cop check in at Vlakdormat. Anytime the police saw Vlakdormat security on the scene, they would turn tail and let the Vlakdormat officers handle the situation, no questions asked. Franklin figured that was mostly because cops had an uncanny track record of getting themselves sucked into other dimensions—maybe that explained why they refused to acknowledge that other dimensions existed.

"They've parked in front of City Hall," said Franklin, watching Helena and Flastcaster through the video feed from the CVT on a large flat screen built into the dash in front of him. He couldn't believe how good the picture and sound quality were coming from the CVT.

"What if it's not one of the other personalities?" William asked. "What if she just snapped?"

Franklin looked back at William. "She didn't," he said. He didn't know that for sure, but he had promised Helena the benefit of the doubt, and he planned to give it to her until she gave him reason not to.

Franklin turned back around in his seat and stared intently at the screen. Helena was facing Flastcaster as they got out of his brown station wagon. There was a wild, irrational inferno in Helena's eyes that made her practically unrecognizable. Flastcaster popped open the station wagon's trunk. Helena reached in and pulled out a clear plastic garbage bag filled with supplies. Franklin couldn't tell exactly what was inside, but he spotted several loose electrical wires coming out of the top of the bag.

"The secret to taking over the world is to take politics out of the equation altogether," Helena said to Flastcaster. Her voice was deep and almost sensual. Flastcaster looked practically mesmerized as she spoke. She had ripped both sides of her ankle-length blue jean skirt, and one of her primary goals seemed to be showing off as much of her legs as possible. "And we do that by barbecuing the politicians."

"That's not Helena," William said.

They were only a block away from City Hall. Franklin hoped they could make it there before whichever personality had taken Helena over started throwing people.

"They must be insane," said Agent Strexit. "There's gotta be plenty of security there."

"Trust me, she's not worried about security," said Franklin.

"I'm not really sure what we can do to stop her, either."

"Dr. Bryce?" said Strexit. Apparently Strexit had no idea what he was getting himself into.

"Do you have anything stronger than four HR120s?" Franklin said, "Because that's what *she* eats for breakfast."

"In that case," said Strexit, "we suck her into a pocket dimension until the dominant personality reasserts itself."

"Good idea," said William, leaning over Franklin's shoulder to see the screen. Helena and Flastcaster were almost through the front doors.

Strexit pulled their slender vehicle into the City Hall parking lot. Franklin and William hurried out of the car and were followed by four other security officers.

"How exactly do you plan to get Helena into a pocket dimension?" Franklin asked as they sprinted for the building.

Strexit pulled out a small, green, cone-shaped devise. It was a portable aperture, programmed to transport anyone it was aimed at into a pocket dimension once it was activated. Franklin had no idea that Vlakdormat security was equipped with portable apertures. In practically every dimension, a single portable aperture cost more than a house. That was why most people used stationary, camouflaged apertures.

"Vlakdormat spares no expense," said Strexit.

As they ran up the wide, concrete stairs to the main entrance, Franklin looked back to see three police cars turning around in the parking lot and hurrying off. Having seen Vlakdormat security cars, they knew something was coming that the police force didn't know how to handle. Strexit smiled and shook his head.

Strexit led them into the building, and Franklin immediately spotted Helena and Flastcaster walking nonchalantly down the brightly lit hallway in front of them. Flastcaster, holding an open plastic container in his right hand, trailed a steady stream of gasoline behind him. There were four security guards in blue uniforms and several men and women in business suits lying on the ground unconscious. Helena stopped Flastcaster at the end of the hallway, but they didn't turn around. Gasoline created a pool between them. Franklin wondered if Helena had noticed that he and Strexit were there or if it even mattered to her. She lit a match.

Strexit aimed the portable aperture at her and prepared to activate it, but Helena didn't drop the match. Strexit hesitated. Helena thoughtfully watched the small fire as it danced in her hands. She suddenly blew it out and flicked the match away. Then she pulled a box of matches out of the plastic bag and crushed it effortlessly in her fist. Flastcaster looked like a kid whose parents wouldn't buy him an ice cream cone.

"You should have stayed in therapy," she said. She looked straight up into the sunlight pouring down from the skylight above her. "You'll want to move now."

Franklin cupped his hand around his mouth to yell to her, but she was gone before he had the chance. She shot up through the skylight above her, and Flastcaster moved out of the way to avoid dozens of shards of falling glass.

"I have a new theory," William said. "I think she's Superman."

Flastcaster reached into a back pocket made of duct tape and pulled out another match, but Strexit was already feet away, pointing the portable aperture at him.

Flastcaster was smiling ear to ear as he gave Strexit the

match. "This isn't exactly what I was hoping for, but it's the next best thing," he said to no one at all.

He was handcuffed and shoved in the back seat of the security vehicle between two guards. William and Franklin squeezed uncomfortably into the front seat, but neither of them minded much. Franklin was just relieved that Helena had gained control before one of the other personalities had the chance to kill anyone.

"You should have listened to me," Franklin said to Flastcaster as they rode back to Vlakdormat. "You know you're going to spend some time in jail."

"I know," said Flastcaster. A goofy smile was still plastered across his face. "But I did it."

"Did what? I thought what you wanted was to rule the world."

"That's my ultimate goal. First I needed to prove I'm a real super villain. I was arrested for a major crime while wearing my costume. Now I'm well on my way."

Franklin couldn't believe Flastcaster had really been willing to hurt anyone, and now that he had proven how serious he was, there was no point in arguing with him. All Flastcaster needed was the wrong kind of encouragement. "I'm happy for you," he said. "Really."

Franklin and William went back to Krawkson Klub that evening—they both needed a stiff drink. This time, neither of them felt like going home during karaoke hour, although stabbing the Quaxor twins might have seriously improved Franklin's mood. He knew that whatever the Vaklock beasts drank would be extremely strong, so he asked for that. What he ended up with was the same thick black bubbling crud that Eva Crill had been drinking that morning. Such was the luck of having two first names.

"Not having a Threpnoidian Dragonfly tonight?" William asked.

"I'm kind of boycotting Threpnoidian products at the moment."

"Oh? Why?"

Franklin didn't feel the need to dignify that with a response.

"Come on. Grothman was one rogue Threpnoidian. That doesn't say anything about the whole race."

"Ever wonder why we all love their products so much?" Franklin asked.

"Not really. I just thought they tasted good."

"Or maybe they're using their persuasion powers to make us *think* they taste good."

"I never thought about that . . . or maybe you're just extremely paranoid. You know, you really should see a shrink."

"Maybe I'll do that.

"How's Helena?"

"I don't know yet. I have an appointment with her tomorrow."

"I'm sorry you had to do what you did."

After Helena had cleared her head for a few hours, she had come back to Vlakdormat. Franklin had security put her in a holding dimension, which looked just like a plain white brick room except a person could only access the aperture from the other side. After telling Helena he trusted her, Franklin felt terrible for having her locked up. She said she understood, but that almost made it worse.

He tried to take a sip, but his drink seemed to be

simultaneously trying to take a drink out of him, so he set it down and looked at William's mustard drink gloomily. Maybe he would finally have to resort to whatever that was.

"It's just until we find a more permanent solution," said Franklin. "None of this is Helena's fault."

"Tell that to Eva Crill. She's already told Dr. Caslom she'll put in her resignation if he doesn't get Helena transferred."

"I didn't know that," Franklin said. "Aren't we supposed to be helping people? People just like Helena? Isn't that our job?"

"Yeah," said William. "But Crill saw her past, or lack thereof. She sees Helena as a drone—no more a person than an HR120. Crill doesn't want her transferred to another facility. She wants Helena transferred to a holding dimension permanently."

"Good thing it isn't up to her, then," said Franklin. "What do you think?"

"Honestly? Helena scares me a little. She can't help it when one of the others takes over. When she's in charge, her intentions are good. She obviously cares about what happens to you. And sometimes I'm really glad to have her around. But I can't help wondering . . . for every Grothman she stops, how many Flastcasters is she going to help?"

"I know," said Franklin. "But she saved my life twice."

"And so you feel like you owe her. I understand; she saved me too. And I know Crill's totally nuts, but she might be on to something. Everything about this girl makes her look like some kind of weapon. What if, at the end of the day, no matter how hard she tries, that's all she knows how to be?"

Franklin wanted to treat Helena like just another patient. She had come to him, and it was his responsibility to be there for her.

But she was a force he couldn't possibly understand. Everyone she came near was in potential danger. On the other hand, when she was at the right place with the right mind, she was a hero. As he wrestled with it all in his head, Franklin looked down at the table and realized that his side was almost completely covered in the thick bubbling liquid.

"It looks like it's growing," Franklin said.

"You know you're supposed to drink it before it does that," said William.

"No, I didn't know that."

"It doesn't stop growing until you drink it. You might want to go find a Vaklock somewhere before we all drown."

Helena entered Franklin's office, sat down across from him, and waited for him to begin, as she always did at the beginning of their sessions. There was no rage in her eyes. She held her usual composure as if nothing had happened. Had he been asleep for the last twenty-four hours, he never would have guessed her body had tried to go on a psychotic killing spree.

"We have a problem," said Franklin.

"I know," Helena said. "Her name is Sandra."

Franklin slowly nodded. "This wasn't your fault. I shouldn't have left you alone with Crill."

"If you hadn't, *you* might have been the one Sandra went after," Helena said. "I've become a liability. I'm willing to leave."

"You'd be a liability wherever you went. What we need to do is find out why that is. You don't have amnesia."

"What?"

"Dr. Crill found out that the reason you don't remember

anything before six months ago is because you didn't *exist* before that."

Helena stood up and slowly moved toward the window. She lost some of her composure.

"The Unexplained Phenomena division has seen me five times," she said. "Dr. Drake has run every test he knows of. I've been probed, prodded, and wrapped in layers of plastic wrap. All he could tell me is that I'm not a robot. Am I some kind of clone?"

"I don't know. But I agree with Dr. Crill. The skull can't be wrong."

"Then why?"

"Why what?"

She turned to face him, and for the first time, he could see real pain on her face. "Why are you helping me?"

"It's what I do, Helena."

"But I'm not even human."

"Probably not, but neither are a lot of people, and I don't hold it against them."

"But what if someone made me—built me to do something terrible?"

"That's exactly what Dr. Crill thinks," said Franklin. And he didn't mention it, but it was the same line of thinking William was on, and that bothered him.

"And what do you think?"

Franklin shrugged. "It's possible. So are a number of other explanations."

"I might lose control again. I could hurt you."

"It's worth the risk," Franklin said.

"Dr. Bryce—"

"I know that you and Sandra are not the same person. I don't care what Crill thinks. I'm not giving up on you. Don't give up on me."

She looked back out the window and didn't say anything for a long time. Franklin stood next to her and watched the traffic outside as it moved beneath them. The sun was almost blinding, and everyone seemed to be out, running errands, going to and from jobs, taking their children to the park, having lunch with friends. It was like looking through a portal to another dimension but not being able to enter it.

"Dr. Bryce," Helena said finally, "if Dr. Crill can put information in someone's head, do you think she could take something out?"

"Helena. . . ."

"I want them out. I want to get rid of them. Permanently."

CHAPTER 11

Dimensions Are People Too

FRANKLIN WALKED THE HALLS OF VLAKDORMAT, RUBBING HIS FOREHEAD. He wished that for just one day, nothing remotely exciting would happen to him. Years ago, when his life had been completely uninteresting, he had, of course, longed for the exact opposite, and he knew that he was proving the age old human contradiction of man only wanting whatever he didn't have. But he didn't care. Back when he had wanted a more exciting life, he never would have imagined robots trying to kill him or his name having anything to do with his fate. And when he had tried to go back to that life, it had made him unhappy.

All he could do now, it seemed, was wait around and see what new, bizarre situation would land in his lap next and try not to get killed. If that was the life that truly made him happy, he thought, perhaps he was the one who needed a shrink.

Franklin stopped at Bethany's desk to pick up the paperwork on his new patient. He looked over the pages for a moment and then glanced up at her in dismay.

"Do you even check these before you give them to me?" Franklin asked.

"I know, some of the answers don't make sense, but the guy was really weird. He made me kinda uncomfortable."

Franklin lay the paper down in front of her and pointed at the species field. The patient had scribbled the words "half Jexarite."

"What does that mean?" Franklin said. "Did he *look* like a Jexarite?"

"Oh yeah," said Bethany. "I saw the scales *and* the double layer of teeth."

"What's the other half?"

"He didn't say. Maybe he's got some Cherokee in him or something."

Franklin shook his head and walked toward his office.

"Hey, look on the bright side," Bethany called from behind him. "At least he's not an HR120."

Mr. Havst was a short, chubby man with pale green, scaly skin and a depressed expression on his face. Without the advantage of telepathy, it was difficult to determine whether or not he was actually depressed. Many of Franklin's patients looked especially troubled at their first session, and sometimes they weren't upset at all. Some of them seemed to think that they couldn't be justified in going to a therapist unless they at least looked like they were on the edge of suicide. It was like being embarrassed to go to the doctor's office because you weren't sure if anything was really wrong with you.

Franklin got up from behind his desk and held out his hand, greeting Havst. "It's good to meet you," he said.

Havst hesitated.

"Do they not shake hands in your dimension?" Franklin asked.

"No," said Havst, "we butt heads. But that's not it. I just . . . make it a habit not to get too close to people."

Franklin offered him a seat on his leather armchair and pulled out his clipboard. "Why is that, Mr. Havst?"

"It's Borflostmikite, Dr. Bryce."

Franklin's eyes widened. Borflostmikite was listed on the patient sheet as Havst's first name, but Franklin had avoided saying it because it was so long and hard to pronounce. Even after Havst said it out loud, Franklin didn't know if he could get the whole thing out. "If it's all the same to you, I think I'll stick with your last name. After all, we only have an hour."

Franklin smiled, but Havst didn't find his joke funny at all. As Franklin looked down at Havst's paperwork, which he had only skimmed before, he noticed that the Jexarite had an anger management problem. Franklin made a mental note to stop trying to be funny. Havst had a lot of very sharp teeth.

"I have a secret," Havst announced, "one I've been living with my entire life."

"Go on," Franklin said.

"You deal with people like me all the time, right? People who are . . . different?"

"Yes, I do. And it's understandable that you feel that way. You're a stranger from another dimension. It must be difficult fitting in here."

"I'm not talking about that. I'm the only one of my *kind,* Dr. Bryce."

"I don't understand."

"I'm not just a Jexarite. I'm something else, too."

Franklin nodded. "You wrote in your file that you're only half Jexarite, but I certainly can't tell by just looking at you. Is that your secret?"

"The other half isn't a species. It's something else."

Franklin doodled on his clipboard. He was afraid Havst was about to get metaphorical, and he wanted to look engaged.

"When I get angry, something happens to the people around me. That's why I'm afraid to get too close."

"They don't respond well to your anger."

"Well, no. They disappear."

"They what?"

"They *disappear.* And they don't come back until I get angry again."

"I'm afraid I'm not following you."

Havst hesitated. "They get sucked inside of me, like a vacuum. And then later, they get blown back out again."

Franklin couldn't tell if this was still a metaphor or if Havst was serious. He drew a large question mark in the middle of his paper.

"I'm a *dimension,*" said Havst.

Franklin slowly looked up and dropped his pen. "You're a. . . ."

"I know how it sounds."

Franklin opened his mouth but nothing came out. He tried to make eye contact with Havst to show he was taking him seriously, but he couldn't stop his eyes from darting around the room. This was too much, even for his brain to wrap around.

Havst's face grew longer than it already was. "You don't believe me."

"A *dimension*?"

"I promise you, I'm not making this up."

Franklin grasped around his head for words, but he ultimately decided this was one of those times in which saying nothing was far preferable to saying anything. "Go on," he said.

"It's hard enough being a Jexarite. Shedding your skin every six months, growing a second set of eyes. . . ."

"You have another set of—"

"Will have, in about a year."

"Oh. Congratulations."

"Thanks. I've heard it really hurts."

"Sorry to hear it. But go on."

Mr. Havst paced the floor. "I've never known how to deal with it. When people find out, they get scared. Sometimes they hate me. I can't keep friends. I'm an outcast in Jexar. A freak of nature."

Franklin wasn't sure what would be the appropriate thing to say next, so he decided to fall back on a classic. "And how does that make you feel?"

"It makes me . . . angry."

"Do you have any idea how it happened?"

"None. My parents are outcasts just like I am. Ever since I started . . . sucking people into myself, their lives haven't been the same. No one wants anything to do with someone with an unstable dimension for a son, even now that I'm fully-grown and on my own. And no one who knows what I am wants anything to do with me. But sometimes when I think about that, I get mad, and then the whole thing starts all over again. I need to control my anger. Maybe then I can stop it, for good. Will you help me?"

"Of course I will," said Franklin. He took a deep breath and hoped he could make good on his word. "That's what I do."

Franklin was looking at the longest table that he could recall ever seeing. The room seemed to have been built around the huge, mahogany conference table, which was so long that at least twenty slightly overweight people could be seated on either side of it. But it was only wide enough so that just one normal-size person could sit on each end. The first time Franklin had attended a meeting in this office, he had thought the table's size a little excessive—considering it was an office, not a conference room—and the office was only occupied by a single individual.

That was, of course, until he met that individual, Dr. Akbar Caslom IV, office manager and head therapist of Vlakdormat's Abott City branch. Caslom was a Makverian, and he was basically an accordion (sans the buttons and keys) with legs, arms at his furthest ends, and a cone-shaped head in the center. His skin was a pearl white. In his natural state, Dr. Caslom was as long as the table in his office, and, while he was far more comfortable at this length, he had the ability to compress his segmented body so that he could fit in or through anything a normal-size human being could. Franklin had always wondered what kind of fantastic material Caslom's suits must have been made out of and how he kept his ties from wrinkling up, but he never asked for fear of being impolite. Suffice it to say, Dr. Caslom was not as wide as he was long.

Dr. Caslom slinked his way into his spacious, top floor office where Franklin, Dr. Eva Crill, and Dr. Drake R. Drake were already seated at the conference table. They all sat on one side together, with several chairs between them. Dr. Caslom gracefully came to his full length, his specially tailored gray suit stretching out along with his body, and he sat down on a matching wood bench the length of the table. His large, melon-like head remained at the center of his body, and his arms stretched out like his torso did, so that he could reach the file folder in front of him. He opened it and called the meeting to order.

"This meeting has been called to discuss the future of Helena Kathryn," said Dr. Caslom. He spoke in his usual high-pitched voice, but his expression was a somber one. He didn't seem to like what was happening with Helena any more than Franklin did. "Franklin, you said that Helena has requested that we look into the possibility of extracting her multiple personalities," Caslom said.

Franklin nodded slowly. "Yes, she has."

"But you've also stated in your reports that there is no evidence of any sort of psychosis. You believe these personalities were put in or programmed in by whomever or whatever brought Helena into existence."

"That's the most reasonable conclusion, given tests run by Dr. Crill, Dr. Drake and myself."

Caslom looked more serious and suddenly dropped his formal tone. "Franklin, is this even a patient we should be handling?"

"I'm sorry?"

"Helena has no mental illness. She isn't the problem—the other six women in her mind are."

"I'm pretty sure," Dr. Crill said, "that I can get rid of those personalities for you."

Franklin took a deep breath and fought the temptation to glare at her. "I've spoken with several of her personalities already," he said. "They each have their own emotions, opinions, and ambitions."

"And what if those emotions are just simulated?" Dr. Crill asked. "What if someone programmed that homicidal maniac to take control of her body and attack any female therapist who happens to have a pet velociraptor?"

"Yes, Dr. Crill," said Franklin sarcastically. "I'm sure that's exactly what happened."

"You get my point."

"But what if those emotions are genuine?" said Franklin. "We can't just eradicate six sentient personalities."

"You're going to make an ethical dilemma out of this, aren't you, Dr. Bryce?" said Crill. She adjusted her fluffy Repzothian hat, which seemed entirely unnecessary since it was floating two or three inches above her head.

"I think it already is," Franklin responded.

"I tend to agree," said Dr. Caslom. "If there is a chance that these personalities are somehow self-aware, we have an obligation to not harm them. And if that's the case, it may be that those six personalities are whom we should be giving psychiatric attention to—not Helena herself. If any of them agrees to that, we have to help, no matter the risk. We have all taken an oath."

All four of them raised their right hands.

"To aid the confused, the obsessed, and the psychotic," said Franklin.

"The depressed, the uncertain, and the insane," said Drake.

"The suicidal, the compulsive, the otherwise mentally ill, and anyone else who is unfit to counsel or perform therapeutic services on him or herself," said Caslom.

The three of them all looked to Crill to finish the credo. She sighed.

"As long as they are sentient and able to communicate in some fashion, regardless of race or races, gender or lack of gender, dimension of birth, religious beliefs or lack thereof, favorite color, or the possibility that they have been genetically engineered or are robots, or are a combination of several robots."

"You know, I'm starting to wonder if we shouldn't talk to headquarters about rethinking that last part," Drake said.

"But Franklin," said Dr. Caslom, getting back to the problem at hand. "Precautions must be taken. We must avoid another incident like what happened last week."

"Helena is still in a holding dimension," said Dr. Crill, "to keep her from trying to kill me. I hope you're not thinking of cancelling that particular precaution."

"I'd like to," Caslom said. "Considering what she's done for this office, I don't like treating her like a prisoner. Franklin trusts her, and I trust his judgment on this."

"And I trust your trust," said Dr. Crill. "But we can't trust the other personalities."

"True. But if it weren't for Helena Kathryn, Dr. Grothman might still have complete control of this facility with his Threpnoidian persuasion powers. We all owe her a great debt."

"I'll be sure to send her a thank-you card," Franklin could barely hear Crill say under her breath. "It'll have a picture of a velociraptor eating a robot on the front."

Dr. Caslom either failed to hear her comment or chose to ignore it. He said to her, "Do you believe you can extract the personalities without destroying them?"

"Well, I've never done it, of course. I'm certain I can get them out. I just don't know what will happen to them if I do. I can usually save memories. . . . But personalities? I can't promise anything."

"At the moment," Dr. Caslom said, "Helena is, regrettably, too dangerous to be allowed free movement about Vlakdormat. Hopefully you can make some progress with the other personalities, Franklin."

Crill gave Franklin a look. He knew she hoped that Caslom would either send Helena away from Vlakdormat, or, at the very least, order the personality extraction. She didn't consider Helena to be a person at all. Crill was the coldest human being Franklin had ever met, and he wondered why and how she ever became a therapist.

"I leave it in your capable hands," Caslom said. "If there is a better solution than extracting her personalities, I'm certain you'll find it. But ultimately, Franklin, the decision will be yours. I cannot, in good conscience, allow Helena to make this decision on her own. You have the support of everyone here. Good luck."

Eva Crill's face reddened. She stood up and leaned over the table, practically sneering at Caslom.

"You have to order the extraction," she said.

Dr. Caslom remained cool and collected. "The last time I checked, I was the one in charge, and you were thinking about resigning."

"She may be in a holding dimension now," Crill said, "but she comes here every day for her sessions. Forget the damned oath. What if she escapes Dr. Bryce's office? And what about the HR120s? They didn't show up until Helena Kathryn did. Obviously they're connected to her. She's more dangerous than anyone is admitting. Surely you can see that."

"What I see, Dr. Crill," said Caslom, "is your failure to understand the delicate nature of this situation. We have the most equipped and secured facility in the city. Vlakdormat has been threatened, attacked, shrunk to the size of a walnut, and sucked into another dimension. And yet, here it still stands today. Each of those incidents happened because we insisted on helping someone too dangerous to be involved with. Each time we managed to survive, and each time we helped a patient to live a better life. Every branch of Vlakdormat in every dimension has this policy, and I refuse to change it here."

Crill opened her mouth, paused for a moment, and then closed it in defeat. Once Caslom's mind was made up, there was nothing in the multiverse that could change it. She slumped back in her chair so abruptly that her Repzothian hat failed to follow. It floated ahead of her, nowhere near her head, until she grabbed it in an embarrassed huff and put it back in place.

Caslom stretched out his slinky-like arm, picked up a large plastic bowl from the center of the table, and passed it around.

"That's all I have today. Thank you all for coming. Enjoy a lollipop on your way out."

After they had all left Dr. Caslom's office, Franklin caught up with Drake and stopped him in the hallway. He was nearly half a foot taller than Franklin, a few years older, and he wore a thinly trimmed goatee. They had been acquaintances for the last three years, since Drake was transferred from another branch of Vlakdormat in the Rekvoloskian dimension, although he wasn't a Rekvoloskian. All Franklin really knew about Drake was that he had lived in over a dozen different dimensions, that he specialized in interdimensional computer technology, and that he was really, really lucky.

"I have a question for you," said Franklin.

"Shoot."

"Have you ever met a dimension?"

Drake raised an eyebrow. "Is this a trick question?"

"No. I know it's bizarre, but I had a new patient today who claims he's a dimension."

"That's not possible."

"I know it sounds strange, but impossible? Considering some of the things I've seen, I find that unlikely. Stranger things have happened."

"No, they really haven't. A living dimension defies everything we know about the multiverse. If you think of reality as a blanket, dimensions are all threads of that blanket. They're all connected, which is why portals can open from one dimension to another. Dimensions are networked, like computers."

"So?"

"So if a dimension was a living being and it went inside another dimension, that dimension wouldn't be part of the network anymore. Which would probably cause the whole thing to break down."

"But the patient works like a dimension," said Franklin. "He can suck people into himself, just like an open portal."

"There must be some other explanation. He can't be a dimension."

"You're sure."

"Positive."

"But you could be wrong."

"No."

"Why?"

"Because I'm Drake R. Drake."

Franklin folded his arms. "Now you're just being arrogant." Drake laughed at his joke and they said goodbye. Franklin knew he was probably right—Drake was practically never wrong. Having the same two first names had the opposite effect on a person as having two different first names. It made Drake the luckiest kind of man in the multiverse.

CHAPTER 12

A Better Explanation

FRANKLIN AND WILLIAM SPENT THEIR LUNCH HOUR IN VLAKDORMAT'S RECREATION ROOM ON THE GROUND FLOOR NEAR THE LOBBY. They often shot a game of eight ball together on the pool table, but it had recently been replaced with a Nixothian table, which was about twice the size of a regulation human pool table. The Nixots played the game much differently than humans did. Not only did the pockets occasionally disappear and reappear somewhere else along the table, often forcing a player to change his entire strategy, but obstructive objects like spinning rods and small metal walls would also occasionally appear in the middle of the table, making the game more like miniature golf than pool. It was certainly more challenging, but Franklin didn't enjoy it as much. He didn't subscribe to the common axiom that just because something was enhanced by someone from another dimension, it was automatically better.

They played anyway, and William almost had Franklin beat. Franklin still had four solid balls left on the table, while William only had the eight ball left to sink. But Franklin still had a fighting chance, because William had to get the ball past two spinning rods, a dragon head whose mouth was constantly opening and closing, and a ramp which would send the cue ball hurtling off the table and onto the floor if it wasn't avoided. And the corner pocket he was about to shoot for had just become a center pocket on the other side of the table.

"I don't know why the Nixots thought they had to make this harder," William said as he struggled to line up his shot.

"Maybe it was too easy for them. I've heard that Nixots born with a knack for geometry. Maybe they're worse at miniature golf."

"Well, I'm great at miniature golf, and this isn't miniature golf. This game needs a par."

"I don't know why you're complaining. You're winning," said Franklin. William hadn't exactly gotten so far ahead of Franklin on his own merits. He had hit a jackpot castle earlier in the game that instantly sunk half of his balls.

"I swear, I'm going to write the makers of this thing," William said. "I'll try to get them to at least install a couple of pinball flippers on it."

William shot the cue ball and it collided with the eight ball, which barely missed a spinning rod and rolled directly into the mouth of the dragon.

"You didn't call that," said Franklin. "I win."

"What do you mean you win? It didn't go into a pocket!"

"The eight ball is gone and it isn't coming back until we insert more coins. So apparently, according to the Nixots, the dragon head *is* a pocket. And I win."

William shook his head and sat down on a bench behind the table. "I'm beginning to understand how you feel," he said.

"What do you mean?"

"A Nixot stole your telepathy and sold it on Interdimensional eBay. Now a Nixot screwed me in a game of pool. Either that whole race is evil, or they just hate therapists."

Franklin laughed and sat down beside William.

"So, how's work?" William asked.

"Interesting. I have a patient who might be a dimension."

"That's impossible."

"That's what Drake said."

"You should listen to him. He's always right."

Franklin sighed. "I also had a meeting with Caslom today."

"Oh. How did it go?"

"Pretty much how I figured it would. I'm stuck making the decision about Helena."

"Wow, that's tough. Maybe as tough as playing this stupid game."

"He is right, though. She's my patient, and it isn't the kind of decision she can make on her own right now."

"Yeah. If you do what Helena wants, you might be killing six innocent human beings. Except for the innocent part in one case —and probably the human part entirely."

"What do you think I should do?" Franklin asked.

William hesitated. He looked uncomfortable, like he had hoped Franklin wouldn't ask that question. "I know what *I'd* do."

"You'd go through with the personality extraction."

"It's risky, but maybe not as risky as doing nothing. We almost saw firsthand what Sandra's capable of. I wouldn't want to see her come out again."

"But like you said . . . the moral implications."

"That's why I'm glad it's not my decision."

"We don't even know it would work. Or what it might do to Helena."

"But we know what could happen if you leave them there."

Franklin chalked his cue and sighed.

"Look. I know she's your favorite patient," said William. "Most of us would kill for a case like hers. But I think you're too attached."

"Our relationship is purely professional," Franklin said.

"I'm not questioning that. But Helena's different than your other patients. They don't usually go out of their way to save your life. You have to be careful. I know you want to trust her, but we just don't know enough about her."

Franklin was starting to wish he hadn't asked for William's opinion.

"Just be as objective as you can be, "William said, "and don't give it too much thought. You know what they say about ethics?"

"No, I don't."

"Ethics is like a time travel paradox. If you think about it too hard, your brain will explode."

When Franklin came home that evening, he found Lera sitting on the couch and staring out the window.

"So now you've graduated to windows," said Franklin as he closed the door behind him. "Did you finally get enough points from your wall-staring game that you actually get to stare at *things* and *people* now?"

Lera turned around and frowned. "I'll have you know that I'm the Veritzu World Champion in Verullia, and I'd appreciate it if you didn't make fun of the game just because your limited brain capacity won't allow you to comprehend it. Besides, everyone knows that only children play Veritzu with a window. It's like bowling with bumpers or bicycling with training wheels."

Franklin shrugged. "Then what were you doing?"

"Watching the HR120s across the street."

Franklin looked at the window and froze. There was a brown TV repair van with tinted windows sitting in front of the house opposite from theirs. Franklin remembered seeing it the day before when he came home from work. The HR120s were waiting for a moment when Franklin was home and Lera wasn't. They would never attack him in front of people because it would compromise their cover, which is why Franklin felt safe enough to drive by himself and go out in public. But an empty house was another story.

One of the HR120s, dressed in gray overalls, got out of the van and glared at the house. Lera opened the window and poked her head out. She waved at the HR120 and he immediately turned the other way. He pulled out an extension cord and pretended to untangle it.

"Lera! Don't play with the HR120s."

"Why? It's hilarious."

Franklin jerked her back and closed the blinds. The HR120s were getting desperate. They had been looking for a moment of opportunity for a month now, and since they had claimed Franklin, he guessed it all had something to do with Helena. They probably thought that the longer Franklin had access to her, the more he could learn about her. Unfortunately for him, that assumption wasn't exactly the case.

"I'm just trying to make them nervous," Lera said. "Thought I ought to remind them about the risk they're taking. If they get too close, who knows what my intuition might pick up?"

Franklin and Lera sat at their dining room table, and Lera sorted through the day's mail. He asked her about her day, but she simply said it was fine.

"You never elaborate. Work is always fine," Franklin said.

"Well, it was. I'm not lying or anything. If I had anything interesting to say, you wouldn't understand it anyway. I doubt you'd appreciate the difficulties of translating Threpnoidian into

Grakthem." Grakthem was a language that sounded a lot like popping bubble wrap.

"You're right. I wouldn't understand."

"And that's why I don't bore you with the details." Lera opened an envelope, unfolded a piece of paper, and frowned. "Our cell phone bill went up again."

Several months earlier, they had switched to interdimensional cell phones and had regretted it ever since. The roaming charges were ridiculous. And they were forced to go with a company from the Pliscott dimension because it was the only one that covered all of the dimensions they ever went to. Lera showed Franklin the bill. The Pliscotts had also knocked a few more dimensions off of their coverage list.

"If they weren't Pliscotts, I'd refuse to pay that," Franklin said.

"Yeah, but you know what Pliscotts do to people who don't pay their electric bills."

Franklin thought about that and shuddered. The Pliscotts were some of the most vicious creatures in the multiverse, especially when it came to utilities. Franklin decided to change the subject.

"So I got a new patient today. Thinks he's a dimension."

"But that's—"

"Impossible. I know. Drake R. Drake and William said the same thing."

"But you think there might be some truth to it?"

"I just have a hard time believing that anything is impossible. The first thing I learned when I discovered that there was a multiverse was not to be surprised by anything, no matter how far-fetched it seemed. And now, a guy who sucks people into himself whenever he gets mad says he's a dimension, and all of the resident interdimensional experts say he can't possibly be one."

"All right," said Lera. "I'll admit that it wouldn't be the first time the laws of physics have changed their minds. There was a time on Verullia when gravity just turned itself off for five minutes and then came back on, like a power outage."

"See?"

"But there could be a million explanations for that. How could a dimension be a person *and* be inside of another dimension?"

"I don't know, since the only dimensions inside of real ones are pocket dimensions."

Lera abruptly stood up from the table. "Wait a minute. Do they come back out?"

"What?"

"The people who get sucked into this guy. Do they come back?"

"Yeah. As soon as he gets angry again."

"How do you get into the Krawkson Klub?"

"The same way you get into any pocket dimension. Through an aperture."

"But it's hidden, right?"

Franklin nodded.

"And you can only access it during very specific circumstances, right? Like driving thirty to thirty-seven miles per hour straight at a clump of trees."

"Lera, what are you getting at?"

"Mr. Havst sucks people into himself, but only when he's angry."

Franklin's eyes widened. His wife was a genius. "But you

don't think he's actually sucking people into *himself* at all, do you?"

"No," said Lera. "I think he's the aperture to a pocket dimension."

CHAPTER 13

What Can't Be Stolen

"KILLING PEOPLE, EVEN THE PEOPLE IN YOUR HEAD, IS WRONG," SAID FRANKLIN TO THE MIRROR IN HIS OFFICE. The mirror didn't respond, but he could only imagine how Helena would. This thought had kept him up most of the night, and, after a lot of reflection, he had decided that William was right—if you think about ethics too long, you do risk exploding your brain.

He was practicing what he would say to her later that afternoon, and he didn't have the slightest idea as to how he would tell her that he couldn't authorize the extraction of her personalities.

"And some of your personalities aren't too bad. Kay says she makes really great homemade apple pie."

"Am I interrupting something?" said a voice from behind him. Franklin turned around, expecting to see Mr. Havst, early for his appointment. But instead of a chubby man with scales, he saw a slender man with orange skin and bat wings. Franklin folded his arms in disgust. Rajel Chirok was the last thing he needed right now.

"I didn't think I'd ever see you again, Chirok," Franklin said.

Chirok's wings folded behind him and he bent over in a graceful bow. "I'm sure you'll understand if I tell you Rajel Chirok is not my real name."

Franklin ignored him and activated the speakerphone on his desk. "Bethany, I specifically told you not to let in any Nixots without my expressed permission."

"I know," came the voice of his secretary, "but Mr. Chirok

said it was the most important thing I'd ever do, and I just couldn't throw away a chance like that."

Chirok smiled. "You'd better hang on to her, Franklin. She's a natural."

Franklin instantly understood. Bethany was acting exactly as he had when he was affected by Grothman's Threpnoidian persuasion powers. "So, you don't put all the powers you steal up for auction," Franklin said.

"Of course not. Some of them come in handy for stealing more." Chirok continued, "It's ironic, isn't it? You never could read my mind, even when you did have telepathy. But now I can read yours. You don't like me very much, do you?"

"Look, as much as I'm enjoying this little reunion, we're both wasting each other's time," said Franklin. He picked up a stack of blank computer paper, set it down in front of him, and thumbed through it as if it were important paperwork. "I don't have any more powers for you to steal. So why don't you run along and try to con a Yivynox or something."

"Don't you know anything? Love powers are so last year. No, what I'm after is brand new. It'll be the hottest commodity since heat vision."

Franklin reached under his desk. "I don't know what you're talking about. I don't have anything you want."

Franklin pointed a bottle of window cleaner at the Nixot and smiled confidently. Chirok laughed.

"For a minute there, I thought you were reaching for a weapon."

"Don't you research your powers' weaknesses before you steal them?" Franklin asked.

As Franklin sprayed Chirok with several blasts of window

cleaner, the door opened and Mr. Havst walked inside.

"Am I interrupting something?" Havst asked. Chirok wiped his now-drenched button-down shirt.

"As a matter of fact, you're not," Chirok said, inching closer to Havst. "I'm here to see you."

Chirok held out his hand and Havst pulled away, just as he had when Franklin had tried to shake hands with him.

"I don't shake hands," Havst said. He looked at Franklin, who was still pointing his bottle of window cleaner at Chirok like an anxious cop. "Dr. Bryce, if this is a bad time. . . ."

"*Shake* my hand," said Chirok, impatiently.

Havst looked confused. "No," he said.

"What's wrong, Chirok?" asked Franklin. "Lost your touch?"

Chirok threw his outstretched hand down at his side in frustration. He walked behind Franklin, leaned over his shoulder, and whispered, "How did you know what would happen?"

"Two words: *Nitzu Trivisknot.* Oh, and don't read the English version. It's worthless." Franklin was relieved—not just because Chirok couldn't use his Threpnoidian persuasion against Havst, but also because he knew Chirok's telepathy wouldn't work now, either. There was nothing worse than having Rajel Chirok digging around in his head for secrets.

Chirok's wings batted angrily. He pulled out a small, white envelope from his pocket.

"I had hoped we could conduct this transaction without incident, but I suppose I'll have to do this the more reckless and less-thought-out way."

Franklin knew exactly what Chirok was trying to do, and he held back a laugh. "You're wasting your time," Franklin said.

"Mr. Havst doesn't have any superpowers."

Chirok narrowed his eyes and held his right arm in front of himself, spreading his fingers wide. He shot a wave of neon-green energy from his palm that sent Franklin flying up against the opposite wall.

"Mr. Havst, why are you here?" Chirok asked him, leaving Franklin lying in a daze on the floor.

"I think the question is, why are *you* here?" said Havst.

"All right, I'll go first. I'm here to take your curse away from you." Chirok fumbled with the piece of paper in his hands.

Franklin moaned and rubbed his bruised side as he tried to stand up.

"How do you know about that?" Havst asked, wide-eyed.

"I have connections all over the multiverse. I know about a lot of people's secrets, especially about the special powers they keep to themselves. I know yours has ruined your life."

Franklin finally stood up and limped toward them. "Don't listen to him, Mr. Havst. He's not here to help you. He thinks he can steal your ability and sell it for a profit."

"Is that true?" asked Mr. Havst.

"Dr. Bryce's opinion of my business practices is not the issue here. Why should you care what my intentions are? If you no longer want the burden of being a dimension, then I can help you."

Havst shook his head and clenched his fists. "But you're going to *help* me whether I want it or not, aren't you?"

"Please, I only want—"

"Oh no," said Havst. The chubby Jexarite stood just inches away from Chirok and stared straight up at him with his hands on his hips. "You might be taller, you might be stronger, and you might have a little piece of paper that steals things, but you don't intimidate me. What makes you think I won't use my power right now?"

"The fact that I can give you the one thing you've always wanted. A normal life."

Franklin began to feel a slight breeze across his neck. "Is it getting chilly in here or is it just me?" he asked aloud.

"You're not interested in what I want," Havst said. "You want to exploit me. You're just like everyone else. If they don't hate me, they want to dissect me."

The breeze grew stronger. Franklin looked at Havst and saw that he was reddening in the face. Franklin grabbed hold of his desk.

"If they don't call me a freak, they want me for their school mascot. And you want to call my condition a gift and use it for your own benefit."

Chirok threw his hands in the air and let the piece of paper fly. "All right. I give up." The paper ripped and folded itself until it was a perfect cube and was hovering in mid-air, just like the one he'd used only a few months earlier to steal Franklin's telepathy. "You're absolutely right. And your powers will be mine before you even have a chance to use them."

Before long, the breeze became a strong wind. Papers flew off of Franklin's desk and spun about the room like they had been swept up by a cyclone. Franklin's wavy hair ruffled in the wind, and he shielded his face with the hand he wasn't using to hold himself steady. He caught a glance of the paper cube, which was vibrating violently but wasn't being affected by the wind at all. Franklin wondered just what kind of paper it was made of.

Havst practically barked in his anger. "Then let's just see

what's faster—your little toy or a dimensional vortex."

As the wind blew even stronger, Chirok jumped into the air and flapped his wings against it, trying to make his way to the door. He looked back at the cube and suddenly appeared very concerned.

"What's wrong?" Franklin yelled. "Don't you have any powers to keep you from getting sucked into a vortex?" He was being only half sarcastic. A part of him hoped Chirok had some way to stop what Havst was doing. Franklin didn't want to get sucked into the aperture any more than Chirok did.

One by one, the wind picked up Franklin's couch, his glass table, his leather armchairs, and his desk chair and sent them toward the aperture that was Mr. Havst. Franklin was amazed to see his furniture seem to disappear just as it reached Havst's wide stomach. Chirok continued to beat his wings faster and faster until he was panting, but it was no use. He made it to the door handle but was slowly pulled away from it until he found himself inches away from Havst. He finally disappeared into the aperture behind the furniture.

Franklin was now holding onto the desk with both hands, his legs flailing in the air behind him, but now the heavy oak desk itself was being dragged across the carpet toward Havst, screeching against the floor as it went. Franklin looked behind him to see Havst grab the cube out of the air. Before Franklin even had time to wonder what he was doing with the cube, Havst and the practically empty office disappeared.

CHAPTER 14

The Truth About Mr. Havst

FRANKLIN FOUND HIMSELF LYING IN A PATCH OF TALL GRASS, RUBBING HIS SIDE. Having been sucked into another dimension and having fallen several feet to wherever he was now, he had a bruise to match the one he'd gotten from being thrown up against a wall. He looked up to see a yellow opening in the sky that was spitting sheets of crumpled paper onto the ground. His oak desk was lying next to him. One of its legs had almost snapped off in the fall. He felt fortunate that the desk hadn't landed on him.

Franklin sat up and instantly forgot all about his favorite desk. He was being observed by a giant eyeball the size of a Greyhound bus that was hovering six feet off the ground. He didn't want to make any quick movements, uncertain as to what a giant eyeball might do if it felt threatened. Or maybe this was a vastly intelligent eyeball that had taken over this pocket dimension and had set itself up as the supreme ruler. For all Franklin knew, the eyeball could be responsible for turning Havst into a pocket dimension aperture and this was how it lured subjects—or victims—into its domain.

Franklin looked around cautiously and found Chirok slumped over one of the leather armchairs, having landed on Franklin's pair of "Therapist of the Year" coffee cups. Their shattered remains were littered among the grass around the chair. Chirok got up and felt his midsection, which had been cut in two places by shards of coffee cup. His forest green button-down shirt was missing a couple of buttons and was ripped in the middle.

"Not only did you steal my telepathy," Franklin said, "but now you've broken my favorite mugs."

Chirok picked up a large piece of one of the cups that still had some writing on it. "You were Therapist of the Year?"

"Technically, no. It was another version of me from Dimension 0.65. We met a couple of years ago. The mugs were mementos."

"That's pathetic."

"And now you've broken them."

"What's also pathetic is that you're worried about coffee cups when we're stuck in a pocket dimension with no way to open an aperture. And there's this huge disembodied *eyeball* staring at us."

"Maybe you should have thought about that before you tried to steal Havst's powers," said Franklin. He walked away from his office furniture, and Chirok reluctantly followed. The huge eyeball turned to each of them, looking up and down and studying them.

"That thing is freaking me out," said Chirok.

"That's what you get," Franklin said. "You steal people's powers, you should expect to get stared at by a giant eyeball. In fact, you should consider yourself lucky. It could be a lot worse. It could have giant *feet* and step on you."

Chirok looked annoyed.

"Hey, here's a thought," said Franklin. "Maybe it's got *heat vision.*"

Chirok backed away from the eyeball. "Don't give it any ideas."

"It's not like it can hear you. It doesn't have ears."

"You're really enjoying this, aren't you?"

"Absolutely."

Chirok ignored him, closed his eyes, and put his hands

together.

"What exactly are you doing?"

"Concentrating. Leave me alone."

Chirok took deep breaths and squinted his eyes, hard. He grunted a few times. Nothing happened.

"What are you trying to do?" asked Franklin.

Chirok opened his eyes and sighed in defeat. "I'm trying to teleport us out of here."

"And now you've lost *your* powers?" said Franklin. He threw his arms into the air. "This day couldn't get any better."

Chirok looked down at his hands. "It must be something about this dimension. And I don't see why you're gloating. You're trapped here too."

"There's a difference between me and you. You went into this without knowing anything. It's kind of like the window cleaner. I did my homework."

"Wait, you're saying you . . . know how to get out of here?"

Franklin smiled.

"For the record, I was going to teleport us both out. I wasn't going to leave you here," Chirok said.

"That's very kind of you. And I suppose you were going to give Mr. Havst a cut of the profits you made off his dimension powers too, right?"

"Let me explain this to you," said Chirok, sounding more like the sly businessman he had been earlier. "I live by a different ethical code."

"You mean one without ethics?"

"I come from a long line of career criminals. My father, his father, his father. . . . I think his father was a hot air balloonist. . . . But then his father before him. . . . It's in my blood, Franklin. I am what I am."

"And the rest of us just have to understand, even while you're getting rich at our expense."

"All I expect you to understand is that I can't change."

"Fine. Then I can't get us out of here."

"You're joking. You'd spend the rest of your life being stared at by this giant eyeball, just because I won't change my lifestyle to conform to your ideals?"

"That's about the size of it," said Franklin. Of course, he had no intention of staying there, and he knew it would only be a matter of time before Havst got angry again and the aperture opened.

But he wasn't about to tell Chirok that.

Franklin was generally open-minded and he appreciated people with different standards than his own, but Chirok had no standards at all.

"There's nothing here," Chirok said. The Nixot was really starting to lose it. "What are we going to eat? The eyeball?"

The eye floated closer and stared at Chirok. Somehow, it looked a little angrier.

"I wouldn't suggest it," said Franklin.

"I don't think you can get us out of here at all. You're just trying to humiliate me."

"You did that all by yourself. Believe what you want, but you've got a choice. You give me your Interdimensional eBay password, and I'll tell you how to get out."

Chirok snickered. "You really think I'm going to fall for that? I'm the master of bluffs. I've won over a dozen superpowers just by playing poker." For a brief second, Franklin wondered if Nixothian poker was anything like Nixothian pool.

He started to walk away from Chirok. "Fine with me. Enjoy your eye."

Franklin looked behind him and watched Chirok as he walked along the thick grass. The eyeball flew higher and hovered directly over Chirok's head. Chirok moved to the right, and the eye moved with him. Frustrated, he moved back to the same spot, and still, the eye stayed with him. Before long he was running in circles, but the eye just kept floating along above him, having no trouble keeping up with him. Franklin wondered if the eye had arbitrarily chosen not to like Chirok or if it understood anything they had been saying and was taking Franklin's side.

Chirok finally gave up and sat on the grass. The eye dropped several inches and stared at Chirok's neatly cropped hair. "I can't stand this," Chirok said. "No powers, no eBay, no food . . . and there's this enormous eye just looking at me! Why is it there? What is it thinking?"

"You sure know how to keep your cool," Franklin said. He kept his distance, but he had stopped walking. This was too entertaining to miss.

"Taunt me all you want. Nothing is going to make me give up that password. Not even this eye."

Franklin shrugged and took another few short steps away from Chirok.

The eye moved down and positioned itself squarely in front of Chirok's face. Chirok looked nervous. He blinked, and the eye immediately rammed hard into him, knocking him to the ground. Franklin held back a laugh.

"What was that for?" Chirok said. The eye said nothing. It just floated there until he stood up again.

"Oh, I get it. Well, forget it, pal. I am not having a staring

contest with you."
Chirok blinked again, and the eye smashed into him a second time, much harder. Chirok grabbed his scraped elbow and looked up at the eye in contempt.

"I bet you can't out-fly a Nixot," he said.

Chirok jumped into the air and flapped his wings. He rose higher and higher into the sky until he was flying away from the eye as fast as he could. The eye followed, slowly at first, and then it picked up speed. The eye was gaining on Chirok fast, and before, long it was obvious to Franklin that the eye could have flown circles around him. It came up from behind and effortlessly rear-ended Chirok. He reeled in pain, but kept flying. The eye hit him again, and this time Chirok flew under it and darted the other way, trying to lose it. But the eye flipped over, caught sight of Chirok, and shot toward him again. It shot three narrow red blasts out of its pupil, each narrowly missing Chirok. The eye was missing him on purpose, trying to surprise him. It worked. Chirok slowed down and the eye slammed into him a third time.

Franklin ran to Chirok as he rubbed sore muscles and bruises.

"I thought you were joking about the heat vision," Chirok said.

"It was just a guess. You probably shouldn't make it any angrier or it might really try to fry you next time."

"That thing is *not* made of eyeball," said Chirok. "Steel hurts less than that."

"So, I was wondering," Franklin said, "about that password. . . ."

"Fine. I'll tell you."

"And make sure you get it right. I know a dimension who'd

love to suck you right back in."

Suddenly, the landscape in front of them seemed to rip apart, and there was a yellow tear just above them once again, about twice the size of the menacing eyeball.

Chirok gave Franklin an evil-looking smile and strode toward the aperture. "I guess you'll never know."

Franklin noticed another aperture directly behind them, and he saw a few papers fly out of it. Franklin grabbed one out of the air. It was a piece of stationary with his name on it. Mr. Havst was still in his office. The wind picked up fast and they were soon sucked toward the aperture. This time, neither of them fought it.

After they entered the vortex, Franklin found himself on the floor next to Chirok, staring up at Mr. Havst. The Jexarite was smiling down at them.

"Welcome back," Havst said. "Now that you're here, I'd like you to meet some friends of mine."

He opened the door to Franklin's office, and two fat, scaly, sharp-toothed Jexarites walked in. They were identical twins, and they each wore the same deadpan expression. Franklin and Chirok got up off the floor to meet them.

"What are you two doing here?" said Chirok.

"You know them?" asked Franklin.

"They're the guys who told me about Havst's powers."

"We are the sons of Grithmardmozone and Chiroroma Lemt," said the man on the right. "Do you remember our name, Chirok?"

"No, I don't. You just called yourselves Bob and Rupert before. What's going on here?"

"Thirty years ago, your father stole our father's wit and imagination."

"My father. . . . You mean you set me up?"

"He stole their father's *what?*" said Franklin.

"Like I said before," Chirok said, "Dad was a con artist, just like me. But he wasn't into superpowers. He was more old fashioned than that. He had little paper cubes that could steal your logic, reason, or even your personality traits."

"Too bad you didn't take up your dad's trade," said Franklin. "Maybe you could've stolen yourself some character."

"We have completed our right of vengeance," said the Lemt on the left.

"What did I do to you?" Chirok said.

"The offspring of a Jexarite has the duty to avenge his father's shame. We have lived by this code for thousands of years."

"But I'm not a Jexarite," said Chirok.

"We are more enlightened than we were thousands of years ago," said the Lemt on the right. "We no longer discriminate between species. We have humiliated you with the Sinister Eye of the Havst pocket dimension and stripped you of your powers. Your father's debt is repaid."

Chirok's wings beat behind him defiantly and he stepped forward. "Pocket dimension? You said he had the powers of a dimension."

"We needed to lure you to him," said the Lemt on the left. "As far as I know, it's impossible for someone to be a dimension."

Mr. Havst pulled Chirok's paper cube from his pocket. "And I got to keep your powers as payment for my services," he said.

Chirok grabbed his shirt pocket. "No . . . the plixtress. It's gone! It must have fallen out when that stupid eyeball hit me."

"What's a plixtress?" Mr. Havst asked.

"It's a device that transports the cube to my location after it has absorbed the powers around it." Franklin thought about that. Since no one else in the room had any real superpowers—and also because Chirok couldn't get out of the room fast enough as he had when he had stolen Franklin's telepathy—the cube must have absorbed all of Chirok's powers. The pocket dimension had nothing to do with why his powers wouldn't work. "Give that back," Chirok said.

"Come now, Mr. Chirok," said Havst. "You know I'm far too powerful now for you to stop me." Havst said.

The Jexarites started to leave. "Wait," said Franklin. Havst turned to face him. "You made it all up. Your family being outcast, your life a living hell because you thought you were a dimension."

"I made most of it up," said Havst, "except for opening the aperture when I get angry. I get mad really easily."

"How did you do it?"

"Do what?"

"Become the aperture to a pocket dimension?"

"I bought the ability on Interdimensional eBay. It's a new development in pocket dimension technology: the personal aperture. It didn't sound very useful at first, but I found a use for it. I'm sorry to deceive you, but there are a lot of opportunities in the multiverse for a man with my newfound talents." He patted his right front pants pocket. "I keep the pocket dimension itself with me at all times, right here in my wallet."

"You realize what you've done makes you no better than Chirok," Franklin said.

"No, I am better. Which one of us ended up with his powers? I assume you'll understand if I don't make it to our session next week."

As the Jexarites left, Franklin looked at his empty office. Havst hadn't kept the aperture open nearly as long this time since Franklin and Chirok had come through the aperture so quickly; nothing he had lost from his office came back with them. But he wasn't worried about that. He was far more concerned that he had let himself be bested by another con artist in the same game. This time it was Chirok who had really lost everything, and, while that reality came with a certain amount of poetic justice, Franklin took no pleasure in it.

Chirok was heading for the door himself when Franklin stopped him.

"This must be hard for you," Franklin said.

"You must be loving this."

"Not really." Franklin reached into his back pocket and produced a small leather-bound day planner. "I have some openings in my schedule next week if you want to talk about it."

"You want me to come in. For therapy."

"My services are open to anyone who needs them."

"But I stole your telepathy and got you sucked into the crappiest pocket dimension imaginable."

"Yes, you did. And you strike me as someone who could use some time with a licensed professional."

Chirok opened the glass door and looked back at Franklin. "What times do you have available next Wednesday?"

"Wednesday's open."

"I don't want to be rehabilitated."

"I think you're far too gone for that."

Chirok gave him half a smile and then walked out the door.

Helena arrived at Franklin's office only an hour after he returned from the pocket dimension. He didn't plan to start replacing furniture until the next day, so he and Helena sat on brown folding chairs.

"Sorry about the office," said Franklin.

"What happened?" Helena asked.

She looked positively dismayed as Franklin told her the story. When he finished, she turned to leave.

"We can postpone this until tomorrow. . . ."

"That's all right. You're the most down-to-earth person I'll talk to all day."

"I don't think you really know any down-to-earth people."

Franklin thought about that and couldn't help but agree.

"Franklin, have you given any thought to my request?" Helena asked.

Franklin swallowed. After hours of practicing what he would say, he couldn't remember a word of his speech. "Dr. Caslom has decided to give me the final word."

"And?"

"I understand why you want to do this, and, under different circumstances, I might be inclined to agree with you. But with circumstances as they stand, you have to understand the ethical considerations. What if what we'd really be doing was condemning six other women to death? And there's no way to really know what it might do to *you.* I want you to know that I'm terrified to leave things the way they are, but there's no other choice."

Helena smiled. "Good answer."

Franklin looked at her in disbelief.

"If you had said anything else," she said, "I would have

snapped your head off."

"Who am I talking to?"

"I warned you, *Doctor* Bryce. Anything she can do I can do better."

"Laura. Good to see you."

"You got lucky this time. And we both know you're not exactly overflowing with luck these days. Helena still wants the rest of us dead. You're going to make sure that doesn't happen."

"Threats aren't going to help."

"You don't even know how long you can keep us in that holding dimension before we break out. Mark my words, Bryce. This is a fight I intend to win. You've stepped into a war zone. You'd better pick a side."

A few moments later, Helena's dominant personality returned.

"You're not going to let me go through with the personality extraction." Laura's overconfident, impulsive expression was replaced with one of Helena's disappointment.

"No," Franklin said. "At least not yet."

CHAPTER 15

The Personality Dilemma

FRANKLIN KNEW HE SHOULD NEVER HAVE PARKED IN THE PARKING GARAGE. Bad things always happened in parking garages, especially after dark. Granted, events probably were never quite as dramatic as *this,* but Franklin was beginning to expect the worst. Mostly because, at least lately, the worst was what he always got.

Franklin was surrounded by fifty HR120s. No one in history had been ambushed by that many of them, since they were so worried about covering their identities. But if it were going to happen to anyone, Franklin wasn't surprised it was happening to him. Still, fifty seemed like overkill. Franklin knew he couldn't have taken on one HR120 with half its limbs missing. And to add insult to injury, they were all eating greasy cheeseburgers and ignoring him. He couldn't help but wonder how long they all must have taken in the drive-thru.

All at once, the entire crowd took a few steps back, and suddenly, six other people materialized in front of them before Franklin's eyes. But they weren't HR120s. They were humans, all female. As one of them approached him, Franklin wondered if this really was a parking garage or the set for a bad episode of *Star Trek.*

"Look around you, *Doctor* Bryce," said the woman. She was clad in a black, skintight, one-piece suit and holding a dagger at her side.

"Laura?" said Franklin. He began to do the math. There were *six* of them. How could this happen? And where was Helena?

Laura reached behind her and pulled a seventh woman from out of nowhere. Laura threw Helena to the ground, her face bloody and her long blue backless dress was in tatters.

"Choose," Laura said.

Franklin bent down to help Helena, but she was completely lifeless. He grabbed her wrist but he didn't feel a pulse. There was no way to be sure that meant anything.

"*Choose*!" the six of them said in perfect unison. Laura smiled dementedly. "Us or her?" she said.

The five women and the little girl each raised an arm. Their upraised arms instantly transformed into spinning saw blades. They moved forward silently and in perfect mechanical unison, as though programmed to do so. They crowded around Helena's broken body and held their blades over her.

He leaped at one of them, whom he assumed was Tracy, the cheerleader, judging from her pink and blue miniskirt and pompoms. She effortlessly threw Franklin to the ground and continued toward Helena.

When he managed to get up, he realized he was too late. They had already gotten to Helena; her body was lying in six neatly cut pieces, blood oozing out and staining the concrete.

The sound of whirling saw blades came closer, and it wasn't long before Franklin was facing all six of Helena's other personalities, all ready to dice him up as they had Helena.

"You murdered her," said Franklin.

"No," Laura replied, looking at the saw blade on her arm. "We defended ourselves. She wanted to do the same to us."

"What about the HR120s? What are they doing here?"

"They're just having lunch."

"Do you know what the connection is between them and

Helena?"

"Why would I know that?" Laura said, "I'm just saying what you're already thinking."

"What?"

The saw blades came toward Franklin, ever so slowly. He tried to move out of the way, but his feet wouldn't move.

"You're in a *dream,* stupid," Laura said. Then she dropped her saw down on his head.

Franklin awoke and found that he was no longer paralyzed, and the impending danger of saw blades was gone. He looked around and found himself in the comfort of his own king-size bed, lying next to Lera, who looked at him as though he had just fallen from the ceiling.

"Are you doing all right?" she asked.

"I'm good," he managed to say. His heart was racing, and he was covered in a river of sweat.

"Just checking—because as long as we've been married, I've never known you to scream, 'there's too many cheeseburgers' and 'don't kill me, don't kill me.' At least, not in the same night."

Franklin sat up and tried to rub the sleep out of his eyes. Lera affectionately put an arm around him, and Franklin gave her a faint smile. "I know you haven't been sleeping well since this whole HR120 thing started, but it's getting worse. You haven't been yourself for over a week."

"What do you mean?" Franklin asked her.

"You haven't shaved in three days. You haven't been to Krawkson Klub all week. And you ate all the Verullian Nitileen bars."

"So?" That wasn't so strange. Verullia had the best

chocolate in the entire multiverse.

"You'd have to be pretty run-down to eat *that many* Nitileen bars." And he had to admit, she had a point. Just one Nitileen bar had as many calories as four chocolate cakes.

"Lera, I told you, I'm just—"

"When are you going to tell me what's going on?"

Franklin folded his arms. "You're the one with the amazing intuition. You might as well tell me."

"All right," said Lera. "It's Helena. You decided not to extract her personalities, and you're not sure you made the right decision."

He sighed. "As long as they exist, I can't trust Helena."

"One of them threatened you, didn't she?"

"It wasn't the first time. The strange thing is, I don't really blame her. Laura's just scared. She's not like Sandra. She's just trying to survive."

"You mean if you were in her position, you might be doing the same thing."

"Exactly. And now she's preparing for war. I think she's capable of anything. And she's not even the worst of them."

"Do you think they're sentient?"

"They could be."

"Then there's only one answer."

"I know."

"But if something happens . . . if this does come to a war between Vlakdormat and Helena's other personalities. . . ."

Franklin didn't have his wife's intuition, but he knew what she was going to say. She said it anyway.

"If that happens, you have a weapon," she said. "And in *that* instance, you can't be afraid to use it."

Franklin entered the office of Dr. Drake R. Drake in Vlakdormat's Unexplained Phenomena Wing and was struck by the sheer number of trophies and plaques in the room, all of various sizes. They took up most of the space on the walls, while the rest took up an entire bookshelf and poured over onto his desk. Franklin wasn't really surprised, given that Drake was the luckiest kind of man there was. He had awards for just about everything: bowling, spelling bees, science fairs, pie and hotdog eating contests, and even one for memorizing decimals of pi—he knew it to the 453rd decimal.

Franklin was especially intrigued by the plaque given to Drake by authorities in the Repzoth dimension for his help in cleverly defeating a renegade lava man, further proof of Drake's incredibly good luck and Franklin's excruciatingly poor luck. Drake stopped a lava man and lived to tell about it. The closest Franklin had gotten was marrying a woman whose ex-husband was a lava man.

"What can I do for you?" Drake asked him as he entered the office.

Franklin picked a bronze trophy about the same size and shape as a two-liter soda bottle and admired it. Drake had won first place in a science contest for some invention called a "photonically retroactive hypersensitive viscillator." Franklin had no idea what that meant, but it certainly sounded impressive.

"You seem to be quite the scientist," said Franklin.

"Yes, among other things."

"So I've noticed." Franklin set the trophy back on the shelf. "I need a favor."

"Is this about Helena?" Drake asked.

"How did you know?"

"When isn't it? After Grothman and Flastcaster, she's the only thing anyone in this building seems to talk about these days. And then there's that thing with Crill."

"You know that wasn't Helena's fault."

Drake nodded. "I was there when she took Grothman down. We all owe her."

Franklin smiled. "Thanks. That means a lot."

"What do you need?"

"I'm not entirely sure. But things can't remain the way they are."

"You want me to find a way to make her safer, so that she doesn't have to stay in the holding dimension. And so certain people will stop talking about personality extraction."

"Exactly. Is it possible to suppress the personalities? Or to give Helena more control over them?"

Drake sat at his black, metal computer desk and rubbed his goatee contemplatively. "I can look into it. But Franklin, those solutions aren't exactly without their moral questions either."

Franklin had considered that, but he didn't have a choice. He couldn't just kill the other personalities, but he couldn't let them come out any time they wanted to. Assuming he could help it.

"One's worse than the other," Franklin said.

"I understand," said Drake. "Don't worry. I'll come up with something. At least a temporary solution."

"I hope so."

"You don't have to hope."

Franklin supposed not.

Helena and Franklin had been sitting in his office for twenty minutes for her daily appointment. He had managed to replace all of his furniture after the incident with Havst and Rajel Chirok, and the armchairs and desk were almost exactly like his old ones. He still couldn't find the right glass coffee table, and there were a few things he was lacking, like filing cabinets and coat rack. He wished the room was less bare so he'd have something else to look at since his conversation with Helena wasn't really going anywhere.

"You really don't have to keep apologizing," Helena said.

"I know. But I don't like that you're still having to spend most of your time in a holding dimension," said Franklin.

"But it's a nice holding dimension. Lots of space, plenty of furniture. I even have interdimensional cable access. I don't really care for television, and there's never anything on, even with twelve billion channels, but—"

"You don't belong there. You haven't done anything wrong."

Franklin used to look forward to his sessions with Helena. In many ways, she was both his easiest and most challenging patient. Some of her personalities were difficult, but Helena herself was always so cooperative. She never yelled or refused to say anything or broke down in hysterical crying fits. But lately, their appointments were more like interrogations. His main concern had stopped being her wellbeing; now it was making sure she didn't kill anyone.

"You know I don't have a problem with this," Helena said. "I know it's necessary. And nothing has changed between us. I still see you every day, and you're still helping me cope with the others. Thanks for the concern, but trust me, I'm fine."

Franklin gave her a faint smile. "Sometimes I wonder why I make you sit here every day."

"What do you mean?"

"You're taking this a lot better than your personalities."

"Like Laura."

Franklin nodded.

"I'm sorry she threatened you," Helena said. "They're all nervous and agitated, and I can't say I blame them. I was talking about killing them all."

"What do you mean you *were* talking about it?"

"I just want to stop them from hurting anyone. Laura seems so much more real to me now. The way she reacted . . . it could just be a defense mechanism. Or it might be something more genuine."

Franklin sighed. "I'm not sure there's any way to really know."

"No, but when one of the others gets possession of my body, I can see and hear what's going on, just like they can when I'm in control. I know I'm the dominant personality, but I can't be sure there's really any difference between me and them."

Franklin leaned forward and held Helena's hands in his. "That's the one thing I'm absolutely sure of. There's definitely something different about you."

"But how do you know that?"

"Because you're mature. You learn and grow. You may not know who you are or where you come from, but you change. They are who they are, and they don't strive to be more."

Helena thought about that. "Even so, I was wrong. We can't do anything to them without knowing for sure."

"I'm glad you feel that way. I was a little worried. After all, once you have your mind made up, it's not like there's much I could do to stop you."

CHAPTER 16

Checkmate

FRANKLIN TRIED NOT TO STARE AT THE BROWN UNMARKED VAN ACROSS THE STREET AS HE WALKED UP THE DRIVE TO HIS HOUSE. Despite his nightmare about Laura, his day had been pretty good, at least when he compared it to all the others he'd had lately. But coming home was always the same story—some vehicle near his house that didn't belong there sat all night—and it was hard to stay in a good mood knowing the HR120s were always watching. The sun was already starting to come down, and there was no one else outside. Could the robots get to him before he reached the door and before Lera could run outside and watch them long enough to pick up something with her intuition to use against them? Franklin picked up the pace, and he skipped every other step as he climbed the staircase to the door. He unlocked it and closed the door fast behind him.

He started to take his shoes off, and then he noticed that all the lights were off in the house. He went back to the front door, peeked through the curtains next to it, and looked at the driveway. He had made a fatal error. Lera's car was gone. She wasn't home. Or maybe she was in their bedroom taking a nap, and he was just being paranoid. Maybe she had cleaned the garage and moved all the gardening tools and the lawnmower and her collection of five-foot, granite statues of former Verullian presidents so that the car could finally fit in the garage.

Franklin shook his head. The idea was so silly. Lera didn't take naps. And she wouldn't have gone through that kind of trouble, even if his life depended on it. Franklin looked through the window again and saw exactly what he expected to see.

HR120s.

There were three of them, dressed like cable repairmen, coming right up his driveway. His dad used to say the worst things always came in threes. Granted, the last time Franklin was chased by HR120s, there had been four of them, but if there was such a thing as fate, he guessed that the fact that there were three of them meant he was really screwed this time.

He turned both locks on his front door and stared at the HR120s. Surely that would slow them down. If he had been watching himself in a movie, he would have laughed.

Franklin turned a corner, opened the door to his garage, went inside, and locked the door behind him. His only chance now was to open an interdimensional portal and go through it before the HR120s got to him. Most interdimensional portals were stationary; sending the right electrical signal could open them at any time, but only in one place. There was a device hidden in one of Lera's statues in the garage that opened a portal to Verullia—that portal was part of why they had moved into this particular house—but since he hated visiting Lera's family and accompanied her as rarely as he could, he wasn't exactly sure which statue it was.

Every male Verullian grew to be exactly five feet tall, so all the statues looked virtually identical, with only subtle differences. Verullian politicians always wore a mustache, suit, and a black pointed hat. And unfortunately, the statues weren't labeled. You'd have to be a Verullian history buff to tell which one was which.

The statues were strewn randomly about the far end of the garage. Franklin hid behind a pair of them, pulled out his interdimensional cell phone, and tried to call Lera's phone. For a few seconds, he heard nothing but dead air. Then, a deep male voice came over the line.

"We're sorry," said the overly enthusiastic, automated voice. "The customer you're trying to reach is out of his, her, or its available service area. If you would like to report a newly discovered interdimensional portal, press one. If you would like to complain about your service, press two, but remember that this may cost you your firstborn child or item of equivalent or greater value. If you do not believe in portals or alternate dimensions, have a pleasant day living in denial."

Where could she possibly be? And whatever had possessed them to purchase their phone service from the Pliscotts?

Franklin ducked low as he heard a faint whirring sound on the floor above him. There was a pop, and then the sound of something small and round hitting the wood floor and rolling across the room. A locked door was about as effective in keeping HR120s out as a "Keep Out" sign. Franklin could now hear three even sets of footfalls. The HR120s wouldn't waste any more time now that no one could see what they were doing.

The handle on the door to the garage jiggled. Then there were three raps. Franklin didn't respond.

"Dr. Bryce," came a voice from the other side. "Please let us in so we can kill you."

That offer being less than motivating, Franklin remained silent and concentrated on getting out of the garage and into Verullia. He remembered that there were only twenty-two presidential statues, because Verullians lived very long lives and their presidents served life terms. After a president died, his wife continued to run things until she died, because, at least according to Lera, the wife was pretty much in charge once her husband was elected anyway. The only real detail Franklin could remember was that the portal device was in the statue of the president who had served the shortest term.

Another energy blast blew the door off its hinges and into a group of tools hanging from the wall adjacent to it, which knocked several rakes, brooms, and a snow shovel to the ground. Franklin could hear the light, calm footsteps of the HR120s as they entered the garage; these sounded more like the footsteps of door-to-door copy machine salesmen than those of merciless killers.

He was careful to breathe quietly, but he couldn't be sure it would help. For all he knew, the HR120s had heat sensors or DNA scanners or x-ray vision. And even if they didn't, he couldn't evade them for more than a moment. If they didn't already know his exact position, they would blast everything in the garage—the riding lawn mower, the seven-foot-tall plastic Christmas tree, the collection of National Geographics that he had been collecting since he was eleven, and most importantly, the Verullian statues—until they found him. And if they hit the president with the interdimensional portal device, he was as good as dead. He could never hope to reach the button that opened the garage door and get out without being vaporized.

Franklin concentrated on what he had learned about Verullian history from Lera. The youngest president's name was Thram-Setlic, Threm-Spetmik, something like that. Why was his term the shortest? He wasn't the one who declared war on Yivynox, nor was he the one who had that scandal over interdimensionally exporting illegal time machines. What was it?

One of the HR120s taunted him. "Don't embarrass yourself like this. We can detect a single needle out of acres of haystacks.

We can see you, Dr. Bryce."

Franklin closed his eyes in defeat. Only a miracle could save him now. He stayed where he was on the off chance the HR120 was bluffing.

The two statues in front of him disintegrated. Franklin was now sitting right out in the open in front of three HR120s in overalls, their weapon arms pulsing with energy and aimed right at him.

In what were certain to be his last few seconds of existence, Franklin's life didn't flash before his eyes as he might have expected. Instead, he found himself regretting all the questions he would never have the answers to. He would never know why his wife hadn't come home that day. He would never know who had built the HR120s or why they pretended to be human beings.

But above all else, Franklin realized that he would never know just what was in a Threpnoidian dragonfly.

"Before we eliminate you, we need you to tell us what you have learned about Helena Kathryn and who else you've told," said the HR120 who had spoken before.

Franklin's eyes widened. He had been right the whole time—all of this was about Helena.

Franklin thought for a moment, trying to look less panicked than he was. There was no escape now. But he could at least delay the inevitable.

"I'll only tell you what you want to know if you answer a question of my own. Is Helena an HR120?"

"We have the weapons trained on you, so we're asking the questions, if it's all the same to you," said the HR120.

"And I'm going to die anyway, so why not tell me?"

"What do you know about Helena Kathryn?"

Franklin should have known that trick only worked in action movies. He didn't answer. The HR120 standing between the others put his open-barreled arm centimeters away from Franklin's forehead, and the situation was suddenly much more real. Franklin wasn't in a parking garage; he was in his own garage. And the HR120s weren't eating cheeseburgers. This wasn't a dream. There was nothing to interpret, nothing to learn or to grow from. Franklin had done all he would ever do. This was the end.

The next sound he heard wasn't the eardrum-exploding sound of the wave of energy Franklin knew was coming. It was the catchy, seven-note ring tone of his cell phone. He answered it. The HR120 held his fire.

"Franklin, you have to get down here," said William on the other end.

"Wait," Franklin said. He let out a long gust of air and listened to his heart jack hammering in his chest. He put his hand over the receiver and spoke, quietly and deliberately, to the HR120s. "If you kill me now, he'll get suspicious and have Vlakdormat security here in seconds. Then they'll know what three HR120s' faces look like. You have a lot more to worry about if they're onto you than you would from the police."

The HR120s shot irritated looks at each other. It was the first time they had looked unsure about anything. They lowered their weapons.

Franklin put the phone back to his ear. "What is it, William?"

"It's Helena. She's gone."

"How?"

"She *teleported,* Franklin. Drake asked to see her. She was being escorted by security, and then she just vanished."

"I'll be there as soon as I can. William, you *have* to stay on the line until I tell you to hang up."

"Okay."

Franklin's mind was a junkyard of facts, ironies, and unlikely coincidences. Lera was gone. He was supposed to be dead but he wasn't. One of Helena's personalities had apparently picked just the right moment to take over, use a new superhuman ability, and go missing again.

If he weren't a trained professional, it might have all been enough to drive him mad.

But as he stole a glance back at the presidential statues, he suddenly realized what he had been missing. He tried to put everything else out of his mind and focus, once again, on the presidents. He was reminded of something important by what William had said. Teleportation. That was the key.

Thram-Spetmik was the Verullian president whose foreign relations were so bad because no other dimension's leaders took him seriously on account of his unbelievably cartoonish voice. And his voice sounded so ridiculous because he had lost his nose in a tragic teleportation accident just after he was elected. Franklin spotted the statue with the missing nose and walked toward it, holding the phone out so the HR120s could see that he still had his leverage.

He reached behind the statue and found the small flat oval button that activated the portal switch. He pushed it, and a small red swirling vortex instantly appeared over his head. This one didn't suck everything around it in like Mr. Havst's pocket dimension aperture had—natural portals didn't usually do that.

Just as Franklin was about to jump up into Verullia,

something very strange happened. He grabbed on to both sides of his head and screamed a scream no one could hear.

The air was filled with a ringing at such a high octave that only dogs could have heard it had it been any higher, and the robots' eyes each began rapidly blinking and glowing a bright red. When the sound finally stopped, the HR120s' arms transformed back into human appendages. One of them approached Franklin. He held the phone out in front of him and backed into a corner, accidentally knocking another rake off the wall. Even under such deadly circumstances, Franklin couldn't help but wonder how he and Lera had wound up with so many rakes.

"Our mission has changed," the HR120 said, "We must attend to the Helena."

The Helena?

"We will delay your demise for the time being. You must grant us access to Vlakdormat," he said.

"That is never—"

"If you don't, she will be as good as dead."

CHAPTER 17

The Off-Switch

THE HR120S FOLLOWED FRANKLIN UP THE STONE STEPS TO THE MAIN ENTRANCE OF VLAKDORMAT. He couldn't believe what he was doing. Ten minutes earlier, he had expected to be a pile of dust. Instead, he was escorting three deadly robots into the sanctuary that had kept him alive for the last several months. But once they were inside, Franklin would breathe easier. If they tried anything, he could activate the positronic deactivation switch. (Unless, of course, this was all an elaborate trap, and the HR120s had found some way to disarm the switch.) But what choice did he have? Helena had disappeared, and the HR120s obviously knew something about her that Franklin didn't.

Two practically identical well-built, black-clad security guards met Franklin at the door. Sometimes Franklin wondered if Vlakdormat security only hired people of an exact height and build, or if they were really all clones. One of them stepped forward, indicating that he was the other man's superior.

"Where's Agent Strexit?" Franklin asked him.

"Dealing with the current situation." He said it seriously but with no sense of urgency, as if there was a "situation" happening all the time. "I'm Agent Roxer. You can't bring guests in here right now. We've got a Code H," he said with barely any inflection in his voice.

"Helena has her own alert code?"

"New protocol. This has been happening a lot lately. She's our biggest liability right now."

"These three men know how to find her," Franklin said.

"She's already been located," said Roxer. The other man remained motionless but nodded slightly. "She's in Dr. Crill's office. That's where Agent Strexit is now."

"What?"

"We must get to her immediately," one of the HR120s said.

"Who are these men?" Roxer asked.

Franklin hesitated. He thought about telling a lie, but he couldn't think of a good one. "They're HR120s."

Roxer paused and looked like he might produce some kind of a facial expression. He pulled out a hand radio and pressed a button on the side of it. "This is Agent Roxer. Activate code—"

"No," Franklin said. "Don't shut them down unless they try something."

"We call a temporary cease fire," one of the HR120s said. It was uncanny how similar his voice was to Roxer's. "We are here only to revive the Helena. No one else has the means."

"It's not a good plan," said Franklin, "but it's all we've got."

"It isn't a plan at all," Roxer said. The other agent nodded in agreement. "If the HR120 is right, then our mission has been accomplished for us. Helena has been neutralized."

Franklin had never hit another man in his life, but if Roxer hadn't been armed, Franklin probably would have sucker punched him.

"Get Strexit. I want to talk to him," Franklin said.

"No need. My orders were—"

"Don't you report to Strexit?"

"Yes."

"Then this isn't your call," said Franklin. "Helena Kathryn is a patient at this facility, and her wellbeing, as long as she isn't a danger to anyone, is your priority. So get Strexit."

Roxer looked like a robot checking his memory banks for validation. Franklin wouldn't have been surprised if the positronic deactivation switch could shut him down. He made no visible reaction to Franklin's defiance and instead held down the button on the side of his radio again. He said Strexit's name several times, but all that came over the radio was static. Roxer turned to leave, but then looked back at the HR120s again.

"If they try anything," Franklin said, "you've got the deactivation switch."

"Fine, until I receive new orders. Follow me," Roxer said.

He led Franklin and the HR120s at a brisk pace up a stairwell to the next level and down a long, narrow, winding hall to Eva Crill's office. They found Helena just as the HR120 had said, lying on the ground unconscious—just like in Franklin's dream.

Laura's voice rang in his head, telling him to make a choice. But he had already made one, though it made him sick to his stomach. He had chosen to trust his enemies in order to save his friend.

"What happened?" Roxer asked Strexit, who was staring blankly at Crill's sarcophagus.

"That looks really scary," Strexit said. Then he noticed her massive collection of medieval weapons from various dimensions. "And that's terrifying."

It hadn't occurred to Franklin that Strexit had never been in Crill's office before, but considering what Strexit dealt with as chief of Vlakdormat security, it didn't make a lot of sense that anything in that room should be especially surprising to him. Yet he looked completely overwhelmed. Franklin put a hand on his shoulder, pointed at Helena, and asked him how she had been knocked unconscious.

"I don't know who that is," Strexit said. Roxer finally looked almost distressed.

"Agent Strexit," Roxer asked him, "what is the last thing you remember?"

Strexit's eyes darkened as he thought about that. His forehead crinkled and his mouth tensed up. "Nothing."

Eva Crill stepped out from behind a bookshelf. "Oh," she said. Then she said it again.

"What did you do?" said Franklin. At first, he only feared the worst. He very quickly decided to expect it.

"She just appeared. I didn't even know she could do that," Crill said in a mouse-like voice. Franklin had never seen her so elusive.

"What did you do?" he asked again.

"What she asked. I tried to remove the personalities. It all happened so fast . . . Strexit ran in, Helena dropped to the ground. . . . I didn't realize how bad it was until now."

Strexit wasn't paying much attention. He was standing, perplexed, in front of a tall bookshelf. "Why do you have a book called *Changing Minds Just Because I Can?*"

One of the HR120s said, "You cannot tamper with the Helena's mind."

"You did something to Strexit. You made him lose his memory," Roxer said.

"I did more than that," said Crill, biting down on her lower lip. "I made him lose his personality."

"Stand back," an HR120 said. Franklin obeyed, but everyone else just stood where they were, each trying to process what had happened.

"They're going to revive Helena," Franklin said. "We'll sort everything else out after that's done."

"Strexit's not in charge anymore, and no one outranks me," Roxer said. His voice had turned darker, more passionate. "I cannot, in good conscience, allow Helena to be revived. She is a major threat to security."

"I must say, I quite agree," Crill said. Franklin ignored her.

"I'm not going to debate this with you," Franklin said to Roxer. "She's my patient, and I take full responsibility for her. I want her revived."

"And as you said to me minutes ago, this isn't your call. I'm Strexit's next in command. We've stood by helplessly as she has attempted to murder personnel—"

"My point exactly," Crill said.

"—and as she has attempted to terrorize this city."

"Helena Kathryn has done no such thing," Franklin said. "She isn't responsible for the actions of her other personalities."

"Which are conveniently incapacitated," said Roxer. "And I intend to keep them that way." He spoke into his radio. Franklin made eye contact with the HR120 who had done most of the talking and saw his eyes flash bright red for a split second.

Roxer started to give a command. "Activate code Alpha—"

Before Roxer could say another word, the HR120's arm transformed into the familiar energy weapon he had tried to use on Franklin and blasted Roxer. The security guard disappeared in a flash of light. There wasn't a particle of him left. Both of the other security guards immediately produced portable pocket dimension apertures and aimed them at the HR120.

"Can you fire that before I fire this?" the HR120 said, training his weapon arm on the officers. After a moment of hesitation, they lowered their weapons.

"No one do anything else," Franklin said. Everyone backed away from the HR120s. Franklin couldn't believe what he had done. They hadn't been in the building for fifteen minutes, and a man was already dead. It was Franklin's fault, and the worst part of it was, he still knew he had done the only thing he could have.

Franklin expected the HR120s to hook themselves up to Helena's brain or something, but instead, they all raised their hands into the air. A small, purple cloud suddenly appeared over their heads and swirled menacingly. It began to grow, and bolts of red and yellow electricity surged within and around it. The lights in the room began to flicker. Franklin, Strexit, and the other officers backed up toward the door, and Crill hugged the bookshelf she was hiding behind for dear life. Once the cloud was so large that Franklin could no longer see the ceiling, it shot a bolt of blue lightning and struck Helena's head. Her chest heaved and her eyes sprang open.

Then the cloud disappeared, and in a few moments, the lights stopped flickering. Helena sat up slowly and took a deep breath. She looked at Franklin in relief. He was standing as far away from the HR120s as possible.

"What happened?" she asked. She noticed the HR120s, and Franklin wondered if she could instantly tell what they were, regardless of the overalls. He wasn't looking forward to telling her about the risk he had taken and the price he had paid for it.

"We have reactivated the Helena," one of the HR120s said. "Our work here is finished." The three HR120s turned to leave.

"Wait," said Franklin, "we had an agreement. You called a truce."

"It was the only way," the HR120 said. "If that man had

deactivated us, the Helena would never have been revived."

Franklin knew the HR120 was right. If he hadn't acted, Roxer would have pulled the positronic deactivation switch. Franklin knew he hadn't had it in himself to stop the HR120. But he wasn't glad it had happened. He would never knowingly trade one person's life for another, but that's exactly what had happened.

And despite his remorse, Franklin also realized that he had recognized the cloud the HR120s had used. It was similar to the one Stephen Zarcadmium had used when he gave Franklin his telepathy. He wondered what that meant.

"At least tell me why you needed magic," Franklin asked the HR120. "Since when do robots use magic?"

The HR120 ignored the question. "Our business together isn't over, Dr. Bryce. We are still watching you. As long as you are near the Helena, your life will be in danger."

Franklin asked a security officer to help Strexit find his home, and Franklin and the other guard escorted the HR120s out of the building.

When they returned to the front steps outside of Vlakdormat, Franklin looked out at the parking lot in amazement. It was completely filled with cars that had men and women standing next to them. Some of them were in business suits, some in casual dress, and some in working clothes like the ones dressed to look like cable repair men, all waiting patiently for the three HR120s to revive Helena.

"HR120s?" Franklin asked the robot who had threatened him earlier.

"Yes," he said.

"I thought you HR120s were discreet. . . ."

"Sometimes we must take risks for the safety of the Helena. That's something you should have no trouble understanding. Every HR120 in this area was alerted when the Helena was in danger." He held up his wrist and pressed it lightly with two fingers. "It is done," he spoke quietly into his wrist. His eyes flickered green as he said it.

The HR120s immediately stepped into their cars and began to drive single file out of the parking lot.

"A word of advice," the HR120 said to Franklin before the three of them left. "That sort of risk-taking may not be something you want to make a habit of."

CHAPTER 18

Bad Moves

FRANKLIN, DR. AKBAR CASLOM IV, AND DR. EVA CRILL SAT AT DR. CASLOM'S ENORMOUS TABLE IN HIS OFFICE. Franklin knew there was a good chance he might lose his job, and he couldn't blame Caslom if that was his decision. Firing him was very likely what Franklin would have done in Caslom's position. But so far, Caslom had much more to say to Crill than he did to Franklin.

"I believe I was more than abundantly clear on this matter," said Caslom. He spoke with a slightly higher pitch today, and that marked the difference between slightly agitated and completely furious. "The decision to perform the extraction of Helena Kathryn's other six personalities was Franklin's, and Franklin's alone. You made your case before, and I disagreed. Surely you knew there would be consequences to this action."

"I didn't have a choice," Crill said. She looked at Caslom with the deepest contempt.

"You most certainly did not. As I said, it wasn't your choice to make."

"Why am I the only one who can see it?" Crill said. "Does it take a Matrulian skull to figure it out? A person with no past is a person with no future. Add to that six mysterious personalities and two first names, and the end result is disaster. Yes, I realize actions have consequences. And your decision to allow Helena Kathryn to stay here will be the end of us all."

Franklin was surprised to hear Crill talk to Caslom like that. She had spoken against him before, but never so verbosely.

"You may be able to see into a person's past, but you cannot look into the future," Caslom said. "And since it is against Vlakdormat's policy to even attempt to do so, I must assume you have not."

"No," Crill said.

"Then you don't know what the outcome of Helena's presence here will be," Caslom said. "I regret that one of her personalities tried to kill you, but that doesn't give you the right to take matters into your own hands. Because of what you did, Dr. Bryce found it necessary to give HR120s access to our facility. For all we know, they may have gathered information to penetrate our positronic deactivation device. And most importantly, a man was killed."

"That was his choice. I didn't know these were life and death circumstances when I decided to help Helena eradicate her personalities. I can't be held responsible for that."

"Tampering with something powerful that you don't understand . . . that is always a potentially life and death situation. And you are also directly the cause of the loss of Agent Strexit's personality."

"Not that he had much of one to begin with."

"Dr. Crill."

"Besides, I can get him another one. Probably a better one."

"*Dr. Crill,*" Caslom said again.

"Yes?"

"I want your letter of resignation on my desk tomorrow morning and your office cleared out."

"And what about Franklin? You know, I didn't let HR120s in here. I didn't let a powerful, unstable being with a psychotic personality in here."

"Franklin will be reprimanded," Caslom said.

"Really," Crill said to Franklin, "you know, I always respected you, Dr. Bryce. Accepting the multiverse for what it was and managing to get a job here, of all places, only a few years after you stopped being part of the small-minded, pathetic masses. But you're as delusional as they are. You think you can control something you don't understand, and that's the real crime. The only thing I tried to do was stop this insanity before we all have to face the consequences."

"That won't be something you'll have to worry about any longer, Dr. Crill," Caslom said. "Goodbye."

Crill scowled and turned to leave. Before she reached the door, she stopped and whispered into Franklin's ear in a crisp, biting way.

"Someday, you're going to need me. And when you do, I'll be there, despite all of this."

She slammed the door behind her. When she was gone, Caslom directed his stern gaze at Franklin.

"One month without pay," he said.

"Sir, if I go home," Franklin said, "I'm dead."

"You may stay. You're just not getting paid for the next month."

"That's fair."

"Fair? I should fire you. You knowingly let HR120s in here, and it got Roxer killed."

"It was the only thing I could do."

"You sound like Crill."

"I was trying to save my patient," Franklin said.

Caslom nodded slightly. "I realize that. And who knows? I might have done the same thing in your place. Have you spoken to Helena yet?"

"No. I have an appointment with her tomorrow."

"I want to help her. But Crill's stunt has made something very clear. Helena's presence here is more dangerous than any of us imagined."

"So what do you want me to do? Put her out on the streets?"

"I want you to find out everything you can about the HR120s. And Franklin? If you ever do anything like this again, you'll be joining Dr. Crill in the unemployment line."

Franklin had never seen Helena look so upset. It was usually difficult to tell how she felt by just looking at her, but now, sitting uncomfortably on the leather chair across from his, she looked as if she were on trial for murder. He knew how she felt. He hoped he could convince her that it hadn't been her fault and help her cope with what had happened. It was easier for him to focus on someone else's demons than to face his own.

"I'm glad you came out of this all right," Franklin said. "We got lucky. It seems you have some kind of build-in failsafe that keeps anyone from tampering with your personalities. The HR120s used some kind of magic. Any idea what it was?"

"No," Helena said. "I don't know anything about magic, much less why robots would be using it, or how it's connected with me."

"Neither do I. There's obviously still a lot we don't understand about you."

"We know almost nothing. Except that I can never get rid of the others, can I?"

"It certainly looks that way. Do they know that?"

"Yes."

"Then at least that war is over. They won't be fighting for

survival after this."

"I'm sorry," Helena said.

"For what?"

"I had to protect you."

"What are you talking about?"

Helena looked away and closed her eyes. "It was my fault. Roxer, Strexit . . . everything."

Franklin swallowed nervously. "You're telling me it wasn't Laura? Or Sandra?"

"No. I teleported. . . . I didn't even know I could. . . . I was on my way to see Dr. Drake, and I had been thinking about how badly I wanted to stop all of this. Laura was willing to kill you . . . Sandra too. I didn't have another choice. I thought about being in Dr. Crill's office, and suddenly, I was there, standing right in front of her."

Franklin stood up and paced the floor. He was devastated. "So you asked her to extract the others."

"Yes. I didn't plan it. I never wanted to run off and try to fix everything myself."

"That's exactly what you did."

"One minute I was in a hallway and the next, I was in her office. It all happened so fast. I was there, she was there. . . ."

That had been Crill's reasoning. Franklin didn't say anything for a long time.

"I trusted you," he finally said.

"I know."

"I had to let HR120s in the building! A man died because of me!"

"I couldn't be responsible for. . . . I didn't want you to get hurt. That's why I did this."

"I think that's enough for today," Franklin said. He sat down at his desk, put on his reading glasses, and looked through some paperwork.

"Dr. Bryce—"

"I'll see you tomorrow," Franklin said without looking up at her. He could feel her staring at him for a long time, and then she was gone. When he looked up, he wondered if she had just walked away quietly or if she had disappeared into thin air. She might have been right outside in the hall. Or she might have been on the other side of the globe.

Franklin found himself once again in Drake R. Drake's award-filled office. Drake had made some progress on the project Franklin had asked him to work on, but Franklin had another reason for being there.

"It's an addendum to the Vlakdormat sensor net," Dr. Drake said, holding up a tiny metal computer chip between his index finger and thumb. He explained that Helena's brain patterns altered slightly when one of the other personalities was in control. All Drake had to do was match up the personalities with their specific patterns, upload the data into the chip, and insert it into the sensor grid.

"So the sensor net will constantly scan Helena's brain?"

"Exactly. Security will know every time one of the others takes over and who it is. I've talked this over with Dr. Caslom, and he said that if it works, she won't have to stay in a holding dimension anymore. We'll have protocols in place for each personality."

"That's great," Franklin said.

"You look . . . disappointed."

"No, I'm fine."

"I heard about what happened with Crill. I'm not sure you did the right thing, but I am sure you did the only thing."

"Thanks."

"Ever think about changing your name?"

"I don't think it would help."

"You're probably right. As soon as I get those brain scans from Helena, we'll have this thing up and running."

After his last conversation with Helena, Franklin wondered if she might have left and planned on never coming back. But hours later, he had checked with security, and she had reported to the pocket dimension room, just as she always did.

"I need to talk to you about something else," Franklin said. "Have you ever run across any magic involving a purple cloud?"

Drake raised an eyebrow. "No, but I know some sorcerers who can do some pretty bizarre stuff with marshmallows."

Franklin described how the HR120s used blue lightning from a purple cloud to bring Helena back to consciousness. Drake looked at him in disbelief.

"I've never heard of anything like that. Why would robots be using magic?"

"That's why I came to you. I've seen this before—a purple cloud—but it fired green lightning instead of blue. Everything else about it was exactly the same."

"I'm familiar with most known forms of magic in the multiverse, and I swear I have never heard of anything involving clouds, purple or otherwise," Drake said. "When did you see this before?"

"Five years ago." Franklin told Drake all about Stephen Zarcadmium, their sessions, and his telepathy.

Drake sat down at his desk and logged onto one of his many computers. Franklin looked over his shoulder as he went through a data bank of interdimensional magic on the Multi-net—the Internet that connected many of the dimensions in the multiverse. Drake's search came up with no results for anything having to do with a purple cloud.

"Whatever this magic is, someone's keeping a lid on it," Drake said.

"Then we need to talk to Stephen Zarcadmium. He might know something about the link between Helena and the HR120s."

CHAPTER 19

Franklin Would Rather Be Franklin

DR. FRANKLIN BRYCE WAS WIDELY RENOWNED AS ONE OF THE GREATEST THERAPISTS IN HIS DIMENSION. He had won Therapist of the Year twice. He consistently appeared confident but never cocky, and he always wore a genuine smile. He seemed to have the power to raise the spirits of whomever he was around, as though every person in the multiverse was his very dear and personal friend. But his real superpower was his telepathic ability, which aided him in his occupation as well as his daily life.

Or, at least, that was the story of the Dr. Franklin Bryce from Dimension 0.65. Franklin hadn't talked with him in two years and was surprised when the other Dr. Bryce walked into his office. Franklin had always been a little jealous of his counterpart, but the other Franklin's smile and charisma worked its charm on him just like everyone else. And it was nice to know he was doing so well for himself in at least one dimension.

"It's been a long time," said Franklin's counterpart. "How are things?"

The answer that came into Franklin's head was long, complicated, and the honest truth. Things were insane. Robots were out to get him. Helena was somehow connected with them, and some of her alternate personalities were also out to get him. A man had just been killed by those robots, another man had lost his personality, and both Franklin and Helena were partially responsible. And to top it all off, Franklin had been staying at Vlakdormat for the last three days because Lera was missing and he still couldn't get through to her interdimensional cell phone.

But Franklin didn't say all that. What he said instead was, "Things are good."

The other Franklin laughed. "I doubt that. Your wife told me what's been going on. HR120s . . . really, Franklin. There are a lot of less-deadly robots you could have ticked off."

"You saw Lera?"

"Just a few hours ago. She sends her love."

"Is she all right?"

"She seemed fine. She said she'll be back home in a couple of days."

"What exactly was she doing there?"

"She's on assignment," his counterpart said. "That's all she told me."

"Assignment? She's a *translator.* Does she expect me to believe she's put in two full days of overtime translating?"

The other Franklin shrugged his shoulders and sat down on Franklin's couch. "It's a little strange to take out your frustrations about your wife on yourself."

"I'm sorry. Things are a little hectic."

"A little? Your head sounds like it's going to explode. As soon as your wife gets back, I recommend the two of you take a vacation."

"So you're my therapist now?"

"Hey, if you can't trust yourself. . . ." His counterpart smiled, and Franklin couldn't help but smile back.

"I guess I'll just have to wait until she comes back. Thanks for coming in person."

"You're welcome. But seriously, are you sure there's nothing else I can do for you? It sounds like this Helena Kathryn has been a real handful."

"Did Lera tell you *everything*?"

"No, but I can't turn the telepathy off. Helena's a topic that's pretty close to the surface. Right behind the security officer you feel you got killed and your most recent near-death experience."

"Thanks, but I don't think there's much you could do."

Franklin's counterpart shook his head. "I don't know how you do it. Your life's constantly in danger, but you still go to work every day. I haven't lost my telepathy or met a Helena Kathryn, and we don't even have HR120s in my dimension. I wonder why *you* get all the bad luck."

It occurred to Franklin that the reason was obvious—he had two first names—but then again, so did his counterpart. It seemed unlikely that the other Franklin would have such good luck while his own life was such a mess. But Franklin wasn't about to mention that to him. He had only recently realized that he had two first names, and maybe that was part of the multiverse's curse.

"I guess you just live in a nicer dimension than mine," said Franklin. "Maybe that's where Lera and I will take that vacation."

The only other place besides Vlakdormat where Franklin could safely go until Lera returned was Krawkson Klub. Franklin was sure the HR120s didn't know about it. He had gone there several times since this whole business started, and they had never tried to attack him there. Franklin knew they would never try to kill him in a crowd, anyway. He was getting restless inside Vlakdormat and decided that tonight he would enjoy a drink with William. They hadn't spent any time together in over a week; Franklin had been too preoccupied with Helena and the HR120s. Franklin's counterpart had stayed at Vlakdormat all afternoon, enjoying the contrasts between the two dimensions, so Franklin invited him to join them.

"Tell me something you know that Franklin doesn't," William said after taking a sip of the mustard-like beverage he always ordered. "After all, you're still telepathic, so you'd know."

Franklin's counterpart laughed. "That would be rude," he said.

"Oh no, go on," Franklin said, smiling. "It'll be interesting. Enlighten us."

"Something Franklin doesn't know. . . . How about the ingredients in a Threpnoidian Dragonfly?"

Franklin looked down at his dark green, murky beverage. When he thought the HR120s were going to vaporize him in his garage, the thing he regretted most was not knowing what was in the Threpnoidian Dragonfly. It didn't make sense, but now a part of him felt that as long as he avoided knowing, he would be okay. The day he found out that would be the day he died. "No, don't tell me. I don't want to know," he said.

"Oh, come on," said William.

"It's my favorite drink, and I just know it's going to turn out to be something completely disgusting, and I'll never want to try it again."

"It's really not gross at all," said the other Franklin.

"No," Franklin said.

William sighed and dropped it. "So how did you get your telepathy, Other Franklin?"

"You can call me Franklin."

"But that's weird. You're the same guy, but you're not the same guy."

"If it would make you feel better, I could introduce you to *your* counterpart in my dimension," the other Franklin said.

"Really?" said William.

"Sure. I might have to pull some strings . . . . In my dimension, you're the President of the United States."

"*Really*?"

"No."

Franklin laughed and took a sip of his Threpnoidian Dragonfly, happy that its secret had yet to be compromised. William folded his arms in mock embarrassment.

"But really, Franklin," said Franklin to his other self, "how did you get your telepathy?"

"It was a gift from an old patient. I helped him through an especially rough patch."

Franklin's eyes widened. "His name didn't happen to be Stephen Zarcadmium. . . ?"

The other Franklin smiled. "We've lived closer lives than I realized."

"You don't happen to know how to contact him, do you?"

"Sure," said Franklin's counterpart. "After he gave me my telepathy, I asked for his address so I could send him Christmas cards. He's moved a few times, but he's always forwarded me his address. Really great guy."

"Wish I'd thought of that," Franklin said. But he was overjoyed. This was the best luck he had had in weeks. Granted, the odds of it being the *same* Stephen Zarcadmium were astronomical, but this Zarcadmium might at least be able to point him in the right direction. It was a better lead than anything Drake had been able to drum up. Franklin asked his counterpart if he could get him the address later that evening.

"I'll do you one better than that," the other Franklin said. "Come back with me to my dimension tonight."

"How are the video games there?" William asked.

Franklin laughed. "As long as your Vlakdormat has a positronic deactivation switch, I'm game."

"You don't think the HR120s are the only killer robots in the multiverse, do you?" his counterpart said, smiling. "But before we go, I think I'll have another Dragonfly myself. They have a lot of important nutrients, you know."

Franklin shook his head and downed the rest of his drink.

CHAPTER 20

We've Been Here Before

FRANKLIN FOUND DR. DRAKE R. DRAKE WORKING LATE IN HIS OFFICE IN THE UNEXPLAINED PHENOMENA WING. Since Drake had been helping him to solve the mystery of the HR120s' magic, Franklin decided to invite him along. Plus, having someone as lucky as Drake around was never a bad idea.

"Don't you ever go home?" Franklin asked him.

"Actually, no," Drake said. "I have an incredibly strong work ethic. Bought it on Interdimensional eBay. It really comes in handy at times like this."

Franklin wasn't sure if Drake was joking or not. He told him about their plan to visit Dimension 0.65 and look for the Zarcadmium his counterpart knew.

Drake nodded. "That's not a bad idea. I'm starting to think that magic cloud might have been borrowed from Zarcadmium's dimension."

Zarcadmium had once told Franklin that his world had disintegrated. Franklin wasn't sure exactly when that had happened, but it might have explained why Drake hadn't found out anything about the magic in his databases.

"Maybe it was indigenous to his dimension," Drake said. "It might have been a well-guarded secret. There's a strong possibility that another Zarcadmium would know about it, assuming he's from a similar dimension."

"It's too much of a coincidence," Franklin said, explaining that his counterpart also got telepathy from the other Zarcadmium.

"This is assuming he's not the same Zarcadmium."

Franklin raised an eyebrow. "So he went through *two*

homicidal depressions, went to two different Franklin Bryces to help him recover, and gave both of us telepathy as a reward for our troubles?"

"I suppose not," Drake said. "Still, it's a start. Let me know if you come up with anything."

"You're not coming with us?" Franklin asked.

"I . . . don't think so," said Drake. He looked a little nervous. "Caslom's got me putting together a list of everyone we know of who is an HR120, and a list of possible suspects."

"He's determined to figure this out," said Franklin. "The alternative is handing Helena over to them."

"Well, it's too bad we didn't have a vested interest in them sooner. From what I can tell, they've been in our dimension quite a bit longer than we've known about them. And they've covered their tracks very well. It's almost impossible to tell if someone is an HR120—besides the few cases that have gone insane and tried to kill people."

Considering what had happened to Calvin Stanley, Franklin couldn't believe he had never thought of tracking down HR120s who had malfunctioned. Drake really was a genius.

"So do the insane HR120s have anything in common?" Franklin asked.

"I've found twelve instances of people who seem to have been malfunctioning HR120s. All of them either wound up 'dead' or missing. There was a thirteenth instance, but that one could easily have been some other random robot. The twelve all had varying occupations, were at various stages of life . . . but they all had an affinity for one thing: environmentalism."

Franklin blinked. "What?"

"All twelve of them belonged to environmental activist

groups. They donated a great deal of their income to supporting environmental causes—recycling, global warming, and tree-saving campaigns, you name it."

"You're telling me that the great, dangerous, mysterious HR120s are *tree huggers*?"

"Sure looks that way."

"Maybe that's just a sign they're going crazy. Maybe they get obsessed and then go insane."

Drake shook his head. "I know of a few people who are HR120s for certain, people who haven't malfunctioned yet. All of them are also actively involved with environmental groups. So unless every one of them is about to blow a gasket or something. . . ."

Franklin sat down on one of Drake's chairs and put a hand on his forehead.

"Look, Franklin, I'm not saying I understand it, I just—"

Franklin exploded into a fit of uncontrollable laughter. It was a full minute before he could say anything. He clutched his chest and tried to breathe. It was at this moment that he finally realized how truly bizarre his life was.

"I'm sorry," he said, wheezing. "But you're . . . you're telling me that the HR120s are here to unleash their evil plan to, what . . . stop *pollution*?"

"I just call it like I see it," said Drake, but by this point, Franklin's laughter had become contagious, and Drake was finding it difficult to hold back a few chuckles of his own. "I'll keep digging," he said.

"You do that," Franklin said as he struggled to stand up. "I'm going to get a glass of water."

Franklin's counterpart gave him directions as he drove the two of them and William to a portal that led to Dimension 0.65. It was on the second floor of a parking garage on the other side of the city. Once they were there, the other Franklin activated a small hand-held device like the one Lera had hidden in the statue of a Verullian president, and a swirling red and green vortex appeared. It had begun to get nippy outside all week, and the vortex reminded Franklin that it was nearing the Christmas season.

The irony of being in a parking garage so soon after his disturbing dream about the HR120s wasn't lost on Franklin, but he was more preoccupied by the irony of finally getting the chance to get out and go somewhere that wasn't home, Vlakdormat, or Krawkson Klub, only to enter a dimension that looked almost identical to his own, except that, while it was seven pm in his dimension, it was the heat of day here. As they drove back across Abott City, now the Abott City of Dimension 0.65, the only differences that were immediately noticeable were a couple of billboards for a local radio station with different call letters than in Franklin's dimension, a Taco Bell and a Burger King on the wrong sides of the street, and an independent gun store where the independent paintball gun store should have been.

As the three of them walked into the main lobby of Vlakdormat, Franklin felt like he was in an episode of a low budget science fiction series, making an episode about a parallel universe but just slightly redressing all the sets. This didn't feel like a vacation. It was more like someone was playing a practical joke on him and had just moved everything around. They walked out of an elevator and into the laboratory of the Unexplained Phenomena wing, just like the one Franklin had visited earlier that morning. The dozens of flat screen computer monitors were all in the same places along the walls, the same big screen monitor was on top of the same kiosk in the center of the room, and, as Franklin looked across the way, he could see into Drake's office window, where impressive trophies and certificates took up every inch of wall and shelf space.

"Welcome to Dimension 0.65," said a feminine voice from behind them. "Or at least, I'm told that's what you call it where you're from. I'm Drake R. Drake." She was a tall, slender, confident-looking woman of about thirty, wearing a white lab coat over a short black dress and a pair of thin-rimmed, dark blue glasses sat on her nose.

William's eyes lit up as he stared at her and they darted to the first place Franklin might have expected them to. "I'm glad not everything's identical," William said.

The female Drake invited Franklin to shake her hand. He hesitated for only a second, regaining his composure so as not to appear rude.

"You look surprised," she said.

"I know a different Dr. Drake."

Drake smiled. "I'm not what you expected?"

"Absolutely not," William blurted. "You look *way* better than—"

"William," Franklin said. "Nothing that's happened in the last five years of my existence has prepared me for the end of that sentence." He looked back at Drake. "It's a pleasure," he said.

"I'm glad you all made it here safely," she said. She looked genuinely amused by William's outburst. She shook his hand, and he looked as though he might not wash it again. "Franklin, were you planning on showing your guests around the facility?"

she said, and Franklin was confused for only a second until he realized she was, of course, talking to his counterpart. "I'd show you what we're working on in here, but I haven't had much to do lately. Nothing unexplained to explain for a few weeks now."

"Maybe later," the other Franklin said. He looked almost suspicious of Drake, and Franklin wondered if something was going on between them. "We're actually on a little mission. We're looking for Stephen Zarcadmium."

"Yes, I remember him. Nice guy. A little suicidal, but that's not always a bad thing."

"Excuse me?" said Franklin.

"Nothing. I'll see you boys later. I've got a little self-destruction of my own to attend to."

"Is everything all right?" Franklin's counterpart asked.

"I just had a talk with the new therapist we brought in to replace Dr. Crill," Drake said.

Franklin was more than a little concerned. This was all starting to sound too familiar. "What happened to Dr. Crill?" Franklin asked.

"She was fired for illegal personality experiments," Drake said. "She tried to give Agent Strexit a new personality. He wound up a vegetable."

"I'd hate to be that guy in any dimension," William said.

"So who's replacing her?" Franklin's counterpart asked Dr. Drake.

"The best therapist I've ever met. I had one session with him, and that's all I needed. In just a few minutes, I'll be totally cured."

Franklin and William looked at each other and their eyes widened simultaneously.

"Dr. Drake," Franklin started, but he hated to even ask. "What's the good doctor's name?"

"Dr. Grothman," Dr. Drake answered. "Amazing man. Drowning myself has never made more sense."

The other Franklin excused himself and then pulled Franklin aside, whispering. "Something's wrong with her. She's not even *thinking* like herself. You know what's going on, don't you?"

Franklin quickly explained about Grothman and his persuasion powers. The other Franklin had never heard of him before. Franklin might have expected some version of Grothman to attack this Vlakdormat at the same time as he attacked Franklin's, but this was weeks later. Maybe this was the same Grothman. "We need window cleaner, and we need it now."

"I'm not going to ask," said the other Franklin. "But I shouldn't have any trouble getting us some. I'm impervious to mind control."

Franklin's counterpart explained that it was an ability that came with his telepathy. As long as he was mentally focused, other people's telepathy wouldn't work on him. He thought he might even be able to extend it to keep Franklin and William's minds safe as well.

William threw his arms in the air and looked at Franklin. "Why couldn't Grothman have shown up back when you could do *that*?"

"Start focusing," Franklin told his counterpart. "He may have already gotten to everyone else in the building. William, I think you should stay here."

William protested profusely. "Why? I know about Grothman. I can help you guys."

"Someone should probably stay here and keep Dr. Drake from

killing herself."

"Oh. Well, in that case. . . ."

"Franklin, show me to the janitor's closet so we can arm ourselves."

Franklin and Franklin snuck stealthily into the main lobby. They each hid behind supporting beams, craning their necks to see what was happening behind them. They held two bottles of window cleaner apiece, like pistols at the ready. Doctors and patients passed by them, unaware of their presence.

Franklin was still amazed at how similar this dimension was to his own. It had always seemed to him that interdimensional travel should completely destroy the balance of the multiverse, making parallel dimensions far less parallel to each other. But here was another Franklin Bryce and another Vlakdormat, defined by the very existence of other dimensions, just as he and his Vlakdormat were. Was the multiverse somehow balancing itself, adjusting to the fact that interdimensional travel was altering most dimensions? Lera had once told him that as far as anyone knew, portals to other dimensions had only started opening about a thousand years earlier. Before that, everyone assumed that theirs was the only universe.

Franklin, came a voice in his head. His counterpart was telepathically communicating with him, which was odd, because it was in the same voice all of his own thoughts were in. *I'm trying to concentrate, remember? You're thinking too much and it's distracting me.*

The other Franklin was right. This was hardly the time to be dissecting the complexities of the multiverse. Franklin couldn't help but envy his counterpart for being able to send a message telepathically. He had become a far more powerful psychic than Franklin ever had been.

I see several humans, a Cimclox, and a Vaklock beast, the other Franklin said telepathically. Franklin had never had a Cimclox as a patient and had only met one once or twice. They were short yellow furry quadrupeds with large mouths, no teeth, and short, pointy tales. *What are we looking for?* the other Franklin asked.

A man with three red horns on his forehead, Franklin thought to his counterpart. That reminded him of something he wished he had thought of earlier. *Either that, or a giant red robot suit.*

As if on cue, the ground began to shake and a booming voice came from everywhere at once.

"I heard there was a Dr. Franklin Bryce in the building," said the voice. "I absolutely *hate* people with that name."

Out of the corner of his eye, Franklin could see the colossal suit coming toward them, but this one was different than the one he had watched Helena rip apart. It was larger, shinier, and it had a flat, rectangular screen picturing a giant face at the head where Grothman's face could be seen before. Nothing could be seen at all behind it, and the face consisted only of a pixilated mouth, nose, and triangular eyes. It was wearing a huge grin.

But the voice was definitely Grothman's. And judging by his comment about Franklin's name, it was indeed the same Grothman Franklin had met before.

Do we go now? asked the other Franklin.

No. He's protected behind that suit. We have to find a way to disable it.

Any ideas?

Not really, said Franklin. *Last time I had a superpowered mental patient to beat him up. You seem to be fresh out of those.*

"Your patients are pathetic, Bryce," Grothman said. His favorite thing in the multiverse seemed to be the sound of his own voice. "They don't need to be comforted. They don't need to be rehabilitated. They need to be taken out of the picture. They're taking up space that could be used by sane and productive individuals."

What is this guy's problem? asked the other Franklin.

I'm sure if we let him go on long enough he'll do a whole monologue about it, said Franklin.

The tile shook harder beneath his feet as the robot suit came closer. Franklin had no idea how they were going to stop it. He wished he had brought Helena along, but he'd had no way of knowing this was going to happen. He wondered what was next —wannabe super villains in orange duct tape or giant, floating eyeballs?

We could always try tripping it, said the other Franklin.

Or maybe we could paint a convincing-looking tunnel on the side of a wall and hope he runs into it, Franklin said to his counterpart. *I don't think we can outthink him. He's telepathic, remember?*

"I know you're here," said Grothman on his loud speaker. "I can hear your thoughts."

No he can't, said Franklin's counterpart. *He caught our thoughts briefly when he entered the room, but I'm blocking his telepathy now. He didn't even hear us long enough to realize there are two of us. We can use that to our advantage.*

But you can still read his mind? Franklin asked.

Yes, but I'm having a hard time keeping it up.

Franklin's head was silent for a while. Then the other

Franklin thought of something. *I think we can shut the whole suit down.*

How?

He's added A. I. to his robot suit.

Artificial intelligence meant that the suit had a positronic brain. If they could get to the positronic deactivation switch, they could knock his suit out just as if it were an HR120.

Franklin looked over to his left and found a control panel on the wall, in the same place it was in his dimension. Even if Grothman had already gotten to the security officers, he could activate the switch automatically with the right security code.

Alpha 394, said Franklin's counterpart.

Keep blocking his telepathy, said Franklin. *I'm going to make a break for it.*

Franklin took off toward the panel, knowing full well that Grothman could see him and could easily pick him up and throw him to the other side of the room or maybe even aim a missile at him. But Grothman was such a windbag that Franklin was betting he would ramble on long enough for Franklin to activate the switch.

"I don't know what you hope to accomplish," Grothman said. "You can't hope to stop me. You don't have the means."

"If that's true," said Franklin, opening the panel and typing in the code, "then why aren't I trying to kill myself?"

The robot suit instantly fell to the ground, its digital, demonic smile disappearing from its face. The helmet opened with a hydraulic sound, revealing the three-horned Threpnoidian reeling in pain.

Franklin's counterpart joined him, and they each pointed their Windex bottles at Grothman. He looked up at them angrily, and then his eyes widened with surprise.

"*Two.* . . . What?"

Both Franklins sprayed Grothman with their window cleaners.

Grothman sat up painfully and narrowed his eyes at Franklin. "*You.* . . ."

"Did you really think you could pull off the same tired routine at another Vlakdormat?" Franklin asked him. "Then you're even dumber than I realized. You walked into a facility with a positronic deactivation switch while wearing an artificially intelligent robot suit?"

"This is just a minor setback," said Grothman. "As I told you before, I will not rest until the entire multiverse is ridden of the mentally ill."

Franklin's counterpart looked at him. "This guy needs some serious help."

"I offered, but he wasn't interested."

Five Vlakdormat security officers appeared on the scene. Franklin frowned. They had never shown up so quickly in his dimension when *he* was in danger.

Grothman quickly reached into his pockets, but he looked distraught. Five men were aiming portable apertures at him. He couldn't possibly activate his before one of them sucked him into theirs.

Franklin looked at his counterpart in disbelief. "That was too easy. I mean, really, *too* easy. I guess my life *would* be a lot simpler if I'd never lost my telepathy . . . and here I was starting to get used to it. . . ."

"I really can't believe it," said Grothman.

"Believe what?"

"Your counterpart, the Franklin of this dimension. He let his guard down. I can read his mind."

Franklin looked at his counterpart nervously.

"Even with all of your successes, you're just as gullible as he is," Grothman said. "I'm going to ruin your life just like I ruined his. You have *two first names.*"

"Get this guy in a pocket dimension," Franklin said to the security officers. "And if you guys have one, make it a bread dimension."

CHAPTER 21

The Corvadian Speaks

ONCE FRANKLIN AND HIS COUNTERPART HAD SUBMITTED A STATEMENT TO VLAKDORMAT SECURITY, THEY WENT BACK TO THE UNEXPLAINED PHENOMENA WING TO PICK UP WILLIAM AND RESUME THEIR MISSION. But when they arrived, neither William nor Drake was in the laboratory. They walked the length of the room, trying to determine what could have happened to them and fearing the worst, until they came to the other Drake's office. There was shattered glass all over the floor. They found William bent over, his head sticking out an open window. One of his white sneakers had fallen off, and he struggled to keep both of his feet—one in a shoe and one in a plaid sock—firmly planted on the carpet, and out of the glass.

Franklin ran to him, and as he looked out the window, he saw the female Drake hanging from a ledge just beneath it and trying not to look down at the busy street below. Her office was on the opposite side of the entrance to the building, directly over four lanes of city traffic, and it was rush hour. Half of her blonde hair had come out of her ponytail and was hitting her face in the wind. William had hold of her hand, but he was having a hard time lifting her up by himself.

"I tried to stop her," William said between deep breaths.

"This wasn't my idea, believe me," Drake yelled up to them. Franklin was glad Grothman's spell had worn off when it did. He grabbed William around the middle and pulled him backward, careful to avoid the broken glass. The other Franklin stood by to help, and soon Drake was inside and out of danger. She sat down in her desk chair and breathed hard.

"You guys got here just in time," William said. "She really is lucky."

"Thank you," Drake said. Franklin almost said something, but he quickly realized she wasn't talking to him. Her attention was completely on William. "It was like someone else was in control. I kept talking about killing myself, but it wasn't really what I wanted to do."

William leaned down in front of her and grabbed her hands. "I know what it's like. Franklin and I went through it too."

"I don't think I would have made it if you hadn't been here."

"No reason to think about it. You're okay now."

William and Drake looked deep into each other's eyes for a long time without saying anything, both of them smiling.

The voice of his counterpart filled Franklin's head. *There's no reason William needs to be with us when we go see Zarcadmium.*

You're right, Franklin said to his counterpart. The two of them said their goodbyes to Drake and told William they would be back for him later. He thanked them as they left, but his eyes never left Drake's.

Are you going to tell your Drake about this? asked Franklin's counterpart.

I doubt it.

The two Franklins sat on a comfortable leather couch in Stephen Zarcadmium's apartment. It turned out it was only fifteen minutes away from Vlakdormat, in one of Abott City's ritziest neighborhoods. It was a spacious loft with wood floors and bright white walls, decorated with futuristic-looking octagonal oak chairs and coffee tables and original paintings of vast landscapes and skylines that revealed the complex architecture of Zarcadmium's home dimension. Adjacent to the kitchen was a small bar, with bottles of champagne already on ice and three glasses sitting next to them. The other Zarcadmium had never struck Franklin as especially posh, and he wondered if that Zarcadmium lived nearly so well.

"It's wonderful to see you, Dr. Bryce. Or should I say, Dr. *Bryces,*" Zarcadmium said. He was just as Franklin remembered him, a stout, fat man with one gold eye and one bright pink eye and a demeanor that was both charming and somewhat domineering.

"So you're from another dimension," Zarcadmium said to Franklin. "What brings you here, running around town with yourself?"

"I was wondering if you could tell me something about the magic you used to give this Franklin his telepathy."

Zarcadmium frowned. "I'm afraid I don't know much of anything about magic. I bought it from a man . . . Chirok, I think his name was. Rajel Chirok. I bought it from him and gave it to Dr. Bryce for helping me out of my depression."

It always seemed to come back to the Nixots. If Franklin had a dime for every time that happened, maybe he could buy some luck powers from Rajel Chirok.

Franklin's counterpart looked surprised. "That's right. Completely different from how Franklin got his."

Franklin explained to Zarcadmium how the other Zarcadmium produced a huge purple cloud that had struck him with lightning and given him his ability.

"I'm sorry, I've never heard of anything like that,"

Zarcadmium said. "The telepathy I had came in an envelope that turned into a cube and floated in mid-air. Isn't that an odd coincidence?"

It certainly was. Franklin couldn't believe both he and his counterpart had been given powers by two different versions of the same man, in two entirely different ways. Now he was right back where he had started.

"There was very little, if any, magic at all in my dimension," Zarcadmium said. "We were a technologically-based people. We got too ambitious, too far ahead of ourselves, and we ultimately destroyed our whole planet with that technology. But I've come to terms with all of that. Now I'm a lawyer."

Franklin's counterpart put a hand on Zarcadmium's shoulder. Franklin could tell that the other Franklin was still reeling from the realization of having two first names, and Franklin appreciated the other's attempt at being comforting.

"It was certainly worth a try," Franklin said. "Maybe your Zarcadmium got his magic in some other dimension."

"This is all rather confusing," said Zarcadmium. "I'm quite sorry I couldn't be more helpful. If there's anything else I can do."

"No, thank you. I'll figure it out. Sorry for bothering you."

"No bother. I'm glad to have the company. You should stick around. I have champagne. And we could make a meatloaf."

Franklin smiled. "I should be getting back. Unless, of course, you've got another box of telepathy lying around somewhere."

"I'm fresh out," said Zarcadmium. "Suit yourself."

The two of them left Zarcadmium's apartment completely empty-handed, knowing no more than they had before they entered Dimension 0.65.

"Franklin," said his counterpart as they walked down a flight of stairs beneath the starry night sky. "That idea you had earlier, about the multiverse trying to balance itself . . . that is just a theory, right?"

"What do you mean?"

"Do you think I'm going to lose my telepathy like you did?"

"I don't know," Franklin said. "Honestly, I hope not. Just . . . don't let the two first names thing get to you too much. It's probably better if you just ignore it."

Considering the differences between interdimensional time zones, Franklin had barely slept three hours before he got up from a cot set up in his office and started work the next day. He spoke with Drake, but neither of them were any closer to finding Zarcadmium or anything more about the purple cloud magic. And the only thing they had been able to drum up about the HR120s was that they appeared to be a bunch of conservationists. Not that Franklin had anything against the environment, but robots obsessed with saving the Earth seemed to Franklin almost a contradiction in terms.

And now he was having his first session with Helena Kathryn since she had told him she was the one who tried to eradicate the other personalities. She was the last person he wanted to see right now.

So it was lucky that she had come today not as Helena, but as Kay, Franklin's favorite of the six other personalities. He felt a little guilty for having a favorite, but Kay was soft-spoken, well-mannered, and was the most down-to-earth of all of them. He had only met her a couple of weeks earlier, and, so far, all she seemed interested in doing was listening to him and learning all she could about the world she rarely had a chance to experience. Compared to an always-frightened little girl, a psychotic girl, a cheerleader, a paranoid woman, and a complete recluse, Kay was a breath of fresh air.

"Don't be too hard on her," she told Franklin. "I'm not, and she tried to kill me. She only did what she thought she had to."

"I know that, but it doesn't make it right," Franklin said.

Kay paused and grinned.

"What?" said Franklin.

"You're *trying* to be mad at her, aren't you?"

"Of course not."

"I think you are. You know that what she did was wrong, but you're having a hard time staying upset with her."

"I didn't like having to keep her in a holding dimension, or having people question whether or not she should even be here. She's my patient. I wanted to help, no matter how dangerous she was."

"It's more than that. You wish she wasn't your patient at all."

"What are you implying? That I have *feelings* for Helena?"

Kay laughed. "Of course not. What I meant was, she saved your life. Twice."

Franklin sighed. "She . . . you all . . . have an incredible amount of power. Every time I turn around, she has some new ability. Who knows what you're all capable of?"

"You like her, and it's easy to want to trust someone you like, even in the situation Helena's in. But after what she did, you know you probably shouldn't."

Franklin wasn't entirely sure why he was opening up to Kay, but she had such a way with people that he couldn't help himself.

It was hard to imagine such a socially adept personality among all the others.

"I can't stop her. She can do *anything* she wants. *You* could do anything you wanted. Despite what we've tried, I'm pretty sure we can't keep her here. But before the other day, Helena never used her powers to do anything but help people. How am I supposed to respond to that?"

"I didn't mean to hurt you, Dr. Bryce."

Franklin froze. The ease and confidence on Helena's face instantly transformed into grief and guilt.

"Some of them threatened to hurt you," Helena said, "and that's why I had to try to get rid of them. But now I can't."

Franklin didn't know what to say.

"You're right. If I wanted to leave, you couldn't stop me. And I've thought about leaving. Because, even though they know I can't kill them, they're still there, and they might come out at any time. Some of them are still dangerous. But wherever I went, I'd be in danger of hurting someone."

She and Franklin looked at each other for a long time.

"This isn't really about trust," Franklin said. "You have at least one monster inside of you, but you're not a monster. Just promise me something. Don't make any rash decisions like that again without talking to me first."

"I won't," said Helena. "Thanks for letting me stay."

Franklin couldn't explain what he felt about her. He had never allowed his patients to affect his personal life before. But Helena was more than a patient. Lately, she had *been* his personal life. She was directly linked to the forces that wanted him dead. And that connected the two of them in a way that was completely perplexing. It was like sitting with both his savior and his mortal enemy at the same time.

There was a knock at the door.

Franklin and Helena immediately snapped out of their trance. Franklin pushed a button on his desk. "Bethany, do you still make appointments for me or is our policy just to let people walk right in now?"

"I figured you'd want to see this guy, no matter who you were with," said his secretary on the speaker phone. "And he said he wanted to make an entrance."

The door swung open and Stephen Zarcadmium walked into the room.

"There's a rumor going around that you're looking for me, Dr. Bryce," he said, smiling. "I'm here to give you your telepathy back."

CHAPTER 22

Zarcadmium Is Here To Help

FRANKLIN WONDERED IF HE WAS DEVELOPING A CASE OF FANTASTIPHOBIA, THE FEAR OF TOO MANY THINGS GOING ONE'S WAY. After returning from Dimension 0.65 with no luck finding anything out about the HR120s or the purple cloud magic that had been used to revive Helena Kathryn, the last thing he expected was for Zarcadmium to suddenly show up in his office. Franklin had almost gotten used to his bad luck, and news this good was almost more than he could handle.

Now, as he walked along the busy city traffic in the cold winter afternoon air, Franklin felt overwhelmed. It was all too insanely easy. Stephen Zarcadmium was here to restore his telepathy at the precise moment Franklin was desperately looking for him. Was it just coincidence? Franklin still had two first names, so probably not.

Franklin had been sitting in bewilderment in front of Zarcadmium while Helena, more skeptical than ever, had asked the tough questions. He couldn't even remember now what they were or how Zarcadmium had responded. He had to get away from it all, to give himself some time to think about everything that had happened, so he just got up and left. Yes, he had more appointments that afternoon. Yes, it wasn't safe to leave Vlakdormat while his naturally-intuitive wife was still away, gallivanting about the multiverse. And yes, Franklin was shivering uncontrollably because it was about thirty-five degrees outside and he had forgotten to take his coat with him. But he knew that Zarcadmium's timely appearance was so good it somehow had to be bad.

"You shouldn't be here," came a voice from behind him. As Franklin turned around, a man rode a bicycle past, staring at Helena in awe. He continued to stare behind him as he rode. She was wearing a light blue winter coat with a matching hat and gloves.

"Neither should you. You can't just teleport in front of people like that," Franklin said.

"Considering that this city seems to be a hot spot for portals, I doubt it's the strangest thing he's ever seen. I'm more concerned about you."

Franklin shook his head and continued walking, shivering more now that he had been standing still for a moment. Helena walked alongside him. He said, "I doubt the HR120s are going to attack in broad daylight, especially with all this traffic. If they killed me, they'd also have to kill every rush hour commuter on forty-seventh street."

It was Helena's turn to shake her head, but only slightly. She was obviously not in a joking mood.

"You can't let him do it," Helena said.

"Him who? Do what?" Franklin asked, as if he didn't know.

"Zarcadmium. I know what it would mean for you to get your powers back, but you can't let him use his magic on you. I don't trust him."

"Why not?"

"Too convenient. You've been researching him and, suddenly, he's here."

"It's not like it's the first coincidence that's ever happened," Franklin said. "After all, I did see an HR120 killed in my office just before all of this started happening. And that was completely unrelated." Franklin thought about that for a moment as his eyes gradually began to grow. "Or, at least, I don't think it was related. . . ."

"I had a feeling," Helena said, "when Zarcadmium walked into your office."

"You mean, like a hunch?"

"Yes."

"Since when do you have hunches?"

"I can't explain it. But Zarcadmium isn't here to make you telepathic again. Or, if he is, that's not all he's come to do."

"Did I miss something?" Franklin asked, stopping in his tracks. "Did you get another power? Is *everyone* telepathic besides me?"

"I'm not telepathic."

"He said he heard I was looking for him. Maybe that's why he decided to come when he did. He came, found out I'd lost my telepathy, and figured that's why I was trying to find him."

"Don't forget that the HR120s did the same magic Zarcadmium did. You can't believe *that's* a coincidence."

Franklin sighed. "I know. I'd like to believe him. If I had my telepathy again, at least I'd *feel* more powerful. I know that doesn't make any sense."

"No, I understand."

They began walking again. "There's something you don't know," Franklin said. He told her about Dimension 0.65 and the other Stephen Zarcadmium, who had known nothing about the purple cloud magic.

"So it's even more convenient than I thought. Franklin, you were just there *yesterday*. Don't you think if he were here just to restore your telepathy, he would have already done it?"

"So what are you thinking, then? You think he's working with the HR120s?"

"No," Helena said. "I think they're trying to play on your weaknesses—maybe they found out you're looking for Zarcadmium. I think this Zarcadmium *is* an HR120."

Franklin was glad he wasn't a scientist, especially at an interdimensional facility like Vlakdormat. Sure, it helped to know something about species from other dimensions and their cultures to do his job, but at least he didn't have to know anything about their *technology*. Drake's laboratory was now filled with weird equipment Franklin had never seen before. Dozens of cables were connected between the floor and the ceiling, and each had several green and yellow bulbs that flashed from time to time. He couldn't imagine what they were for. He had to walk between and around several of the wires just to get to Drake, who stood in the middle of the room at the main computer terminal.

All of the monitors along the steel walls showed the information Drake had obtained so far on the HR120s and Stephen Zarcadmium. Considering how little information they had, Franklin assumed that Drake was taking up so much space with this text just to make himself feel better. The text was all in a very large font.

"So let me get this straight," Drake said after Franklin explained his predicament. "You want me to run a test to see if Stephen Zarcadmium is an HR120."

"We have to be sure," Franklin said.

"That would certainly explain why Zarcadmium is the only other person we know to have used that magic. But even if he is an HR120, he won't register on my sensors as a robot."

"So you can't do it?"

"I didn't say that," Dr. Drake said. "The only way to tell if someone is an HR120 is to pull the positronic deactivation switch. If he keels over, he's a robot."

"Oh." Franklin hadn't thought of this before. But what if Zarcadmium, although an HR12o, was somehow the same Zarcadmium who had given him his telepathy? If so, then pulling the positronic deactivation switch would mean killing the man who had helped to make Franklin who he was. Then again, why an HR120 would become suicidal over the destruction of some random planet was completely beyond Franklin.

"If he is an HR120, he was probably sent here, like all the others, to kill you," Drake said. "Only this time, he came in the guise of someone you know, someone you've trusted before. If he happens to be a robot and we kill him before he kills you, is that really such a bad thing?"

But Franklin had already come to that conclusion on his own. The real question now, if they were right, was where to find the real Stephen Zarcadmium?

"No, I have no ethical reservations about deactivating robots that are trying to kill me. But what if it doesn't work?"

Drake shrugged. "Then he's not a robot. In that case, you'll just have to decide for yourself if you can trust him. But be careful. Even if Zarcadmium isn't a robot, there is still a major connection between him and the HR120s."

"I know."

"When is your next meeting with Zarcadmium?"

"In about twenty minutes."

"Then I'll pull the switch in twenty-five, unless you hear from me. If I don't call, it means I pulled the switch. All you have to do is wait to see if we're going to have to clean up a robot corpse."

Franklin turned to leave, but Drake stopped him. "I know you're hoping that this is somehow all a misunderstanding and that he really just wants to help you out. But for the record, I don't think you need it."

"What?"

"Telepathy. Think of it as a set of training wheels. It got you on your feet, but now you've grown up."

Franklin smiled. "I do my best."

"That's all anyone can do. Granted, I know that's easy for me to say, having won the Rekvoloskian lottery eight times, but it's still the truth."

Franklin started to leave, but he found himself hung up on one of the wires between the floor and the ceiling. He struggled with it for a moment and then finally got himself untangled. He looked back at Drake.

"What are these for, anyway? Some improvement to your sensors or something?"

"My sensors are as close to perfect as they will ever be. No, these are Hrastadom lights. I put them up every year."

"Hrastadom? Isn't that a Rekvoloskian holiday? You're not Rekvoloskian. . . ."

"No, but like I said, I keep winning their lottery. I figure it can't hurt my luck to observe some of their cultural practices."

"I don't think you could hurt your luck if you walked under a ladder holding a black cat while bending over to pick up an upside down penny lying on a sidewalk crack."

Dr. Drake shook his head, sadly. "I'm not so sure. My luck seemed to be holding just fine until Zarcadmium and those blasted HR120s."

As Franklin left the laboratory, Drake's words echoed over

and over in his mind. As he got off the elevator and then slowly walked to his office, Franklin finally began to realize the scope of everything that was happening. The HR120s had managed to affect everything around him, even to the point that Drake's luck was wearing thin.

"I didn't mean to startle you earlier," Stephen Zarcadmium said as Franklin returned to his office. Franklin sat down behind his desk, moved aside a few stray pieces of paper, and set down his clipboard.

"That's all right," Franklin said. "I was just surprised to see you here. I've been trying to find you for a while now."

"So I've heard," Zarcadmium said. He leaned forward in his chair. "What's the clipboard for? Am I in therapy again?"

Franklin laughed. "No. Just force of habit. I even take notes when I'm having conversations with my wife."

Now Zarcadmium let out a chuckle. "That's not bad advice."

He looked and acted exactly as Franklin remembered him, exactly like the man he had met in Dimension 0.65. Same short, round physique, same gold and pink eyes, and the same witty retort. Even when Zarcadmium had been suicidal, he had been witty. The jokes then were bleak and disturbing, but witty nonetheless. It was hard for Franklin to imagine this man being a robot. Franklin glanced at his watch. Only two minutes left before Drake pulled the switch.

"I'm sorry I haven't stayed in touch, but my business takes me all over the multiverse. I design pocket dimensions now. Why were you looking for me?" Zarcadmium asked.

"Actually, I was hoping you could restore my telepathy," Franklin lied.

"I figured that was it. Your secretary mentioned that a Nixot stole it."

"One of these days, I'm going to give Bethany a script," Franklin said, sighing. This time, he wasn't lying. The incident with Rajel Chirok had been extremely embarrassing.

"How long has it been now?" Zarcadmium said. "Six years?"

"Almost," said Franklin. He glanced at his watch, then looked back at Zarcadmium. Franklin stared into his eyes for what felt like an hour. Franklin imagined Zarcadmium's eyes being the aperture to another dimension, and all he had to do was step inside, take a look around, and he would know everything he wanted to know.

But it wasn't that easy. Franklin wasn't telepathic, and eyes weren't really the window into someone's soul. Not if that person knew how to hide his feelings behind an expression. And Zarcadmium had an incredible poker face.

"Is something wrong?" Zarcadmium asked.

"Just lost in thought."

"I can see how that might happen to a therapist."

Everything was wrong. Drake hadn't called, which meant that he had either pulled the positronic deactivation switch and Zarcadmium wasn't an HR120, or something had prevented him from doing so. And if Zarcadmium wasn't an HR120, what, exactly, did that mean?

Franklin hid his surprised that Zarcadmium wasn't dead. "I've been wanting to ask you for years. Where did you get your magic?"

Zarcadmium nodded. "It used to be a trade secret in my dimension, but I don't suppose there would be any harm in telling you about it now. The magic was passed down for generations but guarded, so that only Corvadians had access to it. I'm the only one left who can harness the purple cloud."

"That would explain it," Franklin said. "When I couldn't find you, I went to Dimension 0.65. I thought the Zarcadmium there might know something, but they must not have had that magic in his Corvadia."

Zarcadmium looked intrigued. "I've never been to Dimension 0.65. What's it like?"

"I have better luck there."

"Why don't you move, then?"

"Because if I wanted to be Dr. Franklin Bryce there, I'd have to kill myself."

Zarcadmium laughed. "And we wouldn't want that. You know, I've never met another version of myself. What's he like?"

"Exactly like you, right down to the eyes." Except he wasn't exactly the same. This Zarcadmium was hiding something.

"If he's from a close parallel Corvadia, his eyes would look the same as mine. Every Corvadian looked this way. I think at one time in our ancient past, there was a freak race of Corvadians. All of them had gold eyes on the *right* side, but they were persecuted and wiped out centuries before I was born."

He told it like an amusing anecdote, and Franklin smiled nervously.

"It's possible that only some versions of Corvadia had our magic. Maybe my Corvadia was even the only one."

Franklin wasn't going to get anywhere this way, so he decided to go for broke and say the riskiest possible thing he could say.

"You're not the only one," Franklin said.

"Excuse me? I thought you said. . . ."

"I've met another race with the purple cloud magic."

"What kind of race?" Zarcadmium asked. His intrigue

turned into concern.

"Robots. They've been after me."

"And they have *magic*?"

"Homicidal robots aren't exactly unusual, I realize, but these are different. They can do anything a human being can do. And they know how to use the purple cloud. It was just like the one you used."

"HR120s?"

"You've heard of them."

"I've heard of them. Always trying to destroy or conquer something. Why can't they just be productive members of society?"

"Is there a chance it isn't the same magic?" Franklin asked. "What spell did they do?"

"They revived Helena, the patient of mine you met earlier. She was unconscious."

"What color of lightning did they use?"

"Blue."

"Then we have a problem. It's definitely Corvadian magic." Zarcadmium abruptly stood up and grabbed his blazer from a hook on the wall.

"Where are you going?" Franklin asked.

"I'm sorry I can't give you your telepathy right away, but I have to find the robots. In the wrong hands, that magic is extremely dangerous."

"How . . . dangerous?"

Zarcadmium looked at Franklin in a way that ignited his imagination. It was a look that said, "Anything you can think of, that's how dangerous it is."

"I can do a spell to take the magic away from them, but it's going to take several hours of preparation and all of my strength. It sounds like you've had more than a few brushes with them."

"Just enough that I've had to spend most of my time around a positronic deactivation switch and use my Verullian wife as a body guard," Franklin said. He was still suspicious, but if Zarcadmium was involved with the HR120s in one way or another, he would have already known all of that.

Zarcadmium said, "Can you compile a list of everyone you know to be an HR120?"

"I suppose I could."

"Please," said Zarcadmium, opening Franklin's glass door. "I can't stop them if I don't know where to look. Get those names together and bring them to me at seven tonight. I'm staying at the Marriott just a few blocks south of here. Room 242."

"I'll be there," Franklin said, shaking Zarcadmium's hand.

"Maybe I'll be able to do more for you than just give you your powers back. Hopefully when this is over, you won't have any reason to run from the HR120s anymore."

The phrase *too good to be true* rang in Franklin's brain.

When he had made it through the maze of Hrastadom lights and back to Drake's main computer console, Franklin noticed that the computer screens around the laboratory had changed. Instead of embarrassingly large text, they now all pictured a mess of circuitry, plugs, and wires that were in no way reminiscent of the Hrastadom lights. Franklin had no idea what he was looking at.

"While we were talking before, my sensors picked up something unusual," Drake said, walking over to Franklin and motioning toward the largest of the monitors. He stroked his well-trimmed goatee as he looked up at it. "Do you recognize this?"

"It looks like the inside of a computer, if I had to make a guess," Franklin said.

"You're not too far off. This is, in fact, the inside of a very advanced CVT."

Franklin raised an eyebrow. "Your sensors can pick up a tracer?"

"My sensors could pick out a specific subatomic particle in a room filled with dozens of different species."

"But they can't read HR120s?"

Drake held his hands up in front of him. "Hey, I don't know of *anything* that sophisticated."

"Where did it come from?"

"You. You're wearing it right now."

Franklin fumbled around his navy shirt and then his khaki pants, but since the tracer was likely cloaked, he knew he'd probably never find it. "Who put it there?"

"It's not one of ours. But luckily, the sensors can also give us a time index. They can tell us how long this thing has been active."

Drake pulled a small metallic cylinder out of a drawer in the computer terminal. He ran it over Franklin's stomach, his chest, his arms, and when he got to Franklin's neck, just over his left shoulder, a yellow light blinked rapidly and the cylinder started chirping.

"Unbutton your shirt," Drake said. This was probably the only situation in which Franklin would be willing to cooperate with that request without question, so he unfastened the top three buttons. Drake took a tiny pair of pliers from a drawer. With the pliers, he gripped hold of something and snatched it from Franklin's neck, and pulled away. Franklin was amazed that he never felt something on his neck, not even when Drake was yanking the CVT off. He buttoned his shirt back up.

Drake went back to his console, put his tools away, and pushed a few buttons. His eyes grew large as every monitor in the room showed the same six numbers.

"What does that mean?" Franklin asked.

"I've pinpointed the time they bugged you, down to the second. And you're not going to like it."

Franklin began to understand. "Over a hundred hours. Four days."

"It was planted the same day the HR120s revived Helena," Drake said.

"Which means," Franklin said, "that they must have put it on me while they were here."

"It's certainly not one of ours. So my best guess is that they used it to spy on you in Dimension 0.65, and that's why Zarcadmium is here now."

"But Drake, we've already established that he's not an HR120. Unless you didn't activate—"

"I did," Drake said. "But how else would he have known you were looking for him unless he was involved with them?"

Franklin thought about that for a moment, then headed back toward the forest of Hrastadom lights. A plan started to formulate in his mind.

"I'm going to test your theory," Franklin said. "And I think I have just enough in savings to pull it off."

CHAPTER 23

Going Shopping

FRANKLIN COULDN'T BELIEVE WHAT HE WAS ABOUT TO DO. To stoop any lower would be like stealing his own superpowers. But he had to know the truth. He still wasn't sure Zarcadmium was working with the HR120s. But there was obviously something his old patient wasn't telling him, and he was going to find out what it was if it killed him. Franklin was through waiting for the danger to come to him.

Rajel Chirok walked into Franklin's office and shook Franklin's hand.

Chirok was shaking his head. "When you said you needed a favor from me, I could hardly believe it," said Chirok. He was wearing a light blue silk shirt, matching pants, and a black fedora hat on his head.

"Not a favor. I want to buy something from you."

Chirok was taken aback, and his wings beat once behind him. "*You*? Could it be I'm finally rubbing off on you?"

"Hardly," said Franklin. He had, in fact, hoped that he was starting to rub off on Rajel Chirok. They had been in sessions together for a couple of weeks now, and, thanks to Franklin's advice, Chirok was already starting to add some legitimate items to his Interdimensional eBay auctions. Now, by asking to buy one of the illegal items, Franklin was not only breaking the law, but he was also condoning Chirok's business practices. Franklin may have had a personal grudge against him, but he still wanted to see Chirok become a better man. And he took some perverse pleasure in taking Chirok's money for therapy sessions.

"I need a power," Franklin said.

"What sort of power?" Chirok asked, putting his fingers

together greedily.

"Persuasion," said Franklin. "Threpnoidian, preferably."

Chirok frowned. "I should have known better. You get my hopes up like this and then you ask for one of the hardest abilities to come by. Is this some kind of joke?"

"No joke," Franklin said.

"But you've read the *Nitzu Trivisknot.* You know that the Threpnoidians are the only race left that still has that power."

"So you finally read the *Trivisknot* yourself. Good for you. But I know you used to have the power yourself."

"Emphasis on *used to.* That was before a guy *you* said was a dimension stole all of my powers."

"You kind of deserved it."

"That's not going to help you now, is it? I've been able to build some of my stock back up, but it's only been two weeks. I haven't been able to keep very many powers for myself and stay in business. And it's not like I know how to get into Threpnoidia any more than you do."

"Then how did you get that power in the first place?"

"I got lucky. Found a Threpnoidian settling down with some chick in the Bramzit dimension. A man, even a Threpnoidian man, is never more vulnerable than he is at his own wedding ceremony."

Franklin didn't believe him. Chirok was too good at what he did to not have something up his sleeve. "I know you have sources. I need it in three hours."

"Well, when you put it that way, I guess I'll just take a quick run around the multiverse and see if I can't find any Threpnoidians getting married in the next three hours. It's impossible, Franklin, especially without most of my powers."

"Then there must be some other way. It's a matter of life or death."

"Whose life?"

"Mine."

Chirok laughed. "And the truth comes out. I should have known it would take nothing short of a brush with death to convince you to do something underhanded. There is one possibility. And you can breathe easy, because it isn't even illegal. Verullian magic."

Franklin took an involuntary breath. Lera had never mentioned anyone in her dimension using magic. Her species had a few special abilities, but, as far as Franklin knew, they were all biological.

"Verullians are full of surprises. I'll bet the next time you see your wife, you'll find out something else about her you didn't already know."

Franklin ignored that comment. Lera was the last thing he wanted to discuss with Chirok. "So what do I need to do?"

"Hell if I know. It's not like I've ever met your wife."

"About the *spell.*"

"Oh."

Chirok grabbed a blank piece of paper out of an open drawer in Franklin's file cabinet and started writing out some directions. "You'll need a few items, mostly stuff you can find around the house. I'm also writing out the incantation. You'll want to place the items exactly as I'm outlining, and you'll need someone else with you to speak the incantation."

"Why?"

"Because you'll have a banana in your mouth."

Franklin was driving his Ford Taurus to the grocery store, with William in the front seat. He only had one hour left to complete the spell and become persuasive. But they had been very productive; they had only three more items to purchase for the spell. They had found most of the items lying around William's house, and now they were only lacking a banana, some cooking oil, and two eggs. There was now an old math textbook, a used sock, and a bowling pin in Franklin's trunk.

"I bet you're glad now that I'm such a pack rat," William said.

"Not that I'm complaining . . . but a single bowling pin?" Franklin asked.

"I never said I only had one. That's all the spell called for. I'm sure the other eight are somewhere."

"*Eight?*"

"You'd be surprised how many different interdimensional species bowl. I prefer playing Jexarite style. They only use nine pins, and it's a lot easier. The bowling ball not only rolls at the pins, but it shoots lasers at them."

"Isn't that a little too easy?"

"The hard part is dodging the lasers that shoot *away* from the pins."

"It still sounds better than Nixothian pool."

William rolled his eyes. "Are you kidding? It's better than Nixothian *anything*."

A few minutes later, Franklin parked his car in the grocery store parking lot. The sun had gone down, but there were a lot of cars parked in the lot, which Franklin was grateful for. It was far more dangerous being here at night than walking alongside traffic during the daytime. Helena had offered to come along and protect him, but Franklin had declined the offer. If Zarcadmium really was lying and knew as much about Helena as the HR120s did, he was likely to bail at the first sight of her. Franklin couldn't risk it.

"Franklin," William said, stopping him before they reached the store's entrance. "I just want you to know that I think this is the most insane plan you've ever come up with."

"Thanks," Franklin said, starting to move again. But William firmly grabbed his arm, stopping him.

"I mean it. I know I'm the only one of us who ever gets drunk, but I'm going to be the voice of reason here, anyway. There's a very good possibility—no, a *probability*—that Zarcadmium is leading you into a trap."

"Thank you, conscience, but I already knew that one."

"You're about to pit Verullian magic, which you'd never even heard of before today, against Zarcadmium's magic."

"Do you have a better idea?" Franklin asked. William didn't seem to. "I'm tired of waiting around for the HR120s to vaporize me. I'm tired of trying to fill in the blanks to this insane puzzle. This has been going on for months now. Every time I think I'm closer to understanding what's happening, I have to start all over. I need to know what this magic is and how Helena's connected to it. This is the only way I can see of doing that."

"And what if you're wrong? You don't exactly have the best track record when it comes to things like this."

"Then why are you even here?"

"Because I'm your friend. You need me."

"You just said it was a bad idea."

"It is. And I was really hoping I could talk you out of it."

Franklin walked away from him and went through the

automatic doors. William hesitated for a moment and then followed him inside.

"I've made up my mind," Franklin said when William had caught up with him.

"I should never have told you about the bowling pin," William mumbled.

They entered the produce aisle. Franklin picked up a banana and put it in the cart. "And what's with this spell, anyway?" William said. "What, exactly, does a banana have to do with being persuasive? If the spell called for a semester of public speaking classes, that I would understand."

Franklin ignored him and they continued walking.

"Look, I understand that you have to see this thing through, but you need to know that I'm not doing this for Helena. I'm doing it for you."

"We've been over this," Franklin said. He was beginning to wish he hadn't brought William along.

"It's not her I'm worried about. It's the other six personalities."

"The HR120s have power over her—they might be as dangerous to her as they are to us. It's as important to her that we get to the bottom of this as it is to me."

"You shouldn't trust her. And you know that."

Franklin sighed. "I don't know anything, except that she's my friend. I'm not going to turn my back on her, no matter how dangerous she is."

"You're more loyal than I think I could be. But for the record, I don't think this is going to end well."

Once they had left the store with the rest of the items, Franklin drove back toward Vlakdormat. They parked on the side of the street three blocks away from the Marriott where Zarcadmium said he was staying. All they had to do now was perform the spell, meet Zarcadmium on time, and hope it didn't get them killed.

William was right. This was a bad plan. But considering all the trouble they had gone through, rummaging through closets, suitcases, boxes, and a highly splintery toy box to find a single bowling pin, Franklin couldn't imagine backing out now.

Following Chirok's written directions to the letter, Franklin and William carefully set up the objects in order to perform the spell. Franklin sat in the driver's seat with a used math book in his lap, one naked foot on the floor mat and one in William's used sock soaking in a pot of cooking oil with the two eggs on either side, a bowling pin in his left hand, two dollar bills in his right, and a partially peeled, half-eaten banana in his mouth.

Now Franklin not only felt insane, he felt stupid.

"There's something about this spell that still seems off," William said. "I mean, it's a good thing all of these things even exist in both dimensions. What if the eggs are actually supposed to be from some Verullian chicken? And what about the money? All the spell calls for is legal tender. Is two dollars enough? And what's the exchange rate?"

Franklin put down the money and pulled the banana out of his mouth. "William, we only have twenty minutes left to do this."

"Right, right. I hope I'm pronouncing this incantation right."

Franklin hoped so, too. After looking at the words Chirok had written down, he wished he had studied some Verullian when he married Lera. But the few words he had been forced to speak at their traditional Verullian ceremony had been enough to completely turn him off to the language. Those thirteen words had taken him a full six minutes to say.

Franklin put the banana back in his mouth as William fumbled through the incantation.

"Tritgraspolak fritmig roswalegag protirmof freeveeveev," William chanted. He said it three more times, and then he chanted the words once in reverse order, per Chirok's instructions.

"How did Chirok remember all of that?" William asked in disbelief.

"Maybe he stole himself a photographic memory," Franklin said after he pulled the banana out of his mouth. He began putting the items back in a plastic bag.

"So, did it work? Are you persuasive?"

"Let's find out," Franklin said. He held out his hand. "Give me your wallet."

"No." William shrugged. "Maybe it doesn't work on humans."

Franklin sighed. "If it doesn't work on humans, it's not likely that it'll work on a Corvadian, either."

"So I guess that's it, then."

Franklin put his cell phone to his ear.

"What are you doing?" William asked.

"Calling Helena."

"What? Franklin, didn't we just have this conversation?"

But Franklin spoke to Helena anyway. He gave her their location and told her to get there immediately.

"It's too dangerous to go in there by ourselves," Franklin said.

"Which is why we *don't go*," said William.

"I have an appointment. If I don't show up, Zarcadmium will know I suspect him of something."

"That's the back-up plan? Storm the castle and try not to get killed?"

"It's not far from the original plan," came a voice from the back seat. Franklin and William looked behind them, startled. Helena was sitting there comfortably.

She said, "I think this is a bad idea, Franklin."

"Hallelujah, there is a God," said William.

"You're not coming with me?" Franklin asked.

"Of course I am," said Helena. She opened her door and began to step out. "I've come to realize how stubborn you are, and you're going to do this with or without me. Without me, you probably won't survive. I just wanted you to know I thought it was a bad idea."

"I swear, Franklin," William said, "if I miss my date with Dr. Drake on Friday because I'm dead, it's your fault."

Helena was confused. "Long story," Franklin said. "Different Drake. Female Drake."

"Oh," Helena said, and she left it at that.

The three of them got out of the car and looked toward the hotel.

This could be it. The night Franklin captured Stephen Zarcadmium and got all of the answers he had been searching for. Or it could be the end. Either way, dead or alive, Franklin knew things would never be the same again.

CHAPTER 24

Return of the Purple Cloud

THIS WAS THE PLAN: HELENA WAS TO STAY IN THE HALL UNTIL FRANKLIN YELLED FOR BACKUP. William was also to wait in the hall, in case that didn't work, to call Vlakdormat security for help.

And Franklin was to bluff like he had never bluffed before.

"Right on time," Zarcadmium said, answering the door in room 242. Franklin smiled, shook his hand, and walked inside. Besides Zarcadmium and the generic furniture one would expect in a hotel room, it was completely empty. There was no luggage, no clothes lying around, and, either room service had just been in, or the bed hadn't been used at all.

"Before we get to business, it's time I fulfilled my promise," Zarcadmium said. He closed his eyes and raised both of his pudgy arms into the air. A small, purple cloud appeared, hovering above them. It began to grow as Zarcadmium opened his eyes.

Franklin raised an eyebrow. "I thought you said you had to conserve your strength to stop the HR120s."

Franklin could make out a slight humming noise coming from both sides of the room. Zarcadmium's smile grew wider and more devious as the sound grew louder. The humming was all too familiar, and Franklin realized now that William's fears were well- founded. This was an ambush.

So much for bluffing.

"You mean to stop *them*?" Zarcadmium asked, holding his arms out to both walls. Six male HR120s phased through the walls, three on each side. They wore black business suits and matching ties, as if they were on their way to a convention. The cloud now filled up the entire ceiling. Franklin's eyes widened as he noticed the red lightning surging in and out of the cloud.

Franklin pointed his finger defiantly at Zarcadmium and took a step forward. "Stop what you're doing. Turn the HR120s off, and then turn yourself in to the authorities."

Zarcadmium folded his arms. "In case you need me to spell it out for you . . . I'm here to kill you." Magic obviously wasn't the Verullians' strong suit.

"You know, this wasn't my first choice. Without you, I wouldn't be here, Franklin. But you got too involved. Things have to play out a certain way, and you're getting in the way of that."

Helena appeared out of nowhere and was on one of the HR120s that stood next to Zarcadmium in a flash. She had both of its arms ripped off before the others could react.

Zarcadmium was red with anger, and he lifted his arms again, looking up at the purple cloud. His eyes glossed over and turned from gold and pink to pitch black. Franklin wasn't sure exactly what was going to happen, but on impulse, he leaped toward the door.

Red lightning blasted from the cloud and burned a hole the size of three Franklins in the wall behind where he had been standing. Parts of another HR120 flew over Franklin's head. The other four robots looked at each other, then quickly phased back into the wall.

Franklin lifted himself off the floor. "What happened to you?"

"You helped me to see the point in living," Zarcadmium said, "to see that the destruction of Corvadia was only a bump in a very long road. The key to that road is the Helena. But despite everything you've done for me, *no one* is going to stand in the way of our cause."

"What cause?"

"I'm sorry," Zarcadmium said, and he looked like he truly was.

Franklin rolled out of the way as Zarcadmium lifted his hands yet again and another bolt of red lightning blew a hole in the ground.

"That's enough," came a new voice. "Put your arms to your sides and stand at attention."

And Zarcadmium did. His eyes returned to their original colors.

Rajel Chirok walked into the room. His wings beat behind him a couple of times in annoyance. "I can't believe I'm doing this," he said. "Zarcadmium, come here."

Zarcadmium mindlessly stood next to Chirok. On the other side of the room, Helena was still ripping into an HR120. Franklin watched in horror as she destroyed any semblance of its humanoid persona, just as she had done to the first. Wire, metal, and flesh covered the once-spotless hotel room.

William hesitantly peeked into the room and froze. He, Chirok, and Franklin stared in disbelief, each of them knowing there was no point in saying anything to Helena. They couldn't stop her if they tried.

Franklin had seen Helena in a fight before, but never like this. The HR120 wasn't moving, much less putting up a fight, yet she slashed and ripped at what was left of it as though her life depended on it. She wasn't anything like the woman Franklin knew. She was a force of nature, primal, carnal. One of her other personalities might have taken over, but after what

Zarcadmium had said, none of them had reason to hate the HR120s more than Helena did.

When there was hardly anything left to shred, Helena stopped and slowly looked up at Franklin. She didn't say a word, just gave him a slight nod and then walked away from her mess. She, William, Chirok, and Zarcadmium, under Chirok's power, left the room. But Franklin stayed for a long time, staring at the remains of Helena's onslaught.

He finally had Zarcadmium, and he was still alive. But all of that fled Franklin's mind as though it had never mattered. Only one thing mattered in that brief, terrifying moment. Helena Kathryn—not one of the other six—was angry, and she was ready to act on her anger.

Franklin caught up to Chirok as they walked away from the hotel into the vaguely lit parking lot under the black, cloud-filled sky. He did his best to avoid Helena's stone-faced gaze. He hardly recognized her.

"How did you know?" he asked, focusing his attention on Chirok. He stopped, and at this demand, everyone stopped with him.

"It occurred to me that the spell only works on Verullians."

"You picked a fine time to remember that."

"Yeah, but look on the bright side. It could really come in handy, considering who you're married to."

"You remembered how to spell every word in a Verullian incantation, but you couldn't remember that?" William asked.

"Faulty photographic memory," said Chirok. "It happens sometimes when you buy used abilities. Sometimes I can't remember what I had for lunch the day before, and sometimes I remember someone else's memories."

Franklin looked at Zarcadmium's blank expression. Minutes earlier, he had been filled with purpose and passion, willing to do things he knew were unthinkable for the sake of his cause. Now, he was nothing more than Chirok's puppet. Franklin could punch him until he bled to death, and there would have been nothing Zarcadmium could do about it. And for a brief moment, he thought about it. Franklin had once considered this man a model of the terrible places a person could come back from, and now he realized he had helped to save a monster.

"So what do we do now?" asked William.

"We take Zarcadmium back to Vlakdormat and put him in a holding dimension until he wakes up. Then we'll see if we can finally get some answers," Franklin said.

Franklin stood in front of a large steel door in Vlakdormat's basement. Behind that door lay the pocket dimension room, where Zarcadmium was being held in a holding dimension with Rajel Chirok, who had agreed to stay and make sure he didn't leave, at least until Franklin had asked him some questions. Franklin was sure Chirok would ask for some kind of compensation, and he would deal with that when the time came.

Franklin put his eyes up to a small, square device next to the door, which scanned his retina, and then the door automatically opened. There was, at first, nothing behind the door. The pocket dimension room, which accessed all of Vlakdormat's other pocket dimensions, was itself a pocket dimension. And like all pocket dimensions, there was an entrance condition. The doorframe was the aperture, and Franklin had to walk backward through it in order to enter.

As Franklin slowly went inside, reality seemed to transform

into a vast, blank, white space that looked like it went on forever. The only thing inside this space was a computer console, similar to Dr. Drake's. Franklin punched a few keys, and a giant, six-foot loaf of bread appeared in front of him. It was the aperture to the dimension he'd had Zarcadmium taken to. Franklin was about to proceed, when another figure came backward through the pocket dimension room aperture. It was Rajel Chirok, drinking a can of Dr. Pepper and eating a Twinkie.

"You're supposed to be watching Zarcadmium," Franklin said.

"I have been. In fact, I've been here all night. A guy gets hungry watching another guy sleep all night. Besides, he's still asleep, and I've only been gone a minute."

Franklin decided to take this opportunity to ask a question that had been burning inside him since the hotel. "Why did you lie to me? You said you couldn't get Threpnoidian persuasion powers that quickly."

"I didn't. I found a Threpnoidian fugitive in the Brallnak dimension last week. Threpnoidians are almost as distracted when running from the law as they are when they're getting married."

"You should have told me."

"Look, I have absolutely no interest in getting involved with the HR120s. They don't need any more superpowers. And I knew that no matter how much money you were prepared to spend on it, it wouldn't be enough. But—and I wouldn't be telling you this if *anyone* else was here—I didn't want to see you get killed, so I decided to offer my own services."

"Well, that's at least something," Franklin said. They entered the pocket dimension, and this time the entrance condition was a retinal and fingerprint scan from a faculty member with clearance, which Franklin had. But when Franklin and Chirok stepped on the soft, fresh ground of wheat bread, Stephen Zarcadmium was nowhere to be found. The entire pocket dimension was less than the size of a football field, and the terrain was completely flat; he had nowhere to hide. If they didn't see him, he wasn't there.

Franklin shot a furious glare at Chirok.

"Don't look at me. Even with whatever magic he has, he shouldn't have been able to get out of here." And Chirok was right. He had no way of knowing where Zarcadmium was, which meant that even if he had some way of getting out of the pocket dimension, he could end up absolutely anywhere. Most magic was rooted in some kind of logic, and everything Franklin had heard and read told him that if a person wanted to transport himself somewhere, even with magic, he had to know exactly where he was and exactly where he wanted to go before he could get there. The only exception he knew of was Helena, who seemed to be able to will herself wherever or to whomever she wanted to go, whether she knew exactly where her destination was or not. She had teleported to Franklin when he had run away from Vlakdormat in the middle of his conversation with Zarcadmium earlier the previous day, and she couldn't have known where he was going. But Helena was not a being to whom logic seemed to apply.

To get out of the bread dimension, Franklin had to press his thumb and forefinger on a precise clump of bread near where they had entered. He then walked through where the invisible aperture should have been, dragging Chirok along with him. But nothing happened. They were still inside the bread dimension.

It didn't take Franklin long to realize what had happened.

Chirok hadn't used his magic to teleport out of the pocket dimension. He had used it to change the exit condition for the aperture, and then he had left. Plain and simple. From there, he either snuck out of the building somehow or used his magic to teleport himself, assuming he could do that, once he knew where he was.

"What do we do now?" Chirok said. He sounded worried. This wasn't the first time they had been trapped together in a pocket dimension.

"Relax. If I'm not back in thirty minutes, Helena will come after me." Franklin had instructed Vlakdormat security to allow her to leave her holding dimension and teleport into the bread dimension if he didn't come back in a half hour.

"Well then, nothing to worry about," Chirok said.

Franklin grabbed Chirok by his expensive suit collar. Chirok batted his bat wings several times in protest, but Franklin held his ground.

"Zarcadmium was my last chance."

"It isn't completely a lost cause."

"What are you talking about?"

"He's very good at hiding his thoughts, even when he's being controlled by persuasion powers. It's impressive. But while he was sleeping, I could get through to his thoughts. I got two things. He's the ringleader. Zarcadmium isn't working with the HR120s. . . . He *built* them."

Franklin loosened his grip on Chirok as his eyes grew larger. "And what's the second thing?"

"Helena. They're grooming her, Franklin. The lack of a past, the personalities—it's all part of her training. Helena is going to lead an army of HR120s to take over the world."

CHAPTER 25

Getting Answers the Verullian Way

FRANKLIN HAD BEEN AT IT FOR HOURS. Almost twenty-four straight hours, although he was hardly keeping track. He couldn't remember when he had last slept or ate, and he didn't care. He sat at a computer terminal in Drake's laboratory, the Hrastadom lights still shining brightly behind him. He had been researching nonstop, ever since Helena had rescued him and Rajel Chirok from the bread dimension.

Back in the bread dimension, as soon as Chirok had told him about Zarcadmium's plot for Helena, the HR120s, and global domination, Franklin did two things. First, he tried to punch a hole in the wall, which was entirely ineffective because they were standing in a field of bread which had no walls. And secondly, after he cursed himself inwardly from embarrassment, and after he was finally out of the pocket dimension, he went to the Unexplained Phenomena Wing and sat down at Drake's main computer terminal. Franklin didn't ask, but Drake didn't stop him. Drake had his system set up to connect with more of the multi-net than the computer in Franklin's office. It was more complicated than the Internet. Some dimensions couldn't access sites from other dimensions, but Drake had personal connections which gave him more access.

Dr. Caslom called Franklin a few hours later and told him to take some time off. Normally he would have declined, but at the moment, there were more important things than his job, and he was glad that he had one less thing to worry about.

When Franklin had watched Helena rip apart the HR120s in the hotel room, he was absolutely mortified by the intensity of her seemingly mindless carnage. But after learning that

Zarcadmium had built the entire race of HR120s and included Helena in his sinister plot, Franklin was beginning to think that maybe she had the right idea. Things were starting to look extremely dire. Perhaps it would have made more sense to warn the rest of the staff at Vlakdormat or possibly even explode in a fit of panic.

But Franklin only had one thing on his mind. All he really wanted to do was kill robots.

"Franklin, don't you think it's time you got some rest?" came William's voice from behind him. Franklin ignored him and continued tapping away at the keyboard.

"Look," William said. "I know you're upset. Chirok told Dr. Caslom what he told you, and Dr. Caslom filled the rest of us in."

Franklin swiveled around in his chair to face his friend. "But you haven't told Helena?"

"No. That . . . didn't strike any of us as a good idea, just yet."

"Good," Franklin said, looking back at the computer. "I'm not sure how to break it to her. I've never had to tell anyone they were an unwitting participant in a world domination plot before."

"I don't think you should tell her at all, Franklin," said another voice. Dr. Drake stepped into the room behind William. "At least, not yet."

Franklin turned to face both of them and folded his hands in front of him. "You think she's in on it? You think she has known about Zarcadmium this whole time? Some vastly complicated ruse she's been setting up from the first. . . ?"

"Not necessarily," Drake said. "I'm not assuming anything, and neither should you."

"Even if Helena has no idea how she fits into this whole mess, we have no idea what could happen if we gave her that information," William said. "Trying to eradicate her personalities triggered some internal off switch, remember? What if we told her she was destined to jump start Armageddon and it triggered a self-destruct mechanism and she exploded? Or what if she suddenly turned all the really good fast food places into McDonalds?"

Franklin sighed. "I know, and you're right. But I can't sit back and do nothing, knowing what's going to happen if we don't stop it."

"What have you been doing, anyway, Franklin?" William asked.

"Searching Interdimensional eBay."

"For twenty-four hours?"

"It's a big multiverse. There are a *lot* of people selling superpowers."

"Superpowers? Last time you tried that, I ended up ripping my house apart looking for a single bowling pin, and it *still* didn't work."

"We have to stop waiting for them to come to us. They have abilities we can't even fathom."

"So you think we should all blow our life savings on second-hand superpowers and try to take out the entire race of HR120s? That's your plan?"

Franklin shook his head. "I know how it sounds. . . . But this isn't about me anymore. Every person who works here has either met Helena Kathryn or, at the very least, has heard of her. Now we know why the HR120s have been after me, and you can bet that Zarcadmium would like nothing more than to take out every person who may have influenced Helena in some way. Not only do we have information about her, but we're affecting her, every day. If she's supposed to become the general of the HR120s, I doubt Vlakdormat was the environment Zarcadmium intended for her to grow up in."

"The HR120s and Zarcadmium have been in the building now. They may have been gathering inside information to dismantle the positronic deactivation switch," said William.

"Exactly. They're coming for us. It's only a matter of time."

"But Franklin, you still can't bank on gaining superpowers in time. They're unreliable, and, considering interdimensional shipping, whatever you buy might not even arrive before the HR120s attack. What you need right now isn't superpowers. It's booze."

Franklin cracked a smile but quickly took it back. He knew William was right. It was insane to think he could take on the HR120s single-handedly. But Franklin just wanted to do something, anything.

His interdimensional cell phone beeped, which was odd because it hardly ever made any noise at all. Franklin wasn't even sure why he was still carrying it with him, considering how rarely it worked. He opened the phone and looked at the display. He was glad he had it this time.

"What is it?" William asked.

"Lera. She's back."

Franklin stepped inside his home for the first time in days. He supposed it was finally safe, now that his Verullian, super-intuitive wife had returned. Although, considering that she had mysteriously disappeared for a week, he wasn't completely certain he should trust her. He had never questioned his wife's loyalties before, despite her often bizarre behavior and complete lack of tact. But lately, nothing had been what it seemed, and *anyone* could potentially be an HR120.

It hit him as he unlocked his front door that if his wife turned out to be an HR120, this was absolutely the last place he wanted to be.

Lera stood in the living room with her arms folded, staring intently at the television.

"Lera, where have you been?" Franklin asked.

But Lera just shook her head and put a finger to her mouth. She looked back at the TV. Franklin frowned, annoyed. He stood next to her to see what was so important that Lera couldn't even say hello to her tired and worried husband whom she had abandoned for the last week.

"There were no witnesses to any of the three murders, and police have no suspects at this time," a female news anchor said on the screen. "All three men, all killed within one hour this morning, were prominent environmental activists in the city."

Franklin was pretty sure he knew what that meant. The police probably left several things out of their official report, including the circuitry and wires most likely found during the victims' autopsies. Someone was targeting HR120s.

"It's Helena, isn't it?" Lera said, finally turning to Franklin. She pointed the remote at the television and switched it off.

"I don't know. Probably. She's the only person I know of who could do that to three HR120s, especially so fast. And considering the two she obliterated the other day. . . ."

"You had another run-in with them?"

"I think two, since you left. And I'm perfectly fine, so thanks for asking."

"Franklin, I—"

"About my first question," Franklin interrupted.

"I've been to over a thousand dimensions in the last few days," she said. Franklin raised an eyebrow. Lera had said that almost in a monotone, as though programmed to.

"I spoke with the Franklin from dimension 0.65," Franklin said. "He said you were on assignment. What was he talking about?"

"The Bureau assigned me to a certain sector of the multiverse. I was searching for other Helenas. There aren't any."

The Bureau? Other Helenas? What in the multiverse was she talking about?

"Okay, slow down. What do you mean, she's the only one?"

Lera was now looking at him with a cold, empty expression Franklin had never seen before. She was always so animated, like someone who either drank coffee all day or never needed to. But now, she looked like a nervous politician reading from a teleprompter. Something was definitely not right about her, yet Franklin was thinking less and less that she was an HR120. If she were, he would already be dead.

A zombie, maybe, but not an HR120.

"She's an anomaly. There is, or at one time were, at least two versions of every single person in the multiverse. This is a scientifically proven fact. When I reported Helena's connection with the HR120s to the Bureau, they began an extensive investigation of the entire multiverse, as we know it. The Bureau then discovered a connection between Stephen Zarcadmium's magic and the HR120s."

Franklin shook his head in disbelief. For the last three years,

Lera had told him she was an interdimensional translator. But she had been lying to him, for probably the entire time they had been married.

First, Franklin had found out that Helena was the lynchpin in a plan for world domination, and now this. On the bright side, at least William still seemed to be exactly who he said he was.

"Lera, you're a . . . *secret agent*?"

Lera nodded her head, still mechanically. "I work for the VIBI—the Verullian Interdimensional Bureau of Investigation."

"And when, exactly, were you planning on *telling* me?"

"I wasn't."

"Then why now?"

"Because you asked."

Franklin didn't understand. He turned off the TV and sat down on his recliner.

"What else have you been hiding from me?" he asked.

If Lera had been herself, she probably would have defended her actions, explained that she had a perfectly good reason for keeping her occupation from him, and that he was lucky to find out at all. But Lera wasn't herself. What had happened to her while she was away?

"I have two ex-husbands you don't already know about, which makes twenty marriages altogether," Lera said. "I've also died twice, but one doesn't really count. I was revived in less than thirty seconds."

Franklin shook his head with disbelief as he stood up from his chair.

"Franklin. . . ."

"Yes?" Franklin wiped the sweat from the back of his neck.

"I think it might be a good time for you to go back to work

and do some research. Maybe look into those murders."

"Yes," Franklin said, nodding. He put on his jacket and started for the door. "That's probably a good idea."

"We can finish this conversation later. You know, when I'm less insane."

"Sure, absolutely," Franklin said nervously. "Less insane. Good. Bye."

Franklin left his house, got in his car, and drove toward Vlakdormat. Before, he was glad to finally get away from work for a few minutes. Now, he couldn't get back there fast enough.

Franklin returned to Dr. Drake's lab, where Drake was diligently working at his computer terminal. The screens around the room that had previously pictured information about the HR120s now played video feeds of news reports about the three environmental activists who were killed that morning.

"I see you've already heard," Franklin said to Dr. Drake. Drake lifted his eyes from his monitor and frowned.

"I thought you went home," he said.

"I did, but then I heard about this."

"I'm looking into it. Go, really. Be with your wife."

"Dr. Drake, I don't want you to take this the wrong way, but at the moment, I'd rather be here with you."

Drake laughed. "Didn't go so well, did it?"

"Not so much."

"You'll patch it up. I'm sure she had a good reason for being away so long."

"A little too good. Drake, do you mind if I ask you a question about the multiverse?"

"It's what I'm here for," said Drake, smiling.

"What would it mean if there was only one version of

someone? I mean, one version in the entire multiverse?"

"Well," Drake said, walking in front of his terminal and stroking his goatee in a scientifically thoughtful fashion. "I honestly have no idea."

"Could it happen?"

"No. Or at least, it's not supposed to. It's a textbook fact that everyone has at least one counterpart."

"But what if there was a fluke?"

"Like a person being a dimension?"

"Good point. But hypothetically, what if it did happen?"

"There are some things that only exist in absolutely one place in the multiverse, but they're the most powerful things imaginable. Zarcadmium's magic, for instance, seems to be completely unique."

Franklin nodded. "So this hypothetical person would have to be rather powerful."

"I would assume so. But there are so many parallels of every dimension that it seems virtually impossible."

"Or maybe just very improbable."

Franklin couldn't understand it. Zarcadmium built robots, not people. Helena was certainly a lot more than a robot. How could Zarcadmium have made such a technological leap, going from HR120s to Helena Kathryn? And as vast as the multiverse was, as many times as Corvadia was probably destroyed, how was Zarcadmium the only version of himself to have thought of it?

"What is this about, Dr. Bryce?" Drake asked.

"I wish I could tell you. It's . . . a secret. But thanks for your help."

"No problem. But when you get mysterious, I get nervous. You still have two first names, in case you've forgotten. You aren't planning anything crazy, are you?"

"No," Franklin laughed. "And William was right—Interdimensional eBay is out of the question. The cheapest power I found was $3000, and all it did was turn hard rockers into country music fans. I guess I got a little carried away."

"That's understandable. But just remember, you're only human. No matter how knowledgeable either of us gets about the multiverse, that's something you and I will always have working against us."

"Then how did you beat a lava man single-handedly?" Franklin asked.

Drake smiled. "That's *my* little secret."

Franklin chuckled and stood in front of one of the larger screens. It pictured the three environmentalists who had been killed. They were all grown men, each looking between thirty and forty years old.

"So about these murders," Franklin started.

"I told you, I'm looking into it."

Franklin looked back at Drake. His smile was gone.

"You think it was Helena," Franklin said.

"Hasn't it crossed your mind? Considering what she did to those HR120s, and just yesterday. . . ."

"Are you sure they were all HR120s?"

Drake hesitated. "No," he said after a few seconds. "That's kind of why I didn't want you involved."

"Have you confirmed that at least *one* of them is an HR120?"

"No. None of them were on my list, but that isn't saying much. To know for sure, I'd have to examine one."

Franklin rubbed his forehead and closed his eyes for a second. "If we knew they were HR120s, then she'd—"

"Then she'd technically be doing you a favor. I know. But what if she's just targeting environmentalists and hoping to nail a few HR120s along the way?"

"Helena wouldn't do that."

"Helena doesn't know what we know—what Zarcadmium is planning. But she does know they have a vested interest in her, and she knows it's hurting the people close to her. So she's pushing against them, and pushing hard. And there's always the possibility it's one of her personalities doing the pushing."

"So what if it is her? What do we do about it?"

"You and I both know I couldn't hope to stop her, no matter how lucky I am. So believe me when I say there isn't much we can do, at least about her. But these murders give me an idea. What we need is an HR120."

Franklin's eyes grew. "And you thought *I* was the one with the crazy plans."

"If we could get a hold of a dead HR120, I might be able to find some weakness against them. We know that they malfunction sometimes, which means their design is flawed somewhere. I might also be able to access the positronic brain and get some specifics about Zarcadmium's plans."

"How, exactly, do you plan on getting one?"

"I don't know. First, I have to find out if any of the men who were murdered are really HR120s. If one of them was, I can probably get a hold of it."

"You're going to try and steal a body?"

"Believe me. If the police found an HR120, they'd be glad to see it missing. The less evidence of robots masquerading as people, the better for them. In their eyes, the more help we give the government in covering up these sorts of things, the better."

Franklin shook his head. “Wouldn’t life be easier if everyone would just admit that beings from other dimensions are all over the Earth?”

“Probably, in the long run,” Drake said. “But you’d certainly have a lot more business.”

CHAPTER 26

Playing With Lava

BETHANY SAT AT HER DESK JUST OUTSIDE FRANKLIN'S OFFICE, FILING HER NAILS. She always seemed to be doing that, and Franklin wondered how someone's nails could possibly stay so long after being constantly chipped away like that. Franklin said hello and then stood there, staring at his office door.

"She's in there waiting for you," Bethany said.

"I know," said Franklin.

"I thought you were taking some time off."

"This isn't a therapy session. I just need to talk to Helena."

"Oh." Bethany put the nail file down and picked up a comic book. On the cover, some colorful, caped superhero Franklin didn't recognize dangled another caped character over the side of a building. "Then I guess I shouldn't bill her for this one. Oh, wait. Helena doesn't actually pay for her therapy bills, does she? She just saves your life occasionally, and you call it good."

"Bethany, your job is in no way affected by whether a patient pays or not, so why do you care?"

"If you don't start making better business sense, we're all going to be out of jobs. Helena's got multiple personalities, right? So the way I see it, she's not just one patient; she's seven. Not only should she be paying, but she should be paying seven times the normal amount. Plus physical and emotional damage fees for all the times one of her personalities has gone crazy and tried to kill someone."

"I'm a therapist, not a lawyer."

"Good thing, too. You'd make an awful lawyer."

Franklin reached for the door handle and then stopped again.

"Since when do you read comic books?"

"The last thing I want is to look like the stereotypical, air-headed secretary," Bethany said. Then she popped a bubble with her gum.

Franklin walked into his office and was surprised to find that Helena was seated comfortably, also chewing a piece of bubble gum.

"Tracy?" Franklin said.

"How's it hanging?" Tracy said, propping her feet up on the table. Franklin took a seat at his desk. He glanced at his calendar and saw three appointments from the day before that he had missed. One of them was a new patient, Thakroid Mastyar, who had an extreme addiction to invisibility because of his fear that no one ever noticed him anyway. For the first time, Franklin felt guilty about ignoring his responsibilities. No matter how he justified it to Caslom, William, and Drake, there were other people besides Helena who needed his help. And now, it was likely he would never see Thakroid Mastyar, a man who truly needed his help, again.

Franklin took a deep breath and tried not to look distracted. "Tracy, I really need to talk with Helena."

"Can't help you," Tracy said. "Helena doesn't want to see you."

"What?" said Franklin.

"To be honest, we're all a little freaked out. The way Helena ripped apart those robots. . . . She was totally scary."

"I know. But this is important."

Tracy stared off into space for a minute, chewing her gum loudly and obnoxiously. Franklin wondered how, exactly, the personality of a cheerleader figured into the plan for Helena taking over the world.

"She's afraid to take control again," Tracy said. "She says she's afraid of hurting someone."

Did that mean she was responsible for the deaths of those human environmentalists? "Tell her I understand. Nothing has changed between us."

Tracy stared off into space again, looking almost bored. She rolled her eyes and bobbed her head back and forth. "Jeez, she is so wordy sometimes. Okay, Helena says she knows the question you want to ask. She's been watching the news, which is extremely boring, by the way. The answer is no. She didn't do it. Someone else killed those guys."

That was good news, assuming Tracy wasn't covering for Helena or one of the others. But that left Franklin without any leads on the murders and whether or not the victims had been HR120s. For now, there was only one thing left to do.

William was right. Franklin desperately needed a drink.

Franklin and William sat at a triangular table watching four gold and silver, scantily clad Broxite dancers. Green, red, and purple lights flickered spastically around them as they did a strange routine to a foreign kind of music that sounded a lot like techno, only it used a lot of cowbell. They danced on the small stage in the center of Krawkson Klub, while Franklin and William were in a secluded corner at the farthest end of the club. At least it was as secluded as it could possibly be in a nightclub that was always packed, since it was always night in the pocket dimension.

William applauded as one of the dancers did a back flip over another, then disappeared and reappeared right in front of the other three. It was the kind of dance that could only be done by a select few species, partly because it involved a fair amount of teleporting, but mostly because people often found themselves doubling over in laughter listening to Broxite music.

But Franklin hardly noticed the music or the dancers. His mind was trapped in a darker, less psychedelic place.

"I've lost it," Franklin said.

"What?" William yelled, holding back a chuckle. "I can't hear you over the cowbell."

Franklin raised his voice. "I said I've lost it."

"Lost what?" William yelled, cupping his hands around his mouth.

Franklin frowned, annoyed. "My *mind*!"

William shook his head. "Things are just hectic. Relax a little, and you'll be fine. Okay, so Helena might be evil . . . but she probably doesn't know it. And look on the bright side. At least Lera's back to ward off Zarcadmium's robotic minions."

"Yes, I know." But even Lera had become a problem. Franklin had no idea what he would say to her when he got home that night, but he was more worried about what else she might say, or more to the point, what information she might divulge.

"Is something else going on I don't know about?" William asked. "I don't mean to be insensitive, but shouldn't you almost be used to these weird surprises? They've become almost a matter of course."

One of the Broxite women—a silver one—suddenly materialized on top of William and Franklin's table. Franklin jerked back in surprise, and the woman smiled at him seductively, her red eyes blazing. Franklin flashed her a look of irritation and she snarled at him.

"There is something else," Franklin said once the silver dancer had disappeared and reappeared back on stage in a one-armed handstand. "It's Lera."

"Did something happen to her while she was away?"

"I don't know. Maybe. She told me things . . . things she didn't seem comfortable saying."

"What sorts of things?"

"The kind that aren't anyone else's business. I can't really talk about specifics. But I don't think she would have said what she did if something hadn't happened to her. Maybe she's possessed."

"By what? A being that makes you tell the truth all the time, thus ruining your entire life?"

"You're right. It's crazy."

"No. Actually, there's a being that does that. It's called a Hikstip. It's from Repsothia."

"Oh. Well, I guess she could have picked one up on accident. She did go to a lot of dimensions while she was away. . . ."

William slumped back in his chair, suddenly looking very disturbed. "We've made a big mistake," he said.

"What are you talking about?"

"Remember that spell we did the other day, when we tried to give you temporary persuasion powers? The one Chirok finally told us only worked on *Verullians*. . . . What, uh . . . what if we actually did it right?"

Franklin took a drink of his Threpnoidian Dragonfly. A very long drink. "Oh, hell," he said quietly. Even over the Broxite techno, William could tell what Franklin had said. He nodded in agreement.

"But it wears off, right?"

"Yes. Chirok said it would only work for a couple of days. But what if I still have it when I get home?"

"Has she hidden anything of yours, recently?" William asked.

"That's not funny. I *violated* her." Franklin was still angry that Lera had kept her occupation from him, but he knew that someone in her position was required to keep secrets. Now he wished that he hadn't found out, at least in the way he had.

"You didn't do it on purpose. She showed up at a really inopportune time. Just tell her what happened."

"I'll talk to her tonight."

"In the meantime, try not to think about it. Or Helena. Or robots. Or work."

"What else is there to think about?"

"Gold and silver girls, obviously."

Franklin shook his head, intentionally looking away from the Broxite dancers. Going out for drinks was his idea, but doing it at Krawkson Klub during Psychedelic Dance Hour was William's.

"Sometimes I wonder what made you ever decide on psychology as a profession," Franklin said.

William smiled a devilish smile. "Let's just say that my counseling methods are a little different from yours."

When the dance routine was over, the Broxites disappeared, the music ended, and the club returned to its usual, dimly-lit atmosphere. Some unfamiliar hard rock music played, softer than the techno, and it was sung in some annoying language in which every word began and ended with the letter *T*.

Franklin and William had been drinking together quietly for a while when, all of the sudden, Franklin's feet felt very hot. He leaned down under the table and found that his shoes were melting. He pulled them off in a panic, careful not to touch the burning liquid that had melted them and was flowing across the ground. He lifted his feet onto his chair and wrapped his arms around his knees. After looking at Franklin, baffled, William glanced down and then had much the same reaction, although the liquid hadn't quite reached his feet yet.

"Is it Lava Hour or something?" said Franklin.

"If it is, I'm finding a new club," William said. "Where's it coming from?"

They followed a short trail of lava with their eyes, and it led to a larger, octagonal-shaped table closer to the stage. But specifically, it was coming from under the chair of an enormous, conspicuous-looking, seven-foot-tall lava man who had no drink and appeared to have brought his own chair. He was a Draxan—Lera had told Franklin a lot about them—but he had never met one before. The lava man's chair was far larger than the rest and seemed to be made of some sort of fireproof metal.

The Draxan turned to see Franklin and William, smiled hospitably, and tipped his black-rimmed hat, which was, naturally, also fireproof. He motioned for them to come over to his table, and Franklin and William complied. Franklin wasn't in the habit of declining an offer from a man who didn't need a match or a lighter to burn him alive, and apparently, neither was William.

"Greetings, gentlemen," the lava man said as he placed three poker chips in the center of the table. He held five playing cards in his black, gloved hands, and Franklin noticed a bit of smoke coming from the tips of them. It wouldn't be such a loss if the cards were to completely burn up, Franklin noted to himself. The monster had a very lousy hand.

"My name is Requarr," said the lava man. "Sorry about your

shoes."

"That's all right. I've got more."

"I'm a lava man," said Requarr.

"Funny," said William, "that was my second guess." Requarr suddenly looked less friendly, and William tried to look less sarcastic.

Franklin decided to try to break the ice. He introduced William and himself. "I've never seen you here before," he said.

"I'm new to this dimension. Grapzoth here told me about this club and invited me here to play cards."

Grapzoth was a Vaklock beast who sat across from Requarr, dealing cards. He smiled and waved a huge, clawed and furry hand at William and Franklin. Two other enormous gentlemen sat at the table, and both were species Franklin wasn't familiar with. One of them looked like a gigantic carrot, only his skin color was bright red and he wore a black necktie even though he didn't really have a neck. But also similarly to a carrot, he had no limbs. His cards hovered just above the table in front of him. Either his arms and hands were actually invisible, or he was using some form of telekinesis. The other player was literally a mammoth of a man. He sat upright, but he had gray and blue fur and huge tusks coming out of his mouth.

"Would you gentlemen care to join our game?" Requarr asked.

"Sure," Franklin and William said in unison. If they had said no, they would have been refusing not one enormous creature of terror, but four, each with his own unique ability to destroy virtually anything or anyone.

"Deal these two in, Broff," Requarr said to the giant carrot man. Broff growled something in his own language that rattled the floor beneath them. He dealt the cards, either invisibly or with his mind, and two stacks of poker chips slid across the table, one in front of Franklin, and another in front of William.

Franklin and William exchanged nervous glances. What was the proper way to play cards with these kinds of creatures? Draxans were known for their destructive tendencies, although Franklin hadn't expected them to be as polite as Requarr was. And Vaklock beasts generally ate humanoids as a regular part of their diet. Franklin was especially unsure about what to do, since he had been dealt a royal flush. Sometimes bad luck worked in mysterious ways.

They placed bets and began to play. No one had mentioned exactly what kind of poker they were playing, but Franklin wasn't about to ask. Broff, the carrot man, dropped two cards and drew two more. On his turn, William asked for three more cards, and Broff obliged. The game seemed to be five-card draw, which was good, because it was one of only two types of poker Franklin had played before. The Vaklock and the mammoth man both took one card. Requarr growled, burned up three cards in his hands, and took three more.

Now Franklin understood why there were a dozen more decks of cards sitting next to the carrot man.

"So, Requarr," Franklin said, knowing it was his turn and feeling entirely uncertain as to what the best course of action was. What would be least offensive to four card-playing monsters? Beating them at poker or trying not to? He said, "You said this was your first time in our dimension. What brings you here?"

Requarr smiled. "You're stalling," he said. Franklin swallowed, slowly. "Play first. The answer will be forthcoming."

"All right," said Franklin. He looked at Broff. "No cards."

The Vaklock and mammoth man shot terrifying glances at Franklin. He wanted to take it back, but he was sitting right next to Requarr, who could cook him to a golden brown in seconds.

"Have you ever bluffed a lava man before, Dr. Bryce?" Requarr asked.

"No."

"Good. Then this should be interesting. And to answer your question, I'm here because it's the wrong season in Drax."

"The wrong season . . . for what?"

"Hunting."

Franklin was sweating profusely, but he couldn't decide if that was because he was frightened of Requarr or merely because he was sitting next to him. "What do you come here for? Deer?"

"No," said Requarr. "Robots. I hear this is the perfect time for robot-hunting in your dimension."

Franklin and William made eye contact again. The Vaklock beast bet ten and the mammoth man raised him five.

Franklin hesitated, but he knew there was one question he absolutely had to ask, no matter the risk. "Have you . . . have you already started? Hunting, I mean."

"Yes, but no luck yet," said Requarr. "I'm hunting an especially powerful type of robot. Very strong, very fast. They're called HR120s. I got a tip that they were posing as various members of environmental groups. I took a few environmentalists out, just to see if I might get lucky, but it was a no-go. Lots of blood, but no wires. I'm going to try a new approach tomorrow."

Franklin's heart sank in his chest. Helena really hadn't killed those men. It was Requarr. And the worst part was, they were *all* human, and Requarr didn't care. The whole thing was a sport for him, no matter who died.

"Well, good luck," Franklin said, playing dumb and hoping that Requarr couldn't read the horror on his face. "I hope you find some. Personally, I didn't even know there were any robots here. How did you find out about them?"

"My ex told me. She's a Verullian. She recently dropped in at my home, Drax, to say hello."

Franklin felt as though reality was slipping away from him. How could everything go so incredibly wrong? He wasn't even anywhere in the multiverse, he decided. Sometime in the last week, he had just gone straight to hell, and he had the lava man to prove it.

"What's her last name?" Franklin asked, quietly.

"I wouldn't know," Requarr said. He seemed a little suspicious of the question. "Seems every time I turn around she's remarried again." Requarr saw the last bet and looked back at Franklin.

Franklin had no idea what he was going to do once the game was over, but he had gotten himself into something he certainly had to finish.

"I fold," Franklin said.

CHAPTER 28

Let's Kill Robots

LERA WAS SITTING ON THE LEATHER COUCH IN THE LIVING ROOM, STILL WEARING THE SAME TWO-PIECE BLACK OUTFIT SHE HAD BEEN WEARING EARLIER AND STARING AT THE WALL AS SHE OFTEN DID. But Franklin was fairly certain she wasn't playing Veritzu. She had a far more distant, less focused expression on her face. Lera was lost in thought, and Franklin guessed she had probably been that way for several hours.

"How are you?" Franklin asked, sitting beside her. He wasn't sure what else to say, and he was still uncertain as to whether his powers of persuasion had worn off.

"How do you think?" said Lera, still looking at the wall. "I can't believe you made me tell you all of that."

"I didn't mean to."

Lera's entire body began to glow red. That only ever happened in one of two situations, and judging by the look on her face, Franklin guessed it wasn't the fun, unmentionable-in-public kind of glow.

"Don't think I didn't recognize the spell, Franklin. It was Verullian."

"I know."

"So you *accidentally* did a persuasion spell that only works on Verullians."

"It wasn't for you," said Franklin. He explained how he had gotten the spell from Rajel Chirok in order to get answers out of Stephen Zarcadmium. "I didn't know it wouldn't work on him."

"You expect me to believe that?"

"I'd have thought your intuition would have told you I'm not lying."

Lera's tension slacked a little. "The spell seems to have worn off, but my intuition is a little glitchy. Verullian spells can have that side effect. You haven't told anyone? About my job, I mean."

"No, I wouldn't do that. But you should have told me."

"I couldn't. In fact, now that you know, I'm supposed to kill you. But I think I can persuade the Bureau to make an exception."

"Good. I've got enough people trying to kill me right now. I promise to keep your secret."

"Thank you."

"Why does Verullia even have an interdimensional investigation bureau?"

"Verullia is a lot like the United States. It's one of the most powerful dimensions in the multiverse, so our government thinks it's our job to police everyone else."

"We obviously have a lot to talk about, but now isn't the time. There are a couple of things you need to know." Franklin hesitated for a moment. A part of him thought that the last person who should know about Helena's part in Zarcadmium's plan was a secret government agent. But Lera was his wife, and the last thing Franklin needed was more secrets. Besides, he was fairly certain that the entire dimension of Verullia couldn't take Helena on.

Lera raised an eyebrow and scoffed.

"What?" said Franklin.

"Zarcadmium is going to use Helena in a plan for world domination."

"How did you know? Did the Bureau figure it out?"

"No. Like I said, my intuition is cutting in and out. But what I don't get is, if he's going to use someone as powerful as Helena, why go after one little planet? I really would have expected *dimensional* domination at least."

"It's still a problem, Lera."

"I know, I know. And Helena hasn't found out?"

"No, and she didn't kill those environmentalists. Your ex-lava-man is in town. Did you know he's a robot hunter?"

"Of course I did. That's why I invited him here."

"*Lera*!" Franklin snapped. "They weren't HR120s he killed! He's killing people."

"He . . . enjoys that, too," Lera said. She backed away from Franklin a bit. "The Bureau's paying him to take out HR120s . . . but I didn't think he'd go after humans. The Bureau wanted to distance Helena from the HR120s—it was obvious they had hostile intentions. I was instructed to take any measures to do that."

"Your plan's turning out to be a little counter-productive." Franklin scribbled an address on a piece of paper and handed it to Lera. "Can you contact him?"

"Sure, but—"

"Do it. Have him meet me at that address. Tell him I want to meet him for another poker game."

"You played poker with a lava man? Wow. . . . Franklin, you went off and got a spine while I was gone." She looked at the address Franklin gave her. "Isn't this in the middle of nowhere?"

"Tell him there's an aperture to a pocket dimension there. Another club."

"I really think you're over-reacting."

"Lera, why did you divorce him?"

She hesitated. "He burned up one of my favorite cities."

"I'm not over-reacting."

"So what are you going to do? Give him a therapy session?"

"No, I'm going to call Drake and then we're going to make him stop."

"Is there something I could do to help?"

"No," Franklin said darkly. "I think you've done plenty already."

Franklin and Dr. Drake stood in front of an abandoned shack, waiting for Requarr. They were in a large field, away from the road, with few trees and no power lines. Franklin shivered as a winter breeze blew past them. He was banking on Drake's trophy being enough evidence that he could really beat the lava man.

But since he had no idea as to how Drake had done it the first time, Franklin had his doubts. He had borrowed a portable pocket dimension aperture from Vlakdormat security just in case, but he would only use it as a last resort. The last thing Vlakdormat wanted was to hold a lava man against his will. The Draxan government wouldn't take kindly to that, and it would cause far more casualties than Requarr had already inflicted.

"Good to see you again, Dr. Bryce," Requarr said as he made his way up the hill a few hundred feet from Franklin and Drake. "Imagine my surprise when I learned that you were married to my ex-wife. Small multiverse, I suppose."

"I hope that doesn't bother you."

"On the contrary. You strike me as a good man, for a human. I hope we can become better friends. So, where is this aperture Lera spoke of?"

"There is no aperture," said Franklin, crossing his arms. "You're at the end of the line."

"What is this? Did I offend you in some way back at the club?"

"I was more offended by the three people you murdered."

"Ah. Then you probably won't appreciate the fact that I killed two more on my way here. I saw a couple recycling aluminum cans and figured I'd better take them out, just in case."

Franklin boldly stepped forward, almost forgetting what Requarr could do to him if he really wanted to. "How can you throw life away like that?"

"I'm made of lava," said Requarr. "I throw away life without even knowing about it. Plus, your kind lives about an eighth of the Draxan average lifespan. Not a big loss to me."

Franklin whispered to Drake. "Are you sure you can do this?"

"Absolutely," Drake said. "You're about to witness the true luck of having the same two first names. Do you want me to kill him?"

"No," Franklin said, taken aback. Drake seemed rather sure of himself. "Not if you don't have to. Just scare him—make him go back to his dimension."

Drake nodded and stood in a fighting stance in the tall grass in front of Requarr.

"What is this?" said Requarr, sizing up Drake, who was tall by human standards, but still puny by Draxan standards.

"I might not look like much," said Drake, "but when this is all over, your lava buddies are going to write a song about this day.

They'll call it *Requiem for Requarr.*"

"No," came a new voice. Helena stood behind Drake and moved toward Requarr. "Let me handle this."

"How did she do that?" said Requarr.

"Helena, please," Drake said, "I can handle this."

How had she even known they were here? She had proven that she was capable of simply willing herself to wherever Franklin was, but why now? How did she know what he was up to?

Helena shook her head. "I'm sorry, Dr. Drake, but this is something I have to do." She pushed Drake out of the way and faced off against the lava man.

"This should be interesting," Requarr said.

He shot an enormous wave of lava at Helena, who immediately teleported into thin air. Drake rolled out of the lava's way. Once he was standing up, he went back to Franklin by the shack.

"She's insane," Drake said.

"From where I'm standing," said Franklin, "she's got a better shot than you do."

"I'm not even going to try fighting him now. With Helena here, my luck probably won't even work."

Helena reappeared behind the lava man. She lifted her arms and rose a few feet above the ground. Requarr turned around just in time to see her legs impact his face. Requarr went straight to the ground.

"Did she just. . . ?"

"Yes, Franklin," said Drake. "Helena just drop-kicked a lava man." Of course, Helena's legs were on fire, so she teleported again. When she reappeared, this time standing over Requarr, who was still lying on the ground, the fire was gone.

"Give up yet?" she asked.

"What *are* you?" Requarr said, astonished.

"I don't know, but people ask me that a lot. Most of them are people I've beaten in fights."

But Requarr wasn't finished. He jumped up from the ground and tackled Helena, but when he rolled toward Franklin, Franklin could tell that Helena had teleported out of Requarr's grasp.

"Are you noticing a pattern here?" said Helena, floating a dozen feet above him. It was strange for Franklin to see her fly. She had only done that once before, at City Hall with Flastcaster.

Requarr let out an angry growl. He shot two thick streams of lava downward from both arms, propelling him up like he was riding on a fountain. He rose higher and higher, but Helena effortlessly stayed above him. She was toying with him. He shot gobs of lava up at her, but she easily dodged them. Finally, Helena shot toward him like a bullet. She then sped around him in a blur, and Franklin couldn't make out what was happening.

After a moment, Helena was gone again. The lava man screamed in agony as he fell several stories to the ground below. Helena appeared next to him, nursing a nasty burn on her hand. Anyone else's hand would have turned to ash.

Lying at Helena's feet was one of Requarr's arms. Helena looked around, seeing that the whole field had caught fire. She sped around the area in a circle and was a blur again. Soon, the fire was gone. Helena stood next to the lava man once again.

"You're finished," Helena said.

"It'll grow back," said Requarr.

Helena smiled. "How long will that take?"

Requarr didn't answer.

"So do we keep fighting?" Helena asked. "Risk you losing the other one?"

Requarr cradled the stump where his arm used to be and looked at the severed limb, smoldering on the ground. "What do you want?" he said.

"I've been following you," said Helena. "You're good, but there's no missing a seven-foot-tall lava man. Once I saw you taking a stroll in the business district, it didn't take long to figure out who was behind the killings. Then I followed you here and found out my friends had also discovered you. The difference between us is that they want you to leave. I don't."

Franklin felt sick. What was she doing?

"I have a proposition. You're probably not used to being at someone else's mercy, so I'll make this simple. Help me find and destroy HR120s, and *only* HR120s, and I'll let you live. Kill any more humans, and you're a dead lava man. Or, you can go back where you came from, forget about your hunt and never bother this dimension again."

Requarr sat up and looked at her with contempt. "How do I know you won't kill me anyway?"

"Because I'm not like you. I only kill if I have to. The HR120s, for instance, have to be destroyed." She looked at Franklin and Drake. "My friends' lives depend on it."

She and Requarr stared at each other for a long time. Finally, Requarr spoke.

"My arm will grow back in a day. Then . . . we'll kill robots."

CHAPTER 28

Real Power

FRANKLIN KNEW HE SHOULDN'T HAVE EATEN THAT BURRITO. Not because it gave him heartburn or gas, but because he had bought it at a fast food place in the Traldor dimension. Drive-thru food in his own dimension was often bad enough, but Traldorian fast food was famous—and, in some cases, infamous—for temporarily bestowing unusual abilities on its devourers. (Something about the grease, apparently.) Of course, this was the precise reason Franklin had tried the burrito. But now, as a result, a strange and somewhat unfashionable gold and silver circular symbol about two inches in diameter had formed on his forehead.

It was the day after he had eaten the burrito, and Franklin had been at work for three hours, avoiding everyone he could. He knew he would lose the symbol on his forehead eventually because every fast food restaurant in Traldor made it their top priority to ensure that the powers their food gave were temporary, in order to avoid unwanted lawsuits. But he hoped it would wear off sooner rather than later, because every person who looked at the symbol was flashed by a beam of light and was blinded for several minutes. It wasn't the most desirable superpower for a therapist to have.

Franklin had tried everything he could think of to be ready for an attack by the HR120s. He didn't know when it would happen, but considering recent events, Franklin was certain that it would be soon. Aware of Zarcadmium's involvement but not of his plans for her, Helena was out every day with Requarr, hunting HR120s. But that didn't do much to relieve Franklin's worry. He didn't trust Requarr, who had no regard for human life and was only helping Helena to ensure his own survival.

Jesse Barnes walked into Franklin's office for his third therapy session. He had sought Franklin's services because he was unprepared for the sizable interdimensional portal that had been appearing regularly for the last few weeks in the middle of his basement. This was, of course, a pretty routine case for Franklin. Portals were found in all kinds of places, but for whatever reason, the basements of regular people with no knowledge of the multiverse were quite common.

What was uncommon about Barnes—a young, tall, and well-built Eagle Scout in his early twenties—was that he wasn't so concerned about the portal itself or about the occasional three-headed Quaxor that came out of it, but he was more concerned about the fact that he hadn't seen it coming. Being a life-long, knot-tying, uniform-wearing, motto-quoting Boy Scout, Barnes prided himself on being prepared for absolutely everything. Even now, as he was temporarily blinded by the freakish symbol on Franklin's forehead, Barnes was putting on a pair of sunglasses.

"I think this is going to be my last session," Barnes said, rubbing his temples. He was obviously unhappy, but Franklin could tell that it wasn't because of the portal, or because of the headache. Barnes had the look of a man trying to get a refund for something at Wal-Mart without the receipt.

"What's the problem? Has the portal disappeared?" Franklin asked.

"No, it's still popping up. I'm actually starting to get used to it. Thought I might put in a karaoke bar and try to make some money on the side."

"The Quaxors do love their karaoke."

"But I've had to get used to this whole thing on my own.

You've been almost no help whatsoever."

Franklin froze. "Really?"

"You came highly recommended by some other Scouts who have been involved with these sorts of things. But you haven't delivered."

"We've only had three sessions."

"Because you've cancelled half of them."

"I don't like to talk about my private life with my patients, but I've been having . . . robot problems."

"Word gets around, Dr. Bryce. I've heard the rumors."

"From whom?"

"It's a big lobby. Doctors, techs, patients . . . everyone is talking. What you're in the middle of is huge. You've got robot problems, lava problems, multiple personality patient problems, big magical cloud problems—and I have no idea what that one's about. If what people are saying is true, you've brought so much of this stuff *here* that this place probably won't be around much longer. And I doubt there's a Boy Scout alive who's prepared for what's coming."

Barnes stood up and placed a small, brown rectangular package on Franklin's desk. He put an arm on Franklin's shoulder. "Your check's in there, as well as a gift. It might come in handy."

Barnes gave Franklin a faint smile and left. Franklin closed his eyes for a few seconds. He wondered if there was something more he could have done. He wondered, as he often did, if telepathy might have solved the problem. But as he opened his eyes again and picked up the package Barnes had left him, he realized the problem wasn't his therapeutic advice. It was the lifestyle he had been forced into. Franklin now had two jobs.

Staying alive had become a full-time occupation, and there was barely enough time for the other. He had been doing both so long that it felt like he was only pretending to be a therapist so he could hide in a building with a positronic deactivation switch.

Franklin opened the package, and inside was a copy of the Boy Scout Handbook. Barnes was right. Franklin didn't know how merit badges and canoeing would help, but the message got through. He had to be prepared for what was coming, and he couldn't do that without being completely devoted to preparation. Until the HR120 problem was solved, he couldn't do his job.

"Another one bites the dust, huh Dr. Bryce?" came the voice of Franklin's secretary over the loud speaker.

"What is it, Bethany?"

"I wasn't supposed to bother you until your session was over, but since Mr. Barnes just left. . . . And by the way, that's the third one you've lost this week, in case you're keeping score. . . ."

"Bethany—"

"It's Dr. Caslom. He wants to see you as soon as possible. It sounds important."

This could only be about one thing: Helena. And considering how good news seemed to be recently, Franklin knew he wasn't going to like whatever Caslom had to say.

He reluctantly put a navy blue and black striped stocking cap over his forehead to hide his new, less-than-fashionable superpower. The hat didn't go with his suit and it looked completely unprofessional, but his boss was the last person he wanted to blind. And it didn't look nearly as stupid as an Eagle Scout in full uniform wearing sunglasses indoors.

Franklin stepped into Dr. Caslom's elongated office where the accordion-like Makverian took up an entire end of his conference table, looking especially contemplative. Caslom held out one of his slinky arms, motioning for Franklin to take a seat across from him. Caslom was generally lighthearted, or as lighthearted as anyone running a major psychiatric facility could be, but now he looked as serious as Franklin had ever seen him, maybe even a little uncomfortable. With no one else in the room, Franklin sat exactly in the middle of the table so he could make direct eye contact with Caslom.

"Franklin," Dr. Caslom started, but then he looked at the ceiling and took a deep breath. "I make hard decisions every day," he finally said.

"Yes," said Franklin, waiting for Caslom to elaborate. He didn't. Franklin nodded nervously, unsure of what else he should say to that.

"I've thought about it. It's really all I've thought about. But Zarcadmium and now the lava man, I just. . . . Do you remember when life was simpler?"

"You mean when robots weren't trying to kill me, and my patients actually had pasts?"

"Exactly."

"Vaguely," Franklin said.

"I've been here a long time, Franklin, and I've seen a lot of strange things. To most of our patients, I'm one of those strange things."

"Well, it's like you always say, normal is a four-letter word."

"By the way, are stocking caps fashionable indoors now? Was there a memo I missed?" Caslom was staring at Franklin's hat.

"Long story. Suffice it to say, you wouldn't like it very much if I took it off."

"People don't realize what all goes on here," Caslom said,

returning to the topic at hand, although Franklin still wasn't entirely sure what that topic was. "They don't know that our jobs can be more dangerous than anything. Sometimes running Vlakdormat is like bungee-jumping into a volcano. But despite rival interdimensional cultures and lawsuits and bizarre, non-exchangeable foreign currencies, I have never turned away a patient who was here because she sincerely wanted help. Nor have I turned anyone away who has saved my life and the lives of everyone in this facility . . . on more than one occasion."

"But you're going to now," said Franklin.

"What choice do I have? You and I both know how dangerous she is."

"What about what you said to Crill, that the danger doesn't matter? What about what you told me the day you hired me? We take every precaution in order to help anyone who wants it."

"But if what Chirok said is true," Caslom said, "Helena may turn on us. Dr. Drake tells me the HR120s could attack, and if that happens. . . . What if she joins them?"

"We need her. If the HR120s attack, she's the only person I know of who can stop them."

"Yes, and if she isn't on our side, or if one of her other personalities takes over at the wrong moment, she could kill us all, backed up by an army of robots. I hate this. You must know I don't want this any more than you do."

Franklin got up and stood next to the door. "It's not her fault."

"I know that. But despite what she has done for us, Helena may be more weapon than woman."

Franklin narrowed his eyes and burned a deep stare into Caslom. "You don't know anything."

"I know as much as you do. Helena has no past. She's part of some world domination plot. And she can be turned off, like an HR120. We can't even tell her what Zarcadmium is planning because it might turn her into some sort of time-bomb."

"Helena is *not* an HR120."

"No, she's something much worse. Vlakdormat has survived every danger it has ever faced, but this is different. No one in the multiverse has ever seen anything like her. And now she is in league with a lava man."

"He's under her control, sir. He was killing human beings. Helena struck a deal with him to save lives."

"Yes, and now they're killing HR120s."

"I'm not seeing the problem here. . . ."

"Helena is only escalating the conflict. By going on the offensive, she is making things worse for us. Zarcadmium will attack Vlakdormat as soon as possible now because she's depleting his forces."

"I think they're going to attack very soon, anyway, because we know too much about Helena. And when that happens—"

"When that happens, Helena will be nowhere near here. At least, if she'll agree to it. Look, I obviously can't force her to do anything. But I have to do what I can to protect Vlakdormat."

"You're making a mistake."

"Maybe. I want you to know that I don't blame you for what's happening. She's your patient, and you couldn't have known. . . ."

"Thanks. But she's not my patient anymore. Now she's just a liability. And don't worry—I won't tell Helena that she's the lead horseman of the apocalypse. *That* would really be suicide."

Caslom started to say something more, but Franklin was

already rushing out the door. Later that day, Caslom would ask Helena to leave Vlakdormat, and Franklin knew she would agree. She had done a lot of questionable things lately, but Franklin still believed that Helena cared about all of them. And without her, Vlakdormat was doomed.

Franklin and Lera sat at their kitchen table, eating dinner together for the third time that week, which was nice because Franklin had hated eating by himself while she was away, and the cooking at Vlakdormat was nothing compared with Lera's hundreds of years of culinary experience. But eating with her was also awkward.

Lera couldn't lie about her job anymore, nor could she deny responsibility for the deaths of half a dozen humans killed by Requarr, since she had personally invited him to eliminate the HR120s. She couldn't deny it. Not that Lera felt guilty about those deaths; she just couldn't deny it because it had really happened. Since she had come home, Franklin was breaking inside, realizing that she wasn't the same woman he had thought he married. He didn't have the time or the room in his head to worry about that now, but when all of this was over, things weren't simply going to go back to the way they had been before.

"I started making out my will this morning," Lera said.

"Isn't your life expectancy, like, a thousand years?" said Franklin.

"Not if the world ends first. I tried to get transferred, but the VIBI is keeping me here on assignment, so I thought I'd stay on the safe side. And no, I was not leaving you the Verullian presidential statues. I know you hate those."

"Aren't you jumping the gun a little? Zarcadmium's trying

to rule the world, not destroy it."

"He's a deluded eco-terrorist, Franklin. People like him hardly make that distinction."

"Well, he's got a better chance at doing both now. Caslom-"

"It's Helena."

"I know your intuition is back to a hundred percent, but do you have to rub it in?"

"No, it's *Helena,*" Lera said again. She pointed past Franklin at the window behind him. Franklin was shocked to see Helena and Requarr ripping apart a TV repair van across the street.

"Good for them," Lera said. "I was getting tired of those guys staring at our house all the time. Although now I won't have anyone to tease. . . ."

"This isn't funny." One of the well-groomed male HR120s' heads rolled across the street. A Chihuahua yelped and ran off in the other direction.

"I'm just saying, if Helena's going to lead an army of HR120s, it's nice of her to even up the odds first," Lera said.

"I can't believe you. You're my wife. You're supposed to be on my side."

"And what side is that? The gullible, naïve one?"

"Can't you see what she's doing? She's trying to prove she wants to help."

Lera's face darkened. "Franklin, I love you, but you're an idiot. The only way Helena Kathryn can help us, and by *us* I mean the people living on Earth who would prefer it to remain in existence past this week, is to go get herself turned off again and stay that way."

"I'm sorry, Mrs. Bryce," said a new voice. "That's not going to happen."

Helena had materialized next to the table. Her red, silk shirt had a large rip at the sleeve and she had a few burns on her arm and face.

"Are you all right?" Franklin asked.

"I heal fast," Helena said. "Requarr accidentally got in the way when I hit that last robot. He felt it more than I did. Why are you wearing a hat?"

"Long story. I—" Franklin started.

"Crappy Traldorian food," Lera said. She stood up from the table and folded her arms. "I'm Lera. I've heard a lot about you. Thanks for taking care of those HR120s, but we're fresh out of medals. So why don't you go home?"

"I don't have one. Dr. Caslom asked me to leave," Helena said. She didn't sound hurt at all; she said it like it was as trivial as what she had for breakfast.

"Where are you staying?" Franklin asked, shooting Lera an angry look she didn't seem to notice.

"With Requarr, on Drax. It looks a lot like how I might have imagined hell, only with more cars and billboards. And they have ice cream, which surprised me. It'll take a while to get used to the heat, but I'll manage."

"Is Requarr outside?" Franklin asked.

"Yes. He would have come in, but that tends to leave people homeless," said Helena.

"I think I'll go say hi," Lera said. "Three seems like a bit of a crowd right now." And she left the house. Franklin motioned for Helena to take a seat at the table.

"Are you hungry?" he asked. "We have plenty of drostanya left. It's Verullian. Tastes like fish, unless you cook it in the morning, and then it tastes like bacon. It's really fascinating. . . ."

"She doesn't like me, does she?" said Helena.

"Hm?"

"Your wife."

"Oh. She . . . thinks you're evil. Don't hold it against her. A lot of people do."

"That's all right. I understand. It's just . . . she had a look. It was the same one Caslom had earlier today when he asked me to leave Vlakdormat."

"What kind of look?"

"Like they knew something I didn't. Something important."

Franklin sighed.

"Tell me," Helena said. "Tell me what's going on. Everyone's been treating me differently since the hotel. And it's not just because of what I did to those HR120s, is it? Something's about to happen. I can feel it. Please. What has everyone so afraid of me?"

"You're working with a lava man, for one."

"I need his help. The HR120s have to be stopped."

"I know. I actually thought it was a good idea, at first. But what if Caslom's right? What if you're just making it worse?"

"Everything is about to change, Franklin, and I have to do what I can. If I can find enough HR120s, I can cripple them."

"Zarcadmium will just make more."

"And I'll destroy them, too. Eventually Zarcadmium will come for me himself, and when he does, I'll be ready for him. I haven't met anything yet I couldn't kill."

Franklin had never heard Helena talk like this. Zarcadmium wanted a killer and that's just what he was getting. Was this part of her development? Build up enough blood lust, and suddenly she's leading the HR120s? Maybe it was inevitable. Or maybe Helena was just lost and alone, an ill that six other personalities and a lava man could hardly cure.

"Do what you feel is right," Franklin said. "But no matter what connection you have with Stephen Zarcadmium, you don't have to be what they want."

Lera came back inside, and Requarr stood next to the front porch, calling inside. "Good to see you again, Dr. Bryce. How've you been since our last encounter?"

A seven-foot-tall lava man standing in Franklin's front yard was a little surreal, but no more so than the pile of robot parts lying in the middle of the road surrounded by a dozen children speculating about an alien invasion. Franklin knew the police would find a way to cover this up, as well as any lava man sightings that might be reported. He wondered how long Requarr would be out in the open before reality couldn't be buried any longer—before the community was forced to accept it. But that would probably never happen, and the few people who did accept it would soon be patients at Vlakdormat. Assuming Vlakdormat lasted that long.

"Sorry about leading you into that trap before," Franklin said to Requarr. "No hard feelings, I hope."

"No, I understand. You were protecting your own. Lera was just telling me about your species' regard for life despite the fact that you don't live very long. I mean, what's the difference between thirty years and seventy? But I can respect your odd culture, especially since, if I don't, your friend Helena will rip me into so many pieces I won't be able to grow everything back."

"Thanks again for taking care of those robots for us," Lera said to Requarr. She was avoiding eye contact with Helena.

Franklin couldn't decide why Lera was treating her this way. Lera was rarely afraid of anything.

"Not a problem," Requarr said. "They were a lot easier to find once I knew that they try to kill you if you know they exist. All I have to do is walk up to a human and say, 'Pardon me. If you were an HR120, what kind of HR120 would you be?' If their arms turn into energy weapons, they're robots. If they run away screaming, they're not. Piece of cake."

That gave Franklin an idea. He looked back at Helena. "Is there a chance you could kill an HR120 but keep it intact? Drake wants to get his hands on one to study."

Helena shook her head and frowned, obviously still preoccupied with their earlier conversation. "You have to destroy the positronic brain to kill them. Bashing their skulls in is the most effective way. There wouldn't be enough left to study."

"What if you kept the head intact? It would have a hard time fighting without a body, even if it were still active."

"That wouldn't work, either," said Requarr. "Every one of their body parts turns into some kind of weapon."

"I'll work on finding a way to keep more of the brain intact," Helena said.

"We'll have plenty of chances to practice," Requarr said, reassuringly. "So anyway, Dr. Bryce. . . . What's with the hat?"

CHAPTER 29

Slight Difference

COMING OFF THE ELEVATOR THE NEXT MORNING ON HIS WAY TO HIS OFFICE, FRANKLIN MET THE LAST PERSON HE EXPECTED TO SEE THAT DAY. Or at least, the last version of that person he expected to see. It was the female version of Drake R. Drake, from Dimension 0.65. She was standing to one side of the hall, applying some lipstick. When she finished what she was doing, Franklin greeted her and they shook hands.

"I wasn't sure you'd remember me. I know your Drake looks . . . quite a bit different."

"Are you kidding? You're all William talks about."

She blushed a little, and then she rubbed her hands together and looked around excitedly. "So this is Vlakdormat in Dimension 0.1115."

"That's what our dimension is called where you're from?"

"Every dimension has its own system for naming other dimensions."

She explained why the number for Franklin's dimension had four numbers after the decimal point, and what the decimal point was for, but Franklin just nodded and smiled, which was how he often reacted to things he didn't understand. He nodded and smiled a lot.

"Are you here to see William?" Franklin asked.

"I was hoping to run into him, yes. But I was primarily looking for myself."

"Your . . . oh, the other Dr. Drake. Why?"

"I have some technical questions about a project I've been working on, and I figured the best person to ask would be myself. Plus, I've always wanted to see what I'd look like as a man."

Franklin decided to leave that particular comment alone and led the female Dr. Drake to the Unexplained Phenomena wing. When they reached the laboratory, Drake was working diligently at the main computer terminal. He was so engrossed in his work that he didn't even notice the arrival of Franklin and a female version of himself.

"Dr. Drake," said Franklin. "You have a visitor."

Drake batted the air a couple of times with his hand, keeping his head glued to the monitor. "Just . . . just give me a minute. I think I've made a breakthrough."

Franklin strode into the room and stood in front of the computer, bending over to meet Drake at eye level. "Really? About the HR120s?"

Drake was silent for a minute, but he finally looked up at Franklin. "What? No. Quantum physics."

"Oh," Franklin said, disappointed. "Anyway, this is Dr. Drake R. Drake."

The female Drake walked over and shook Drake's hand. He stood up and greeted her warmly, seeming to forget all about whatever his incredible breakthrough was. He also, to Franklin's relief, didn't seem to notice Franklin's hat.

"It's wonderful to finally meet you," Drake said. "This is quite interesting indeed. Do you notice our resemblance?"

"Like brother and sister," said Drake's counterpart. "And mannerisms. I notice you lean on your left hand when looking at the computer. I do the exact same thing."

"And do you have three freckles on your right shin?"

"Indeed. Quite fascinating. Now, I was wondering if you

could help me with something?"

"Certainly."

"I've been working on some new sensor technology to pick up certain brain wave patterns."

"I've done similar work since Helena Kathryn arrived."

Before, when Franklin had invited Drake to Dimension 0.65, Drake had seemed more than nervous about the possibility of meeting another version of himself. But now he seemed to have forgotten all about that anxiety. It had probably never occurred to him that there might be a version of him who was of the opposite gender, and it was interesting to him that they still had nearly everything in common. Whatever awkwardness that he might have expected was nonexistent.

Franklin could tell the two Drakes were about to start speaking science, so he excused himself. "I'm going to go let William know you're here," he said to the female Drake. "Why don't you stay with . . . the other you, and he'll come visit when he has a break."

"I'll just be here, seeing what incredible technological strides I've made in this dimension," she said.

After he had told William about the visitor, Franklin went back to his office, and because he had nothing better to do, he sat at his desk and brooded. Helena had been forced to move in with a lava man, and meanwhile Franklin had few patients and little patience. He knew with Helena's personalities he could never completely count on her if the HR120s were to attack, but now that she was gone completely . . . he felt about as lost as he supposed she did.

"Boss," said Bethany over the speaker. "Franklin's here."

"Franklin who?"

"Franklin *Bryce.* The one from 0.65. And he looks like he wants to punch you in the face."

The one complaint Franklin couldn't make was that his morning had been uneventful. "Send him in."

Franklin's counterpart threw open the door and stood there in the doorway, breathing heavily and looking at Franklin with contempt.

"If you want me dead," said Franklin, "or you're mad at one of my patients, you're going to have to take a number."

"You destroyed it," said the other Franklin.

"Destroyed what?"

"Vlakdormat."

Franklin surveyed the room with his eyes. "No . . . it's still here."

"*My* Vlakdormat. You brought your damned problems with you to my dimension. I went back, and there was . . . there was hardly anything left."

Franklin took off his glasses, got up from his desk, and approached his counterpart. The look on the other Franklin's face was uncannily similar to how Franklin had looked when he'd grabbed Chirok in the bread dimension. "Slow down. What happened?"

"HR120s. Somehow they neutralized the positronic deactivation switch. They burned the entire building to the ground in minutes—I couldn't get there in time. Franklin . . . no one made it out alive."

Franklin's heart skipped a beat. "But you—"

"I was on vacation in the Bramzit dimension."

Maybe learning he had two first names hadn't completely ruined the other Franklin's luck after all.

"A few people were home, off work that day. William's okay. But Drake. . . ."

His counterpart's eyes widened as he read Franklin's mind. It was a look that told Franklin that the female Dr. Drake couldn't possibly be there. "Franklin, the woman here is not her. Dr. Drake from my dimension is dead."

Franklin hit the speaker button on his desk. "Security, code 392 Alpha. Repeat: Code 392 Alpha. That's the positronic deactivation, switch in case you've forgotten. So do it now!"

"You think she's an HR120?" asked his counterpart.

"What else would she be?"

When the two Franklins made it to Drake's lab, William and the male Dr. Drake were standing back, watching the female Drake, now definitely an HR120, who had one of her robotic arms inserted into one of the computer consoles along the wall and was writhing and sparking. The switch had been activated, but it wasn't working. At least, not entirely.

"Drake?" said William. He looked at the two Franklins as they hurried into the room. "I didn't know she was a robot, I swear. She's never done this before. Not even the time I made dinner and undercooked the pot roast."

"That's not Drake," said Franklin.

"Something's wrong with the deactivation switch," said Dr. Drake. "If she's an HR120, it should have killed her instantly."

"She must have tried to neutralize it, like they did in my dimension," the other Franklin said. "Our switches probably operate a little differently, so it only partially shut her down."

"She's still conscious," said the male Drake. "She's still downloading information from that computer, but she's slowly breaking down."

"Any chance there's *not* any information about the positronic deactivation device in that computer?" Franklin asked.

They looked at each other in horror, then ran toward the malfunctioning HR120. Her other arm immediately transformed into an energy cannon, exactly like the others Franklin had faced before, and Franklin and Drake stopped in their tracks.

"Do . . . not m-move," the HR120 said, twitching as if she was being electrocuted. "W-we have . . . already . . . prevailed."

The HR120's eyes glazed over, her arm retracted from the wall, and she fell to the floor, deactivated.

"It was a test," said Franklin's counterpart. "What they did to my facility, my friends! They sent her to impersonate Drake in my dimension, learn about the switch, and deactivate it. Then they destroyed my Vlakdormat, and she came here to see if the switches were identical. To see if the methods they developed would make them immune to your switch. They only destroyed my Vlakdormat in preparation to destroy yours."

"But why?" said William. Franklin could tell William knew what all this meant, that he knew the female Drake was gone, but that he was trying to be strong. "Why not just kill and replace our Drake?"

Dr. Drake raised an eyebrow.

"I just mean they could have done the same thing here. Why did they need to use Dimension 0.65?"

"Because," said Franklin, "there wasn't anyone to stop them there. They don't have a Helena Kathryn."

Franklin, Dr. Drake, William, and Franklin's counterpart sat drinking together at an octagonal table in one of the corners of Krawkson Klub. After what had happened, they couldn't think of anything else to do, but they knew they needed to sort everything out. Things were different now. The HR120s had brought Dimension 0.65 into their war against Franklin, and using their copy of the female Drake as a guinea pig, they had found a way to get through Vlakdormat's defenses, at least partially.

"They're coming," the other Franklin said. "It might be tomorrow, it might be next week, but you're all next."

"I'm sorry," Drake said. "This is my fault. I let her have access to the system, and then she. . . . She was just so authentic."

"It wasn't your fault," said William. "It wasn't anyone's fault." Franklin couldn't imagine what William was going through. Just as he and Drake had been starting to get serious, she was taken away from him. As much as the HR120s had put Franklin through, they hadn't taken anyone close to him. All at once, William had more reason to hate them than Franklin did.

"This all goes back to the first time you went to Dimension 0.65," Drake said, looking at Franklin. "They put a CVT on you."

Franklin agreed. "They probably studied the video and got enough from that to build a copy of Dr. Drake."

"We can't let this happen again," Franklin's counterpart said.

"I didn't mean for you to get caught up in this," Franklin said.

"Well, I'm involved now. I've got as much of a stake in this as you do."

It was strange for Franklin to see another version of himself so angry and dedicated. It was like looking in a mirror. Before, his counterpart was a lot like he had been five years earlier, when he still had his telepathy. That Franklin had an infectious, positive energy and could make you feel better about everything just by being in the same room with you. But now, he and his other self were the same, and Franklin didn't like who they had become.

"We can use all the help we can get," Franklin said to his counterpart. "I know it hurts. We've all lost something. But the only way we can hope to beat this thing is to act."

"I'll drink to that," said William. He, too, was a darker, paler image of the man he had been. The four of them raised their glasses together, but if the other three had known what Franklin was planning at that very moment, they may not have toasted so quickly.

It had taken a while, but Franklin had finally gotten the address he needed from a Rekvoloskian therapist on the fifth floor of Vlakdormat. He pulled up to an old building in the lower part of downtown Abott City and cautiously got out of his car. It was late in the evening, and the cold air smelled like cigarettes and rotting pizza. He climbed the short flight of stairs to the front door. The place was anything but ready for business.

The front glass was cracked, and the old, faded blue paint was chipping away off the walls. There was a small, old sign across the side that used to sport the name of the previous business, but the only letters left were N, R, and A, spaced far apart from each other. Franklin wasn't sure what this place used to be, but he guessed it had nothing to do with the National Rifle Association. No one had used this building in years, judging from its condition and some faded red paint on one of the store front windows that said, "New Year's Sale, 1984." It was a strange place to open a new business, but Franklin figured it was all the new owner could afford. Besides, considering the kind of clientele the business was likely to have, it was probably best to operate far under the radar.

Franklin knocked on the door and was immediately greeted by a female voice from inside. "I'm in the middle of something. Give me exactly one minute and thirty-eight seconds."

Franklin didn't time her, but he guessed she was right on time when the door finally opened, revealing a woman wearing a bright green dress and a red feather boa. She hardly matched the run-down, practically condemned building.

"Did you bring them?" Eva Crill asked.

Franklin reached into his trench coat and produced a manila envelope.

"Right here," said Franklin, handing them to her. She opened the envelope and looked at three 8 x 10 photographs. "You got my message, then?"

"I can't believe you managed it," said Crill.

"It was nothing we did." He explained that the HR120's body sitting in Drake's laboratory was a duplicate of the female Drake and how the positronic deactivation switch had only partially shut her down. "The HR120's completely intact and has a fully functional positronic brain. Drake says we basically paralyzed it."

Crill considered everything he'd said. "I can do this," she said.

"And you're willing?"

"I meant what I said the last time we saw each other. Contrary to popular belief, I have no wish to see Vlakdormat destroyed. But are you sure you want to go through with it?"

"I'll do whatever I have to."

"It's going to take some time," Crill said. "I've never done anything like this."

"I'll get you the HR120 within 24 hours."

"Are you going to be able to convince Drake and Caslom this is a good idea?"

"Probably not," said Franklin. "I'm not sure I've completely convinced myself."

But he knew it had to be done. A lot of people had a stake in this fight, but he was responsible for getting them all through it. And the only way he knew to fight the HR120s was to become an HR120 himself.

CHAPTER 30

Forward: The Only Good Direction

FRANKLIN STOOD OVER THE STAINLESS STEEL TABLE, WATCHING THE LIFELESS HR120. Its head was connected to Drake's computers by a number of multi-colored wires. It was strange to see an enemy wearing the face of a woman who easily might have been Franklin's friend had she not been murdered before he had the chance to know her. As that Drake and William had grown closer, Franklin imagined William might have started bringing her to Krawkson Klub, or they might have double dated with him and Lera. Now that would never happen.

Some of the HR120's components had shorted out, so there were patches along her arms and shoulders where the skin had melted away, leaving wires and circuits completely visible. Amazingly, nothing had shorted out in her face; her blank eyes were still open, and she held an almost frightened expression that looked nearly human. But regardless of appearances, Franklin didn't feel sorry for the HR120. It had been programmed to die for its creator's cause, and that's exactly what it had done. There was no reason to really feel anything for it—pity, hatred, or anything else.

The room was deathly silent as Drake R. Drake tapped keys on three different keyboards and looked at readings on three different monitors along the wall behind the table. The giant screens pictured thousands of characters of code Franklin couldn't read, but he understood that it might be the most important computer gibberish he would ever not recognize.

Although the HR120's body no longer functioned by its own will, its positronic brain was still working. Drake believed he might be able to find information on Helena Kathryn, Stephen

Zarcadmium, or, of more immediate concern, the forthcoming attack on Vlakdormat. Franklin knew the attack might come at any time, although probably no sooner than the next twenty-four hours. Even though the HR120s now had information about the deactivation switch, Zarcadmium would need time to perfect his counter weapon. A bunch of paralyzed HR120s would be as useless to Zarcadmium as dead ones. Still, Franklin had convinced Dr. Caslom to start planning an entire evacuation of the facility within the next couple of days. He hoped they had that long.

"Hmm," Drake said, stroking his chin. It was the most noise he had made in an hour.

"Did you find something?" Franklin asked.

"Yes, but you're not going to like it."

Franklin stood next to Drake and looked at the monitor, although he had no idea what he was looking at. The screen pictured a vertical series of complex moving characters. Some of the characters were circles with triangles inside of them, others were zigzags with hash marks through them, and some were intersecting, straight lines. Watching Drake read it reminded him vaguely of *The Matrix.*

"You're right. This code looks a lot more sinister than the rest. What is it?" asked Franklin.

"A to-do list in its active memory core. It's networked between all of the HR120s, like a newsletter, announcing all upcoming, just-for-robot events. At the top of that list is a message that reads like a publicity flyer. They're having an environmental rally. They're planning a huge protest Saturday morning, picketing things like global warming, landfills, and toxic dumping. HR120s from all over the country are supposed to be in town."

That gave them just under three days to get ready. "Let me guess. This little demonstration is happening real close to Vlakdormat."

"The march takes them right by the building," Drake said,. "This has got to be a front for an attack. The HR120s have always been about staying inconspicuous—they wouldn't just send 5000 of their troops in black suits and sunglasses, if they could help it."

Besides, Franklin thought, if they did that, it really would be *The Matrix*. Or at least the sequel.

"Did you say five *thousand*?" Franklin asked.

"That's the part I figured you wouldn't like. Oh, and you'll like this even less. . . . Zarcadmium will be there."

Actually, that was good news. Franklin had been banking on Zarcadmium's presence, and his plan hinged on it. He pulled out Drake's swivel chair from his desk and took a seat. "At least we know when it's happening," he said.

"I think we'll have just enough time to put your insane plan together," Drake said. "And may I reiterate, once again, that as insane plans go, this is by far the most insane I have ever heard."

"I know I'm not qualified for this. I don't know the first thing about waging war. I read *Sun-Tzu* in college, but I don't remember much of it. I think he said something like, 'never engage the enemy when it's five versus 5000.' But we have something Sun-Tzu wouldn't have had."

"The enemy's game plan? MasterCard?"

"That. And pocket dimensions."

"True, but I'm just worried about the part where you implant your consciousness into an HR120."

"One of us needs to be able to fight the way they do," said Franklin.

Drake nodded. "I only said your plan was insane, not that it didn't stand a chance. You'll be fine, as long as I'm there."

"I hope good luck is enough."

He heard uneven footsteps in the entrance to the lab behind them, and both he and Drake turned to see Franklin's counterpart standing there.

His white shirt was in tatters and a long, deep red cut ran across his left cheek.

"Luck?" the other Franklin said. "That's funny. From where I'm standing, it's looking more and more like we're all going to die."

After they had given the other Franklin some fresh clothes and he had cleaned himself up, the three of them sat in Drake's office. Franklin and Drake listened in horror as Franklin's counterpart explained what had happened to him. Just after they had all had drinks in Krawkson Klub the night before, he and William had gone together and executed a plan Franklin would argue was a billion times more insane than the one he was currently working on: they had attempted time travel in order to learn more about Stephen Zarcadmium. They went back to Corvadia, Stephen Zarcadmium's home dimension, just before it had been destroyed.

"I got out," the other Franklin said. "But William wasn't so lucky."

"What happened?" Drake asked. His arms were folded, and he had been listening in complete disbelief. Time travel was a big interdimensional no-no, an unspoken rule among everyone who knew it was possible. Franklin once had a Jexarite patient who had somehow altered time such that his father was also his son. He had been a patient for most of Franklin's career.

"The door to Limbo only opens at certain intervals in each dimension. I made it out, but just barely."

Drake leaned forward and darkened his gaze. "You went into *Limbo*? You are an idiot."

Over the last two days, Franklin had seen expressions on his counterpart's face he didn't even know he had; he now looked more offended than Franklin could remember ever being. "I don't have the same two first names like some people," said the other Franklin. "And last time I checked, I was the one whose facility was destroyed and whose friends were all killed, so—"

"Look," Franklin said. "I know we're dealing with robots and time travel and very possibly all of our deaths, but we should try to retain some semblance of professionalism."

Drake took a deep breath. "Is William all right?"

"I don't know," said Franklin's counterpart, avoiding eye contact with Drake. "He was attacked by CR120s."

"Did you hit your head while you were getting ripped apart?" Franklin asked. "Don't you mean HR120s?"

"No. I mean just what I said. You see, our plan worked. We found out quite a bit about Stephen Zarcadmium. CR120s are Corvadian Replicas, model 120. Zarcadmium perfected the design there and then brought them to Earth."

Franklin had always assumed Zarcadmium hadn't gone insane until after his world had been destroyed. Of course, Franklin hadn't had telepathy while Zarcadmium was a patient, but he still thought his crude human intuition should have detected some sense of malice in Zarcadmium if he were already building an army of homicidal robots to eventually rule the world.

"He altered their programming so they'd look human?" Drake said.

"Yes, but it didn't take much," the other Franklin said. "Corvadians are physiologically no different from humans, with the exception of their eyes being two different colors."

"Weird," Franklin said. "Oh, and *bad*. You left William at the mercy of HR120s!"

"I didn't have a choice. If I hadn't left, they would have killed us both. This way, we can go back in time and rescue him before the CR120s attacked us."

"No," said Drake.

"What do you mean, no?" said Franklin.

"Solving a time travel problem with time travel is like trying to disinfect a wound with gasoline. Unless you're a Vaklock beast."

"So what do we do? Leave him there and let him get killed by robots?" Franklin asked.

"Nothing good ever comes from time travel," Drake said. "You know that first hand."

Franklin flashed Drake an intense look of irritation. He had hoped that maybe, somehow, Drake was the one person Bethany hadn't blabbed to about the time travel incident, but obviously, he had no such luck. He supposed Drake had been a good friend for not bringing up the single most embarrassing thing Franklin had ever done since working at Vlakdormat before this moment. It had happened almost a year earlier, after Rajel Chirok stole his telepathy.

As Franklin stared at his computer monitor, watching

Rajel Chirok auction his future away, Franklin still believed there had to be something he could do about it. Franklin wasn't good at letting things go. Growing up, he had never been satisfied after a fight with his parents or one of his friends until he felt that everything that needed to be said had been said. So when Rajel Chirok had stolen his telepathy, he didn't know how to move on. He had seen patients levitate his office furniture with their minds, he had seen people phase through solid objects, and he had even seen a species, the Flop-Qua, who had evolved an umbrella that popped out of their heads whenever it rained. He had spent over four years witnessing the impossible. There had to be more difficult tasks than getting his telepathy back from an interdimensional superpower dealer, even after it had already been sold.

Franklin had heard hushed whispers here and there about time travel and how it was forbidden, both in Vlakdormat and in most professional businesses around the multiverse. But Franklin couldn't imagine how his going back a day, just to tell himself not to see Rajel Chirok so he could keep his telepathy, could possibly harm anyone or make any grand, sweeping changes to the timeline. He helped people of different species from all over the multiverse every day. If anything, wouldn't he be making the future better by ensuring that he kept the tool he needed to do his job?

So the next day, after asking some of his patients about how someone, hypothetically of course, might go about traveling backward in time, Tramsey the Vaklock beast told him about Limbo. Franklin had to sell his BMW and settle for a Taurus to afford Limbo, but it was still a lot cheaper than buying his telepathy back would have been. Plus, this way, Rajel Chirok didn't win. Someone needed to teach that guy a lesson, and maybe after this, he'd think twice before he . . . wait. If Franklin changed the time line, Rajel Chirok wouldn't remember any of it, so he wouldn't learn anything. Man, time travel was confusing.

Franklin paid to go to Limbo, and the friendly and polite cosmic salesmen there sent him twenty-four hours back in time, as Franklin requested, to just a few minutes before he would sit down with Rajel Chirok for their session. Franklin briskly walked through the front doors of Vlakdormat, stepped onto the elevator, and made his way to his office. When he stepped off, Dr. Caslom, his accordion-like body spread out to its maximum length, stood there, blocking his path.

"You don't belong here," Caslom said.

Franklin's heart raced. "What do you mean?" he said. "I'm just on my way to my next session."

"You're already in your office. The you that belongs in this time. You're a you from twenty-four hours from now. You know time travel is against company policy, Franklin. We're very strict on this matter. That's why we have a tachyon detection grid."

Almost nothing got past Vlakdormat security. Of course they could detect tachyons. As fast as Limbo had sucked him into the past, Franklin's common sense returned to him. How could he have rushed into this, guns blazing, without even the vaguest of strategies? He made every rookie time travel mistake from the movies. He could have gone back as far as he'd wanted to and warn himself. Why the day of the incident? Why minutes before the incident? And why Vlakdormat, where someone could catch him? If it hadn't been tachyons, it might have been his secretary, who knew there were two different versions of Franklin in his office and would surely report that. Franklin's secretary who, at this very moment, was peaking up from behind her computer screen and making eye contact with him over Caslom's extended gray suit. She had that look on her face that said this was the juiciest thing she'd seen in months, and everyone in the building would know before he made it back to the future.

So despite Vlakdormat's strict no-time-travel policy, Caslom let Franklin off with a warning, since he'd been caught before anything had happened and in consideration of everything he'd been through over the last day. And that was the embarrassing part. Franklin was reprimanded by Caslom, didn't get his powers back, was the laughing stock of the office for weeks, and he didn't even have a good story to tell. His entire visit to his own past lasted less than five minutes, and the only thing he did was get a stern talking to from his boss, who then felt the need to give him the same stern talking to when he returned to the present, despite Franklin's insistence that, from his perspective, he had just heard the same speech minutes earlier.

"This is different," Franklin said to Drake.

"Franklin, you're not seriously considering this," Drake asked.

"No, I'm not considering. I've already decided. I'm willing to transfer my own consciousness into an HR120 to save Vlakdormat, and I'm willing to risk altering history to save my friend."

"You're going to transfer your what into a *what*?" said Franklin's counterpart. "I mean, I read that in your mind earlier, but I just assumed it was a bizarre passing thought."

Drake ignored him and continued arguing. "You know, people with two first names who try to be this heroic almost always get themselves killed."

"Then I'll just have to make sure I'm one of the almost," said Franklin.

"You know what Caslom will do to you when you get back."

"When we get back, I'm going to suck Stephen Zarcadmium in a pocket dimension he can't purple-cloud his way out of and put him in rehab for however long Corvadians happen to live. I'll deal with the consequences after."

"One other thing you might want to know before we do this," Franklin's counterpart said. "William probably won't come quietly. When we get there, he's not going to want to be rescued."

"What?"

"When we got there, he told me why he had really gone there. It wasn't for information, like it was for me. William is going to try and kill Zarcadmium."

CHAPTER 31

Don't Make It Worse

FRANKLIN FINISHED PACKING A SMALL OVERNIGHT BAG AND SWUNG IT OVER HIS SHOULDER. He didn't know how long he would be gone, and he couldn't imagine going back in time again without a clean change of clothes.

He knew this was a bad idea, but what choice did he have? This wasn't simply a matter of going back in time to change something that had already happened and was supposed to happen. Someone was in the past who didn't belong there, and Franklin had to go back to save the present as much as to save William. Without Zarcadmium, the last five years of Franklin's life would never have happened, and whether that life might have been better or worse wasn't for Franklin to judge. It had happened, and what had happened was meant to happen.

Franklin took a long look at his bedroom. He looked at the polished wood floor, the king-sized bed, the ancient marble Rekvoloskian end table that was worth 15,000 *drastonites*—Lera assured Franklin that was a lot—which Lera had bought years ago, and it was her favorite table. And now, he might never see any of it again. Not only was Franklin going back in time, which was a lot like jumping into the eye of a tornado, but he was very likely going up against HR120s three days before he was ready for them. His mind wasn't in a killer robot body yet, and he couldn't borrow a portable aperture from Vlakdormat security, partly because Caslom would know what it was for, but more importantly because pocket dimensions didn't transcend the boundaries of space-time. He could take the aperture with him, but not the dimension. If he tried to use an aperture in the past, nothing would happen at all.

Franklin hesitantly left the bedroom and almost had a heart attack upon entering the dining room. Lera was sitting at the table sipping a cup of tea with Helena, who was listening intently as Lera told her one of those ex-husband stories Franklin had sat through at least fifty times.

"So then Requarr said something like, 'You probably don't accept a lot of invitations from destructive forces of nature, but since I just accidentally set your garage on fire, I think the least I could do is take you out for a slice of pie.'"

Helena laughed politely and looked at Franklin. He was almost as shocked as he had been the first time he saw a purple cloud.

Lera said, "This probably strikes you as odd, dear, but I invited Helena here."

"For tea?"

"For time travel."

"Oh. I guess that makes sense. . . . Wait, no it doesn't."

"Lera didn't think it made sense to let you and the other Franklin go up against an army of HR120s by yourselves, so she gave Requarr a call, and I got here as soon as I heard," said Helena.

"I don't like Helena," Lera said. "But we've had a woman-to-woman talk. She's quite comfortable with it. Just because I don't like her doesn't make me stupid. You need her, or you're all going to wind up dead."

Just when Franklin thought he had his wife figured out, just when he was starting to fear he couldn't trust her anymore, she surprised him.

"But what about your personalities?" Franklin asked. "What if one of them decides to get vengeance on Zarcadmium?"

"They wouldn't dare change the past, especially where Zarcadmium is concerned. It could easily result in our never existing."

"Good point," Franklin said.

"So when do we leave?" asked Helena.

"Right away. Drake's working on computations to open a time portal back to Corvadia."

"A time portal? That sounds difficult," said Helena.

"Not really," Lera said. "Just a lot of math. It's a cinch for a guy like Drake. A time portal is just a regular portal with an extra component. The only reason more geeks like Drake don't use them is because time travel is so dangerous. Even evil geeks generally stay away from time portals."

"I thought you said something about Limbo," said Helena. "Isn't that what William and the other Franklin used?"

"Limbo is a commercial time travel agency," Franklin said. He had used it before, since he wasn't a nerd and didn't know the first thing about manifesting a time portal. "It's too expensive, and I don't want to support an organization that profits from time travel."

They couldn't create the portal in Vlakdormat because the facility had sensors in more places than Drake's lab, and security would immediately know about it. Drake, Franklin, Franklin's counterpart, and Helena all drove out to a cornfield just outside of the city. It was a gorgeous, sunny Thursday afternoon, just at the tail end of winter. Tomorrow was daylight savings time, and the irony in that made Franklin a little nervous.

The other three waited as Drake set up his equipment. A small, square, metallic portal device sat on top of a tall, black, metal tripod. Franklin was familiar with the portal device, but he had never seen the orange cone that Drake connected to the top of it.

"What does a road cone have to do with time travel?" he asked.

"It's not a road cone. It's . . . well, it's necessary. If I tried to explain what it did, you would just accuse me of spouting technical jargon and trying to sound superior."

"I'm really curious too," said Franklin's counterpart. "What's it for?"

"It's an energy-directing unit designed to curve space-time to a precise point so that any interdimensional portal opened in this area will take a person to the designated dimension, back in time to the point set by the cone."

"Why didn't you just say so?" said Franklin's counterpart.

"I understood that perfectly," said Franklin.

Franklin's counterpart was able to tell Drake the exact time that he and William were transported back to the present from Limbo, and Drake entered that information into his machine by wireless remote.

"I just thought of something," said Franklin. "How do we know we're going to the right Corvadia?"

Franklin's counterpart looked nervous. "I hadn't really thought about that. . . . When we got to Corvadia, the guys running Limbo asked us if we wanted to go to Corvadia just before it was destroyed, like they knew exactly what we were doing there. We said yes, and there we were."

The beings who ran Limbo were mind-readers, but they may not have read exactly which Corvadia William and the other Franklin had been thinking of. If they had gone to the wrong one, it was possible that the Stephen Zarcadmium there hadn't built CR120s before going to Earth. But there was really no way to know.

"Your fact-finding mission was probably for nothing," said Franklin. "We don't even know if you were spying on the right Zarcadmium!"

"We can at least be sure that I'm sending you to whatever Corvadia William is trapped in. I got the coordinates off Franklin's Limbo receipt," Drake said.

He pushed a few buttons on his remote control, and a red beam shot out from the nozzle at the front of his machine. A hole in space and time opened in front of them, tearing through reality itself and growing bigger and bigger until it was conveniently large enough for three adults to walk through. Inside the portal, Franklin could see a dark red sky and what looked like the ruins of a once-great civilization.

"Are you sure you want to go in there?" Drake asked.

"Are you sure you won't come with us?" Franklin responded.

"It's nothing against William, but someone has to stay behind in case you don't make it. In case you've forgotten, we've got less than three days before the HR120s turn Vlakdormat into . . . well, *that*," Drake said, pointing at the huge, broken stone structure that was barely standing inside the portal in front of them.

"I'll open another one just like it in the same place two hours from the time you step inside," said Drake. Franklin wished they could somehow communicate through time, but to do that they would have to keep the portal open, and that was too risky. "Don't be late."

"If we're late," said Franklin's counterpart, "it's because we're dead."

"And Franklin?" said Drake. "Find William so I can kill him."

They emerged out of the portal behind one of the dilapidated buildings. What had happened here? The Corvadians were supposed to have destroyed themselves, so it was possible they were looking at the tail end of a war that would ultimately doom the entire race. But Franklin wondered, then, why Zarcadmium had built the CR120s. Was it really because the Corvadians weren't careful enough with their environment, or did they have a more immediate purpose? Maybe Zarcadmium had built them to stop this war. But whatever the reason, they presented exactly the same threat as the ones on Earth did, and Franklin had to do everything he could to avoid them.

Helena asked if they were in the right place, and Franklin's counterpart nodded affirmatively. He explained that when he had been here before, he and William had walked a few blocks north from where they were standing now. "It wasn't hard to find information about Stephen Zarcadmium," he said. "He's the most famous person in this dimension. And the CR120s run the entire city. He set himself up as dictator. Easy to do when you have an unstoppable army of robots."

Zarcadmium had done the exact same thing in his dimension that he seemed to be trying in Franklin's. They were just witnessing the final stages of it: a complete CR120 occupation of the planet. But the question was, if Zarcadmium didn't have Helena here, why did he need her to run his army on Earth?

They peeked around the building, looking for William and trying to stay hidden. The entire city was in ruins. There were a few people in rags wandering around, looking lost and frightened for their lives. The streets were cracked to pieces and littered with mangled road signs. This part of town was probably the business district; there was a multi-story office building ahead of them, but now all the windows were broken and the glass covered the ground below.

"For a guy so concerned with the environment, you'd think he'd clean up after his carnage," Franklin said.

"That's exactly what I thought," said his counterpart. "I don't know how this happened, exactly. There was a war, but no one's talking about it. Zarcadmium took over, but no one is saying why."

"Maybe they're afraid to," said Helena. "Maybe the CR120s limit what they're allowed to discuss."

"I don't know," the other Franklin said. "Seemed to me like they were just really depressed about it."

They watched for William for several minutes, but he never arrived. Franklin was beginning to fear the worst. Time travel was a tricky thing, and interdimensional time travel was doubly so.

"Maybe Drake's calculations were off," said Franklin.

"No, this is the right time and the right place," Franklin's counterpart said. "I recognize that lady across the street." He pointed at a woman who was bouncing a blue rubber ball on the sidewalk. She stared at it without emotion, her head rising and falling with the ball as she bounced it steadily, the exact same height each time. Franklin found it a little disturbing.

"I don't think I'd forget her, either," he said.

"Maybe it's some kind of bizarre time paradox," said Franklin's counterpart.

Helena looked at Franklin with big, sad eyes. Not now,

Franklin thought, immediately guessing that the Alicia personality had taken over. This was not a good time.

"Too red," Alicia said softly and innocently. She looked up at the sky and then back at the rubble behind them. "Everything is red and broken. I don't like it here. It's like a rated-R movie, and I'm not supposed to watch those."

Franklin's counterpart put a hand on her shoulder. She was immune to his telepathy, and he didn't realize what was happening. "You okay? I think maybe the time travel's getting to you. I've seen cases like this."

"No," Franklin said, "that's not it. Damn, we don't have time to deal with this."

Helena covered her ears at the sound of Franklin's expletive.

Franklin knelt down and took Helena by the hands, as if she were much shorter than he was. In fact, Helena was about three inches taller. "Alicia, everything is fine. Just stay with me and Franklin."

"Two Franklins." Alicia pointed at the other Franklin. "I've seen him before. Is he evil? Is he an evil clone?"

"No, he's not evil. He's just . . . my brother. From another dimension."

Alicia looked at Franklin, then back at his counterpart. She violently shoved Franklin's hands away from her, knocking Franklin flat on his back. She took off running across the street.

Franklin's counterpart started after her, but Franklin grabbed him by the shoulder and held him back. "It's all right. She's just afraid."

"So am I. She was supposed to be our protection."

"Yes, but if we run out in the street, we'll be spotted by a CR120. Even as a little girl, I think she'll protect herself if she has to. We just have to wait for Helena to take over again."

Franklin's counterpart looked at his watch. "How long will that take? We've only got an hour and a half."

"No telling. When Sandra took over, it was for the better part of an afternoon."

"Great. In the meantime, we have no bodyguard, and William isn't here. *And* we might have to risk leaving Helena here, too."

"It could be worse."

"How?"

"She could be Sandra."

Franklin was startled by a light tap on his shoulder. He spun around to meet a young man in tattered clothes wearing a gun holster at his belt and a leather strap across his chest with compartments for small supplies. If Franklin had to guess, he would have said the man was a member of some underground resistance movement.

"Please, you must come with me," the man said in a raspy voice. His gold and pink eyes were wide with mad excitement.

"We can't," said Franklin. "We're looking for someone."

The Corvadian frowned and pulled a small, green pellet from the leather strap. He threw it to the ground and a green mist rapidly filled the air around them. Franklin tried to cover his mouth, but he had already breathed in too much. In seconds, everything was dark.

"They awaken. They awaken."

Murmurs and whispers filled Franklin's ears as he regained consciousness. When his eyes began to focus, he saw several people sitting on the floor, cross-legged, gathered around like he was about to tell a story. Still a bit drowsy, he tried to think if he knew any good ones and then remembered where and when he was. His counterpart was lying on the floor next to him, also looking slightly delirious. They were in a large sewer tunnel that looked surprisingly how Franklin might have expected. Metal pipes lined the walls and the ceiling, and the group was surrounded by streams of sewer water. The air was dank and cold. Apparently sewers weren't that different between dimensions.

"We are so glad you have finally arrived," said the man who had kidnapped them. The others wore similar rags and weapons, but they were all different ages, and about half of them were women.

"What the hell are we doing here?" asked Franklin's counterpart. "Actually, scratch that. *How long* have we been here?" He didn't wait for an answer; he glanced at his watch and suddenly looked concerned. "We've got fifteen minutes, Franklin."

The kidnapper stood up and walked in front of his troops, ignoring the alternate Franklin's confusion. He seemed to be their leader. "I am Adam Maktorboram. We thought you would never come, but here you are. Our saviors."

"Don't even tell me there's some kind of prophecy," said Franklin's counterpart. When he grabbed his forehead and shook his head, Franklin realized his counterpart had read their minds, and that there really was a prophecy.

"Didn't you know? It was foretold thousands of years ago that two twins with mono-colored eyes would grace Corvadia with their presence and save it from an impending doom. Our world is about to end, and here you are," said Maktorboram.

This was precisely the reason time travel was supposed to be avoided: the unavoidable, unexplainable time paradox. Did the prophecy refer to some unrelated twins with mono-colored eyes, and the two Franklins just happened to coincide with that prophecy? Or was the prophecy actually referring to the two Franklins—in which case they were destined to travel back in time and save Corvadia from destruction? Except, being from the future, Franklin already knew that Corvadia was supposed to be destroyed; unless they were, somehow, really in some other version of Corvadia, in which case not saving it could have dire consequences for the entire multiverse. Not that Franklin had the slightest idea about how to save an entire dimension from destruction, even if he wanted to. On the other hand, it was equally likely that the prophecy was never supposed to come true, even coincidentally, in which case they might have already screwed up time beyond repair.

But while Franklin was considering all of these possibilities, the other Franklin had come to another, more immediate conclusion. "Adam?" he said. "I'm just wondering . . . how, exactly, do you know your world is about to end?"

"Lord Zarcadmium has been advertising it all week," Maktorboram said. "Even with his CR120s, he couldn't save the world from pollution, so now he's going to destroy it on purpose. Put it out of its misery, as it were. He's making the whole planet throw this big End of Everything party. But we're revolting. We're an underground resistance movement." He said it proudly, like they deserved medals or something.

"And what are you doing to stop Zarcadmium?" asked Franklin's counterpart.

"Nothing, really. Once the CR120s figured out there was a

resistance, they flooded the sewers with a toxic compound and killed most of us. Turns out a small percentage of Corvadians were born with an immunity to it. That's us."

"How many of you are there?"

"Just us," said Maktorboram. He took a quick head count. "So about sixteen."

"Sixteen? In the entire resistance movement?"

"We're not really resisting the end of the world. Zarcadmium's got that crazy mojo no one knows how to stop. Plus robots. We're pretty much just resisting the party. But hey, now that our glorious saviors have arrived, we've got nothing to worry about."

In fact, they had everything to worry about. Stephen Zarcadmium had used his purple cloud magic to destroy his own dimension. And if history repeated itself, he would do the same to Franklin's.

"We have to leave now," said Franklin, standing up. He used his best, deepest savior-of-the-universe voice.

"Are you going to save the world?" asked Maktorboram.

"Of course," said Franklin's counterpart, speaking with the same fake confidence. "We go now to fulfill the prophecy of Corvadia. Then we will disappear, and you will never see us again. Now, how do we get out of here?"

Maktorboram gave them directions and then apologized for the kidnapping. "We just wanted you to know there were still some among us who believe in the ancient teachings of Ned, the prophet from another dimension who had only one color of eyes."

Obviously, these people didn't realize how common interdimensional travel was. Franklin couldn't help but wonder if the prophet Ned was a time traveler who had screwed up the past by accidentally spawning a new religion. In fact, he thought, there were a lot of religions that probably got started that way.

When the two Franklins were back on the surface, they broke out in a sprint, heading for the building where they had come out of the time portal.

"We've got six minutes to find Helena," said the alternate Franklin. Franklin's watch said they only had four, and he hoped that Drake's watch wasn't running fast.

"Let's just get there and pray that she's close," said Franklin.

"You know, we might have just changed the whole future of the multiverse by that little stunt we pulled back there," said Franklin's counterpart.

"I was thinking the same thing."

They arrived at the meeting place, and the time portal was already open. Helena was standing next to it, holding the broken head of a CR120, wires dangling beneath it.

"Where have I seen this before?" said Franklin.

"They attacked me when I was a little girl," said Helena. "I mean, when I was being controlled by a little girl. What happened to you two?"

"We got kidnapped by a cult who thought we were here to stop Zarcadmium from destroying everything," said Franklin's counterpart.

"Zarcadmium? He destroys *his own* dimension?"

"It looks that way," said Franklin. Helena's eyes wandered furiously.

"We've really got to go."

"I know," Helena whispered. They stepped into the time portal without William, but they were not altogether empty-handed.

CHAPTER 32

Fire At Will

"I'M SURE THERE'S A GOOD EXPLANATION FOR THIS," SAID DRAKE. They were all standing in the cornfield once again, as if nothing had happened. As far as anyone else knew, nothing had—Drake had brought them back to the present just seconds after they had left. "Unless William's on some other plane of existence or something fancy like that."

"Could time travel do that?" Franklin asked.

"I don't know," Drake said. "I honestly haven't done a lot of research on time paradoxes because there's not a lot of demand for literature on the subject. Why write a theoretical paper on something everyone's afraid of doing?"

Franklin surveyed the area. The machine and the orange cone looked the same. The field, the corn, the puffy clouds, the sky, and the sun all looked the same. Drake was still wearing the same gray suit and had the same brown, well-groomed goatee.

"Is something else wrong?" Drake asked.

"No," said Franklin. "Unless it is. You tell me. Are there still HR120s?"

"What? Of course there are," Drake said.

"And Corvadia was still destroyed."

"Yes."

"Zarcadmium still built the HR120s."

"Yes."

"They're still trying to kill me."

"Yes. And they're coming to Vlakdormat in three days."

"Good—I mean, not good—but good that nothing's changed."

"What exactly happened over there?" Drake asked.

"Oh nothing," Franklin's counterpart said. "We just got sixteen resistance fighters' hopes up, claiming to be their prophesized saviors."

Drake buried his head in his hand and then blinked a couple of times. "Well that's bound to have changed *something.*"

"Wasn't our fault we're the same guy from different dimensions and both have two blue eyes," said Franklin's counterpart.

Helena had been silent during the entire conversation, looking intently at Drake's time portal contraption. Franklin could only imagine how she was feeling, knowing that she was deeply connected to a man who had willingly destroyed his entire dimension.

"Helena," he said softly, approaching her slowly. "You all right?"

"Could it have something to do with *how* we got there?" she asked.

"What?"

"William went back through Limbo. We used a time portal. Is Limbo different, somehow?"

Drake took a deep breath, once again afraid to speak over everyone's heads. He explained that a time portal was just a regular one-dimensional portal, fixed with what he called a "time tag." Limbo worked quite differently. It was an interdimensional conduit, connected not only to every single known dimension, but also to every second of every dimension's existence. It was a place between dimensions and time. You could go into any time and dimension freely in Limbo because time simply had no meaning there. However, once you were inside a dimension, the door back to Limbo only opened at particular times and places.

"Why is that? Is Limbo some unpredictable force of nature?" Helena asked.

"No, it's a man-made force of nature," Drake said. He then looked slightly embarrassed for saying that. "It's run by two all-powerful, all-knowing immortals just trying to make a buck. They set time and space limits so that if you want to go back in, they can charge you more."

"But it's still a lot different from a portal," said Helena. "Maybe that's why we couldn't find William in the past."

"I don't see why that would make a difference," Drake said. "But again, not a time scholar. If you think saving William is worth wasting the cash, then by all means."

Many of Franklin's interdimensional patients knew how to get into Limbo from Earth. The people who were into time travel were addicted to it like a drug, only the effects were usually longer-lasting. He remembered that a portal opened just off the corner of 19th and Mire in the parking lot of an old Taco Bell that was now closed down. The property had never been bought or used for anything since. Apparently having customers falling into Limbo while going through the drive-thru was bad for business. Entrances to Limbo weren't like portals – they were invisible. Franklin sometimes wondered how many construction workers had the pleasure of visiting Limbo while the Taco Bell was being built. The portal opened every eight hours on weekdays and every six hours on weekends. Franklin had done his math right, and one opened at precisely 7:00 pm.

Limbo was as trippy as Franklin remembered it. He, his counterpart, and Helena stood on a thin, metal plank surrounded by what could only be described as a mix of M.C. Escher and

Picasso. Surreal, abstract images took the place of ceilings, floors, and walls. The bizarre images swirled, folded, spun, and bounced everywhere; and a trillion things, places, and people all merged into one hideous montage.

"Is this how we get into a dimension?" Helena asked. "Try to make out which part of this is Corvadia and jump in?"

"No. That's just advertising," Franklin said. Two figures slowly floated down to the plank from out of nowhere.

"This is the best part," said the alternate Franklin. Franklin raised an eyebrow and wondered if he, too, had gone back in time before.

Loud, epic orchestral music filled Limbo as the figures dropped. They wore long, flowing, red capes tied in the front at their necks and sleek black, metallic armor that covered their entire bodies. They wore black, mouthless helmets with an opening at the top to show off their enormous, bare, pink brains. They wore bright red,spiked gauntlets on their hands, which they held out in front of them. They each held their gauntlets a few inches apart, and a blue and green planet spun in the air between them. They hovered inches off the ground, their feet never touching down.

"Welcome, Helena Kathryn, Franklin Bryce, and Franklin Bryce," the deep, booming immortals spoke in unison. It sounded like there were large speakers hidden in every wall, on the ceiling, and in the floors; their voices came from everywhere at once.

"We are the keepers and creators of Limbo. I am Gralkor."

"And I am Roklarg."

"Together, we represent the beginning and the end," said Gralkor. "And for a reasonable price, you can visit the dimension of your choice somewhere in the middle."

"We're here to find—" Franklin started.

"William Vanderhorst," said Roklarg. His brain pulsated as he spoke. "Yes, he is in Corvadia. We will send you there for our usual fee. We take cash or credit card, but please no personal checks. Some customers have been writing bad checks lately, and it's simply not worth the hassle at the bank."

"You take U.S. dollars?" Helena said.

"We take any currency that can legally be spent in a dimension we don't hate," Gralkor said.

"But if you're all-powerful, why do you need money?" Helena asked.

"We're not without a certain code of ethics," said Gralkor. "Everyone should work for his wages."

Franklin's counterpart handed his credit card to Roklarg, who swiped it across a slot in the midsection of his armor. The alternate Franklin felt responsible for getting them all into this mess—a responsibility that cost him $245.00. "Now goodbye," Roklarg said. "Remember that the next portal opens in precisely the same spot you will be transported to, in exactly one hour from the time you arrive."

"Wait," Franklin said. "Where exactly in Corvadia are we going?"

"Exactly where William Vanderhorst is. And no, the Franklin from Dimension 0.65 is not already there, so you won't have to worry about a third Franklin Bryce. This isn't *Back to the Future.* We're sending you to the time just after he came back to Limbo," Gralkor said.

"You've seen *Back to the Future*?" asked Franklin's counterpart.

"Who hasn't?"

They returned to the same dilapidated building as before, except this time, there was a lot more going on around it. Three male CR120s wearing the typical black suits and sunglasses were chasing William down the street toward the building, firing their weapon arms at him and missing terribly. They were warning shots. But William didn't stop running. He must have hoped he could make it to the opening to Limbo before they caught up with him.

Helena shot into the air and flew high above the CR120s. She was back on the ground in a flash, only now standing in front of the CR120s with her hands confidently on her hips.

"Turn around or go through me," she said. "Your choice."

The CR120s looked at each other. "Her eyes have only one color," one of them said.

"Her twin must not be far behind," said another. They chose Helena's first option and ran the other way.

"I can't believe it worked," William said when the four of them were safely behind the building again.

"What's that?" said Franklin.

"Getting Helena here."

Franklin's heart began to race. William had planned the entire thing.

"I knew you'd come back for me," William said to Franklin. "I didn't know if you'd bring Helena, but apparently it was a good bet. Now we can kill Zarcadmium."

"You made us go through all of this just so you could—"

"That HR120 killed Drake, Franklin," William said. "I fall for a girl, girl likes me back, girl gets killed by homicidal robots, robots are programmed by homicidal maniac, so homicidal maniac dies. So yeah. I did. Call me insane."

"You're insane," said Helena.

"What?"

Helena said, "Do you really think I'm going to kill Zarcadmium?"

"After what he's put you through?" said William.

"I know he wants to use me in his plans to take over the world, probably worse."

Franklin opened his mouth to say something, but Helena stopped him. He had done everything he could to keep that from her. How did she know?

"I didn't understand it until today. You've all been acting differently since the hotel. Chirok read Zarcadmium's mind. That's the only explanation."

"But how did you—"

"It wasn't hard to figure out. Zarcadmium destroyed his own dimension. What other plan could he possibly have for someone like me? I don't exactly know why he needs me—he did fine on his own the first time. There's obviously more we don't know." She turned to William. "But what I do know is that I'm also alive because of him. If I kill him, I won't exist in the first place."

"Damn," William said. "I didn't think of that. Stupid confusing time travel. But don't you understand? I just wanted to stop him from killing Drake."

"It wouldn't have worked, anyway," said the alternate Franklin. "Think about it. If we killed Zarcadmium here and Franklin never met Helena, there would have been no one to stop Dr. Grothman. He would have taken over your Vlakdormat and mine, making all of us, including Drake, commit suicide."

William said nothing else. Helena uncharacteristically

offered him her hand and he took it. "I know you don't know what to think of me," she said, "but I do care about what happens to you. To your dimension. This isn't just about me. Things have to be left to unfold the way they were meant to."

She had found out Zarcadmium's plans for her, and it hadn't turned her insane or evil. Franklin had tried to keep her from finding out the inevitable truth, and all it had done was get her thrown out of Vlakdormat.

They all stood there, silently, reflecting to themselves about everything that had happened until Limbo opened up again. And the only thing Franklin knew for certain was that all of them needed to start trusting each other.

"Welcome back," said the immortal Roklarg upon their return to Limbo. He and his brother floated inches above the ground, exactly where they had been before, as though Franklin and the others had never left. "We congratulate you on rescuing your friend."

"At least we didn't do anything that might change the future," said Franklin's counterpart. "Unless you count chasing off three CR120s."

"Nonsense," Gralkor said, his laughter reverberating across Limbo. "You couldn't have changed the future if you wanted to."

"Excuse me?" said Franklin.

"Limbo is an exact facsimile of the timeline of the multiverse. It's a chance to experience the past without risking contamination of the future," said Gralkor.

"But I contaminated the future last time I was here," Franklin said.

"Different Limbo. We changed it. We didn't get many

tourists after time travel became more of a taboo, so we changed it."

"How does that work?" William said. "I thought time had no meaning in Limbo."

"It doesn't, but it has meaning for us," Roklarg said. "We like spending money. In lots of dimensions. And if we don't keep track of linear time—all the different types of linear time—we get confused and, therefore, cranky. So we do our best to experience time the same way you do, at least when we aren't here."

"You could have mentioned this before," Franklin said.

"Silly me," said Gralkor. "Forgot to give you a guide book. As you mentioned, time has no meaning *here*. I forget that every time."

"Now I wish we had killed Zarcadmium," said William, "since it wouldn't have mattered. Might've been fun."

"Can we at least be certain we went to the right Corvadia?" asked Franklin.

"Certainly," Gralkor said. "We have kept a close eye on this Stephen Zarcadmium, even as he has wiped himself away from your histories. There is only one with the magic of the purple cloud."

As soon as they returned to Vlakdormat, three very important things happened that would change Franklin's life forever. First, Caslom began evacuating the facility, which was hard on Franklin because it meant he had to finally accept that his and everyone else's careers might be over—not to mention Franklin's life. It meant that his plan would soon be set into motion, and if it didn't work, Zarcadmium would either be running his dimension or destroying it. He was tempted to evacuate too, but he couldn't. It was possible that if they all deserted Vlakdormat, the HR120s would just leave them all alone. But Franklin seriously doubted that Zarcadmium, a man who had erased himself from history, wouldn't cover his own tracks. Franklin had to end this business, not only with the HR120s, but with Zarcadmium, or his life and the lives of everyone he knew would always be on hold and in potential danger.

The second important thing happened to William. Even as Vlakdormat was being evacuated, Caslom terminated William's position because William had gone back in time, making him the third person Caslom had kicked out of Vlakdormat that year. But as much as Franklin hated it, he couldn't entirely blame Caslom. Caslom's official reason was that, although William hadn't altered time, he had proven that he was willing to. Franklin couldn't argue with that. If Zarcadmium had been killed in the past, they would all have been doomed.

But then again, they were probably doomed anyway.

And whether or not William had been fired, Franklin wouldn't have asked for his help going up against Zarcadmium. It was too personal for William. Maybe it was too personal for Franklin, too, but he didn't know what else to do. The HR120s were his responsibility, not William's, and no one close to Franklin had been lost. At least, not yet.

But the last thing that happened terrified Franklin.

When he walked into Drake's laboratory, he immediately noticed that the HR120 was no longer lying on its table. It slowly approached Franklin, holding its hands out toward him. There were no wires sticking out of it anywhere. Its hair was tied back in a ponytail when it had been worn loose before and it was now wearing a black pant suit. Franklin was sure that any moment, its hands would turn into enormous guns.

"I know what you're thinking," the HR120 said. "But I had some time when you went into Limbo. I went to see Crill in your place. You're fighting a war. You can't call the shots and be on the front lines. Somebody has to be the leader if you're not around. And I wasn't about to let you become the enemy that wants you dead."

"Drake?" Franklin said. "*Drake* Drake?"

"Well, the other Drake was technically called Drake Drake too, but yes Franklin, it's me."

"You put yourself in the body of an HR120?"

"It's for the best." It immediately became obvious to Franklin that pronouns were about to become a huge problem when Drake looked down at his/her legs and touched his/her navy blue skirt. "I've never put one of these on before. Does it look all right?"

Franklin looked deep into Drake's eyes for a long time. Eva Crill had put him in the body of the female HR120, but since Drake had become one of his closest friends over the last few months, Franklin could tell that he was definitely in there.

"Where's your body?" Franklin asked. "I mean, are you okay?"

"Crill's keeping it on life support for me," Drake said. "She has equipment to keep me alive indefinitely.

"Won't you go brain dead without, you know, your consciousness in there?"

"Crill's tech can keep my brain stimulated artificially. I took a good look at it before I committed to this, Franklin. Everything checks out. I won't lie and say that I'm not anxious to get back in my own body, but I'll be okay. Your idea was a good one. It just made more sense for someone else to do it."

Franklin sighed. "I guess now there's only one thing that really matters," he said. "Do your arms still turn into guns?"

CHAPTER 33

Discovering the Obvious

FRANKLIN STOOD ON THE DOMED-GLASS ROOF OF VLAKDORMAT, HOPING THE HR120S COULDN'T SEE HIM. Every few minutes, the sky brilliantly lit up in flashes of lightning as Franklin and everyone fighting was soaked from head to toe by a hard shower of freezing rain. Vlakdormat was a tall, monstrous structure, and with all of the rain and carnage below, it was difficult to tell what was happening, even looking through a pair of binoculars. Security officers fired alien energy weapons and sucked HR120s into pocket dimensions with their portable apertures. HR120s turned their own arms into huge, ungodly weapons of terror, firing energy blasts and slicing and dicing with sharp, hideous blades of every kind.

But the most damage was done by Helena Kathryn, who was not at all difficult to spot. She was the only one of them who had the luxury of taking to the air, and she used that advantage to its fullest. She hovered several feet above the raging battle, using her superhuman speed to dive-bomb an HR120 like a lightning strike before it could target her, rip it apart, and then take back to the air again and attack another.

And Franklin finally managed to spot his friend Dr. Drake R. Drake, who had taken great risk to help Franklin's cause by placing his mind in an HR120, which had once posed as a female version of himself, so that Franklin wouldn't have to put his own consciousness into a robot. In all the chaos, Franklin was worried that one of the HR120s had taken him out, but it appeared that Drake's luck was still with him. Drake had transformed both of his robotic arms into massive broadswords, which he was efficiently using to stab into every HR120's face that he could.

Franklin still couldn't get used to seeing his Drake—now a rather attractive woman, even with swords for hands—wearing a skirt and skewering robots.

The end of four long months of hiding from, waiting for, and trying to outmaneuver the HR120s was finally near. Yet Franklin felt like he was doing nothing to contribute. He was supposed to be leading this stand, calling the shots in his grand plan to finally stop Stephen Zarcadmium, once and for all. But here he was, in the pouring rain, completely unarmed, completely defenseless, with no way to communicate with his troops and without so much as a soccer whistle that would make him at least look like he was in charge.

The fight was going well. Franklin's side was losing numbers, but the HR120s were losing more. Helena was taking them out a lot faster than they were killing Franklin's people. This would be a horrendous mess to clean up when they were through. Tears would be shed. Eulogies would be given. Lera would probably take the opportunity to give away things she didn't use anymore to the families of deceased people she had barely known. But the HR120s hadn't reached the doors yet. They hadn't destroyed the place where Franklin worked every day to help those who couldn't help themselves. They were going to win.

Or so it would have appeared to anyone else standing in Franklin's place, holding a pair of binoculars. But Franklin knew better. He knew they were doomed.

He didn't stand a chance against even one HR120, which was why he wasn't fighting the hundreds below. But he hadn't meant to be on the roof, and he had no idea how he had gotten here. Somehow he knew something was missing, something he had to do, or the mission wouldn't succeed.

The same was true about Stephen Zarcadmium; he was supposed to be here. But he wasn't. Without him, Franklin's plan was worthless. If Franklin couldn't stop Zarcadmium, it didn't matter how many HR120s they killed. Zarcadmium would just build more and start the madness all over again. And it wasn't enough to simply capture him. Franklin had to be certain that he never communicated with his robots again, that he never summoned another purple cloud again. But how? Zarcadmium had already demonstrated that he couldn't be held in a pocket dimension, and his magic was the one thing that seemed more powerful than Helena.

"Do you think what's happening down there matters?" asked a voice from behind Franklin. "Do you think it makes any difference?"

Franklin turned to find Stephen Zarcadmium standing behind him on the roof, wearing black leather from head to toe and with his hair greased back with too much product. His head sat crookedly on one side, and he smiled dementedly. Franklin tried to stay collected, but this was just silly. Zarcadmium was a lost, twisted man with misplaced ideals and delusions of godhood, not a comic book super villain. For all the evil he had done, the Zarcadmium Franklin knew didn't consider himself to be a bad guy. That would have been too simple, and were it true, it would have made Franklin's life a lot easier. This wasn't the Zarcadmium he knew.

"Your army is losing," Franklin said.

"This began with you and me, Dr. Bryce," Zarcadmium said. He folded his hands in front of him. He didn't even seem to notice the rain. "It will end with us."

Zarcadmium raised his arms in the air, and a small purple

cloud appeared above him. A bolt of blue lighting shot at him, and he was gone. Franklin leaned over the roof again, assuming he couldn't be lucky enough to see Zarcadmium commit suicide. He saw Zarcadmium, now far away on the ground, as he raised his arms into the air again. The cloud above Franklin's head began to grow, much faster than he had ever seen one grow. But Franklin wasn't focusing on the cloud, regardless of what he imagined it could do to him. He was focused on Zarcadmium. He was focused on his *arms.*

It was too late. The lightning fired from the cloud, a bright, blinding red streak that tore through the night sky and nailed Franklin right in the heart with incredible impact. He flew backward, and it felt like he flew forever, hundreds of miles in slow motion. He saw each individual rain drop as it hit the roof, his arms, and his legs. Franklin looked down and was startled to find that there was no more roof, only the ground and the battle that raged beneath him.

Franklin knew he was falling fast, but time still moved like wet peanut butter. He looked around, searching for Helena, but she was nowhere to be found. Though time moved slowly for him, it seemed to move much faster for the people below him. The battle had ended, and everyone on both sides lay dead beneath him. The bodies drew closer and closer as he fell—HR120s, Vlakdormat security, Drake, Lera, the long, accordion body of Dr. Caslom, the orange remains of Rajel Chirok with one wing ripped off lying next to him, and even Agent Strexit, who must have decided to fight because people without personalities didn't have much to lose anyway.

Zarcadmium had won, and *only* Zarcadmium. Franklin had been to the Corvadia of the past. He knew what Zarcadmium was capable of. And now, this dimension was about to be destroyed, and it didn't matter who was left alive on either side. It only mattered to Zarcadmium that he remained.

Franklin was about to hit the ground. He was about to die. But he took some comfort from knowing that were he to have that day to live over again with all the knowledge he had gained from the first, he might possibly succeed. He finally knew how to beat Stephen Zarcadmium. In that long, painstakingly slow moment just before impact, Franklin laughed. He laughed hard and loud. All he wished was that *someone* were falling with him just then, because what Franklin had finally realized was side-splittingly hilarious. It had been staring him in the face the entire time. It was so obvious that he felt a great sense of achievement just then.

Because, with his luck and apparently his great stupidity, it was a wonder he had lived long enough to figure it out.

And then every bone in Franklin's body broke, his skull smashed into the pavement, and he died.

Franklin woke suddenly.

His eyes scanned his dark bedroom and he felt relieved and unnerved all at once. He was relieved that was alive, but unnerved that he was going to have to battle Zarcadmium all over again, for real. He looked over at his wife sleeping next to him, and was glad he hadn't woken her. It wasn't a dream he wanted to relive right away, and knowing Lera, she would have repeated the whole thing back to him, gleaning all of it with her sense of intuition.

The dream was similar to the one he had had about the parking garage. Both dreams were surreal in their way, but both were horrifying because they had felt completely real. Franklin wasn't the kind of therapist who liked to read into people's dreams, but he couldn't deny that each of these nightmares had a message. The first had reminded him who his friends were and who his enemies were, and it had cautioned him to watch his back. This new dream told him not what to do with his feelings, but what to do with a certain piece of knowledge he had always had but had never thought about before. It told him two very specific things.

The first was that if he proceeded the way he had originally planned, he was going to fail. A bunch of Verullians, Vlakdormat security from multiple dimensions, and the head of the Unexplained Phenomena Division in robot form *might* be enough to at least deal with 3000 HR120s. But that force wouldn't stop Stephen Zarcadmium.

The other thing he now knew was that Zarcadmium, just like everyone else, had a weakness. In fact, he was *so* easy to overcome, Franklin realized, that they might have ended this weeks ago. But Zarcadmium's greatest assets were deception and intimidation, which, combined with Franklin's incredible bad luck and complete exhaustion, had totally blinded him to the fact that his rival had arms.

Yes, everyone else had arms, but no one else used them to create giant magical clouds out of nowhere. Franklin had now seen Zarcadmium and his robots create three purple clouds, not counting the one in his dream, and every time, they had lifted their arms into the air, which meant that it was very probable that all Franklin had to do in order to stop Zarcadmium was to tie his hands behind his back.

If the HR120s happened to blow up Vlakdormat in the next twelve hours, and he survived, Franklin was going to give up psychology and become a private investigator.

His thoughts were interrupted by the ceiling caving in on him. This time, Lera did wake up, cursing in pain. The air filled with dust and smelled like wood. Franklin and Lera were both buried under rubble, but they climbed out from under it with only some scrapes, bruises, and a splinter or two. Franklin asked Lera if she was all right, and she nodded, coughed, and spouted an unnaturally long and impolite sounding word in Verullian. None of the pieces of debris was large enough to trap or kill them, but once Franklin saw who was standing on the remainder of the roof, crouching down and looking through the sizable hole she made in it, Franklin almost wished it had killed them.

"Hi there," said Helena, or whoever was controlling her body. "Sorry to barge in like this. The door was locked."

Helena dropped down and landed at the foot of their bed. She looked around the once-clean room and nodded in approval. "Nice place you've got here, Bryce. Besides the roof damage, of course."

Lera gave Franklin a look as if this was somehow his fault. He ignored her.

"Let me take a wild guess," Franklin said. "Sandra."

"Righty-oh, Cap'n Obvious," Sandra said. She jumped up playfully and landed in a cross-legged position on the end of the bed. She squealed a high-pitched, mad cackle.

"What's so funny?" said Lera. She had begun to glow red and was already standing in a fighting stance next to the bed. Franklin knew it didn't matter to Lera that she couldn't possibly win in a fight against Helena.

"What's funny is that the last words you two are ever going to hear are 'righty-oh, Cap'n Obvious.'"

"You're close," came another voice, "but Sandra's slightly cleverer." Sandra whirled around in surprise, only to get her head ripped off and smashed through once with a very resilient fist.

"Hello, Dr. Bryce," Helena said, standing beside the very convincing corpse of an HR120. She dropped its head on top of the body that had fallen unceremoniously to the floor. She paused for a second, considering the head. Franklin figured that would be a strange experience for anyone.

"I knew it was an HR120," Lera said.

"Then why didn't you say anything?" Franklin asked.

"Would it have helped?"

Franklin smacked himself in the forehead with the palm of his hand, twice for good measure.

"Dr. Bryce?" Helena said.

"Damn," Franklin said. "Not a dream. How did you know it was here?" he asked Helena.

"Requarr and I have been listening to police radio. Someone reported a disturbance at this address, and I knew it could only be one thing."

"Thanks," Lera said. "I'll never be able to picture you now without seeing you ripping holes in my roof or holding your own head. But thanks. I doubt we would have made it."

"They're getting desperate," Franklin said. "They don't care about you anymore, Lera. They must have thought if they could get rid of the both of us before attacking Vlakdormat they'd have a better shot at succeeding."

"But they must know that as soon as they attack, I'm going to be there," said Helena.

"Zarcadmium's a powerful man," Lera said. "Surely his plan

is more complicated than charging 3000 robots on the building."

Franklin glared at Lera for a split second. She didn't know it, but Franklin had no intention of telling Helena anything about the attack on Vlakdormat. "And no, Helena, you aren't going to be there," he said.

"Excuse me?" Helena said.

"Lera's right. Zarcadmium will be planning for that."

"We both know what Zarcadmium wants from me," said Helena. "But look—I figured that out on my own and didn't turn evil. I have to be there. Without me—"

"You're a liability," Franklin said coldly. "An HR120 pretending to be Sandra is a pretty good reminder of that. Not to mention Zarcadmium's clouds. Those robots knew how to revive you. Who's to say they don't know another way to trigger your off-switch."

"You know something I don't," Helena said. Franklin swallowed.

"What do you mean?"

"I know you've evacuated Vlakdormat. You put up a hologram over the building to make it look like business as usual, but I can see through it."

Franklin folded his arms. "Any other new powers you want to let me in on?"

"You want to tell me when this attack is happening?" Helena said.

They both stared at each other in cold, awkward silence for a long time. The dust particles from the broken ceiling were the only moving things in the room.

Lera, of course, was the one to break the silence. "Should I give you two some alone time?"

"This isn't funny," Franklin said. The very last thing he wanted, the worst thing that could possibly happen, would be for Zarcadmium to be allowed anywhere near Helena again.

"You're not going to be there. This is my operation," Franklin said.

"You have *operations* now? So you do know when it's going to happen," said Helena.

"Yes," Franklin said. "And when it does, you're not going to be there. It's best for everyone involved. You know this isn't because I don't trust you."

"I know."

"Then promise me you won't be there."

"I'm sorry, Franklin," Helena said. "I can't make that promise." She bent her knees slightly and gradually pushed off from the floor, effortlessly floating into the air toward the hole in the ceiling. Franklin followed her with his eyes in dismay.

CHAPTER 34

More Than a Demonstration

"THE ENVIRONMENTAL RALLY IS SCHEDULED TO START IN SIX HOURS," DRAKE SAID TO FRANKLIN'S ARMY IN HIS LAB AT VLAKDORMAT. There were thirty people in all, including Drake, Franklin, Lera, Dr. Caslom, and the entire staff of Vlakdormat security. The rest of the building was completely shut down, and they were the only people there. Inside one room, it seemed like they had a lot of people, but once they met up against Zarcadmium and his robots, it would feel like no one at all. Lera had promised there were over 200 agents from the Verullian Interdimensional Bureau of Investigation on their way, but that still put the odds at more than fifteen to one. Hopefully, if Franklin modified his plan correctly, it wouldn't matter.

Drake said, "Everyone has their assignments, so be sure to be in place at—"

"It's not going to work," Franklin said, interrupting Drake. "If we engage the HR120s as planned, we're all going to die. Everyone but Zarcadmium."

"I don't mean to embarrass you in front of everyone," Lera said, "but you can't read the future any more than you can read minds."

"I've thought a lot about this," Franklin said. He considered telling them about the dream, but he decided that it was a bad idea. He didn't want to look like he was having a nervous breakdown just before they went to war. Better to just make it look like a change in strategy. "It doesn't matter what we're able to do to the HR120s—this isn't about them. It's about Zarcadmium. We have to switch our focus to him."

"We already have a plan for him," Drake said. "Vlakdormat security was able to rig up a pocket dimension just like you requested."

The idea was that one of them would suck Zarcadmium in through a portable aperture, and if he produced any unknown energy at all (the kind produced by a purple cloud) he wouldn't have the chance to escape because the pocket dimension would immediately self-destruct and implode in on itself.

"I know, and it was a good idea, but that magic is too unpredictable. We can't beat it with technology. We have to beat Zarcadmium himself, physically."

"Now this plan is finally starting to sound fun," said Lera.

"The only way we can keep him trapped is to make sure he can't use his magic at all. And the only way to do that is to prevent him from raising his arms into the air. No arms, no purple cloud."

"We're going to amputate him?" asked Agent Grax in horror. "I can't authorize that, sir." Grax was the new head of Vlakdormat security, promoted after Strexit had lost his personality. He was a beefy, bald, middle-aged man who had worked at the facility twice as long as Franklin had.

Franklin shook his head. "We're just going to tie him up and make sure he stays that way at all times."

Drake looked at Franklin disapprovingly. It was a look Franklin wasn't used to seeing from him, and it was especially odd coming from the female version. Franklin just couldn't get used to him without a goatee. "How do you know that will work any better than the imploding pocket dimension?" Drake asked. "Maybe he just raises his arms for dramatic effect."

"I can't explain it," said Franklin. "You're all just going to have to trust me."

"This is a lot to take on your word, Dr. Bryce," Dr. Caslom said. It was the first time he had spoken. "Zarcadmium has the ability to—"

"This is what we have to do," Franklin said. "No arms, no magic. I can't explain how I know, but I know. Call it a hunch, call it whatever you want, but I've been around all of this more than anyone here. So any of you who don't want to believe in that, you know where the door is."

Drake folded his arms and bit his lip. Franklin paused for a moment, but he still clearly had the floor.

"We're not going to use an imploding dimension because, if I'm right about this, we won't have to kill anyone, besides some robots."

"It occurs to me that if we have to get to Zarcadmium's arms, we're going to need to catch him first," Drake said, "before he can use any magic on us."

"Any ideas?" Franklin asked.

"What you need is a vacuum," came a new voice from the doorway. Franklin turned to see a winged silhouette on the wall. Rajel Chirok stepped into the light and held out his hands arrogantly. He certainly knew how to make an entrance.

"How did you know we were here?" Franklin said.

"Hey, I was evacuated with everyone else. I knew something was going on, so I've been eavesdropping on these little meetings of yours. Super-hearing—just bought it back a couple days ago."

"You're the last person I expected to want to help with this."

Chirok came closer and placed a hand on Franklin's shoulder. "I'll tell you why I'm here, but it has to be our secret." He pulled Franklin off to the side, then looked back and spoke to the room.

"No one else here has super-hearing, I hope?"

No one said anything, so Chirok turned his back to the rest of the group and huddled with Franklin, whispering in his ear. "I don't want anyone else to know this . . . but I don't want to see you get hurt. And if you tell anyone I told you that, I'll kill you."

Chirok patted Franklin's shoulder and stepped to the middle of the lab. "You're planning to use portable apertures to suck HR120s into pocket dimensions. The problem with a portable aperture, of course, is that you can only pull in one body at a time. And they only work at close range, so you might not be able to get close enough to Zarcadmium to use one."

"You could always use your persuasion powers to make him get close enough," Franklin said.

"Oh no," said Chirok. "Not this time. Three thousand killer robots immune to Threpnoidian persuasion? No thanks. This is your shindig. I'm helping from the sidelines on this one, pal. But what if you had an aperture that was powerful enough to suck everything around it, a football field's length away?"

"I've only seen one thing that could do that," Franklin said. His eyes widened when he realized what Chirok was getting at. He wanted to use Borflostmikite Havst, the man who had once masqueraded as a dimension.

"I don't trust Havst. We could just get the technology he used to make himself an aperture and do it to one of us. Or all of us," Franklin said.

"Too expensive," said Chirok. "At least, a little more expensive than what you'll be paying us. And you couldn't possibly get it in six hours. Besides, you don't trust me, and we've worked together before, so what's the dif?"

"Paying you?"

"Look, it took a lot for me to look up and talk to the jerk who stole my powers, but I'm bigger than petty revenge. I knew Havst was your best shot, so I found him, snuck up on him, beat the crap out him for good measure, and told him I'd split my pay with him if he'd help. If Havst is anything, he's predictable. He'll do anything for a check."

"And how much is this check?" Franklin asked.

Chirok pulled out a piece of paper and handed it to Dr. Caslom. "Sorry, but this is going to require deeper pockets. No offense."

Dr. Caslom looked at the paper, frowned, and handed it back to Chirok. "Get your friend here and give us a demonstration of his ability. Then I'll sign the check."

"Wonderful," Chirok said.

"One thing," said Lera. "What if Havst sucks in a bunch of HR120s along with Zarcadmium and whoever goes to tie him up? Won't we have the same problem in there we would out here? They could provide cover fire for him, and he could escape before anyone ever reaches him."

"That won't be an issue," Chirok said. "It doesn't take a lot to piss off that giant eyeball. And it's got heat vision."

It might be the last Threpnoidian Dragonfly Franklin would ever have, and he had been slowly and deliberately drinking it for the last hour. In a few minutes, an Agvorian comedian was scheduled to perform.

Each Agvorian body part sounded like a different musical instrument, and this particular comedian was renowned in several dimensions for being able to play any song ever written and make it sound just like the original recording. But as much as he probably needed to do so, Franklin didn't feel like laughing. He decided he would leave as soon as the comedian came on stage.

"Is this seat taken?" William Vanderhorst asked, setting down the mustard beverage he always ordered.

Franklin's heart raced a little. He didn't want to see William right now. He didn't want his friend to know what he was about to do. But he invited him to sit down anyway. He wasn't sure he'd ever see William again.

"I never said I was sorry," William said, "for making you come all the way to the past to get me and for getting myself fired." He didn't look great. He obviously hadn't shaved since the last time they had spoken, and Franklin couldn't remember the last time he had seen William wearing a t-shirt. Especially a "Dance Dance Revolution" t-shirt.

"Apology accepted," Franklin said. "You doing okay?"

William sighed. "I've never been a pessimist, Franklin, but I've got nowhere to go. It's only a matter of time before my money runs out."

"You've been in this business for years. You'll find something."

"I got fired from *Vlakdormat.* I won't be able to find another job, here or in any other dimension. And it's not like I've got the capital to start out on my own. Maybe if I'd been fired from that dump you worked at when you found Helena. . . ."

Franklin smiled uncomfortably. "You'll figure it out. You always do."

"And what about you?" William said, changing the subject. "Any HR120 incidents since I left?"

"No," Franklin lied, "nothing in the last three days."

"I want to know if they make it to Vlakdormat. I want to be

there for you."

"I'll let you know."

"So how's Helena?"

"She's keeping her distance, respecting Caslom's request. She's still staying with Requarr."

William nodded. "And what about Franklin number two?"

"He went back to help clean up his Vlakdormat." That was actually the honest truth. Franklin hadn't asked his counterpart to help in the fight for the same reason he didn't want William there. They had both lost too much to the HR120s; they were too deeply involved to be any help to him. As much as he'd rather have them by his side, they were liabilities.

"You think he's okay?" William asked.

"Franklin's a strong guy."

William smiled. "So are you. And that means something, because I realize now that you aren't both the same guy. You never would have gone back to Corvadia with me."

"Thanks. But he and I have just had different experiences."

They both drank quietly together for a few minutes until William suddenly looked very serious and very sad.

"Do you think things can ever be the way they used to be? Before all of this started?"

Franklin gave William an expression of complete sincerity, and he didn't have to say a word. They both knew that whatever the future held, the last few months had changed both of their lives forever.

When Franklin returned to Drake's laboratory, Havst was standing there, surrounded by Franklin's troops. He was letting out a long, hardy belly laugh.

"What's so funny?" Franklin said, folding his arms. He wasn't thrilled with the notion of working with Havst. Plus, it was strange to see anyone who knew what was coming do anything but scowl. That was, except for Chirok, who seemed generally capable of really only one expression, and that was one of cheap, insincere salesmanship.

"Mr. Havst is in the middle of displaying the talent we've called on him for," Dr. Caslom said. "He just sucked Rajel Chirok into himself."

Franklin tried to remain serious, but even he had to admit that it was really funny.

"Let him out," Franklin said.

Havst was furious. "What are you, my boss?" he said. But when Havst got angry, his aperture was always activated, so Rajel Chirok immediately flew across the room from Havst's stomach.

"When I said 'demonstration,' I didn't mean *me*!" roared Chirok.

Havst cracked up again, but this time Franklin ignored him. He took a long look around the room. The 200 Verullian agents had now arrived. They wore Hawaiian shirts and sunglasses, which Franklin thought looked really silly, especially in the middle of winter, but Lera had told him that Verullians didn't get cold and that was how VIBI agents always dressed. They looked like William on his best-dressed day, and Franklin thought his wardrobe was completely unprofessional. They stood at full attention and looked as though theirs was the most important job in the world.

Franklin also noticed that a twenty-seventh security guard had arrived. "Agent Strexit?" he said in surprise.

"We've been retraining him," said Agent Grax.

"I was told I lost my personality," Strexit said. "I still have skills and things. But no memory. And I'm told I'm really boring at parties."

"He can't lead anymore," Grax said, "but he knows how to fight. And he can operate a portable aperture."

"I'm going to need one of those as well," Dr. Caslom said, slinking his way to Franklin's side.

"I'm not sure that's a good idea."

"I fought in the Trasultonia and the Plavquam Wars in Makveria. This is still my facility. Just because you're taking charge of the fight doesn't mean you can stop me from defending this place."

Franklin was hesitant, but he wasn't about to argue. No matter how much he cared about Vlakdormat, Caslom must have cared about it more. "All right. But no one does anything he or she doesn't have to. I'm going to try and end this before any fighting happens, if I can. Is the force field up?"

"Yes sir," Grax said.

"Good. Our lives are more important than the building, but let's keep the fight outside if possible. There's a good chance they won't risk being seen as HR120s, and it would be best if Vlakdormat didn't get destroyed."

"I agree," said Caslom.

Franklin had a stirring speech planned. He was going to talk about sacrifice and honor and the irony of therapists fighting against insane people who blow up dimensions; but before he could say anything else, the room flashed red, a loud, obnoxious alarm klaxon sounded, and monitors all around the room showed different angles of the property outside the building.

Environmental activists. Hundreds of them, all wearing heavy coats and carrying picket signs. The HR120s had arrived, and they were right on time.

When they were outside, Franklin's army stood behind him in three long rows in front of Vlakdormat's large glass double door entrance. Franklin's second-in-command, Dr. Drake, stood next to him with his hands on his hips.

"Drake, you're freaking me out," Franklin whispered as he tried to look commanding in front of the robots.

"I can't help it. I've never had hips before," Drake said.

Franklin had to hand it to the HR120s. They looked like they were conducting a harmless demonstration. The intel Drake had gotten from the HR120's brain was right—there were hundreds of them. As Franklin surveyed the area, he realized that even in their disguises, the HR120s were already setting themselves up strategically. They were lined up and down both sides of the street in front of Vlakdormat, and as many of them as there were, no one would ever suspect they were deliberately "picketing" Vlakdormat. Besides, there was a strip of fast food restaurants that began across the street, and they easily could have been misconstrued as reminding people not to litter.

That was assuming, of course, that they didn't start firing energy beams all over the place.

It had been a cold but sunny afternoon when Franklin had come back from Krawkson Klub, but now the weather had taken a dramatic turn. Dark, menacing clouds now filled the sky, and it made Franklin nervous. It looked too much like his dream. He continued scanning the crowd, but he didn't see Zarcadmium.

Franklin cupped his hands around his mouth and shouted at the crowd, stepping away from his people. "Zarcadmium! We're here, and we're ready for you. We know what you're here for. But you're not getting into the building. We have 200 Verullians staring down your robots, figuring out your secrets with their intuition. The rest of us are ready for a fight if that's what you want, but it's going to happen out here. If your robots stay, they will be exposed to the public. Or you can send them away and we can talk about what this is really about—me and you."

The HR120s didn't react. They just kept waving their signs and chanting about pollution and climate change. But after a few long moments, one short, fat figure emerged from the crowd, wearing a blue coat over a red t-shirt and a baseball cap. He walked across the street and stood in front of Franklin. He took his hat off slowly in a dramatic reveal, but it was already obvious that he was Stephen Zarcadmium. Everyone had to make an entrance.

"I'm impressed," he whispered calmly to Franklin. "I honestly don't know how you figured out when we'd be here. My robots have penetrated your hologram in the office windows, depicting people diligently working at their computers and talking with patients—we know there's no one inside. I had hoped to destroy the building, kill everyone who knows the Helena . . . but it appears now there's no point."

"Why don't you just send them home, then?" Franklin said. "I'd like to talk with you."

Zarcadmium shook his head. "You can't be naïve enough to think you and I are the most important players here, as you suggested. This is really about someone who isn't even here, the only person who could have *really* saved you were this to become a . . . physical conflict."

"You're not getting near Helena."

"You should have invited her."

"I'm still ready for you. You're not going to attack us now. It would only be a matter of time before the media got here, and then the world would know that everyone at this demonstration is an HR120."

Franklin could have ordered Havst to activate his aperture and suck Zarcadmium into the pocket dimension at that very moment. But he knew Zarcadmium was both unstable and unpredictable. He had sent that replica of Helena after Franklin in desperation—who knew what else he might have his robots do? Franklin hoped the Verullians would scare him enough to make him send his robots away. Then Zarcadmium would be alone when Franklin used his secret weapon.

But that isn't what happened at all.

Zarcadmium snapped his fingers, and the HR120s dropped their picket signs. Thousands of robot arms transformed into huge guns and blades. They began walking as one huge unit toward Franklin and his people.

"Is it really worth all this?" Franklin said. "You were always so careful before."

"You're not the only one with a hologram. Mine's just *bigger*. No one outside of Vlakdormat's property can see us. They'll think everything is just business as usual."

Franklin looked at Havst, who was starting to get very angry. But Franklin shook his head, signaling for Havst to try to control himself for now. Giant eye or no, Franklin didn't want to have to fight 3000 HR120s by himself when he and Zarcadmium went into the pocket dimension.

As the HR120s continued to advance, the security guards pulled out their portable apertures and stood ready. Lera tapped

Franklin on the shoulder.

"I'm sorry," she said. "I wasn't completely honest about how far the Verullians are willing to get involved. They're secret agents, not soldiers, and this isn't their fight or a matter of Verullian security."

"You're saying they won't fight with us?" Franklin said over his shoulder.

"That's right. They have a pocket dimension aperture that will get them someplace safe, and they're about to use it. And if I want to keep my job, I have to go with them."

"You knew they were going to do this?"

"It was the only way I could get them here. The VIBI was willing to be here as a deterrent, but they're unwilling to risk the lives of their people in this conflict. I had hoped maybe their presence would be enough to get Zarcadmium to back off. I guess I didn't have much intuition this time."

Franklin didn't know what to say. He was angry she had lied to him, but she'd certainly been trying to help the only way she knew how.

"I don't want to go. But there's not much more I can do than you can. Just use Havst. It's a good plan."

The HR120s began firing.

Franklin gave his wife a very quick kiss goodbye. "I'll see you when this is over."

The Verullians were gone in a flash, which left just the thirty of them against Zarcadmium's entire army. The security guards starting sucking HR120s into pocket dimensions as they took cover from all the energy fire. Franklin himself hid behind a Buick. He glanced around a tire and saw Drake, with broadswords where his arms used to be, slicing at two HR120s.

Drake glanced back and looked annoyed. Franklin suddenly realized the car he was hiding behind was Drake's.

Franklin heard a loud thunder clap over the sounds of energy fire and metal hitting metal. Lightning filled the sky, and then a hard rain began to fall.

HR120s started exploding. Right and left they simply blew up. Franklin looked up and found exactly what he had expected.

Helena.

And she was dive-bombing the robots, just as he had expressly told her not to do.

But more importantly, just like she had done in his dream.

Zarcadmium still stood right in the middle of his forces. They fired with deadly accuracy, never hitting their leader. Franklin had to use Havst soon, but he still wanted to get Zarcadmium more isolated. He just hoped his people could hold out in the meantime. He continued to watch, and when he thought there was an opening in the energy fire near him, he took off in a sprint, hoping to draw Zarcadmium near him. The HR120s seemed more interested in shooting at his friends rather than at him. Franklin thought that if Zarcadmium were like most lunatics with vendettas, he would want to kill Franklin himself.

Franklin caught a glimpse of Rajel Chirok flying over the crowd. He had still been inside the building when the fight started, waiting to collect his pay from Dr. Caslom, but he hadn't managed to get out in time. No doubt he was trying to get away from the fight but he was having a hard time of it, dodging energy blasts right and left.

As he ran away from the battle and toward the street, Franklin heard fewer explosions. He looked behind him and no longer saw Helena in the air or robots blowing up on the ground.

Before he had long to think about it, Franklin was in the air.

"Helena, I told you not to come here," Franklin said.

"But I'm glad she did," said a deep, feminine voice that wasn't quite Helena's. "I really wanted to crash through the ceiling like my robot counterpart. That looked like fun. But unfortunately, you were outside."

It was Sandra, and she was not an HR120 this time. He had never seen an HR120 fly.

"What do you want?" Franklin asked.

"Well, I've always wanted an excuse to get revenge on someone. And I seem to recall that you considered letting Eva Crill try to *eradicate* me one time."

"She did try. It didn't work."

"That's not the point," Sandra said. She held Franklin with both hands and was flying up and toward the building.

Sandra landed on the roof and dropped Franklin unceremoniously to the glass. "I thought it might be fun to just stand up here and watch all your friends die. What do you think?"

Franklin ignored her and looked over the edge. Besides the fact that Sandra was on the roof with him, the only difference between this and his dream was that this time, he had remembered to bring his cell phone with him. He pulled it out of his pocket, but Sandra smacked it out of his hand like lightning and it went careening over the roof.

"So what are you going to do when this is over?" Franklin asked her.

"After I eat you?" she asked. She laughed, but Franklin wasn't sure she was joking. "I might join the Stephen Zarcadmium fan club. Helena hates the guy, but I don't see what the fuss is about. He built us to rule the planet. The man has style."

Franklin looked down again and saw Zarcadmium standing in the middle of the yard, raising his hands.

"Now Havst!" Franklin shouted, but he was sure the Jexarite couldn't hear him. He was busy shooting HR120s with his heat vision and teleporting away from energy blasts.

The purple cloud emerged just underneath the rain clouds and began to grow. Franklin stared at it in horror while Sandra let out an ear-splitting cackle. She waved down at Zarcadmium and grabbed Franklin by the throat. A flash of lightning shot toward the ground where Zarcadmium was standing, and in seconds he materialized on the roof next to Helena.

"Sandra?" he said in bewilderment.

"At your service," she said.

"I thought it might be you. I've been watching you. I like your style. You're a good role model for Helena. I wish she'd take after you more and less after Franklin here."

"You see Franklin?" Sandra said. "Someone around here appreciates me. This body of ours obviously isn't for saving people. Why can't you and Helena get that through your craniums?"

Zarcadmium's smile quickly faded as he kneeled down next to Franklin and looked into his eyes. "I'm sorry it had to come to this, I really am. If I could think of something else to do with you, I would. None of this would even be possible without you, and don't think for a moment I've lost sight of that. You saved me. But my vision isn't complete without Helena, and you're putting her on a path she wasn't meant for. A noble, good path, to be sure, but hers is a higher calling, and if I thought you could understand that . . well, things would be different."

This was the end. Again. Red energy swirled in and out of the cloud above them, and Franklin had no way out. Either Zarcadmium would end him, or Sandra would. Two psychopaths, both thirsty for a vague sense of power, any power. And based on what he had seen, Helena's penchant for destruction as profound as her heroism, and Zarcadmium was right about one thing: without Franklin's guidance, her path was a frightening one.

"Let go of him," Zarcadmium said. "This man deserves to die with some dignity. It is a terrible thing that must be done. It is a crime. Necessary, but a crime, nonetheless. And so, it should be on me, and me alone. So I ask you to stand back, Sandra."

Sandra was reluctant, but she obeyed.

"Sure, whatever," she said. She moved back three paces and looked up at the billowing cloud over their heads. The instant Zarcadmium began to raise his hands in the air, she shot at Zarcadmium and Franklin faster than the lightning that never came. With Franklin and Zarcadmium both tightly in her embrace, she flew directly at a very surprised, very angry Borflostmikite Havst.

CHAPTER 35

Twisted Logic and Secret Weapons

As he was pulled into the vortex, Franklin looked behind him and saw several HR120s, Drake R. Drake, and Helena being sucked in behind him.

Mr. Havst had come through.

The sky was blue again, and there was now an endless green field where Vlakdormat used to be. Franklin was bruised, but he got up as fast as he could, hoping to get to Zarcadmium before he could produce another purple cloud. Franklin looked around frantically, and it wasn't long before he found him. Sure enough, someone had gotten to Zarcadmium before him. It was Helena. She stood beside him with a twisted smile.

"That was a good trick," Zarcadmium said. "I think you had us both fooled."

Helena hit Zarcadmium in the gut and then threw a punch at his face. As he fell to the ground, Franklin pulled a pair of handcuffs from his back pocket and threw them to her.

"You were never Sandra, were you?" Franklin said.

"Of course not. What are the odds Sandra would actually show up the same day an HR120 posed as her?"

"Stranger things have happened. You had me convinced."

"Good. Made it more likely to work. I flew down and asked Drake what your plan was in the middle of the battle. All he told me was to get Zarcadmium isolated. Then I saw Havst and figured this was where you wanted him. Sorry I had to take you with us, but I couldn't risk that cloud being on some kind of autopilot or something."

Franklin fought a smile. "I told you not to be here."

"You're welcome," Helena said.

Franklin was worried that the HR120s that were now inside the pocket dimension would come after him, but there were only about a dozen and they were all preoccupied with the giant, floating eye's heat vision. It attacked them just as Chirok had predicted. Each robot fired several energy blasts at the eyeball, but it simply absorbed them and continued firing its own energy without pause. It destroyed them all in less than a minute, and after it had turned them all into piles of scrap, the floating eye looked almost disappointed. Then it looked at Franklin, who turned his head and focused on Zarcadmium, and it flew off into the distance.

After a moment, Dr. Drake came to Franklin's side. "You got him," he said, cheerfully.

"I just hope I'm right about this," Franklin said. He half-expected another purple cloud to appear out of thin air right above them and fry them all.

When Zarcadmium came to, he struggled to get his hands loose and then looked up at Franklin in horror. "What . . . what have you *done*?" he panicked.

"So," Fralink said, "you really can't use your magic without your hands."

"You have to let me go . . . you don't understand."

Helena stood over him and balled her hands into fists. "I'm going to kill you," she said. "I'll make it quick if you give me some answers first."

"Helena—" Franklin started.

"After everything he's done to us," Helena asked Franklin, "are you really going to try and stop me?"

Helena was playing right into his hands. She had proven she

could be both a hero and a killer, and if she killed an unarmed man deliberately, no matter what he might have done, she would be making her permanent decision right there.

"Let's get some answers," Franklin said. "And then, if you still want to kill him, there's no one here who can stop you."

"I didn't make the Helena," Zarcadmium whispered. Before, he would never have volunteered that kind of information, but now it was as if it didn't matter to him, as if his life was over just because he was wearing a pair of handcuffs. "She was given to me as part of a plan. Someone else's plan."

Helena seemed less tense as she leaned closer, now at least as intrigued as she was angry. "Whose?"

"I was her emissary," Zarcadmium said. "But I failed. *She* gave me the power to destroy a dimension, to see if I was strong enough not to use it."

Franklin and Drake made eye contact, and Drake looked as stunned as Franklin. The difference between this Zarcadmium and the other version of him was that this Zarcadmium hadn't just destroyed his planet . . . he had destroyed his entire *dimension.* As far as Franklin knew, that occurrence was as unlikely as a person being a dimension.

"But then I did," Zarcadmium said. "All I wanted was to *save* Corvadia, but my people were destroying themselves, much in the same way the people in your dimension are. Pollution, war, greed. I invented the CR120s to influence policy, not to destroy mankind. Sure, I built weapons into them just in case. . . . But the rest of my people didn't care enough about Corvadia to end the madness. So I grew impatient, angry. The changes weren't happening fast enough—they weren't happening at all. I used my robots to take over the world. And that incited a civil war. I couldn't change enough minds, even through a global takeover. I decided that a dimension doesn't deserve to exist if its people don't care whether or not it does. So I ended it."

"That's when you came to my dimension," Franklin said.

"The year was 1951 in your dimension. I realized it had some of the same problems mine had, so I decided to try again. I set up CR120s to start an environmental movement and tried to establish them in key positions in the public and private sectors to influence people and policy, and I renamed them HR120s. I altered them so their eyes looked human and they could have human instead of Corvadian children. Gradually, there were a significant number of humans who also supported our cause. And when an HR120 got too 'old,' it would fake its own death and reintegrate into society with false identification, much like the driver's license I gave to the Helena. But after a few months, I just let the HR120s do what they were programmed to do. I fell into a deep depression for decades and did next to nothing."

"Until you started seeing Franklin in therapy," Drake said.

"He helped me to get my life back. I realized my mistake, but that I was on the right track with my mission on Earth. Once I was stable again, I retook control of the HR120s and started pushing the environmental movement further than I ever had. A few years later, s*he* finally contacted me again—the entity who gave me the magic of the purple cloud. Only other time she ever did.

"She said she wanted to use my HR120s to take over the Earth, but that they needed a greater leader than I could give them. She created the Helena and gave her six extra personalities. The six would all provide a well-roundedness that would mold the seventh into a mature, independent personality, and after a time, this training would make Helena ready to lead my robots and do what was necessary to rule the world and make it the very best it could be. She also gave the HR120s the ability to access the power of the purple cloud under one condition, and one only: they could revive Helena were she ever to be deactivated. She wouldn't tell me under what circumstances this failsafe would be triggered, but she said this was in place in case the Helena were to ever fall into the wrong hands. Once the process was completed and the Helena was in charge, your planet would finally become the utopia every world should be. The utopia I tried to create in Corvadia."

Franklin's eyes went wide with horror. This was his own fault, at least partially. If he hadn't helped this madman get his life back, perhaps none of this would have ever happened. And whoever *she* was, she would probably have just found someone else with a bunch of robots and made him her emissary.

"I had the same powers on Earth I had in Corvadia; she never took them from me. She gave me a second chance after my failure with Corvadia. But I couldn't use the purple cloud to create another Helena. She said there was to be only one in the entire multiverse.

"I also used my powers to erase myself from the historical record, so no one could connect me to the HR120s and potentially discover the secret of the Helena. You'd have to go back in time to find any evidence I even existed. My mistake was showing you a purple cloud to give you your telepathy."

"Why tell us any of this?" Helena said.

"Because you asked," Zarcadmium said sadly to Helena. "I have nothing left to live for. My dream is dead. The HR120s belong to her, and she wants you to have them, Helena Kathryn.

I've failed her again. I have always felt the magic, and it's gone now. Even if I could use my hands now, it wouldn't do any good."

"You're bluffing," Franklin said. "You just want us to take the handcuffs off."

"I don't care what you do with me now," Zarcadmium said. "I was supposed to make sure that Helena took complete control over your dimension, but you got in the way. I knew with you around, she wouldn't have the environment she needed to do what needed to be done. You guided her to protect whoever was in jeopardy, and by extension, she protected the status quo. You taught her to be a bodyguard when she was meant to be so much more. I instructed the HR120s to stop anyone from interfering with the Helena's development, but not at the cost of exposing themselves. If their identities were ever compromised, we would be forced to take action before the Helena was ready to lead. So you can see the difficult position I was in. I needed Helena to be a fighter, a killer, knowing full well that peace always comes at a high price. She had the ability to force change, but without my guidance, that would never happen.

"On the other hand, I couldn't take her by force. She has no idea how powerful she is, but at her fullest potential, she will be far beyond the magic of the purple cloud. And unfortunately, the Helena got to you before my HR120s could speak to her, since the first one I sent after her malfunctioned and went homicidal—in your office, of all places. I spent the next three months putting the whole plan on hold while I tried to figure out what was wrong. I couldn't afford the others failing so dramatically while working with the Helena."

"Who is s*he*?" Helena asked.

"*She* is beyond all comprehension," Zarcadmium said. "I have never seen her. I'm not sure she can be seen. She only contacted me through letters. You are her creation, Helena Kathryn, her gift to the multiverse."

"And she wants me to, what, stop pollution?"

Zarcadmium laughed, but it was somehow without any humor. "I'm sure her plans are beyond any I ever had. But I do know that her influence stretches to the farthest reaches of the multiverse. Whatever reason she has for giving Earth to the Helena, it's only the beginning."

It wasn't long before Mr. Havst got angry again and they were all thrown out of the pocket dimension once more and back in front of Vlakdormat. Helena hadn't killed Zarcadmium, and Franklin was grateful for that. But he wasn't sure why. Had he actually talked her out of it, or did she believe Zarcadmium's bizarre story of her birth and decided he might be useful later? He hoped it was the former.

One thing Zarcadmium had said was instantly proven to be true. The HR120s that were left near Vlakdormat (the dozen in Havst's pocket dimension had all been fried by the giant eyeball) were completely under Helena's power. Zarcadmium said nothing to them and they ignored him as he walked by; they simply stood there until Helena gave them orders. She was taken aback by this and wasn't sure what to do.

"You are the Helena," they each said repeatedly.

"Yeah. . . . I'm the Helena," she said finally. "So this is what I want you to do. Keep cleaning up the environment and, uh . . . don't kill people. Or turn your arms into things."

She told Franklin she figured that was best for now. After all, there was nothing wrong with wanting to save the environment, and Helena didn't like being responsible for six other personalities and superpowers, let alone thousands of robots. The HR120s began to walk away, but once each of them had taken a few steps away from the building, they disappeared, as if they were walking through an invisible portal.

"Did you all see that?" Franklin asked.

"We did," Drake said. "And speaking of . . . there were only about fifty of them, total. Where did the rest of them go?"

"And where are the security guards and Dr. Caslom?" Helena said.

"They all disappeared too," Havst said. "But they didn't walk into a void or anything like those HR120s just now. After you all got sucked into my pocket dimension, they just vanished." He pointed at a light post off to the right and center of the yard, which was just about where the HR120s had gotten by the time they had disappeared. "Anyone past that pole was gone as soon as you all were, but they weren't sucked up by my aperture."

Franklin looked at Zarcadmium, but he didn't say a word. Franklin couldn't tell if he really knew what had happened or not. He seemed completely indifferent. But the purple cloud he had made twenty minutes earlier still swirled in the air above the building.

"This is really bizarre," said Franklin. "I'm going to check it out."

"But there's no telling where you'll end up," Drake said. "It could be a void into nothingness."

Franklin pointed at Zarcadmium. "We all just survived *that*," he said. "I'm going to take my chances. And if this is something he did, I doubt he'd just kill off all of his robots. Especially not before he knew he was beaten. I'll be back for you."

"I'm coming with you," Helena said.

"Fine," said Franklin.

Franklin gave Zarcadmium to Dr. Drake to deal with for the time being, instructing him to put Zarcadmium in a holding dimension for now. There was still a chance he was lying about everything, but if he could still use his magic and escape from a pocket dimension, it was pretty weak strategy for him to suddenly give control of his robots to Helena, whose destiny had apparently been "contaminated" by Franklin and Vlakdormat.

Franklin and Helena cautiously walked past the light pole and into the unknown. The world ahead of them looked exactly the same once they crossed the barrier, except for the weather.

"Weren't there just storm clouds above us?" Helena asked. "Wasn't it *raining*?"

The sky was now perfectly clear, and it was night. Thousands of stars twinkled brightly above them and a large crescent moon shone brilliantly in the distance. All of the businesses on the strip were now closed, and there were hardly any cars parked in the lots, unlike twenty seconds earlier.

Franklin turned around to see Vlakdormat again, which had changed along with everything else. There were no lights in the windows, no cars in the lot. Zarcadmium's menacing cloud hovering over the building was gone with the rest of the clouds.

"Can you teleport us?" Franklin asked.

"To where?"

"My house. This doesn't add up. There isn't a time change from a normal dimension and a pocket dimension. I need to check something I'm familiar with, to see just how much has changed."

Helena nodded. She wrapped Franklin in her arms and her forehead furrowed in concentration. Then, they were gone.

When they materialized in Franklin's yard, he immediately noticed a new car in the driveway. Now he was especially suspicious. When had Lera had time to buy a new car? Did she drive it there from Verullia? Franklin doubted that. It was a Lexus.

He unlocked the door, and the two of them tiptoed into the living room, which was completely dark. They stealthily headed into the pitch-black bedroom. Franklin squinted his eyes, trying to see if Lera was sleeping in the bed. As his eyes adjusted, he definitely saw a person-sized bulge in the sheets. After another second or two, he noticed a second bulge.

Franklin immediately hit the lights. Both bulges moved around in a panic, until a head peaked out from under the sheets. And it wasn't Lera's head. Hers popped up second.

"I can explain this," said William Vanderhorst. "And by the way, we're glad you're still alive."

"There really is a very good explanation," Lera said. "But it's a long, long story."

CHAPTER 36

Meanwhile

FRANKLIN HAD KNOWN THERE WOULD BE ADJUSTMENTS TO MAKE, BUT THIS WAS RIDICULOUS. It seemed he couldn't leave his dimension for twenty minutes without all hell breaking loose. He hadn't forgotten the victory he and Helena had just won in defeating Zarcadmium and the HR120s; now the homicidal army of robots that had been after him for the last four months would finally be leaving Franklin and his dimension alone. But somehow, coming home was almost worse for Franklin than robots trying to take over the world.

Franklin was an expert in counseling families with domestic disputes. He knew that people were most irrational when dealing with those closest to them. Now he was beginning to understand why some of these sorts of cases ended in murder. His first mad inclination was to ask Helena to do the job for him, but he decided to let Lera and William explain themselves before he did or said anything at all.

As Lera led them all out of the bedroom, a wave of emotion overcame Franklin. Lera and William both wore pajamas, and imagining them together made Franklin's throat dry. The house only made him sicker. The rooms were the same, but the décor was all wrong. The walls had been repainted to that ugly shade of light green many Verullians were so partial to. Lera had tried to use that color when she and Franklin first bought the house, but Franklin had talked her out of it. He peeked from the hall into the living room and noticed a large flat screen television that hadn't been there that morning. The entire set of furniture in the living room was new. And as they entered the kitchen, he noticed a framed portrait of William and Lera in formal dress, hanging next to a clock on the wall above the kitchen table.

Surely they couldn't have made these changes in twenty minutes, and even if they had, a complex practical joke couldn't explain how day had mysteriously turned into night. Lera shouldn't have even been there; she had gone back to Verullia with the other agents in the middle of the battle with the HR120s. It was painfully evident that this wasn't a simple love affair. William was now completely clean-shaven and there was a confidence in his eyes that hadn't been there earlier at Krawkson Klub. Standing in the kitchen, staring at Helena and himself, William and Lera both looked concerned, perhaps even apologetic, but not the least bit guilty.

Helena said exactly what Franklin was beginning to realize. "Either this is an uncannily similar parallel dimension to ours . . . or we're in the future."

"The latter," Lera said. "Now please, both of you, take a seat. I'll make some coffee. Things may have changed a lot in the last three years, but don't worry. We still have coffee."

"*Three years?*" said Franklin. His dry throat made it come out more like someone scratching a vinyl record than someone talking.

"Like I said, it's a long story," said William. "But we'll try to give you the short version. At least until you're ready to hear the rest. Are you sure you even want to do this now. . . ? Because we could play a game of cards, watch a movie. . . ."

"I think I have an idea, at least about the time differential," Helena said. "When anyone reached a certain point on the grounds, they disappeared. They must have crossed into another time frame, into the future. And whatever caused that to happen . . . the purple cloud must be producing it."

"She's a genius," William said, somewhat sarcastically. "That's our theory, too. The cloud is causing time to move more slowly around Vlakdormat than outside it. Three months after you were all sucked into Havst, a lot of the HR120s and Vlakdormat security suddenly showed up outside of Vlakdormat, as confused by the time differential as you are. For them, almost no time had passed at all. Of course, three months is a little different than three years. . . ."

"We did everything we could to get you out," Lera said. "I checked with every multiversal contact I had, but all of the usual methods of dropping a magical force field have no effect on this thing. The only other expert who may have had an idea was Dr. Drake, and he was in there with you."

"Drake," Franklin said. "I can't believe I forgot about him. He's still in the field. He was going to put Zarcadmium in a holding dimension and then go home."

"I don't think he could do that any faster than five minutes," said Helena. Her brow furrowed in concentration. "If twenty minutes inside the field equals three years here, then Drake won't be back for at least . . . nine months."

"Where did you learn how to do *math*?" William asked her.

Helena smiled. "For that matter, where did I learn how to *fly*?"

"We have to get Drake out of there. Who knows what might have happened to his *body* in the last three years," Franklin said. He would never forgive himself if Drake was trapped in an HR120 for the rest of his life.

William nodded. "Good call. Eva Crill hasn't been in the city for months. Her shop closed down almost a year ago."

"But there is an upside," Lera said. "If he won't make it back for at least nine months, you have that long to get him out. Remember that for the few minutes you've been here, Drake hasn't even moved an inch. But good luck. I'm not telling you not to try, but the VIBI, with all its resources, couldn't even figure out how to drop that field."

"Why did he do this?" Franklin said, still avoiding eye contact with both Lera and William. "What would Zarcadmium gain by changing time?"

"We think it was a backup plan," Lera said, "in case he lost the battle. He, his robots, and Helena would be outside the time displacement field with you trapped in a slower time. That may have given him enough time for Helena's development to finish and his plans for world domination to unfold."

Helena nodded. "It's a smart plan. He probably didn't expect that he and I would both get sucked into Havst's dimension on the other side."

"Exactly," Lera said. She fiddled with her wedding band, and Franklin noticed it wasn't the same one she had been wearing last time he saw her.

Franklin stood up and rubbed his hand across his neck. "I can't take this."

Lera put down the pot of coffee she had just brewed and started toward him. "I know this is going to be difficult for you, but we really need to—"

"You got *married*!" Franklin said. "Again! So what happened? I didn't come back after a few months because of a time displacement field that you *knew about*, and you just couldn't wait anymore?"

"There was no way to know what happened to you," Lera said. "When you didn't come back with everyone else, we thought you were probably dead."

"*Probably*? Surely you knew this could happen. But I suppose marriage isn't as permanent to you as it is for some of the rest of us. After all, when you're 312 years old—*315* now—it doesn't have to be. You just keep marrying into species that die before you, and you can sample just about every kind of man there is!"

"Franklin, that's not fair," said Lera.

"Sure it is. William's lucky husband number twenty-one now, right? Or did it take even less time to declare me dead? Maybe you've been married two or three times since I ran off and *saved the world*."

Lera had been trying to be patient during Franklin's outburst, but it was obvious by the faint red glow around her arms and legs that it was starting to get to her. Franklin didn't care. He felt like both she and William had betrayed him. After learning her other secrets, that she was a VIBI agent and that she had more previous husbands than she had once told him, Franklin was already beginning to suspect Lera wasn't the woman he thought he had married. But now he was certain of it. He turned his back on her and started to walk away. The world outside might not be the way he remembered it, but if he really had been thrown into the future, the last place he wanted to be was a warped version of his own home in which Lera was married to his best friend and he didn't live there anymore.

"Please wait," William said. "There's still a lot you need to know."

"Not from you," Franklin said coldly.

"You have to understand, we really didn't know what happened to you in there. Three years is a long time," Lera said.

"I guess I wouldn't know."

Helena still sat at the table, processing everything but staying quiet.

"We understand you're going to need some space, but it might not be a great idea to go outside right now," William said.

"Why? Did some *other* army of robots take over the world while I was gone?"

"No. And I guess the HR120s don't have big master plans without the big boss to give them orders. The world's . . . more or less fine. But trust me, *you* don't want to be out there until you know more about what's been happening."

"I'll find out on my own. Any news has to better than this."

"I'm coming with you," Helena said.

Franklin nodded and they started for the door.

"Before you go," said Lera, "at least tell us what happened in Havst's dimension."

Franklin hesitated and then gave her a slight nod. "We stopped Zarcadmium. But it looks like he still got the last word."

Franklin and Helena walked silently for several blocks away from the house. Franklin was irrational and angry, and he didn't care. He stared straight ahead and walked at a brisk pace. Helena had no problem keeping up with him, of course, but she followed him without comment for a long time. She was giving him time to think, and he appreciated that. But after about twenty minutes, she finally broke the silence.

"Franklin, where are we going?" she asked.

"I don't know."

"We don't have to stay on foot. I can teleport us anywhere you—"

"I *don't know,*" Franklin said again.

"All right. Good. We'll just keep walking until you've come to terms with the fact that Lera married your best friend and you have no job to go back to. How long do you think that's going to take?"

Franklin stopped walking. He looked up at the clear, star-filled sky and took a deep breath. Then he smiled and shook his head slightly. "You might want to jump back into the time displacement field and try me again in a few minutes."

"I'm really proud of you," Helena said.

"Proud? Why?"

"Your entire life has been turned upside down. Again. Of course this is hard. Of course you're not happy. But even after everything that just happened, you didn't faint, you didn't have a heart attack, and you didn't kill anyone."

"I thought about that last one," Franklin admitted.

"We have to look on the bright side. We're alive. We beat Zarcadmium . . . more or less. I'm not evil. But we need to slow down. It's two in the morning."

"It was six in the evening a few minutes ago."

"Still, you need some rest. Something to eat."

"So it's three years later and now you're *my* therapist."

"You looked like you could use one. Except for occasionally being possessed by other women, I probably wouldn't make a bad one. I did learn from the master."

"How is it you're taking all of this so much better than I am? Forty minutes ago, I had to talk you out of killing Zarcadmium."

"Because I didn't have anything to lose. Three more years doesn't change anything for me. I still have no life, no purpose. But I'm grateful. That's better than having a sinister purpose.

And I didn't kill him, as much as I wanted to, which means killing may not be all I'm good for."

"I guess I have rubbed off on you a little."

"Do you have any money?"

"What? Do I owe you a therapy bill now?"

"No. We need a place to stay for the night."

"Oh. Sure, I should have enough cash for that. Anywhere but the Marriot is good."

CHAPTER 37

Might As Well Be a New Dimension

FRANKLIN AND HELENA ENTERED THE LOBBY OF THE VIKUS HOTEL, A NEW ESTABLISHMENT THAT HAD BEEN BUILT AFTER THE BATTLE AT VLAKDORMAT. It was a large five-story classy building with four marble pillars on either side of the glass double doors in front. But the first thing that caught Franklin's eye was a Vaklock beast checking in at the front desk. It was Franklin's old patient, Tramsey.

"Apparently he never found another therapist," Franklin told Helena, "because he's gone out of his mind."

Franklin and Helena walked to the desk and Franklin tapped Tramsey on the shoulder. The hulking mass spun around, a little annoyed at first, but his hideous armadillo face lit up when he recognized Franklin.

"Dr. Bryce? What are you doing here?" he asked. "It's so good to finally see the legend himself in person, now that he's a celebrity. I guess it's not 'doctor' now, though, is it? Sorry about that."

Franklin took Tramsey by one huge arm and guided him to a corner of the room next to a large, plastic floor plant where no one could hear them.

"Tramsey, what are you talking about?" Franklin said. He lowered his voice. "What are you doing here? People can *see* you."

Tramsey looked confused. "That's what happens when you walk into a room with people in it. Are you feeling okay?"

"Tramsey, you've got to get out of here. Do you want to wind up on the front page of every paper in the country and then be part of a huge government cover-up? They'll lock you in a big, metal room and you'll never see the sun again."

Tramsey looked at Helena and his eyes grew larger. "You're *that* Dr. Bryce? I can't believe it! You're alive!"

"Yes, isn't it fantastic?" Franklin said. "I'm alive and completely confused. Now I need your help. What can you tell me about what's been happening?"

"You've been behind the time displacement field since. . . . Oh, wow, that was *years* ago. . . ."

"So what can you tell me?"

"You mean about why I'm in a crowded hotel lobby filled with humans? Or why I said that thing about you being famous?"

"Yes."

"Things are a little different now. I'm still not eating humans, though. That hasn't changed. But there are a couple of things in the city, interdimensional-type things, that the government hasn't been able to cover up. Things that are really hard to ignore."

Helena was straining to understand Tramsey through his thick, guttural, growling accent, but she seemed to be making out most of it. "Like a building that looks like business as usual, but when someone goes inside, they never come back," she said.

"Yeah, like that," Tramsey said. "Some people are even starting to accept other dimensions and interdimensional species. Others, especially some parts of the government, are denying that, but they don't have a better explanation. The President has even mentioned it a couple of times. He just kinda laughs, says how ridiculous the idea of alternate dimensions is, and moves on to something less important."

Helena and Franklin exchanged surprised glances. The world

had not only changed, but it was in a delicate, possibly unstable transition period. America officially recognizing the existence of the multiverse was like America making official first contact with aliens from another planet. It would eventually mean official public recognition of other dimensions by the U.S. Government, formal agreements with foreign dimensions, interdimensional trade, and a number of new forms of legislation.

Or, it could just as likely be the catalyst of an interdimensional war.

"So you're saying this new hotel is friendly to people from other dimensions?" Helena asked.

"Absolutely," Tramsey said. "The owner is a huge supporter of . . . um, organizations trying to spread the word about alternate dimensions. He's working the front desk tonight. You ought to meet him."

"We will," Franklin said. "We were just about to check in."

"You and *her*?" Tramsey said. "Wait, aren't you—"

"Married?" Franklin said. "No. Yes. Kind of. Long story. Helena and I don't have anywhere else to go tonight. This isn't what you think."

"*Oh,*" Tramsey said. "I understand. Lera's married to Vanderhorst."

"You know William?"

"Yeah, see him all the time at . . . um . . . bridge club."

"Tramsey, there's something you're not telling me."

"There are a *lot* of things I'm not telling you."

"What is it?"

"I don't think I should be the one to tell you. Maybe you should ask your . . . ask Lera."

"I tried. She won't tell me anything either. Tramsey, who

did you think I was? Why am I supposed to be famous?"

"You'll find out. Look, I don't like these kinds of confrontations. And when I get nervous, I get hungry. There are a *lot* of humans here, and the last thing I need right now is another relapse, so could you just—"

Franklin sighed. "We'll just check in now. Nice to see you."

When Franklin and Helena walked back to the front desk, the white-haired hotel manager, Mr. Vikus, was practically glowing to see them.

"Good evening, Senator," he said to Franklin, holding out his hand. Franklin shook it, but he had no idea what was going on. He had apparently managed to make a career in national politics while simultaneously being inside a pocket dimension for the last three years. As impressive as that would have looked on a resume, Franklin was fairly certain that the manager had him confused with someone else. But he decided not to mention it. The manager may have accepted alternate dimensions, but it was likely that he wasn't ready for alternate *people* yet.

"My friend and I would like a room for the night," said Franklin.

The manager's smile transformed into a look of concern. "Are you sure that's wise? With the upcoming election and all? I know it's none of my business, but—"

"What's wrong with staying the night in a hotel?" Franklin asked.

Mr. Vikus glanced at Helena. "Aren't you *married*? To someone else?"

"Yes. No. *Yes*," Franklin said, remembering he was most likely speaking for another man. "*Yes.*"

"I understand," said Mr. Vikus, speaking more softly and

hunching slightly. "Sorry to mention it. I'll be sure to keep this under wraps. And just to show my appreciation for what you've been doing for the country, I'm going to give you and your friend a free room tonight. I know you're still in the primaries and you haven't gotten the ticket yet, but I'm sure you will. You'll have my vote."

"Thanks," Franklin said, barely managing to get the word out. He looked around the lobby, dumbfounded, as Mr. Vikus typed away at his computer. After a couple of minutes, he handed Franklin the key to his room.

"Enjoy your stay," Mr. Vikus said. "And don't forget my hotel while you're on campaign. I want everyone to know that we support future-President Bryce, and we're multiverse-friendly!"

Franklin and Helena took the elevator to their room on the third floor. As soon as they entered it, Franklin turned on the overhead light, walked to the queen sized bed on the farthest end of the room near the window, and fell to the covers on his stomach.

"I'm running for President," he said into the white down comforter.

"I can't hear you," Helena said.

Franklin rolled over onto his back and folded his arms, staring up at the low ceiling. "I said, 'I'm running for *President*!'"

Helena held back a laugh. "Really? You're going to run against yourself? Or are you going to try to be your own running mate?"

"You think this is funny?" Franklin said.

"I just don't think you should take it so hard. You should've expected it. It's just when you start thinking things can't get any worse that they start getting worse. Besides, it makes sense.

Your counterpart lost everything. What does he have to lose?"

"You think it's him, too."

"What other Franklin Bryce would run for President in this dimension?"

"He must be making quite an impression."

"It sounds like he's using the existence of other dimensions as his main platform. And if this dimension is finally going to start participating with others, it's going to need leaders who know what it's getting itself into."

Franklin shook his head and buried his face in his hands. "Helena, what's happening to the world?"

"What would you have done if you had entered a time displacement field just before you met me, someone else had lived your life, and then you came back just before the fight at Vlakdormat and were given your life back?"

"I'd probably go live the rest of my life in the bread dimension."

"William was right. A lot can change in three years. You've adapted to much worse situations."

"Thanks." But this time, he wasn't entirely convinced. Not only was he about to have to completely start his life over, but his counterpart's seemed to be perfect. He decided to change the subject and try to get his mind off things.

"Do you want a pizza?" he asked Helena.

"I like anything that doesn't have mushrooms on it."

"I didn't know that. Come to think of it, I don't think we've ever really eaten together before."

"I guess not. I'm glad we've lived long enough to get the chance."

"Me too," Franklin said. "I love mushrooms."

"*Anything* but mushrooms."

"Okay, no mushrooms." Franklin picked up a yellow flier from the end table with a list of restaurants recommended by the hotel. The pizza shop listed wasn't one Franklin had ever heard of.

"Helena, look at this." He handed her the flier. The place was called Pocket Pizza, and there was a little cartoon of a green, swirling vortex with a pizza box in the middle of it. Their slogan was, "We deliver anywhere. And we mean *anywhere.*"

"When Mr. Vikus said interdimensional-friendly, he meant it," Franklin said. "Well, we might as well give it a try. I can't imagine it'll be any slower than anything else in this city."

Franklin dialed the number and was immediately greeted by an automated message that said, "Thank you for choosing Pocket Pizza. We're always busy because we're insane enough to serve every known dimension in the multiverse. Please be patient with us. A team member will be with you shortly."

In another minute, a new, live voice came on the line. "Would you like to try some bread sticks with our new Rekvoloskian helterberry sauce?" it snarled in a thick, deep voice. It was a voice Franklin recognized.

"Requarr? Is that you?"

"Dr. Bryce? You're *alive*?"

"Helena and I just got out of the time displacement field. How did you know it was me and not the version running for President?"

"Because he orders here all the time."

"When did you get into legitimate business?"

"I got out of the robot-hunting game a couple years ago. Don't tell her I said this, but it stopped being so fun without

Helena around. Man, does she know how to kill a robot. Anyway, I'm actually running this place. It's a chain—we've got pocket dimensions all over the multiverse. Franklin, Senator Franklin that is, has been helping me drum up some business in your dimension. How did you find out about it?"

"We're staying at the Vikus."

"Nice place. So what'll you two have?"

"Large supreme, hold the mushrooms."

Requarr got the room and phone numbers from Franklin and gave him his total. He was surprisingly professional.

"Requarr, quick question," said Franklin. "How did my counterpart end up a candidate for president? He obviously hasn't been in politics very long."

"No. He hasn't even finished a full term as Senator. But he has a good platform and he's talking about issues no one else will touch. He's even open about the fact that he's from a parallel dimension."

"He's not pretending to be me?"

"No, and he got around the Constitution, too. When he first announced he was running and that he was from another dimension, the press wanted to know how that was even legal, since he isn't a national. He said the Constitution only states a person has to be born in America. It doesn't mention which one."

"I can't argue with that."

"Your driver should be there in about fifteen minutes," said Requarr.

"That fast?"

"It's much faster to deliver with portals than it is to drive across a city in a car. Plus, this kid I've got working for me is one of the best in the interdimensional delivery business. He helped me get this place started. Anyway, I need to get back to work. It's nice to talk to you, and considering that you saved a dimension that produces a lot of revenue, I'm glad I didn't kill you that one time. Call again!"

Franklin hung up the receiver and explained to Helena everything Requarr had told him.

"I really thought I would eventually have to kill that lava man," Helena said. "I'm glad he finally found a job that didn't involve murdering anyone."

"That depends on which interdimensional pizzas are on the menu," Franklin said. "You know, I'm not sure how many more surprises I can handle tonight."

Precisely fourteen minutes after Franklin's conversation with Requarr, there was a knock at the door. Franklin wondered what to expect when meeting an interdimensional pizza man. What species would he be? Franklin just hoped he wasn't a robot.

"Okay, that's going to be $13.25 in U.S. dollars," said the delivery man, "or I have an interdimensional exchange rate calculator if you're paying with some other currency. We'll take anything but Threpnoidian currency because those arrogant, secretive jerks still won't let us deliver to their dimension."

He was a short, college-aged kid with a couple days worth of facial hair and he was wearing a green uniform and hat.

"You're human," Franklin said as he dug into his wallet for the cash.

"Wow, hungry *and* observant," said the delivery man. "My name's Vince. My boss told me a lot about you. Thanks for saving the world and all that."

They exchanged pizza and money. Franklin gave Vince a little less of a tip for making fun of him. "Are you from this dimension or another Earth?" he asked.

"I'm from here. I've been doing this for about four years now. I've known about alternate dimensions since I was five. We had a portal in our basement."

"What is it about basements and portals?" Franklin said.

"My mom was cool about it. She always said we should be grateful for what we had. A lot of people only had cockroaches and cobwebs in their basements. Now I know everything there is to know about the multiverse. Speaking of the multiverse, I gotta book. I've got a delivery to Makveria, and they have really long hallways at their apartment complexes. Anyway, enjoy your pizza."

As Vince left, Franklin and Helena sat down to eat their pizza.

"Franklin, do you remember what Zarcadmium said before we got back?" Helena asked after a couple of slices. "About how there was some other force at work behind everything he was doing? Do you think he was telling the truth?"

Franklin set the slice he was working on back in the box and folded his arms. "Before we fought Zarcadmium, I changed some of our battle strategy. It hadn't occurred to me until the night before that Zarcadmium's power came from his hands. If he couldn't lift them into the air, he couldn't make a purple cloud."

"Then it's a good thing you realized that, before it was too late."

"That's the thing. I realized it . . . in a dream."

"I'm not following you."

"In the dream, we followed the original plan, and *everyone* died, except for you and Zarcadmium. The scene was uncannily close to what really happened—it even predicted that I would be on the roof. But because I changed the plan, it didn't happen that way."

"You're saying you had a dream that predicted the future?" Helena said. There was uncertainty in her voice.

"I don't know. All I'm saying is that there's still something we're missing. Zarcadmium couldn't possibly have built you. And his powers did seem to vanish as soon as we captured him. Maybe there is something bigger. And maybe something or someone *wanted* us to beat Zarcadmium."

Helena looked doubtful. "I'm tired of trying to figure out my own destiny," she said.

"And I really don't believe in destiny," said Franklin. "I think we proved no one can tell you who you're supposed to be when we stopped the man who wanted you to be the general of his robot army."

"I hope you're right. But I'm sorry for everything I've put you through—the personalities, the HR120s, getting flung into the future. You don't deserve all this, and you don't deserve to have two first names."

"Thanks, Helena. Neither do you."

CHAPTER 38

Rapid Fire

THE TELEPHONE RANG. Franklin struggled to get all of the layers of hotel blankets off of himself, rubbed some of the sleep from his eyes, and picked up the phone groggily.

"Senator Bryce," came the voice of Mr. Vikus. Franklin fought the urge to correct him. "Your friend is here in the lobby, crouched behind a potted plant and crying. My staff has tried to talk to her, but she screamed at them like a little girl. Could you come down here please?"

Franklin looked at the digital clock next to his bed. It was only 4:30 am. "I'll be right down," he said.

Franklin and Helena had both slept in their clothes to avoid any awkwardness, since they both had to share the same room. They slept in two separate queen-sized beds, and sure enough, Helena's was empty, and the unnecessary number of blankets was lying in a heap on the floor. But Helena would never act that way. Alicia had taken over.

"Franklin," Alicia said when he found her sitting behind a plant just as the manager had said. "Please, you gotta help me."

"Don't worry. No one's going to hurt you," Franklin said.

"I don't know what to do. Please. Help me." She hugged the large, ceramic pot and turned her head away from Franklin. Alicia was always afraid of something, but now she was terrified.

"What's wrong? Why don't you know what to do?"

"Something's coming."

"Try to calm down. I'm here to help. What's coming?"

"I don't understand. I don't know where I am. I don't know why I'm with all these other girls in this little space. I don't know why there were so many robots. . . ."

"The robots are gone now. They can't hurt you."

"Then why does it feel so scary?"

Alicia turned her head to Franklin, tears streaming down her face.

"I'm not going to let anything happen to you," Franklin said. He took her in his arms and she laid her head on his shoulder. They sat that way for a long time until her head suddenly jerked like she had licked a light socket. She leaped off his lap and stood with her back to him in a tall, confident posture.

"What do you think of this place, Bryce?" she asked him. Franklin began to slowly stand up. "Don't move," she commanded. He sat back down on the floor. "Answer the question."

"All right. It's nice."

She laughed. "That's kind of what I hoped you'd say." She disappeared and instantly reappeared next to the front desk. She effortlessly lifted it from the ground, leaving Mr. Vikus sitting in his office chair, dumbfounded.

"I just thought it would feel good to break something you liked. It does. And just to spell it out for you, I'm the real deal this time."

She threw the enormous wooden desk toward Franklin and he leaped out of its way, barely missing the edge of it as it collided with the wall behind him. The potted plant Alicia had been sitting behind was crushed, along with a glass coffee table.

Franklin looked up from the floor to see Mr. Vikus picking up the phone.

"Don't do that," Franklin yelled. "The police can't stop her. You're just inviting more people for her to slaughter."

"He's right, of course," Sandra said. "But by all means,

invite whomever you'd like. Helena doesn't take on the tough challenges nearly often enough. What I wouldn't give right now for an army of tanks."

Mr. Vikus screamed, "*What* have you brought into my hotel?"

"You can call me Armageddon. You can call me the Apocalypse. Just don't call me Helena. Then I'd have to kill you real slow."

"What do you want?" Franklin said, now walking toward her. He was rubbing a bruise on his forehead but he approached her with confidence. He was as good as dead if she wanted him that way, but she liked to talk. He hoped he could buy himself some time.

"Is this what you do? Throw things around until Helena takes over again? Don't you have some reason for being so dangerous? Or are you really that superficial?"

"What can I say? I just like the color of *blood.*" She turned to Vikus and grabbed his throat, picking him up with one hand. Franklin was reminded of the HR120 in his office, crushing Calvin Stanley's neck. This time, even a positronic deactivation switch wouldn't have helped.

"You want me, Sandra," Franklin said. "You tried to kill me first, remember? Put Vikus down."

"Anyone with such a stupid name really needs to die."

"Really? You can't come up with a better reason to murder someone?"

Sandra shot Franklin a furious glare. She dropped Vikus to the floor and slowly headed toward him. Vikus struggled for a moment to catch his breath, but he was alive.

"Here's a reason for you. You got rid of Zarcadmium. There

was a visionary. God, I liked his style. He said Helena was supposed to be his general, but honestly, I think she's just going to get lost in the bowels of her own psyche like the rest of us. *The Helena* was supposed to rule the world? There's no other way around it: I was going to become the dominant personality! I'm a shoe-in for that job! But now he's closed up shop and whoever the almighty powerful *SHE* is supposed to be, *she* took away his magic and now, no takeover. Which means there's no telling what's going to happen to me now."

"You talked about a challenge, Sandra," Franklin said, backing away from her now like a lion tamer as she neared him. "Isn't this too easy? You kill me and then what?"

Sandra smiled. "Then I'll kill someone else. Someone more fun. And then I won't have to listen to you and your obnoxious lectures anymore."

"But then you'll just go back into Helena's mind and not come back out again for, what, three, four months? You had one shot to really make your mark on the world and you wasted it on Miles Flastcaster, the wannabe super villain."

"So what do you suggest? It's not like you can control me. Each of us has our own nature. Alicia's a sniveling little girl, Laura's the paranoid impulsive, Kay's the over-confident leader-type, Krystal's the shy, insecure chick, Tracey's the immature teenager . . . and I'm a homicidal maniac. None of us chose to be what we are, but I obviously got the best of the draw. I'm going to kill because it's my nature. Hell, I had motive to kill you *before* you crushed all my hopes and dreams for world domination. I'm so sick of listening to you and Helena whine about your first names and your bad luck, your wife's secrets, your patients and their stupid moral dilemmas. So if the only thing I'm able to do in the precious amount of time I'm in control of this body is to bash your brains in, then . . . um. . . ."

The wild, demonic fury disappeared from her face and was replaced with a calm, collected, but somewhat disturbed expression.

"Franklin, that was . . . really genius."

"Helena?"

"No, sorry. I'm Kay. And no, I have no idea what's going on with us. But that was an excellent strategy, keeping her talking like that."

Franklin let out a long sigh of relief. He really hadn't thought it would work, but it was the only thing he could come up with. This was the first time more than one of them had taken over in a single day, much less *three* in just a few minutes.

"Franklin, I have to tell you this before I lose control. Something is about to happen to us. None of us knows what it is, but we can all feel it."

Franklin said, "Alicia was absolutely mortified."

The few guests who were in the lobby had cleared out during Sandra's rage, but Mr. Vikus remained. He had been hiding behind a large stone pillar. Now he came up behind Franklin, careful not to get too close to Kay. "Get out of my hotel! Or I *will* call the police. I have no idea what kind of games you're playing, Senator, but if they can't strong-arm your super-girlfriend, they can at least arrest you."

"We'd better go," Kay said. She turned to Vikus. "I know you can't possibly understand what's happening here, but you should know that if you're opening up this establishment to interdimensional races, this probably isn't the last time you'll have to buy new furniture."

"Guess I'm not going to get his vote after all," Franklin whispered to Kay as they left the hotel.

They stood on the dimly lit street corner near the hotel to decide what to do next. "We've got to get me somewhere I can't hurt anyone," Kay said.

"I don't get it. Some of the others are unreasonable or, at the very least, scared or uncertain. But you seem to be completely rational."

"Nah, I just like being in charge. Every time I'm in control, it gives me the opportunity to be a leader."

"Then why haven't you tried to take over, like Laura or Sandra?"

"Oh, I would, but it's not in my nature. My style is to bide my time until opportunities present themselves. If anything, I'm the opposite of Sandra. I don't take those kinds of risks. I wish things could be different. I wish the seven of us could all be separated into our own bodies and live our own lives. But we can't. I can either deny that fact, like Sandra and Laura, fight against the inevitable, or I can help Helena, and hope somehow that helps me in the long run."

"It's too bad some of the others weren't more like you. Would have made the last few months a little easier on everyone."

Suddenly, Kay frowned, stood one-footed in a karate stance, and side-kicked Franklin in his stomach. He lurched forward and clutched his midsection.

"All that talk was smart once," Laura said. "But you've screwed yourself this time, *Doctor* Bryce. I admit, I don't hate you quite as much as I used to. You did a good thing by bringing down Zarcadmium. All he wanted was to control us, and it's like the Offspring says, I don't want to be controlled. That's all I want. But if this irritating pattern holds, I've only got a few minutes, and I have to make them count. Hope life gets less complicated for you in the future."

Laura disappeared. Franklin reeled in pain but managed to reach his cell phone. He began to open it but immediately pocketed it. There was no way he'd still have service after three years of not paying his phone bill. He hoped Lera had canceled his plan for fear of being hunted down by the Pliscotts.

Franklin used a pay phone behind the hotel building rather than going inside to use the one at the desk. He didn't have time to be berated again by the manager. He dialed Lera's home number, hoping she and William hadn't changed it.

"Lera, I need your help," he said once he had her on the phone. "One of Helena's personalities has taken over and I've got to find her before she hurts someone."

"Is it Sandra?" Lera said. She sounded wide-awake. She and William had probably stayed up all night talking about Franklin's return.

"No, Sandra took over earlier."

"Earlier? Franklin, what's going on?"

"Helena's personalities are taking over every few minutes. So far it's been a different one every time, but there's no telling what else might happen. We've got to get her into a pocket dimension or something."

"All right. I'll get a security team and try to track her down. Drake left his blueprints stored on an internet server, and we added her brain patterns to our sensors just in case she ever came back and we needed them. We should have no problem finding them."

"Lera? What do you mean *we*?"

"I'm sorry. I didn't have the chance to tell you. Vlakdormat was rebuilt on the other side of the city a year ago, and I left the VIBI to become its chief of security."

CHAPTER 39

Starting Over

FRANKLIN HADN'T EXPECTED THE NEW VLAKDORMAT BUILDING TO BE LARGER THAN THE OLD, BUT IT HAD THREE MORE STORIES AND AN EXTRA WING. It looked more like a state-of-the-art government installation than a psychiatric facility, and there were still a ridiculous number of windows. Franklin now stood with Lera and a couple of other security officers in the pocket dimension room, facing a large, flat computer monitor that hovered in mid-air. The room was almost identical to the one in the other building—a white void with a control panel in the middle to access the pocket dimensions. But the floating screen was new.

"Where did all the money come from?" Franklin asked. He was in real shock at the size of the place. He felt like he had when he first toured the original Vlakdormat.

"It took Caslom a few months to get the funding he needed," Lera admitted. "It was a little hard after what happened to the old building. But once some of the other Vlakdormat facilities throughout the multiverse realized that a large percentage of Earth's populace was accepting alternate dimensions, they saw how good business was about to get, and the money followed."

Lera pressed a button on the silver console and the monitor flashed on, revealing Helena standing in another blank, white void.

"Helena is in a holding dimension," Lera said. "We picked her up at a twenty-four hour cyber café while Laura was still in control. She was searching through online yellow pages, trying to locate Eva Crill."

"Figures," Franklin said. "She knows it probably won't work, but she'll try anything. Laura's only goal is survival, ανδ she'll do anything to try and take over Helena's body permanently."

"We managed to surprise her with a portable aperture to get her into this holding dimension. So far, two other personalities have taken over. About ten minutes ago, she was a woman named Krystal. You never talked about her."

"She's the shy, insecure personality," Franklin said. "Never took over for more than a minute or two. She always seemed too worried about what I thought of her, so she always gave Helena control back right away."

"Now she's Tracy."

"That means every single personality has taken over in the last hour. This is the first time anything like this has happened."

"If you want," Lera said, "you can talk to her through the monitor."

Franklin nodded. It was awkward, working with Lera like he would have once worked with Agent Strexit, especially now that she wasn't really his wife anymore. He tried to remain professional and focus on Helena, but that was difficult. He was still angry, and he didn't know any other way to feel about it.

"Tracy? How are you feeling?" Franklin asked through the monitor.

"Other than being surrounded by miles of uneatable marshmallows? Sure, I'm just peachy. Something *bad* is going on, Franklin. I have this feeling, like . . . like a doom kind of feeling. Have you ever had that?"

"Like the world is about to end?"

"Yeah. Like that."

"Sure. I've had that."

"I think all of us popping out at once like this is a warning or something."

"A warning about what?"

"I don't know. But I hope it goes away pretty soon. It's like watching a slasher movie. You know, it's the cheerleader who always gets knifed first."

Franklin looked back at Lera and spoke in a low voice. "Thanks for doing this. I know it isn't exactly in your job description. She's not a patient anymore."

Lera warmly put her hand on his shoulder. "Just don't mention it to Helena. I don't want her thinking she owes me any favors."

Franklin gave her a weak smile.

"Franklin," came Helena's voice on the monitor. "It's me."

"How do you feel?"

"I'm fine. But Alicia. . . . She's gone."

"What?"

"That feeling the others kept talking about? I think we were sensing that one of us was about to go. There's only six of us left in here, Franklin. Alicia is *gone.*"

"But why? What does that mean?"

"I wish I knew. But I've had some time to think, and I know how to do it now. I know how to get Drake back."

Franklin, Helena, and Lera stood across the street from the original Vlakdormat building. A beautiful orange sunrise shone behind the facility, where holographic cars were pulling into the parking lot and holographic therapists were walking through the front doors for holographic work. It was risky for Lera to let Helena out of the holding dimension, since her other personalities were less predictable than usual, but if Tracy was right and it had been a warning about Alicia's personality vanishing, it was fairly safe to assume the pattern of constant personality shifts was over. Still, Lera was ready with her portable aperture, just in case.

"It's only been a few hours," Helena said. "Which means Drake and Zarcadmium can't have taken more than one step since we left."

"Are you sure you can do this?" Franklin said.

"Are you sure you want to come with me?" said Helena. "If we aren't careful, we could wind up coming back another three years in the future."

"So much has changed," Franklin said. "The only thing that makes sense is for the two of us to stick together." Franklin felt strange saying that in front of Lera, but it was the truth. "And like you said, Drake and Zarcadmium are right where we left them. The whole thing shouldn't take more than thirty seconds."

"Which means we should be back in about two weeks," said Helena.

"I still think this is a bad idea," Lera said. "Can't you wait until you're sure another personality won't take over and ruin the whole operation? It's not like Drake's going anywhere."

"I don't see how he could either, but stranger things have happened," Helena said. "Stranger things have happened *today*. We should do this now."

"One more thing," said Lera. "You're going to bring Zarcadmium back, too?"

"Yes," said Franklin.

"After everything he's put us through, wouldn't it be easier to just leave him there?" said Lera.

"Only so he can come back and wreak havoc on us in the future?" Franklin said. "What if it takes him sixty years to get back? He'll have the benefit of youth on most of us. I don't really want to save the world again in my nineties."

"So what you're really saying," said Lera, "is that it's the right thing to do. Well, have a nice thirty-second vacation. We'll see you in two weeks."

Helena grasped Franklin's hand, and in a split second they were on the other side of the field, looking up at the enormous, swirling purple cloud hanging over Vlakdormat.

"What happened?" Drake said. Just as they had hoped, he/she was still turned toward the building, walking with a handcuffed Zarcadmium. "Why did you teleport back here? Don't tell me the world past that mysterious vanishing point is missing or there's no gravity or the HR120s put an end to apple pie."

"No time," Franklin said. He grabbed Drake's shoulder, Helena grabbed Zarcadmium's cuffs, and the two of them clasped hands once again. Then Helena closed her eyes, put her fingers on her temples, and concentrated. In seconds, the four of them were once again across the street. The ominous purple cloud was replaced by a puffy white one, and the holograms were once again hard at work inside a completely useless Vlakdormat.

"What the hell just happened?" Drake asked.

Franklin smiled, grateful that something had finally worked the way he planned. "Gentlemen, welcome to the future."

Franklin, Helena, Drake, and Zarcadmium materialized in an alley behind a five-level parking garage downtown. Franklin wasn't sure the exact date now that they had once again crossed the time displacement field, but this time, they certainly hadn't been inside the field for more than twenty or thirty seconds. The time of day had once again changed, however. Now the air was warm, the sun was shining, and there wasn't a cloud of any color in the sky.

"Helena, we're still five or six blocks away," Franklin said. "Why did you teleport us here?"

"I thought they should know." She looked at Drake and seemed happy to see him, but she avoided Zarcadmium. She probably wished, quite understandably, that they had left him on the other side of the field. "We need to tell them before they find out like we did."

They talked for a full hour. Franklin and Helena explained how much time had passed, what was happening to the status quo, and about the new Vlakdormat. They were careful not to explain too much too fast, but Drake was remarkably unaffected by the news. He was surprised, certainly, but not angry or shocked. After all, he explained, dealing with the future would be a piece of cake compared to what they had all just gone through. He was excited about the prospects Senator Bryce's platform brought. And, of course, he didn't have to deal with suddenly not being married anymore.

Zarcadmium remained quiet but attentive—none of the news could be very surprising to him. He had put up the time displacement field, and his plan had backfired. Now he was thrown into the future with the rest of them, a future moving toward an understanding of interdimensional peoples and cultures rather than one ruled with fear and terror by programmed generals and robots.

"I just have one question," Drake said before they teleported to the new Vlakdormat building. "Do you know where my body is? I hate to complain, but I'd like to get back in it as soon as I can. I'm sure my apartment has been rented out by now, and not only am I going to have to find a new one, but I'll need a whole new wardrobe. I'd really like to start shopping in the men's section again."

"Crill had your body on life support three years ago. Assuming she still has it, it should be fine. But we're going to have to find her. She left the city several months ago," Franklin said.

Drake sighed. "I suppose in the meantime I'll have to go the mall and see if there are any sales," he said. "Hey Helena, I don't suppose you'd want to come with me. I'm sure you need to re-stock your things too."

Helena smiled. "Sure, Drake. Shopping with a woman who is actually a man would not be the strangest thing I've done in the last several hours."

The four of them entered the crystal clear glass doors of the new Vlakdormat. The vast, spacious lobby with its bright red carpet, spiral staircase, glass elevators on both sides of the room, and balconies leading to offices on each floor were enough to awe Franklin the first time he saw them. But the giant welcome home banner really did him in.

His old secretary, Bethany, reached for her phone on the main lobby desk in excited panic, and it wasn't long before dozens of familiar faces and a few new ones filled the room to greet them with warm anticipation. Lera was the first to approach Franklin.

"You didn't have to do all this," he said.

"I'm just glad you made it back in time," she said. "We've

had this banner up for four days. Look, Franklin, we never forgot about you. We just didn't know if you were all right. We all had to go on with our lives. But we've been waiting to do this for three years. You, Helena, Drake . . . you're all heroes."

She ordered a security team to escort Zarcadmium to a holding dimension.

"*She* isn't finished with the Helena," he said to Franklin before they took him away. It was the first thing he had said since they brought him back through the field. "Whatever she has planned, it's going on without me. You can be sure Helena losing that personality wasn't a coincidence."

Franklin felt a sudden chill. He had thought of all of that on his own, but hearing Zarcadmium say it out loud somehow made it more real.

Franklin had the opportunity to get his mind off the inevitable horrors of the future when he was bombarded by old colleagues, each wanting to know every detail of the fight for Vlakdormat. Eventually, they all made way for Dr. Akbar Caslom the Third when he finally approached the guests of honor.

"I don't know how to thank you," Caslom said. He looked at Drake and smiled. "Both of you, actually."

"You could always give us our old jobs back," Drake said.

Caslom looked nervous. "Dr. Drake, would you please excuse Franklin and me for a moment. There is something we need to discuss."

Caslom led Franklin up a spiral staircase, and Franklin supposed he opted for the staircase instead of the elevator because he wanted to talk on the way. They passed a young lady in a navy blue business suit with brown hair down to her waist who had three eyes that matched her hair color. Franklin wasn't sure about her species, and he was surprised to see how many more interdimensional species were employed at the new Vlakdormat.

"There's someone waiting for us in our office. I called him as soon as I heard you were on your way here," Caslom said.

"I appreciate the warm welcome, but you don't look entirely happy to see me," Franklin said.

Caslom slinked up the stairs a little slower, looking behind him at Franklin as he spoke. "That isn't true at all. I'm grateful to see you alive. What I'm not looking forward to is the grave truth we have to share with you. I trust no one has explained yet the real reason your counterpart is running for President?"

"Just that the incident at Vlakdormat three years ago set a chain of events in motion that has made a greater percentage of our dimension's population accept the existence of other dimensions."

"That's only a very small part of it. This way," Caslom said. They came to a glass door with Caslom's name printed on it, and Caslom led him inside. Standing in a far corner, next to Caslom's wall-mounted collection of priceless slinkies and accordions from various dimensions, was a very serious-looking Rajel Chirok. He had traded his usual tacky business suit and tie for a more casual light blue dress shirt and black slacks. The office was brightly lit with three flood lamps on the ceiling, and from the doorway, Franklin could make out a deep gash running down the pale orange skin of Chirok's left cheek. His arms were folded in front of him, and he didn't greet Franklin with the usual sarcastic quip or jibe. Instead, he let Caslom begin their meeting.

"A lot has changed since you've been away," Caslom said.

"I'm guessing you mean more than I've already seen," Franklin replied. "The Vikus Hotel? Interdimensional pizza delivery? This place?"

Chirok silently produced a manila folder from behind his back and dropped it to Caslom's famously-long conference table, which was identical to his old one. Franklin picked up the folder and pulled out a stack of eight-by-ten photographs. The first one was a grainy, black and white picture, taken from a security camera, of a young girl clad from head to toe in black leather, holding both hands in the air and looking straight up at the sky. Behind the girl, Franklin could make out an older, balding Nixothian flying and holding an umbrella.

"This was taken just outside the International Bank of Nixothia," Caslom said. "Notice anything?"

"Looks like she's in the middle of a thunderstorm. Odd time for interpretive dance," Franklin said. The other men didn't crack a smile.

"Look at the next one," Chirok said. Franklin turned to the next photograph, which was a blown-up image of the previous picture, focused on the girl's left shoulder. She was wearing a paper nametag. He could barely make out the name.

"No," Franklin said, shaking his head. He put the pictures back on the table without bothering to look at the others. "I know what this looks like, but it's not. It can't be."

"It is," Chirok said. "The nametag says, 'Hello, my name is SANDRA.'"

"Sandra," Franklin said. "Countless dimensions, countless people, countless different *versions* of each dimension and each person, and you find a grainy image of a woman holding her hands in the air who has a nametag that *might* say 'Sandra' on it, and it spells the end of the world."

"You want to tell me this is a coincidence?" Chirok said.

"When was this taken?"

"A year ago. Look at the next picture."

Franklin hesitated. He felt like he was right back where he'd started, defending Helena to a man who was only interested in the well-being of his patients and those in his employ. But grainy as it was, the person in that picture was definitely not Helena Kathryn. And as he slowly picked up the next picture and looked at it in horror, he understood why Rajel Chirok was here. The woman stood with her hands in the air, and dozens of bright bolts of lightning shot from a gigantic cloud just above her head, all striking the ground everywhere but where she was standing.

"What happened?" Franklin asked.

"It's gone," Chirok replied.

"What do you mean it's gone?" said Franklin.

"Nixothia. The entire dimension. Whoever or whatever *that* is," Chirok said, pointing at the woman in the picture Franklin held, "my entire dimension blanked out of existence hours after these pictures were taken. The bank owner took the camera footage and got out of the dimension as soon as he could. He's a customer of mine. Luckily, he had teleportation powers, too, or he probably wouldn't have made it out alive. He gave me and several other interdimensional business dealers these pictures, hoping one of us would find her and find someone who can stop her."

"As I said, things have changed," Caslom said. "Rajel Chirok works for me now. He keeps Lera, the security team, and others on our staff supplied with certain supernatural abilities, so that if and when the time comes, we can protect this dimension from . . . Sandra."

A woman named Sandra. With purple cloud magic. While

Helena was trapped with Franklin inside Havst's pocket dimension. It didn't make any sense. Purple cloud magic meant that whoever she was, she was directly connected to Zarcadmium and the mysterious *she* he spoke of. And Franklin recognized the demented look on the woman's face; he had seen it on Helena's face before. But how could Sandra be both in Helena's head and out in the multiverse, destroying entire dimensions?

"I'm not surprised no one told you," said Caslom. "People have slowly been embracing other dimensions, but most of them aren't ready to talk about the inevitable truth."

"Which is?" Franklin asked.

"The end of the multiverse itself," Caslom said, dryly.

"Hold on. I knew this was possible. Zarcadmium destroyed his own dimension through purple cloud magic. It's powerful enough to do that. It's horrible, but it doesn't necessarily spell the end of the entire multiverse," Franklin said.

"Nixothia isn't the only one," said Caslom. "Dozens of dimensions have been reported to have disappeared since you were gone. The most recent is Threpnoidia, although that isn't confirmed, since no one can actually go there in the first place. But no company has had a shipment from them in over a month."

No more Threpnoidian Dragonflies? This was serious.

"And there have been unconfirmed rumors of others besides Sandra, other women, visiting and destroying dimensions, in the last three years. They don't always use purple clouds, either. One dimension, Hargothmia, was said to be literally erased, piece by piece, by a little girl with a very large paintbrush," Caslom added.

If these somehow were Helena's personalities come to life, he must be referring now to Alicia. Still, a giant erasing paintbrush? That sounded unlikely. But Caslom was dead serious, and Franklin had never seen Chirok like this. He looked like Franklin's counterpart, just after his Vlakdormat was attacked by HR120s. The difference was, the other Franklin had found a way to reconcile and get on with his life; Chirok looked as if he might never be the same man again.

"The bottom line is, if there aren't any dimensions, I don't have anyone to sell anything to," Chirok said. Franklin smiled a little. Maybe he wasn't so far gone after all. "No offense, Franklin, but having all of those personalities back here makes me nervous. So you can understand why I might not be the happiest to see you back."

"There's something you should both know," Franklin said. "Something is happening to Helena. When we got back from the pocket dimension, she lost Alicia."

Chirok rolled his eyes. "That's good. At least now we only have to worry about one homicidal kid with a magic paintbrush."

"I think this is why Zarcadmium wanted me, wanted all of us, out of the picture," Franklin said. "As long as she has the other personalities, she's dangerous, vulnerable. With our guidance, she's beginning to lose the personalities on her own."

"What does that mean?" Caslom said.

"I don't know."

"Can you be sure she'll be less dangerous without them? Can you be sure just because she's lost this one she'll lose the others?"

"I don't know."

"And so you see our dilemma," said Caslom. "We have proof that at least one of Helena's personalities has a real, flesh-and-blood counterpart and is out there destroying entire dimensions. I'm not just risking Vlakdormat by allowing her here; I'm risking the existence of every being in this dimension. I'm sorry, Franklin, but neither of you are welcome here any longer. I'm certain you'll do your very best to sort this out, and we all owe you our lives."

Franklin might have expected to be insulted, angry, outraged . . . but he wasn't. He completely understood. And had Caslom offered him his old job back, he now imagined he probably wouldn't have taken it. He believed in Helena, despite everything that had happened and was happening; but wherever she went, trouble most certainly followed, just as he knew it would those months, those years ago when she first came to his office and he read her two first names. He had a responsibility to stay with her, to guide her, to keep people like Zarcadmium from getting their warped, greedy, misguided hands on her. That responsibility was his, and his alone.

He offered his hand to Caslom, who gladly took it in his own tiny, clammy hand and shook it. "It was an honor working with you, sir," Franklin said.

"You are one of the finest in your profession. Whatever the future brings for you, warrior, superhero . . . remember, you are a therapist first," Caslom said with a smile.

"Always," said Franklin. He nodded to Rajel Chirok and began to leave, but Chirok stopped him before he reached the door. He handed him a small, white envelope with Franklin's name on the outside.

"You didn't believe me when I told you I had a code of ethics. It's not a long code or anything, but I do have one. You were there for me, even after everything I'd put you through. The only time I chose to help you was when it benefited me—which is how I operate and I don't regret it in the least, just so you know—but I owe you. I'm giving you this for free. Enjoy it; it'll never happen again."

Franklin looked at the envelope for a long time. He knew what this was and what it meant. There was a time when it was the only thing in the world he wanted. Chirok had taken it from him, and Franklin had hated him for that, but a lot had happened since then. He didn't like Chirok, and he didn't condone a lot of things Chirok had done, but Franklin had understood Chirok. Or at least, he thought he had. But now, Chirok had lost the most precious thing to him, and Franklin felt strangely responsible. This woman, Sandra or whoever she was, clearly was deeply connected with Helena, and Franklin had stood by Helena's side since the very beginning. If Chirok had hated Franklin for that, Franklin could hardly have blamed him, and yet, all Chirok wanted to do was give Franklin back what he'd taken from him. Clearly there was a lot more to Rajel Chirok than he had ever let on.

Franklin tucked the envelope away in his jacket pocket, smiled warmly, and shook Chirok's hand. "Thank you," he said. It was all that needed to be said.

Franklin made his way out of the office and down the spiral staircase. In the lobby, he said his final goodbyes to Bethany and then Drake R. Drake, whom Franklin was confident would be getting his old job back. He promised Drake that he would stay on the lookout for Eva Crill and do everything in his power to get his body back. He thanked Lera for all her help in finding Helena and wished her and William the best of luck. Then he and Helena left Vlakdormat to embark on a new adventure: apartment hunting.

CHAPTER 40

The Seventh

IT WAS SURE TO BE ONE OF THE LAST THREPNOIDIAN DRAGONFLIES HE WOULD HAVE THE PLEASURE OF DRINKING, AND, ESPECIALLY SINCE KRAWKSON KLUB HAD RAISED ITS PRICE BY THREE TIMES WHAT IT HAD COST THREE YEARS AGO, FRANKLIN WAS NURSING IT SLOWLY AND DELIBERATELY. He sat at a triangular table in the corner, thinking. It was just after noon, at least by his dimension's time, and though it was usually busy in the club no matter what time it was, the place was unusually empty today. Franklin was glad, because the lack of bustle and activity—and especially the awful karaoke or dancing—gave him time to reflect, on the past and on the future.

Before seeing what the world had become, he thought all he wanted was for things to return to the relative normality they had been before Helena and the HR120s. To sit at his desk, wait for the next patient, then listen to complaints about scaly alien stepparents or pets who turned into cars. To go home to his Verullian wife and wonder what she really did at work, or what her other husbands had been like, or what she really saw in a simple human being who had never done an interesting thing in his life before discovering the multiverse. To nostalgically remember the good old days of being telepathic and longing for that feeling of knowing just what to say at just the right time.

And now, he was strangely content to know that that life was behind him. He was unemployed, separated from his wife, hadn't begun to unpack at his new apartment, and he was unsure how he would pay his bills past the first couple of months; and he was living with the most potentially powerful creature who had ever lived. The multiverse was coming apart at the seams, and somehow, living, breathing personifications of Helena's personalities were responsible. But still, Franklin was content, even though nothing was right at all. Perhaps it was because he finally had exactly what he wanted.

A purpose.

And it was an important purpose. He was playing guide and advisor to the most important person in the multiverse.

"Just got done playing a really great video game," came a tenor voice from behind him. "It's called 'The Seven.' You play as a mental patient with seven multiple personalities—and superpowers—and all you have to do is save everyone, stop robots from taking over the multiverse, and convince everyone you're not evil."

William Vanderhorst, wearing a dark green suit and matching tie, took a seat next to Franklin.

"I think I'll pass on that one in favor of something a little less familiar, like tennis or cooking," Franklin said. "Now what are the odds you and I would both be here at the one hour no one else seems to be?"

"Well, since I'm the owner, it's not that surprising," William said with a grin. "I've been meaning to tell you, but considering me and Lera and everything, I couldn't decide how to drop another bombshell on you."

"Honestly, nothing really surprises me anymore," Franklin said. "I'm proud of you. And you could probably say you get along with my old in-laws and I wouldn't be surprised."

William looked at Franklin in stunned silence.

"No, tell me you don't actually get along with them,"

Franklin said.

"Okay, no, they are pretty awful," William admitted, and they had a good laugh.

"So what happened to Mr. Krawkson?" Franklin asked.

"He passed away a couple years back. He left the club to me."

"You didn't even know him that well."

"He said in his will that you and I were his favorite customers, and since you weren't around. . . ."

"That's okay. I don't think I'm ready to get into the food and drink business quite yet. Maybe I'll hit you up for a job if striking out on my own doesn't pan out."

"You're going solo?"

"Seems like the best idea. I can't work at Vlakdormat, and with dimensions disappearing and Sandra and the others on the loose, I don't want to deal with a place where everyone's in denial about the very idea of alternate dimensions. Besides, when things start heating up again, I can close my doors and the only person losing out will be me."

William shook his head. "When you're not at work, every potential patient is missing out."

"I appreciate that. I'm a little surprised you wanted this job."

"Are you kidding? The only difference between being a therapist and a bartender is the 400 page drink list. Besides, now that I own the place, I get to pick all the acts and events. No more karaoke night."

Franklin laughed. "I'm glad you and Lera are happy."

"It means a lot to hear you say that. You had every right to be angry. You still do."

"Everything looks different me to me now, you know? Like over the three years, the world moved on without me. It gave me a sense of perspective, looking back on it from this lens of the future. Lera and I were never right for each other. We enjoyed time together, don't get me wrong, but I don't know if it was ever anything more than curiosity. I was infatuated with everything extradimensional, and she had never married a human before. I don't think I ever would have admitted this before, but I think I married her because it brought me one step closer to the interdimensional, and all I cared about back then was not being 'normal.'"

"And she wanted to try her hand at a more ordinary home life," William said. "And once she got bored of that, she stopped taking you seriously. I don't think she ever took any species completely seriously that she knew only lived to be a fraction of her age."

"So then why did she marry you?" Franklin asked.

"She missed you. She didn't realize how much until you left. I think I missed you as much as she did. She started wanting all the things she already had but had taken for granted when you left. She and I started getting together just to talk about you a few months after you disappeared, and we started wondering if we'd ever see you again. It wasn't like I was second best or she was rebounding or anything—it didn't get serious until later. The one thing we had in common was you, and that's what brought us together."

"You're a great friend," Franklin said, and the two men got up from the table and gave each other a quick, manly hug. "I wish I hadn't reacted the way I did when I saw you together."

"You wouldn't have been much of a husband if you hadn't. And you know, if we had known you were alive—"

"I know. I'm just glad *you're* both still alive."

William paused for a moment, and then he raised his eyebrows in understanding. "Helena's personalities."

"Or whatever they are. There's really no way to understand anything that's happened since Helena found me."

William stared past Franklin as though he had seen a ghost. A shrill, feminine voice spoke up behind him. "I wouldn't be so sure about that," it said.

Franklin spun around to find Dr. Eva Crill, looking as eccentric as ever, leaning up against a wall next to the stage. She wore a bright orange pantsuit, black gloves, and her long, thick hair was a bright shade of purple, worn up in an elaborate bun.

"I have answers, but they are only for you," Crill said. She looked long and hard at William, who didn't seem to get the hint right away. It was probably hard enough for him to get his mind around the idea of Eva Crill, who he hadn't seen in years, standing in his establishment. He and Franklin always expected her hangouts to be so exotic and bizarre that if they were to go where she frequented, their heads would probably implode. Their brains would fail to process whatever their eyes were seeing.

"William, if you don't mind. . . ." Franklin said.

"Sure, I'll go . . . drink something," William said. He walked into an employee entrance, and Crill and Franklin were now alone.

"About Drake—" Franklin started.

"I've already seen Dr. Drake, and his body has been returned to him."

"Really? Is he all right?"

"Perfectly, and glad to be himself again. The HR120 has been incinerated. But that is not why I am here."

She looked like herself, but she certainly didn't sound like Eva

Crill. By this point in the conversation, she should have already insulted him without realizing it and bragged about her collection of ancient interdimensional artifacts that would have been more impressive if anyone but her had ever heard of them.

"Before we begin, you should know that I am not exactly Eva Crill," she said.

That certainly explained a lot.

"After what you have witnessed over the last three years, I decided it is finally time for the two of us to meet. Let me start with what you know. Helena had six other personalities in her head, each with unique perspectives and characteristics. Stephen Zarcadmium planned to use her for his own petty schemes, and ultimately, she defeated him with your help. When she decided not to kill Zarcadmium, she passed an important test and lost the Alicia personality; Alicia was a representation of childishness and fear."

"Who are you?" Franklin asked.

Eva Crill, or whoever she was, pulled up a seat to the triangular table and invited Franklin to sit with her. "Believe me when I say that is not an easy question to answer. This is Eva Crill's real body, and I am simply borrowing it to speak with you —I will give it back to her as soon as we are through. The best response would probably be, I am the *she* that Zarcadmium referred to when you captured him."

Franklin was speechless. He was speaking with the source of everything that had happened to him since he quit Vlakdormat the first time. He was speaking with the being who had created Helena.

"Tell me this," Franklin said. "Is Helena here to save my dimension or to rule it?"

"When the game is ended, there will be no difference between those two things. You need to know that everything Zarcadmium told you is true, from his limited and warped understanding. I did give him the purple cloud magic, and later, I did tell him that Helena was destined to rule the world. He believed I intended for her to be his general, that I was interested in helping him to achieve his goal of world domination, after he destroyed his own dimension. That was, of course, not my intention, but I wanted him to believe it was. Zarcadmium played exactly the role I chose for him."

"You wanted him to use his HR120s to kill innocent people?"

"You have to understand that this all goes beyond the future of a single dimension. This is about *every* dimension."

"Sandra and Helena's other personalities. They're real? I mean, there are walking, talking versions of them out there?"

"Oh yes. They're real."

"And you created them, too?"

She sighed. "No, I did not create the beings that are destroying the multiverse. Let me go back to the beginning. Before the existence of the multiverse, there were six beings, each with its own unique personality. These beings were cosmic in nature; they had unlimited power to do with as they pleased. Time had no meaning for them. They simply entertained themselves and each other in whatever fashion pleased them, until they decided they were tired of each other. They became arrogant, each believing itself to be the true ruler of the cosmos. There was no one to challenge each of their claims except each other. They would have destroyed each other if they could have, but they were all far too powerful for that.

"So they decided to create an elaborate game, one that would, finally, determine which of the six was the greatest of them all. Together, they created the multiverse, a reality filled with many realities. Each dimension was based on the unique personality type of one of the six, and from those initial six dimensions, thousands more were spawned. Many became alternate versions of others, some more unique than others, but each was, at its core, based on one of six types.

"The goal of the game was to see which of the six types could last the longest, once the destruction of the multiverse began. Whichever dimension was left standing in the end, the being whose type it belonged to would be declared the greatest of the six."

Franklin had known that whatever she had to say would be big, but he certainly hadn't expected to learn the origin of the multiverse.

"And these six cosmic beings created the multiverse just to destroy it?" Franklin said.

"That is the game. Each has its own representative playing piece. Tracy plays for the First, Laura plays for the Second, Krystal the Third, Kay the Fourth, Sandra the Fifth, and Alicia the Sixth. They all have just one goal: to destroy every dimension except for those representing their cosmic entity. Using the personalities and skills given to them by their cosmic entity, they must destroy dimensions while blocking their own from being destroyed. Ultimately, only one dimension will remain."

All at once, it came to Franklin. "And Helena is *your* piece."

"Exactly," she said. "I created the Helena as a blank slate. Her personality was to be determined by how she coped with the other six in her head, each based on her real-life opponents. As she matures, she will continue to lose her multiple personalities, until all that is left is Helena, the unique personality created by overcoming the others. And because she has been allowed to make her own decisions and develop her own characteristics, she will win the game."

"But how can she win a game she wasn't even invited to play?"

"By making it impossible for the other six to win. Just like I created the Helena, I also created your dimension. I masked it by making it nearly identical to other versions of Earth, so that the six would not suspect anything. But this dimension is fundamentally different from any others—its core is not one of the six types. It is a seventh type. I created Helena not to destroy dimensions, but to save *one.* This one. And when the six cannot destroy Helena or this dimension, *I* will be the winner."

"Then let me ask you again," Franklin said. "Who are you?"

"I am the Seventh. When the six created the multiverse, they were careless. They never realized that what they had actually created was another sentient, cosmic being, with powers like their own but without the ability to communicate with them, as they communicate with each other. They have failed to realize that they have created life, only to destroy it. When the multiverse dies, I will die. It is inevitable—there is nothing I can do to stop it.

"So to show them what they have done, to show them I *exist,* I will win their game. And I will do it on their terms. That is why I have chosen my own playing piece,and why I have given Helena personalities based on the six and their pieces. Like me, Helena began as a blank slate, and like me, she is maturing based on overcoming her six opponents."

"That's poetic, really," Franklin said.

"Thank you," said the Seventh.

"But why isn't your goal to keep yourself alive? Those of us who live in the multiverse . . . we'd much rather you stick around than have you win a game."

"The playing pieces represent the combined power of six supremely powerful, cosmic beings. I am only one."

"But you gave the purple cloud magic to Zarcadmium."

"True, but nothing in the multiverse can destroy the six playing pieces."

"Not even each other?"

The Seventh hesitated. "They haven't been able to destroy each other yet. They do not know if it's possible, and neither do I. As long as they exist, I am destined to die. That is the truth. All I have control over is the way I am going to die. Helena is my choice. I choose to win their game, to show them the wonders they have created only to violently tear them apart."

"Why Zarcadmium? Why not just tell Helena yourself what you wanted her to do? Why the elaborate plan?"

"To truly win the game, I must follow the same rules as the six. They are not allowed to communicate in any fashion with their playing pieces. Therefore, neither can I. They are allowed a certain amount of manipulation of the game board, however. There are a limited number of times they can directly interfere, which is why I was able to give Zarcadmium the purple cloud magic and give you clues in your dreams about how to proceed. Sadly, by coming to you in person like this, I am severely draining my own allotment of interference.

"It wasn't enough to only give Helena the six personalities, the inner conflict that would strengthen her character. She also required an external conflict, and that was Zarcadmium, the foe that, once she had defeated, would define her as a hero rather than a killer.

"There was, of course, a sizeable amount of risk in my plan. I have a very specific goal, which required me to do things in a particular way, and in a particular order. I couldn't be certain any part of it would succeed. But there was one variable I did not count on, and that was you. Had Helena not discovered you, had you not offered her your guidance, my plan for her may have backfired. She has the ability to choose her own destiny—to save or to destroy—and without you, she may very well have chosen to become Zarcadmium's general on her own. Zarcadmium didn't know what to do with the kind of power I gave him; that's why I gave it to him. I knew he would destroy his own dimension, and that's the kind of background he needed to be the adversary I felt Helena needed. But had she worked with Zarcadmium, yours would be the very first dimension that would have been destroyed. After all, I can give and take purple cloud magic, but Helena is all on her own. Those are the rules."

"So why tell me all of this now?" Franklin asked.

"So that you would know what is at stake," said the Seventh. "You have proven yourself to me, proven that Helena needs a guide, and I wanted your commitment to that role. The six pieces are already well on their way to destroying the multiverse, and Helena still has five personalities left to overcome before she is truly ready and powerful enough to save your dimension."

"If the playing pieces were out destroying dimensions, why didn't we know about it earlier? Drake and the VIBI could never find any other proof of purple cloud magic besides Zarcadmium and the HR120s, but shouldn't there have been sightings everywhere?"

"The six pieces have been operating for precisely as long as Helena has been, but they all bided their time for months, learning about the multiverse and developing their strategies. Dimensions were destroyed here and there, but the multiverse is a very big place, and your dimension has portals that access only a small portion of it. And after all, if an entire dimension is destroyed, just how much evidence would you expect to be left as to how exactly it happened? The game escalated greatly during the three years you were gone. The shrinking of the multiverse is now a very real threat, one that is terrifying to anyone who has accepted the existence of other dimensions."

The Seventh had put everything in perspective for Franklin. While he was busy trying to figure out how to beat Zarcadmium, a much bigger conflict was already underway. And now he found himself right in the middle of it.

"So I must ask you," the Seventh said. "Are you willing to continue on the quest you have taken upon yourself, Dr. Franklin Bryce of Abott City?"

Franklin never thought he would help save the world, much less be drafted by a cosmic being to prove to some other cosmic beings that the multiverse is more than a game board to settle their cosmic differences. He thought about all the wonderful and terrible things he had witnessed since that fateful day Zarcadmium gave him telepathic powers. He tried to imagine a reality without Rajel Chirok and Interdimensional eBay, Lera and her intuition, Mr. Havst and his pocket dimension with the laser eyeball, Requarr and his pizzeria, the other Franklin and the dimension that was just like his but different . . . and as insane as the Seventh had first sounded, with her strange logic and convoluted plans just to get noticed by some cosmic beings, he knew she was right. If the multiverse couldn't be saved, its memory had to be preserved, by helping Helena to win the Seventh's game for her.

"I decided a long time ago to stick by Helena, no matter what happens," Franklin said. "I'm glad to see I was right. I'll be her guide, for as long as I'm alive."

The Seventh smiled. "Good. I knew I did well creating this dimension—you are proof of that. I must ask one last thing of you. You must not tell Helena of any of this. I designed her so that she would develop without knowing the game, as the six do. I will not create a being simply for my own purposes; she has free will. What separates her from them is that she is not simply a pawn—she is a true player."

"I understand."

"I am counting on you, Dr. Franklin Bryce."

And then, Eva Grill was gone. Franklin finally reached into his coat pocket and produced Rajel Chirok's envelope. He opened it, and a square piece of paper flew out, hovered in mid-air, and began to fold itself into a cube. Franklin smiled. If that cube was about to do what Franklin thought it was, he imagined it would come in handy.

EPILOGUE

A New Player

THE SIX PLAYERS GATHERED IN A POCKET DIMENSION INSIDE THE BRAMZIT DIMENSION. The entire pocket dimension was designed to look like a city park, and the six gathered under the scorching sun around a wooden, rotting picnic table, much like the one they had sat around when they were first introduced to each other three and a half years earlier. This put Krystal somewhat at a disadvantage, as the Bramzit dimension was a Type Three, and if the other five decided to gang up on it together, there would be little she could do to fight them all off. But there was no such thing as neutral territory in the multiverse, and she had ultimately volunteered one of her dimensions as grounds for this meeting on the logic that the others might see it as a favor and leave her dimensions alone for a while, since she had lost the most territory so far in the game.

It was highly unusual for the six opponents to meet like this, but these were unusual circumstances. Since there was no communicating directly with the beings who had created them, they would have to decide together, according to the rules of the game, how to proceed.

"You all know why we're here," Kay said, wiping a thick layer of sweat from her forehead. "I bought a pizza recently and had an interesting conversation with a pizza delivery boy, whose boss likes to talk a lot. There is a new player, who just returned from being trapped in a pocket dimension for three years."

"An old player," Laura corrected her. "An old player whose been around since the game began, and we never knew about it."

"Lighten up," Tracy said. "She doesn't even know she's a player. She isn't even playing the game. Nothing to worry about."

"Oh, there's something to worry about," Sandra said. "Kay mentioned in her letter this Helena person *saves* people. She's some sort of superhero."

"Ooh, does she have a cape?" Tracy asked. "Or a mask? Or gauntlets? We should all have costumes."

"Right, because that's inconspicuous," Laura said, rolling her eyes.

"Talk about inconspicuous. Sandra never took her name tag off!"

"Does a tornado try to cover up incriminating evidence?" Sandra asked. "No. It leaves a calling card. It says, 'I'm a tornado; get out of my way or get dead.' That's what I say, too."

Kay cleared her throat loudly, trying to bring the group back on topic. "If this other girl sees herself as some sort of savior, that's bad for us. We blow things up. That makes us super villains."

"I'm not bad," Alicia said. "Every dimension I killed had mean people in it. They wanted to hurt me, so I hurt them. That's good, right?"

"Where did she come from?" Laura asked. "There are only six. How could there be a seventh when there are only six?"

"There's no reason to panic," Kay said. "We just need to decide what to do about her. We don't even know what she's capable of yet. There have been purple clouds around her, but she hasn't produced one herself."

"How is *that* possible? There's nothing in the multiverse with that magic except us," Krystal said.

"It doesn't matter," said Sandra. "There are no rules about an extra player. And there are no Type Seven dimensions. She's not *in* the game. But she might be able to slow us down, if she wants to. I say we stop her first. You notice how her dimension isn't even on the grid? Let's wipe it out, see what that does to her."

"That's against the rules," Kay said. "The game is to destroy Type One to Type Six dimensions. Type Seven's out of bounds."

"But, uh . . . if we get rid of them all and this Helena's dimension is the only one left… who wins?" asked Krystal. She looked at Sandra and seemed worried she might get smacked in the face.

"Well, the Type Seven wouldn't count, right?" Tracy said. "It's like a, what, a mulligan?"

"I think so," Kay said. "I think we should just ignore her and her dimension. From what's been going around the multiverse about her, it seems she mostly just stays in her dimension. If you don't mess with her, she won't mess with you."

"Whatever," Laura said. "The game is about the last dimension standing. I'm not about to let this wannabe win by default."

"Me neither," Sandra said. "The Type Seven is next on my list."

"Now wait a minute. We haven't come to a decision yet," Kay said.

"I have," said Sandra.

"So have I," said Laura.

Sandra smiled at Laura and started for the portable aperture on the swing set. "Let's go have a little temporary team-up. No way she can take us both."

The other four watched as the two most-feared players headed off for Helena Kathryn's dimension.

JAYMES LOGAN is a full-time father, blogger, and reviewer. *The Girl With Seven First Names* is his first novel. Jaymes lives in Lenexa, Kansas with his wife and son. You can find more of his work at www.geekvolution.com.

12434035R00243

Made in the USA
Charleston, SC
04 May 2012